WORLD
LEADER
PRETEND

JAMES

WORLD

BERNARD

LEADER

FROST

PRETEND

ST. MARTIN'S GRIFFIN
NEW YORK

This is a work of fiction. All of the characters, organizations, and events portrayed in this novel are either products of the author's imagination or are used fictitiously.

www.stmartins.com

Book design by Jonathan Bennett

Library of Congress Cataloging-in-Publication Data

Frost, James Bernard.
    World leader pretend / James Bernard Frost. — 1st ed.
        p. cm.
    ISBN-13: 978-0-312-35223-3
    ISBN-10: 0-312-35223-9
        1. Video games—Fiction.   2. Virtual reality—Fiction.   I. Title.
    PS3606.R65W67 2007
    813'.6—dc22

                                        2006050571

First Edition: February 2007

10   9   8   7   6   5   4   3   2   1

FOR MARY

ACKNOWLEDGMENTS

This book would not exist if not for the efforts of a great many individuals and entities. The author would like to thank the faculty and students at the University of San Francisco's MFA program in creative writing, for their encouragement and gentle criticism; Lewis Buzbee, his mentor, for pushing him to his limits; Jim and Dodi Frost, his parents, for their generosity; his ex-kingdom mates in Drunken Legions KLA, for research material; Irina Kendall, Josh Kendall, and Rebecca Heller, for finding an unusual book a home; and Andrea Frost, his wife, for giving him the time and financial backing to write.

This is my world
And I am
World leader pretend

—R.E.M., "WORLD LEADER PRETEND"

PROLOGUE: THE TWO-HEADED BOY

Two-Headed Boy
All floating in glass
The sun it has passed
Now it's blacker than black
I can hear as you tap on your jar

—NEUTRAL MILK HOTEL, "TWO-HEADED BOY"

EDWARD CALVIN RAWLINGS III is not a crier. He has, in fact, only cried a few times in his adult life.

The first time that he cried was after the accident—not right after the accident, not after he had caught an edge at 73.2 m.p.h.; had caught an edge after coming off a 100-foot precipice during the preliminaries of the European Championships; had caught an edge right before the famous Chamonix left; had caught an edge and gone over; had gone right through the course lining that read *Pepsi-Cola, Pepsi-Cola, Pepsi-Cola*; had gone through the course lining and over a rock-strewn cliff and landed in soft snow, soft snow that although it was soft still twisted his left leg in such a way that it still, to this day, points upward with his knee inverted, inverted the wrong way. The fall also snapped his spine, snapped it irreparably and irrevocably, so that since the age of nineteen, since January 23rd, 1997, since his last day as a budding star, England's best hope for its first downhill skiing winter Olympics medal, he has been immobile in his wheelchair, immobile from the neck down, actually even worse than that, immobile from the upper jaw down, immobile in such a way that he has not spoken since he was nineteen, immobile so that his saliva must be sucked from a tube that enters his mouth in the right corner, from a tube that circles around his right cheek to the back of his neck, where it attaches to other tubes. Edward Calvin Rawlings III, known to his

1

friends and family as Tres, pronounced Trace, all one syllable, did not cry
then. He hadn't cried then because he had blacked out in midair.

He also hadn't cried when he regained consciousness in a hospital in
Geneva, Switzerland, in a full body cast. He hadn't cried when, before anyone had realized that he had finally regained consciousness and needed to be
told what had happened, on the telly that was located ten feet over his head
and angled down at him, on an American station, on ABC, they were replaying it, they were replaying him, with the #78 on his back and the skintight
bodysuit with the Union Jack imprinted on both the front and the back, going through the course lining with *Pepsi-Cola, Pepsi-Cola, Pepsi-Cola* on it. It
was just like on the *Wide World of Sports* when the skier broke through a similar sheet of plastic, spinning, and crashed pell-mell into a crowd of specta-
tors, while a dramatic male voice said: . . . *and the agony of defeat.*

They replayed Tres dropping over the cliff and landing in the soft snow
with a thud. He hadn't wanted to watch it. He had wanted to be told by
someone else, someone other than two smarmy sportscasters wearing yellow
blazers and big smiles and talking into microphones that looked like snow
cones. But he couldn't move. He was physically unable to turn away or re-
duce the volume. And so he heard from two sportscasters, "Let us take a
short break from our regularly scheduled program to have a moment of silence for Tres Rawlings, the talented young English skier who will never walk
again."

Still, this didn't make him cry. What made him cry was when his father,
when Edward Calvin Rawlings Jr., had come into his Geneva hospital room
and called him Eddie. When his father, sighing heavily, on his breath a hint of
The Macallan, which he had sucked out of a small plastic bottle on the way
to Geneva, said, "Eddie, you're awake! Bloody Christ! I was in Lili and Car-
penter's when it happened. I saw the whole thing on the telly. Eric and I were
drinking pints. You missed your turn and went through the railings and over
the cliff. When they showed the stretcher, you didn't move. We couldn't
believe it. And then, just like that, they switched over to Colin Montgomerie
putting for birdie at the Scottish Open."

Edward, Tres's father, went on, went on to explain how quickly he and
Tilda had hopped on a plane from London, how quickly they had got to
Geneva, how distraught his mother was, but Tres couldn't listen. Edward
was calling him Eddie. His father was calling him Eddie. His father had never
called him Eddie. His name was Tres. He was the third. Uno. Dos. Tres. His

father called him Tres because he was his father's namesake, the third in a proud lineage, and now, suddenly, his father was calling him Eddie. He wanted to communicate this, to tell his father not to call him Eddie. But he couldn't. His mouth wouldn't move. His fingers wouldn't move. His father was calling him Eddie.

The tears that were in Eddie's eyes built up for an hour. He didn't cry in the hospital room while he was forced to watch the finals of the European Downhill Championships, while his father rambled on, soused on whiskey, oblivious to the fact that his son Tres, his son Eddie, was facing the telly and wasn't listening to what his father was saying. He didn't cry when Pierre Foucault, Tres's archenemy, that irritating Frenchman who had pumped himself so full of steroids that there wasn't a square inch of his brain remaining for higher thought, appeared on the telly, appeared in front of reporters after standing atop the podium and listening to La Marseillaise with tears in his eyes, tears that Tres knew had been induced by a pearl onion that Pierre attached with a safety pin to the underside of his collar for such occasions, tears that Pierre had bragged before the competition would win him another night with some Swiss hottie, tears that Pierre claimed made this Swiss hottie say, "Pierre, it makes me purr when you cry," something that Tres could never actually see anyone saying; Tres still wasn't sobbing, although his eyes certainly contained moisture, when Pierre, a big bulge under his collar and a bloody torrent of onion-induced tears dripping down his face, said, "Tres Rawlings was a good friend. Let us not think of victory. Let us pray for Tres."

Tres wouldn't let his father see. He could hold this back. His eyes were clouding though and would have teared over if the nurses had double-pillowed behind his head, but they hadn't, they had single-pillowed him, so the tears just sat there, a lake of tears in his eyes sat there clouding his vision while his father waved good-bye to him, waved good-bye curling his fingers to his palm, waved good-bye like you would wave good-bye to a 3-year-old, waved good-bye and said dramatically, "Adieu, Eddie, adieu."

When Edward the Second left, Edward the Third cried, cried for the first time in his adult life. He was crying because his father was calling him Eddie and would call him Eddie from that day forward. While Eddie cried, that Pepsi commercial came on the telly with the supermodels that are drinking Pepsi and tickling a baby, a baby who is so pleased that supermodels are tickling his belly that he will be a "Pepsi drinker for life."

While Tres cried, a single thought formed in his mind. *I will never drink Pepsi again.*

The second time that E.C.R. III cried was eight months later. This spout of tears was much more unprompted and surprised Tres with its force. That morning he had arrived at Heathrow Airport after a Swissair Flight from Geneva. He had flown first class. They had removed seats 2C and 2D and inserted his wheelchair into two grooves. The stewardess that had inserted his wheelchair into the grooves had smiled at him and then told him that she was going to strap him in. She had leaned all the way over him, so that her breasts rested on his right leg, so that her short, pleated skirt stuck up behind her at a perfect right angle to her long legs. When she did this Tres had an unspeakable urge to reach his hands up those legs, to slide his hands under that skirt, to squeeze that firm ass. Not that he would have if he could have, but that was the urge he had. That was the urge that a nineteen-year-old boy, recently paralyzed from the upper jaw down, naturally had. Tres had wanted to get under that skirt, and he had fantasized about this for a good two minutes, a two minutes that would have given him, just eight months prior, a full-mast hard-on. Now, it gave him nothing.

When his plane arrived in Heathrow he had been wheeled by a customs officer through customs, and then wheeled by a porter to the baggage claim. His parents had met him there, smiling big smiles. His father was dressed in his finest pinstriped suit, and Tilda was wearing a tangerine dress that Tres had never seen before. Tres supposed that they had expected cameras, had expected the paparazzi to have turned out in droves. But there was no one; there was just a bored porter and a drooling Eddie. The news was over, and they already had a celebrity paralytic in Christopher Reeve. They didn't need Tres. Edward and Tilda still smiled though—just in case.

Tilda was exuberant, "My God, Eddie. Eddie. We're so happy to see you. Oh Eddie, you're a star. The parliament wrote us a check and the bloody queen signed it. They were so proud of you. So proud of what you were going to do for the country. You are going to be happy. We got a van with a hydraulic lift. And we've redone the house with ramps. All in three weeks! And your bedroom is nice. I put up pictures of California. You said you wanted to go to California some day and learn to surf. Oh, you're going to love it, Eddie. You're going to love it."

Tilda had said this and Edward had gotten behind him and they had wheeled him out of the airport and into their new white van with the hydraulic lift. Edward strapped Tres down and they had left, making semi-circles around several roundabouts before heading down the familiar cobblestone of his street. Tres couldn't see any of this from his vantage point. His chair was set too low to see anything at ground level. But he could see up. Tres could see the billboards that they were passing. They drove by a Calvin Klein billboard. It was Kate Moss wearing a pair of jeans, an unbuttoned white blouse, and a red tie that was tied unusually short so that it didn't cover her navel. Kate was not wearing a bra and Tres could just make out the outline of the insides of her breasts.

Breasts. Edward and Tilda parked their car in front of 8 Sussex Road, in front of the family's four-story Georgian home. They wheeled Tres out. They wheeled him up a freshly cemented ramp that some neighborhood kid had scrawled in with a finger, or possibly a knife, a cemented ramp that had a heart scrawled in it with letters and symbols inside that read P. F. + T.H. = LOVE. They wheeled him up the ramp, onto a sidewalk, and between two rows of well-trimmed hedges.

Breasts. Edward and Tilda wheeled Tres underneath the awning that covered the front porch and turned right instead of going through the front door. They wheeled him around a porch swing, a porch swing which Tres couldn't remember ever having swung in. They wheeled him around to the side of the house, the side of the house which now had an elevator attached to it, an elevator which was painted primary blue, an elevator which his parents told him was specially designed for Eddie by Sir Norman Foster, the famous English architect. (A knight!) They wheeled him to the elevator, an elevator with no walls, an elevator that was designed so that its inhabitant could look out, could look out at rows of Tudor mansions spiraling down a serpentine drive, could look out at mansions and then smokestacks, and then the moors beyond. It was an open-air elevator. It was also designed, Tres thought, so that outsiders could look in. So that the inhabitants of the Tudor mansions spiraling down a serpentine drive could see the tremendous loss contained within.

Breasts. Tres's parents had stuck him in the elevator and pushed the 3 button. Tilda had said, still cheery, still with her prepared-for-paparazzi smile, "We're going around to get you, but soon we won't have to. They said that they can attach sensors to your brain that will help you work the elevator. Oh, Eddie! They said that you can still do just about anything. They're going to attach a metal cage to your head. It'll be right stunning. They said they can even make it look good, that all the wires and sensors will be inside the metal cage so no one can see them. They're going to attach sensors to your brain and you'll be able to control things on your own: your bed, your elevator, your wheelchair, even a computer! The doctors said that your brain is still intact, Eddie. Don't forget, Eddie, you still have your brain!"

There were no doors in the elevator, so they did not close. The elevator simply started going up. While the elevator went up, Tres thought, *Yes, I still have my brain, but my hair, my jet black hair they will have to shave. I'll lose my hair and my head will look like an Airstream. Like an Airstream or a toaster.*

Breasts. When the elevator reached the 3rd floor Tres's parents were waiting for him. Edward said to Tres, "Did you see the pulleys on that thing, Eddie? The engineering is amazing." Edward removed him from the elevator and wheeled him down the hall to his room, the room that he had lived in the first eighteen years of his life, all the years of his life except this last. He opened Tres's bedroom door in front of him and then wheeled him in. Tres was surprised. He had assumed that his mother had taken down his skiing posters, some of which were actually of him—posters of him making perfect open parallel turns down a steep section at St. Moritz decked out in all white on a pair of K2 Extreme FX 204cms. He was OK with his mother removing these posters; he didn't really need to see himself, full of health, on his bedroom walls. But these weren't the posters that his mother had removed. The posters that she had taken down were his posters of Tyra Banks and Rebecca Romijn, and an old poster of Kathy Ireland riding a bicycle in a bikini.

Breasts. Edward and Tilda had left him there in his newly redecorated room, a newly redecorated room that had in it, instead of posters of supermodels, posters of the lonely, rocky shores and cypress trees of Big Sur, California, a place Tres had never been, and probably never would go.

As soon as his parents left the room, Tres started to cry, rivulets that, because of his new handicap, he couldn't feel going over his cheekbones. As soon as his parents left the room, Tres realized that he would be a virgin until the day he died.

*   *   *

Today, more than five years after his accident, Edward Calvin Rawlings III is crying for the third time. Unlike the first two times, though, the tears in his eyes are not there to mourn what he has lost, but rather, they are there to celebrate what he has gained. Today, staring wide-eyed at four computer screens placed strategically above him, Tres is not a young man paralyzed from the jaw line down, forgotten by friends, teammates, and parents; he is, instead, a king. On each of the four screens above Tres is the following text, white on a field of cornflower blue:

The Lords of The Realm have awarded you 200 acres of land and 250,000 gold coins to build your province. You have been assigned to Kingdom 47, Continent 50. The name you have chosen for your province is Carrot Flowers. The persona you have chosen is Two-Headed Boy. Welcome to The Realm.

Today is the first day of the new age.

BOOK I: THE TWINS

RL TIME: June 20–26, 2000
REALM TIME: YR 1

I sit at my table
And wage war on myself
It seems like it's all, it's all for nothing

—R.E.M., "WORLD LEADER PRETEND"

I. HAVE PATIENCE.

XERXES METICULA IS PLAYING A GAME. The game he is playing is not a 2-person game; it is not chess or checkers or Connect Four, although it has a similarly complicated strategy; nor is the game he is playing a 4-person game, like bridge or poker, or a 6-person game, or even a game for 8. The game Xerxes Meticula is playing is a game being played simultaneously by 60,000 people, people representing hundreds of countries and all seven continents on the 3rd planet from the sun. It is a game unlike any other played by the human race in recorded history, unless you consider the act of waging war a game.

The players of the game of which we are speaking are much more humble about their game. They see nothing particularly extraordinary about it. They have no perception of the man-hours, the acts of manipulation and persuasion, the mental energy, and the physical labor that it took for an entire species to string long strands of copper wire from one end of each continent to the other and then to hurl objects through their planet's atmosphere to connect these continents all so that they could play their game. These players, in fact, perceive themselves and are perceived by others as some sort of subclass, as losers. They do not have the respect of their peers. They are not presented with garlands or roses when they are victorious.

8

These players—these players connected to each other by copper strands of varying widths, widths that, as they increase, increase the speed at which each player can play the game; widths which correspond in modern terminology to standard telephone wires, DSL lines, cable connections, T1's and T3's—as a group tend to be very dedicated to their game. They train for their game, do research, strategize. They play their game every day. They play for hours on end—2, 4, 8, 16, 24. They sneak out in the middle of the night, leaving their husbands, wives, children, or lovers alone in their beds.

Xerxes Meticula, lying as he is in the bed of a bedroom whose walls are plastered with pictures that he long ago cut out of old Dungeons & Dragons guidebooks; pictures of what are called, by those familiar with fantasy novels and games, *orcs*; pictures of blue, bulky half-giants who rarely bother to clothe themselves; pictures of slobbering beasts with disfigured faces who carry maces and pole arms and are always threatening to kill; Xerxes Meticula knows, at this moment, as he stares at the screen of the laptop perched in front of him on his bed, exactly what he is getting himself into, but he is trying to forget, trying to forget that today is his 32nd birthday and that he has managed in one way or another to lose most of the things and people that he cares for.

★ ★ ★

Unlike her brother, Gabriella Meticula is not interested in games. She is concerned only with the words of the cross-stitching that her mother has given her, the one which hangs over her bed on her bedroom wall, the one which reads:

Lo, I am sending my messenger
To prepare the way before me.

Gabriella gets out of her single bed and makes her way to her bathroom mirror. She stares longer into the mirror than a normal person would, her arms dangling uselessly at her sides. She does not wash her hands or apply makeup. She does not brush her teeth or floss. She isn't even really looking into the mirror, but rather at some empty point in front of it. She doesn't do any of these things, because she is thinking, and thinking is more important to Gabriella Meticula than anything else.

What Gabriella Meticula is thinking about is this: she and her brother are in grave danger. As the last of the Great American Dreamers, as the last of the Great American Thinkers, as the last of Those Who Will Rebel, as the Duke and Duchess of the Arizonan Desert, they are in exile. Fraternal twins born under the sun and moon of Gemini in any other day and age, in any place other than 21st century America, would have been treated with great respect: their births would have heralded years of tremendously fertile crops; they would have been considered soothsayers, prophets, or perhaps even royalty. They would have been protected.

As it stands, here in 21st century America, royalty is disdained. A person like Gabriella who considers herself unique, different, gifted, or special, is labeled an egotist or worse. In 21st century America it is important to bury your talents, to not show too much intelligence or creativity or verve. The intelligent child is chastised by his peers, and oftentimes by his teachers, for being stuck up, for being too good for everyone. The creative child, the one who sits in the corner with her stack of blocks, who wants to build her towers in peace, is told to join the group, to share. The child with verve, the one that runs yelling and screaming in mad circles around the classroom, is dosed with Ritalin.

In the eyes of 21st century America, Xerxes and Gabriella, a pair of twins with untold powers, have caused nothing but drought. Xerxes is a failed entrepreneur who, at the age of 32, returned from San Francisco to the house of his parents, returned after wasting billions of dollars of someone else's money, and Gabriella is not even that, she is nothing but an ex–high school valedictorian who was found one night by her friends at Mills wandering the streets of Oakland in a pair of pin-striped pajamas, wandering the streets at 3 A.M. looking up at the stars and conversing with them, telling the stars that she knew who she was, and that she was awaiting the message they would surely send. These friends who she thought were her friends but were obviously not, admitted her to a mental institution where she was wrongfully accused of being diseased, where she was wrongfully accused of being diseased and where she began a pharmaceutical imprisonment that she has yet to figure out how to escape. The people here, the people in America, they don't understand destiny.

Gabriella reaches a hand to the mirror and pulls on it, revealing a small cabinet. She takes out four small amber plastic pill jars. She opens the child-proof caps and places one pill from each jar into the palm of her hand. She thinks for a moment, *no, today is my birthday, I can do without the pills.* She places the pills back in their jars.

* * *

It is 6 in the morning in Rest Stop, Arizona, where Xerxes is lying on his bed interfacing with his computer. Outside his bedroom, behind a window whose shades have not been drawn, whose shades, in fact, have not been drawn since Xerxes arrived here a few weeks ago, the sun is rising. It rises alone and unnoticed like a red Wham-O Frisbee unearthed by a dog in a suburban backyard.

In his bed, Xerxes is wearing a chocolate brown T-shirt with the Cocoa Puffs bird printed on it; the word bubble above the bird reads: *I'm cuckoo for Cocoa Puffs.* This is one of the three T-shirts that Xerxes has been wearing since he arrived here in Rest Stop, since he became an exile from San Francisco. His other shirts include a blue T-shirt with white block letters that reads Uncle Jeffrey, which he wears although he is not an uncle and his name is not Jeffrey, and a mustard yellow T-shirt with the outline of the state of Mississippi on it and the words *We've Come This Far by Faith: The Barksfield/Lyon Reunion 1981,* which he wears despite not being a Barksfield, a Lyon, a member of either extended family, nor religious.

In addition to the T-shirt, Xerxes is wearing a pair of Chuck Taylor high-tops, a pair of shoes which he doesn't bother to remove before getting into bed and with which he has managed to track into his bed a good deal of sand. Next to his laptop on the bed is a yellow notepad filled with algebraic formulas scribbled wildly on its pages. On the screen in front of him are the following words:

The Lords of the Realm have awarded you 200 acres of land and 250,000 gold coins to build your province. You have been assigned to Kingdom 12, Continent 5. The name you have chosen for your province is The Strangely Peaceful Citadel of Blue Orcs. The persona you have chosen is Lady Peace & Love but Mostly Love. Welcome to The Realm.

Today is the first day of the new age.

* * *

In the terminology of gamers, the game Xerxes plays is a browser-based, multiplayer, resource management, team fantasy game. This is not the type

11

of game that most mothers of preteen males are familiar with. It does not involve the firing of virtual artillery or the amazing abilities of Barbie-shaped, sports bra-confined, virtual women. In other words, it is not a game that introduces military tactics and sexual desire to small children.

It is, in fact, a game that the mothers of preteen males, were they to take the time to understand it, would fully approve of. It is a game of math, patience, imagination, and most importantly, partnership. The primary objective of the game is for the 20 players who are members of one's kingdom to attain a net worth that is greater than the net worths of the 3,000 other kingdoms involved in the game. Net worth is the sum of all of one's possessions. This includes the land that one has obtained through exploration or battle, the population of one's province, the soldiers that one has trained, and the gold that one has generated through one's internal economy, traded for, stolen from one's enemies, or looted during battle.

One's net worth appears as a figure at the top of the screen. It changes every hour, every hour being considered a day in the time of The Realm. It is his net worth that Xerxes Meticula obsesses over, that he will stay up deep into the night calculating permutations of.

Because today is only the first day, there is little Xerxes can do. He and the 60,000 other provinces are all under protection, that is, they cannot attack, steal from, trade with, or otherwise affect each other's provinces for 72 hours according to the bylaws of the Lords of The Realm.

Xerxes consults a yellow notepad. He has written very neatly on the top,

- *50% of your buildings are available after building the necessary housing, farms, wizard towers, and guilds.*
- *Banks have no maximum and increase the wealth generated by your peasants by *1.5.*
- *Armories have a maximum of 30%. They decrease your military costs by *2. In the early stages of the game you will spend approximately 50% of your wealth on your military.*
- *Universities have a maximum of 20%. They decrease your science-related costs by *3. In the early stages of the game you will spend approximately 10% of your wealth on developing the sciences.*
- *Once you go OOP your thieves will account for approximately 50% of your income. (This is theoretical. Thieving, of course, increases the chances of counter-attack. The gains, however, seem to outweigh the risks.) Banks do not increase wealth generated in this fashion.*

- Q: *What percentage of banks/armories/universities is the most efficient?*
- A: *Build 30% banks/20% armories until 500 acres.*

These numbers make no sense to you, but they make great sense to Xerxes. He plugs in his numbers. Xerxes thinks to himself: *have patience; follow the rules*. Xerxes logs out. The screen reads:

Lady Peace & Love but Mostly Love, thank you for visiting The Realm. Remember, the Lords of The Realm appreciate your time away and will reward you with a bonus if you stay away for more than 24 hours.

Xerxes needs the bonus that the Lords of the Realm will give him. He must find something else to do with his day.

★   ★   ★

Gabriella Meticula is one of the things gone bust in Xerxes's personal bear market, one of the things that he has lost. Although he feels there is no saving what has been lost, he will go visit her, go visit her on this, their mutual birthday.

Xerxes leaves his computer, puts on underwear and a pair of shorts, and leaves his bedroom still wearing the Cocoa Puffs T-shirt that he wore last night, and for that matter, yesterday, the night before last, and the day before that. From his bedroom, Xerxes enters the first floor of his parents' house, a floor that, despite the fact that he is the only one who occupies it, contains 4 bedrooms, 3 baths, a kitchen, and a large room dubbed the "family room." He walks through this family room, a family room with an odd painting of him in it, a nine-paneled painting of his face as a 10-year-old, of him with blond straight hair cut in a perfectly horizontal line that makes it look like his barber stuck a salad bowl on his head and used it for a mold. The odd thing about the painting is that the boy in the painting has no eyes; the spaces where the eyes are supposed to be are painted jet black.

Xerxes walks through the family room to the stairs. He hops up these and enters the second floor, the floor that his parents live on, a floor that also contains 4 bedrooms, 3 baths, and a kitchen, in addition to a living room, dining room, and 4 balconies. Xerxes passes through the living room and the dining room, rooms done in desert rose and Indian turquoise, and marches past his mother, a mother who wishes him a happy birthday, a mother who asks him if he wants breakfast, some of her egg casserole and home-made sticky buns, a mother to whom he mumbles "no" to quickly, "gotta go ride, gotta go see Gabby."

Xerxes has a strange sense of déjà vu at this interaction. It was as if he were 16, not 32. Xerxes's mind spits fire—16 half of 32, 32 half of 64, 64 being less than the median age of death of all his deceased relatives, 5 on his father's side, 4 on his mother's side, deceased relatives of ages 43, 52, 53, 58, 63, 65, 65, 66, 68, an average age of 59.22.

He is 32. By the law of averages, he is more than halfway, more than halfway to death, his mother only .62 years away.

Xerxes makes his way past his mother in the kitchen and turns a gold-plated knob into the garage, a four-car garage with two electric garage door openers on the ceiling, one for the black Cadillac sedan and the white Cadillac sedan, the other for the silver Cadillac Escalade SUV and his car, a beat-up black Toyota truck with a white number 8 painted on both the driver's side door, the passenger's side door, and the hood. When he still lived in San Francisco he had the numbers airbrushed on by two Honduran men running a detailing operation on Mission St. In addition to the number 8 is the following script on the tailgate,

And the train conductor says
Take a break Driver 8
Driver 8 take a break
We've been on this shift too long.

Xerxes stands on the flat bed of his truck in the garage. Over the truck is a Cannondale mountain bike that he purchased for $5000, not including tax. This was the last purchase he made before he left San Francisco; the last purchase that he made before he declared bankruptcy; before he confessed to his parents that he had blown $25,000 of their money, blown first their initial investment, and then later the investment of 6 VC's; before he slipped away from his office and begged his parents to let him move into the basement of their retirement home in Rest Stop, Arizona; and before he, after settling into the basement of his parents' retirement home, strangely reverted back to childhood, back to age 16, spending his time doing nothing but playing computer games and occasionally riding the back trails of Rest

Stop National Forest to visit his twin sister Gabriella in her apartment ten miles away.

Xerxes presses a white plastic button that opens the garage door for the Escalade and the Toyota. He pedals past his truck, shifts his left gear once from 2nd to 3rd, rapid fires his right gear 4 times from 5th to 8th, a total gear shift of 14 gears, from 10th to 24th. Xerxes accelerates to 22 m.p.h. according to the digital speedometer/odometer/altimeter mounted on his handlebars before hitting the lip of the driveway at full-force. The 100 millimeters of travel on the RockShox of the Cannondale deftly handle the jolt of the lip but the bike still flies off the pavement. Despite the launch, Xerxes remains in control, his crotch is a good foot and a half off the top tube of his neon yellow mountain bike but his feet are still on the pedals. Xerxes lands, still on his $5000 chunk of aluminum, smack-dab on the perforated yellow line in the middle of Buena Vista Court, then banks sharply to the left, narrowly avoiding the curb on the other side, a curb that were he to hit it would send him sprawling down a near-cliff of perfectly round gray rocks that have been placed there by the homeowners association. He takes the turn and then bombs down the last stretch of man-made earth that he will see for several hours. As he nears the end of the court, nears the trailhead, he presses a small red button on the speedometer/odometer/altimeter. It reads, **43.21 m.p.h.**

13 short of the Buena Vista record.

2. CHOOSE A GOOD NAME.

AT THE TRAILHEAD, Xerxes starts his way up a steep ravine strewn with large chunks of sharp, chipped granite. He walks the bike up, absentminded.

Xerxes doesn't see the stocky piñion pines, the taller, thinner Ponderosas, the scratchy scrub oak. He doesn't look behind him to see the green-gray of Rest Stop National Forest dropping to the yellow of the high desert in Rest Stop Valley, rising back up into the rocky oranges of the Mingus Mountains. He doesn't see the aquamarine sky or the white clouds that look like the fluffy coverings of earmuffs. Xerxes only sees the dirt trail below him. He sees the vague shapes of other people's footsteps.

Xerxes isn't really paying attention because he is thinking about the names. He is thinking about the wisdom of the name he has chosen for his province: *The Strangely Peaceful Citadel of Blue Orcs.*

This is a name with character, and because of this other good players will know by the name that he has been in The Realm before. The name has character because orcs are the most warlike race and it would indeed be strange for his citadel to be peaceful.

The name is strategic in another way. Other players will assume that he has taken a defensive tact and in the beginning of the game he will. Later, however, when he secretly amasses a horde of orcish spear throwers, his enemies will be left unawares.

This morning, Xerxes had glanced over the names of other provinces in his kingdom. Some were headed for an early exit. *Third Reich* would instantly be a target. Players in The Realm are a righteous bunch and anti-Semites are summarily destroyed. *666* would probably be ousted quickly too. There are just enough Christians playing the game to make life difficult for someone who has announced their allegiance to the anti-Christ. Other names showed more promise: *sKyLaR'S PlEaSuRe PaLaCe* would provide entertainment; Raven would be a powerful warrior.

Xerxes reaches the top of a ridge where his trail ends at a T. He turns the bike to the right and gets on, riding it fiercely down a fire road strewn with sharp granite. The bike buzzes in staccato like a semiautomatic. He rides this way for miles. Down 500 feet. Up 200. Down 500 more.

His bike gets caught in a jeep rut, the pedals jam between two ridges, and he is thrown over the handlebars. He lands, first on his hands, then on his stomach. He gets up, retrieves the bike, and dusts himself off. His gloves have protected his hands, but a rock has cut a small gash across his abdomen. The feathers of the Cocoa Puffs bird are bloody.

He is back on his bike and now he is climbing an incline in a granny gear. He presses a heart-shaped button on the speedometer/odometer/altimeter. It reads: **160 b.p.s.**

Xerxes races through Rest Stop National Forest in this way, eventually arriving at his sister's apartment. His calves burn. His fingertips are blackened with chain grease, his arms and legs scratched from speeding past scrub oaks. He limps up the steps and knocks on Gabriella's door.

* * *

Gabriella is centered in the lotus position on the orange shag carpet of her one-bedroom apartment, a ramshackle apartment with peeling mustard yellow paint that occupies the backyard of a Planned Parenthood office. The room smells of frangipani. An incense stick hangs out of the mouth of a ceramic frog sitting on a ceramic lily pad. Both the ceramic frog and the ceramic lily pad were sculpted by a friend of Gabriella's at the St. Francis Sanitarium. Candles burn on end tables, on the ledge next to the stove, and on a lamp stand. None of the candles are in candleholders and wax drips and dries on unprotected wood. The candle on the end table is dangerously close to burning out, only a thin film of liquid wax keeps the end table from catching fire.

Gabriella sits in the lotus position with her eyes closed. In her right hand she holds a lit Liggett Ultra Light 100 cigarette. She does not acknowledge Xerxes's presence in the room, although he is panting desperately, although he has dropped his bike in the hallway and left a big black mark on her wall from the rubber of his handlebar grips, although he is greeting her wildly, trilling his r's, "Gabrrrrrrrrriella!" Gabriella does not turn her head in Xerxes's direction. She takes a drag of her Liggett and smiles mischievously.

"I see you, Xerxes. You are burning. You are riding down a mining trail from the top of Mingus Mountain to Jerome and your hair catches fire, catches fire because you are stupidly riding without a helmet, and because some scientist from the observatory is aiming a telescope at you and doesn't realize that he is reflecting concentrated sunlight from the lenses directly at your exposed scalp. You are riding so fast and with such deep resolve that you don't realize that you are on fire. The fire burns a bald spot on the top of your head, then it turns the rest of your hair ash-colored, then you are completely bald, then you become wrinkled and red all over like a sun-dried tomato. But you still ride, you hit the red rock at ungodly speeds, you look at your speedometer: you're going 30, 40, 50, 60, 70, 80. And still you take no notice, you don't notice the buzzards flying overhead, you can't smell your own flesh burning, roasting like a pig on a spit in Oahu, you are just riding. Riding as fast as you can."

"What else?"

"That's it. You walked in and interrupted it. How was your morning ride?"

"It was fine. That fire road is a bitch."

"You sprained your wrist."

"No, just a few scrapes. I did an endo and bent my rim a little, but I should be able to true it back into shape."

"Not your wrist? I was sure it was the wrist."

Xerxes has walked past Gabriella into her kitchen. He opens up her refrigerator. Looks in. "Can I have one of these energy drinks?"

Gabriella tries to change the subject back to something serious. "Xerxes, when are you going back?"

Xerxes will have nothing of it. "Why don't you buy yourself a TV? Don't you get bored here?"

"You're ignoring my question."

Xerxes opens the bottle of energy drink and looks down at the lamp stand. On it are four small black onyx statues of horses rearing back on their hind legs. Carved into them are flames coming out of their nostrils and wings on their flanks. They are the four horsemen of the apocalypse. There is also a bottle of Walgreens sunscreen lotion SPF 15, a box of Odor-Eaters, 3 empty cans of Slim-Fast, a prescription from the St. Francis Sanitarium for 100mg of Zoloft, and Gabriella's Social Security check. Xerxes spies the numbers on the check and says, "Six hundred and forty-seven dollars and twenty-three cents, that has to be rough."

He goes on, "Your carpet smells like cat urine, you should have had them shampoo it before you moved in. Wanna play Scrabble?"

"I can't play, Xerxes. I'm going with Sonya to the Y.M.C.A. Her baby is learning to swim."

"Who's Sonya?" Xerxes is pacing the length of the living room, still sweating from his ride. Gabriella remains on the orange shag carpet with her cigarette; she has forgotten to ash and the cherry on its end is almost an inch long.

"The next door neighbor."

"Does she pay you to help her?"

"No."

"She should pay you."

Gabriella's eyes are still closed. "I see you returning to San Francisco and reuniting with your friends. Your company is no longer the multibillion dollar conglomerate that you and Zahn envisioned. It is now a small family-run nonprofit organization that uses the algorithms that you uncovered to aid other nonprofits in keeping their inventories low."

Xerxes looks at an open CD case on the end table. It is Sinéad O'Connor's *Universal Mother*. The thin film of liquid wax has burned away and the wick is beginning to burn through the varnish.

"I don't get it, Gabriella, why doesn't your medication work?" The smell of burning pine cuts through the thick frangipani. Xerxes locates the source of the burning and blows out the candle, then pours a few drops of his energy drink onto the smoldering table.

Gabriella's eyes are still closed. She is still in the lotus position. Her ashes have fallen onto the carpet. "There are thirty-two candles."

"Gabriella, do you realize that if I hadn't shown up you'd still be on the floor with that dead-Elvis grin on your face with the house going up in flames around you."

Gabriella opens her emerald eyes, takes a drag of her Liggett, and looks up at Xerxes. "That was the point."

3. BUILD UP YOUR DEFENSES.

XERXES HAS WAITED THE 24 HOURS. He has ridden his bike the 15 miles to his sister's apartment and then he has returned that same 15 miles. He has driven number 8 to Taco Bell, had his birthday dinner there, and returned. After all that, he has slept. In the night his calves cramped up like they were stuck in a Chinese finger toy, one of those toys you can buy in Chinatown, in any Chinatown in any city in any country—in New York, Philadelphia, San Francisco, London, Xiangxi—a finger toy that you stick your two index fingers into and pull. The harder you pull the more stuck you get.

Xerxes wakes up at precisely the end of his 24 hours as if he had an alarm clock hardwired into his head. The alarm clock is the cry of his peasants, of *her* peasants, the peasants of his lady, the lady that is he. He can hear them outside the citadel walls demanding food, demanding work, demanding protection. He is awake and he is in front of his computer screen. It reads:

Lady Peace & Love but Mostly Love,

Welcome back to The Realm; for your time away you have been awarded 80,000 gold coins.

Today she must build up her defenses. She clicks the "Military" button and begins to draft soldiers at a rate of 20%.

She will also need more peasants for her draft to be effective. She selects the "Magic" button and then chooses "Fertility" from a drop-down menu. Her spell capacity is limited at this stage in the game, but this one interests her. She clicks the "Cast" button. The hourglass spins. The screen reads:

Your wizards gather the shadows around them and . . .

Your spell is successful. Population growth will increase for the next 15 days.

Lady Peace & Love has done all she can do for now. She is curious what her kingdom mates are up to. She clicks the "Read Messages" button. A message is there from Sir BonZ:

i was king of my KD last age. we did very good. finished eighth on our continet. I ask for your vote as king so we can gorw strong!! Let's kick some @$*@.

Sir BonZ

It is too early to choose a king, the Lady thinks, and 8th on the continent is too low for her aspirations. She has an image of the real-life Sir BonZ: an 18-year-old, possibly Korean, or at least Korean-American; English isn't spoken in the house; a young math wiz, spends too much time in front of the computer, knows what ROFL means, possibly overweight; *maybe*, if the kingdom is lucky, has a sense of humor; *biggest weakness*, a false sense of pride.

The Lady switches to the "Elections" screen. A list of all the provinces in the kingdom is displayed on the left side of the screen; on the right is each province's vote for the regency. She is surprised to see that Sir BonZ has already achieved the necessary votes to become the king. She had expected more of a power struggle, a show of smarts. She had expected that her kingdom mates would hold their votes until they saw whose net worth was climbing the fastest, who showed the most promise. She had expected to be the queen. A mere note to his kingdom mates was all it took. 8th on the continent—things were already diverging from her plan. No matter. A Lady must be prepared for change.

There is nothing for Lady Peace & Love to do but show grace. She prepares a message for the new king:

King BonZ,

Congratulations on your ascendancy to the throne of our fine kingdom. I hope to serve you well.

Signed, Lady Peace & Love but Mostly Love

She clicks the "Send Message" button. Her screen reads:

Lady Peace & Love but Mostly Love,

A courier has been sent with a communication for Land of BonZ. Please remember that inappropriate messages may be cause for removal from The Realm.

The Lady pauses for a moment, taps her fingernails on the plastic of her keyboard. She thinks, a minor slight is necessary, a whisper of dissention. She will not cast her vote for King BonZ. The Lady leaves the space on the right-hand column of the "Elections" screen blank.

Lady Peace & Love but Mostly Love is itching to get things started, but now is not the time. There are still 48 hours under protection. She will once again wait 24 hours and receive her gold bonus. The Lady Peace & Love but Mostly Love logs out of The Realm.

*   *   *

Gabriella likes poetry. She was excited about the trip yesterday, but today she slouches in the truck's bench, picking at a scab on her leg, her face in a scowl. Xerxes talks to Gabriella as if she were a child, in a teasing, singsong way. She is what Xerxes calls the Zoloft Zombie today—spacey, incoherent, lost to the world.

"Gabrrrrrrriella, aren't you excited. Poetrrrrrry. You luuuuve poetry. You know you waaaaant it. And we're going to Arcology. It's a commune with tons of hippies, totally your scene."

Gabriella doesn't respond. Her face is stone and her eyes are crossed like

21

a princess in a Mayan stelae. Xerxes slips a CD into the slot. The whining voice of Isaac Brock from the indie rock band Modest Mouse fills the cab of the truck. Xerxes interprets a line from the music his own way: *One hundred miles is a long drive in a silent car.*

Xerxes stops trying to be entertaining and watches the road. He drives out of Rest Stop and onto State Highway 69, beginning his descent into the desert valley.

The desert is the only landscape that is truly pastel. Monet should have used his color schemes to paint desert rather than Mediterranean villas. Xerxes looks out at creamy grasses, sage green near the root, then a faded gold, then an off-white. His eyes filter in the earth: the dirt, often exposed, is a beige or an orangish pink, a color that interior decorators call "desert rose," but can't actually be desert rose, since there isn't a rose in the universe that could survive this heat. The temperature is climbing—80 degrees Fahrenheit, 90, 100, 110, 120; 35 degrees Celsius, 40, 45. The deeper into the valley Xerxes drives, the hotter it gets; the more sun-bleached and faded everything is. The sun is a slow Clorox.

Five hundred miles is a real, long, drive in a car.

Number 8 is diving into the desert and now everything is the color of dust: the ocotillo, its skeletal fingers rising eight feet into the air; the flapjack prickly pear, rounded and stacked like sand dollars in a jar; the teddy bear cholla, microscopic needles that get under your skin by the hundreds.

They have driven 50 miles. There has been silence. Gabriella breaks Xerxes's private reverie, his observations of color. Xerxes and Gabriella are on similar frequencies but different channels. Gabriella says the words that a Catholic priest utters when he smears ashes on your forehead on Ash Wednesday, "From dust you came, and unto dust you shall return."

Xerxes pushes the petal harder: *Eight hundred miles is a long drive in a silent car.*

It is the second day that Gabriella has shunned her pills and she is beginning to figure things out. For example, she knows that it is the year 1984 in 20th-century America. She knows that Big Brother is here and that we have welcomed him with open arms. She knows that sometimes we play Big Brother himself, sitting in our living rooms watching *Survivor*, sitting at our computers watching *College Coeds: 6 Girls, 6 Web Cams, see it all—rate the stars*; sometimes we let Big Brother in, allow him to rate us: *A,B,C,D,F.* We give

Big Brother our Social Security numbers, our Visa numbers, our Rapid Rewards numbers, our Safeway Club Card numbers. We have held out our arms for the barcode.

Gabriella knows that multinational corporations are blackening our souls, that they are turning us into automatons who must all look and think the same. Everyone wears blue jeans. Everyone shops at The Gap. Every item of clothing has a tag. The tags read:

4,6,8,10,12

S,M,L,XL

W30L32, W32L32, W34L32, W36L32, W38L32, W40L32

Everyone must be healthy. Our streets must be safe, clear of both garbage and shopping cart-pushing pedestrians. The mentally ill, the ones that color our streets with strangeness, the ones that make life entertaining, these people must be drugged so they don't bother us—diazepam, Prozac, Zoloft, serotonin reuptake inhibitors, lithium, monoamine oxidase inhibitors, haloperidol. Depression, that sure sign that it is time to change, that sure sign that we should sell our house, our Mercedes Benz, take our dog to the pound, throw our cat into the alley, leave our wife and kids and move to Montana and live in a shack and write the Great American Novel, should be treated with a drug that steals our memory, that makes us forget who we were meant to be, that kills the inner Kerouac, that keeps us in place, a big dumb smile on our big dumb faces. We 20th-century Americans will be monogamous, we will not smoke cigarettes, we will drink lots and lots of beer but we won't smoke pot, we will drink coffee and soda to keep us amped but we won't snort cocaine. We will have wars on everything that is unpleasant: *War on Drugs, War on Cancer, War on Crime, War on Terrorism*. We will eradicate everything that displeases us with brute force. Everything that might change us and alter us for the better. Everything that may keep us from being #1. *March! March! March!* March with your pink ribbons and your empty thoughts. *Go! Go! Go!* There is no time for rest. There is no time for contemplation. There is no time to be sure you are doing things the right way, there is no time to make sure you aren't royally fucking things up.

Gabriella's Pink Floyd albums tell her something. *The Wall* is the next book after Revelations. The Gospel according to Pink Floyd warns us, admonishes us. Pink Floyd 1:1 tells us this about America: *Welcome. Welcome to the machine.*

Gabriella and her brother are here: Gemini twins, Pagans, misfits, *losers*. They are the oracle. They are the chosen ones. They are the way, the truth, and the light. Someone, somewhere, should design a bumper sticker: recognize true prophecy.

Isaac intones: *Eleven hundred miles is a long, long, long, long ways in a car.*

Three hours and 6 minutes later Xerxes and Gabriella arrive in Arcology.

★   ★   ★

A man wearing a floral dress, pumps, and oversized, gold-rimmed, brown-lensed Marilyn Monroe sunglasses stands on a dais in front of a microphone. The dais is surrounded by a moat of running water. His lips are painted plum and his cheeks are thickly rouged. He is reading his poetry to an audience sitting on throw pillows in a stone-stepped amphitheater with fake Ionic columns. He glowers daringly at the smattering of observers, saying seductively,

"I want a three-piece band in my pussy. I want Charlie Parker playing sax and Dizzy Gillespie on the vocals. I want every man in the Million Man March inside me, poking placards at my vulva. I want a busload of school children in my pussy, squirming uncomfortably in their seats . . ."

Xerxes is sitting awkwardly on his throw pillow. One of his legs is dead asleep. He won't notice this until he tries to stand up, until he falls into Gabriella's lap. He is howling with laughter. Gabriella is reticent, lost in her own thoughts.

Xerxes has volunteered to be a judge at the poetry slam; he flips through the numbers of his scorecard. He flips to 10.9. Gabriella senses danger like a dragon waking from her slumber.

"10.9? You can't give him a 10.9. And, besides, his poem wasn't any good."

Xerxes wants to argue this point. He thinks what the poet read was the most poetic thing he has heard in years, he thinks, *this guy wants to have a pussy. It's beautiful—his big, pink, tiger lily pussy pollinating the planet,* but he doesn't have time to say this, the man is done and the audience is waiting for Xerxes to give him his score.

Xerxes says to Gabriella out of the corner of his mouth, "Quick what would you give him?"

"7."

Xerxes is incredulous. "7?"

Gabriella concedes a little. "7.9."

"Come on, you want poetry to be about flowers and birds? He was brilliant."

"7.9."

The moderator is growing impatient. "Judges, we need your scores, please."

Xerxes brain forms, $X + G/2$. $10.9 + 7.9/2$. He flips the numbers of the scorecard to 9.4. Holds up his hand to let the moderator know he is ready.

A woman sitting to the right of Xerxes and Gabriella at the top of the stone amphitheater holds up her scorecard. She is on her fourth or fifth Budweiser longneck. Her boyfriend whispers God-knows-what into her ear. Her scorecard reads, for the sixth poet in a row: 9.8. The audience and the poets clap politely.

Xerxes's card goes up next. Xerxes bases his scores on a complex formula: Originality plus Eccentricity plus Presentation plus Emotional Content divided by 4. Occasionally, he asks for Gabriella's opinion when he feels he has a male bias. In these cases, if he chooses to include Gabriella's scores, he averages the two scores. For the current contestant, he threw out the rules, but he still feels the 9.4 is fair. He holds up his scorecard. The right side of the amphitheater is relatively happy. Some know the poet, some are on his team, and others just appreciated his reading. They clap. The left side of the amphitheater is strangely silent.

The last judge is a blond woman with a nervous laugh and a tattoo of a gecko on her right shoulder blade. She holds up her scorecard: 6.6. Ouch. The poets on the right side of the room boo and hiss. The poets on the left side of the room smirk smugly. There are whisperings of bias—the blond gecko judge seems to know one of the poets on the left side of the room; she turns to him and giggles. The poets on the right take note. The whisperings become grumblings.

Xerxes recognizes the shift. This is no longer a Poetry Slam but a War of Poets. The right-side poets, the intellectual poets, the young, eccentric, brazen, and brave poets vs. the left-side poets, the dirty, untalented, cowboy poets; the poets who have brought their own judge. Xerxes leans over and whispers in Gabriella's ear, "She's a Russian judge."

Gabriella doesn't get it. She looks at Xerxes comically, a look halfway between confusion and scorn. "You think she's Russian?"

"No, silly. Remember when Nadia Comaneci and Mary Lou Retton were battling it out for the gold medal and the Russian judge kept giving

Mary Lou lower scores than the rest of the judges. The Russian judge was being biased. That girl's a Russian judge."

"The American judges were biased, too."

"You think she's being fair?"

"No, she's drunk and her boyfriend is on the other team."

"This pisses me off."

Gabriella eyes Xerxes coolly. She rises up off her seat cushion. "I'm going to have a smoke."

Xerxes understands what he now must do. The blind judge, the Budweiser judge, is a dummy judge. She will score everyone the same. The blond gecko judge, the Russian judge, is a biased judge, she will score the left-side poets significantly higher each time. Xerxes is the only nonbiased judge left, and therefore only his scores must count. Unless the left-side poets show some unbelievable panache in the next two rounds, then the right-side poets should win. He will have to throw out his formulas in order for justice to be done.

Another poet, a left-side poet arrives on stage and begins to speak,

"My perfect day. My perfect day begins with a blow job. It begins with a blow job and then some bitch making me breakfast. That's right, some bitch. Some bitch who let's me call her some bitch."

The poet goes on in this fashion. Xerxes knows that his words are intended to shock, but the words of the poet are not particularly creative. He would have scored him low anyway, but now he has to think both politically and mathematically.

The Russian judge will score him high: a 9.8 or a 9.9. He must score him high enough so she doesn't suspect him of lowballing and low enough to give the right-side poets a chance to catch up in the last round. Xerxes works through the psychological circuitry. As a rule, he would never score anyone at a Poetry Slam lower than an 8, but he's going to have to dip lower than that to make this work. Fortunately, he's never judged here before and everyone is too drunk to pick up on his judging style.

Xerxes decides on the number 6. It's dangerously high and he's really going to have to nail the last poet, but it will allow him to make a sneak attack—the Russian judge will think her side's victory assured. Xerxes holds up his number 6. The left side of the room doesn't even flinch. They have no idea what's about to hit them.

★　★　★

Gabriella is standing next to a steel barrel with a blue, triangular-shaped sticker on it that says #5 and also, CORROSIVE. She is standing next to the steel barrel smoking one of her Liggett's. She is standing facing a box canyon with craggy, broken walls of maroon-colored rock. Rows of saguaros, their arms pointed upwards like a football referee signaling "Good," line the top of the canyon walls. Gabriella takes a drag and blows the smoke upwards. She watches its heat shimmer in the desert sky.

She is thinking, "Why, why is Xerxes doing it? There is no reason for it. This is not his fight. Not his battle. Why would he abuse his powers? God-damn him. Goddamn him. Why does he always have to win?" Gabriella looks down into the steel barrel. It is filled with dirty dishwashing rags and coagulated canola oil from Arcology's cafeteria kitchen.

* * *

It is the last round of the poetry slam. The poet from the right side of the room reads a poem about his friend who has died from AIDS. It is a remarkable poem. The poet shakes as he reads it. Xerxes scores him a 10. He may have given him a 10 anyway. The Russian judge gives him a 7.4.

The poet from the left side of the room reads a poem about waking up on the sand of a beach in Puerto Vallarta in nothing but his Fruit of the Looms. The tide has come in and salt water hits him in the face. It washes away his vomit. In the poem the poet is in Mexico and he wakes up knowing that his money, his passport, and his virginity are gone. He wakes up in the sand of a beach in Puerto Vallarta with his arms outstretched. He moves his arms up and down and makes a sand angel. He knows he has found Jesus.

This is also a remarkable poem. The Russian judge scores him a 9.9. The 9.8 judge scores him a 9.8. Xerxes calculates the maximum score that he can give the left-side poet to give the right-side poets a .1 edge in the overall voting—a 2.3. Xerxes flips the numbers of his scorecard: 2.3. He holds up the score.

* * *

"Damn him. He had no right." Gabriella drops her Liggett into the steel barrel. The dishwashing rags, gone crispy like Lay's Potato Chips from the dry desert air, catch fire immediately. The dishwashing rags, in turn, catch the coagulated canola oil on fire. There are blue flames. There is thick black smoke. Gabriella sticks her head into the mouth of the flaming, smoking steel barrel. She closes her eyes and sticks her head into the conflagration for as long as she can stand.

★   ★   ★

Several things happen simultaneously in the stone-stepped amphitheater with the fake Ionic columns and the moat-surrounded dais. The boyfriend of the Russian judge yells, "That's bullshit." The moderator of the poetry slam says, "Hold on. Hold on." Many people in the audience, confused about how what was supposed to be a pleasant poetry slam has turned into a display of profanity, jealousy, and over-competitiveness, turn around to leave, not at all interested in the outcome of the scoring, just wanting to get back in their 4WD vehicles and get back to the safety of their homes in Scottsdale, turn around only to discover a thick column of black smoke rising from the back of the amphitheater.

While all this is happening in the amphitheater, Xerxes has leapt up the stone steps; has run to the steel barrel; has found his sister sitting crosslegged on the beige, barren earth, her face gray with flecks of burnt dishwashing rags; has grabbed her hand and pulled her up; has slapped her face to get her moving; has dragged her and run with her to #8; has gotten in #8 and fired the engine and begun the drive up from Arcology and the desert valley.

Gabriella and Xerxes say nothing on the drive up State Highway 69 back to The Ranch.

4. IN THE NEW AGE, YOUR PAST DOESN'T MATTER.

THE NEWS OF HIS COMPANY'S DEMISE HAD COME IN SUCH A PECULIAR WAY. Xerxes was sitting in his office with the door closed. His feet were on his desk. He was throwing a #2 lead pencil at the ceiling, trying to get it to stick in the one ceiling tile that he had left in place, a ceiling tile that he had drawn a dartboard on in Magic Marker. He was throwing the pencil up at the target and thinking about how he would fit his new *Hulk* poster next to the *Storm*, *X-Men*, and *Fantastic Four* posters that he had Scotch-taped over the glass windows so that his employees couldn't see what he did all day, which was mostly daydream and play computer games. He was throwing the pencil up at the target and going through his list of favorite Web sites and clicking on one of the three that he checked every morning when he got to work.

The Web site that he checked that morning was screwedcompany.com, a Web site that listed all the latest dot-com closures, layoffs, and bankruptcies. The "screws" as they were called, were excruciatingly funny, and not only were they funny, but they were usually accurate. They told the tale of how one company had hired security guards to march their employees out of their screwed company; how at another company the workers had gotten wind of their bankruptcy earlier in the day, had all gone out for cosmopolitans, and had come back into the office and stolen as much computer equipment as they could carry; how at a third company the marketing department had printed a T-shirt for the employees' last day of work that read: *MusicExplosion.com: Another Dot Bomb.*

It was a strange system of information gathering that allowed screwedcompany.com to get their news. Insiders at failed dot-coms religiously sent in the "screws" themselves, in some sort of sick penance for the disasters they had caused.

Each screwed company got a rating from 1 to 100 for just how screwed they were.

Xerxes's pencil hit the bulls-eye on the ceiling. The headline on screwedcompany.com read, maximuminventory.com: 100!!!

Xerxes read on:

Co-founder Zahn Mendoza, well into his eighth Sapphire and Tonic at Bimbo's last night, looking dashing in a tailored 1940's Zoot Suit and a thin-red leather tie fashionable amongst the mod crowd, brazenly announced to everyone within earshot, including shock pink-haired Dixie Humes—receptionist, coffee maker, and Employee #3—that the five- and one-dollar bills that he had just placed on the bar top in front of bartender Dan Weathers were the last Abraham Lincoln and George Washington that his company owned and that he, Zahn Mendoza, was "going to go home and fuck Dixie," and leave the job of informing his employees that today was their last day on the job to "shit-for-brains" who "probably has a generator in his dungeon of an office and won't even notice that the power has been shut off." Good-bye maximuminventory.com. And good luck to Xerxes Meticula, maximuminventory.com's unfortunate co-founder. You're screwed! Have a nice day!

Xerxes looked at his poster of *Storm*, her wild, frizzy white hair with a wicked devil's peak, her dark features, her black cape and gold bracelets, her black leather knee-boots and her matching black leather thong, her hands and arms extended with lightning shooting skyward. He hadn't seen this coming at all. Or, maybe he had, maybe his reticence, his locking himself in the office, his hiding in The Realm, was part of a complex system of denial. His own name stared at him on the screen in 12-point Tahoma font like one of those yellow smiley faces with a bullet hole in its forehead: Xerxes Meticula, you're screwed!

Xerxes grabbed another #2 lead pencil from an artsy $100 pencil holder made out of pieces of chain-link fence and threw it up at the ceiling tile. Double bulls-eye! He was on target today!

Xerxes sat calmly at his desk and considered the chain of events that were the most likely to have led up to Zahn's combustion at Bimbo's the preceding evening.

1) 3 months ago, Zahn was, as usual, being overly optimistic about how well his meeting had gone with Amazon.com. When he had held out his index finger and his thumb to Xerxes, and said, "Xerx, we're *this* close. We're gonna make it, buddy," he was just buttering him up.

2) The highly technical document, the 500-page monster that Xerxes had produced for Zahn to give to the Amazon.com executive team, the document that Zahn had read over in 15 minutes, the document that had elicited this response from Zahn, a big grin taking over the Hispanic features on his chiseled face: "This is going to do it, this is going to be the straw that breaks the camel's back," had indeed been the straw that broke the camel's back. The technical document that Xerxes had created to explain the complex logic that would allow Amazon to keep very close to 0 percent inventory by integrating maximuminventory.com's easy-to-use, open source system into their own Web site, had flown right over the heads of Amazon's executive team, and Zahn, not having read Xerxes's document, had blown the meeting.

3) Zahn's increased cocaine use and his subsequent purchase of a brand-new Porsche S had not been, as Xerxes had interpreted, a sign that the Amazon deal had gone well, but that it had gone sour, and that Zahn was going to bilk every penny of the company's money on a good time before the ship sank.

4) Because Xerxes had finished his documentation, and because the Amazon deal was going to keep them in the black, Xerxes had figured that there was nothing wrong with his beginning to settle into relative comfort—locking his door, putting his feet on his desk, buying vintage comic books on eBay, and playing very addictive computer games.

5a)Zahn must have somehow, perhaps in a state of cocaine-induced paranoia, interpreted Xerxes's quietude and hermeticism as a reaction to the obviously declining situation at maximuminventory.com.

5b) Zahn must have also, in this state of cocaine-induced paranoia, begun to resent Xerxes, begun to think that Xerxes now disliked Zahn, begun to doubt their friendship, a friendship that had lasted through grade school and high school, survived four years at Stanford, and finally culminated in the two of them living their dream: their dream of being in business together, of owning a successful business together and then growing old and playing croquet together in all-white clothes and a perfectly manicured lawn; their dream of always being just a little bit off, of never playing golf but rather croquet; their dream of never, ever, doing things in a stereotypical way, of always being a step ahead of the rest of the world, of always being above stuffy business attire, office politics, and gradual decline.

This interpretation, the interpretation that Zahn had decided that Xerxes was no longer his friend, was the only one that could possibly explain Zahn's role in #6.

6) Dixie, Xerxes's girlfriend of 2½ years, the girl that he had, up until two months ago, rode tandem with every day on his Vespa scooter; the girl that he sat back-to-back with every morning at the Atlas Café drinking double espressos in small white espresso cups like two characters in a French novel set in the 1920s; the magic, magic girl with the shock-pink hair, the perma-puckered lips, the slightly crooked teeth; the girl with whom he had spoken so little, had needed to speak to so little; the girl who understood everything about him and about the world that surrounded him; the girl who understood the inherent value of eBay and why it was the only Internet site that truly mattered, the only Internet site that could truly transform the world; the girl who understood that it was the only Internet site that truly mattered and could truly transform the world because on it you

could purchase any make and model of Hot Wheels car ever manufactured. Dixie, the magic, magic, shock-pink girl, had not gone out last night because "she was just a little bored" but because she had transferred her love to Zahn, or, more accurately, as screwedcompany.com had seen fit to print, had taken to fucking Zahn, most likely because of her own recent cocaine addiction.

This was, thought Xerxes, as he sat in his desk chair launching #2 lead pencils at the ceiling, the logical progression. For some reason, a song that he and Zahn used to listen to was replaying in his mind. It was a song titled "Opportunities." The chorus went: *I've got the brains, you've got the looks, let's make lots of money.*

Xerxes had been the brains, Zahn the looks. There had been opportunities and they had pursued them. They were millionaires; millionaires like they had said they were going to be; millionaires who had stuck their noses up at everyone; millionaires who had borrowed insane amounts of money from people that they knew, and later people that they didn't know; millionaires who exuded wild confidence at all junctures; millionaires who were pulling the wool over everyone's eyes and who were OK with it.

And now it was over. The whole thing, the whole dream, over. Beginning. Middle. End. Xerxes threw another #2 lead pencil at his target. This time he missed the ceiling tile altogether. He was 31. His life had followed the bell curve perfectly. Everything had risen, had risen to a climax, and then disaster had struck and now he was, at 31, moving on to the denouement.

So now what? Xerxes wanted to make like a Wonder Twin and transform himself into a rain cloud that would simply float away. How could he leave his office and face them all? How could he face Kristin and her IKEA shelving units full of bonsai plants, how could he face John always listening to the latest emo mp3s, how could he tell them that he hadn't been lying to them, that he really had thought things were "cool" and that Zahn had things under control, that he had truly believed that the company stocks they were working for were more valuable than a decent salary.

He couldn't tell them. Xerxes stood up on his desk and removed the last remaining ceiling tile. He looked up past the exposed girders into the electrical wiring. He had set up this system himself, bundled the T1 lines and coaxial cables, wrapped them in static-free wiring. Above his head were wires that could connect him with half of humanity—at least the wealthier half.

The steps that he needed to take were clear:

1) Attempt to call Zahn and confirm the news. *Most likely scenario:* Zahn doesn't answer his cell and Xerxes leaves a message. The message Xerxes leaves: "Listen, Zahn, I've been trying to get ahold of you all morning. There was a rumor on screwedcompany.com that we need to bury fast. Don't know if you saw it. I'm going to talk to Sandy in PR so she can put out a press release and answer any questions, but I just need to make sure nothing in it is true." The message would assume the best, would show that Xerxes couldn't imagine that his friend would betray him, and would provide Zahn a foundation to pull out of it somehow, to pull a Zahn: "Yeah, well, Xerx we're a little short on cash, but I think there's something we can do. Let's talk to some people. Yeah, tell Sandy that none of it's true. We'll figure something out, Xerx. You and me, buddy. That shit about me and Dixie: *total bullshit*. We'll talk, Xerx. We'll talk. Fuck man, this is some crazy shit. We'll figure it out."

2) Assuming the *most likely scenario*: after leaving his message with Zahn, he would open the bottom drawer of his filing cabinet and then open a small aluminum box with moons welded into it. He would open this box and then pull out a small jar labeled GERBER'S PEAS. He would twist open the small jar labeled GERBER'S PEAS and pour its contents onto the freshly Windexed surface of his glass desk. Pills would cover the surface of his desk and he would look for a large blue pill that he knew was Paxil and another, smaller, blue pill with a V-shaped hole in the middle of it that he knew was Valium. He would take out a pill splitter and split the Valium in half. This is what he would need: 30mg of Paxil, 5mg of Valium. He would place the blue Paxil and the half a blue Valium on his tongue, wait until the salivary gland beneath his tongue filled his mouth with saliva, and then swallow them both with one concentrated movement of his Adam's apple.

3) After waiting 20 minutes for the anti-anxiety effect of the Paxil to kick in, an effect that would allow him to say the things he was going to say without a hint of emotion, and after waiting for the queasy, slowing effect of the Valium, which would allow him to forget the entire experience shortly afterwards,

Xerxes would push the intercom button on his telephone. He would say into the speaker, *"There will be a mandatory company meeting in the Everest Conference Room in 15 minutes. All are expected to attend."*

He would walk into that meeting room—late, of course—looking stoned in that special way that only he could pull off and still be considered businesslike. He would smile. He would stand in front of a dry-erase board and pull at his hair. Everyone would look at him, waiting for him to speak, and he would just stand there for a minute doing nothing, pulling at his hair until it stood straight up.

In that minute, he would have completely disarmed them all, his silence a strange hypnotism. This was his element, putting everyone at ease. Xerxes Meticula, the opiate of the masses. It would all be good after that moment. He would tell them exactly what was happening: the whole truth. They would take it just like he had taken the Paxil, the way everyone took everything in the late '90s—it's all good.

He could do it. The future that he had prepared himself for and that he was living now could continue. Perhaps the company would go under, perhaps he'd have to get Zahn into rehab, perhaps he'd have to suck it up and give Zahn and Dixie his blessing, but he and Zahn could weasel their way out of it.

He could work his way out of this. Yes, he could. His mind could see the next 20 moves, all the way through to the checkmate.

Yes, he knew the moves, but while Xerxes was standing on his desk looking up at the T1 lines, something inside him snapped.

5. YOU ARE NOW OUT OF PROTECTION.

XERXES WAKES WITH A START. How could he let this happen? How could he cut it so close? There are 8 minutes. 8 minutes until his province is out of protection. Xerxes flips the lid on his laptop and logs in. He becomes the Lady Peace & Love but Mostly Love.

She must find some targets fast. Her primary objectives are:

1) Maintain a military that is made up exclusively of defensive specialists, so that she can increase her net worth rapidly without fear of being attacked.

2) Maintain an above-average-sized guild of thieves. Send these thieves out every 12 hours to steal gold from opponents.

3) With the extra gold obtained through thievery, send scholars out to study the Housing and Alchemy Sciences. Housing Science increases the maximum population that can exist on each acre of land. If she is able to keep her acreage down compared to the size of her military, it is less likely that she will be attacked, since the object of a military attack is to obtain more acreage. The Alchemy Science increases the amount of gold that each peasant generates. The added income will allow her to purchase more advanced military units.

The only difficulty in this strategy is the risk inherent in her thievery operations. If her thieves are unsuccessful, a decent-sized percentage of them will be killed in the process, and worse yet, her thieves might get caught, which would mean that her opponent would receive a report that her province had made an attempt on them. Retaliation in The Realm is often swift and brutal.

The Lady Peace & Love but Mostly Love logs into The Realm. The screen reads,

Lady Peace & Love but Mostly Love,

Welcome back to The Realm; For your time away you have been awarded 100,000gc. You have 0 days left of protection in The Realm.

She is now out of protection. She scrolls through the lists of kingdoms, looking for a province with a below average net worth. Ideally, she would find a province that has become "inactive," its player starting the game but getting bored with it and not growing their province. If this player has built a lot of housing so that its peasants will have generated a great deal of income, but quit before attempting to develop a thieves' guild, then there will be plenty of easy gold for the taking.

The Lady thinks she has gotten lucky. In Kingdom 8, Province 19, she finds:

ULULULULU LAND, acres 200, net worth 12,429. An uninspired name that might indicate a player disinterested in the game, an acreage that suggests no attempt at recent growth, and a net worth that suggests that some effort was made to grow beyond the initial 8,000. Perfect. The Lady sets her wizards in motion:

Your wizards gather the shadows around them and . . .

Your spell is successful. Here are the vital statistics for ULULULULU LAND (8:19).

Ruler & Race: Ululu, Human
Land: 200 Acres
Money: 246,424gc
Food: 43,550 bushels
Runes: 0 runes
Peasants: 3,428 (100% Employed)
Networth: 12,429
Soldiers: 378
Swordsmen: 0
Archers: 0
Knights: 0
War-Horses: 0
Max. Possible Thieves/Wizards: 0 (0.00/Acre)
Estimated Thieves Number: 0 (0.00 per Acre)
Estimated Wizards Number: 0 (0.00 per Acre)

** Thievery Advisor **
Money: 589 thieves to steal up to 35,107gc
Food: 157 thieves to steal up to 3,775 bushels
Peasants: 422 thieves to kidnap up to 79 peasants
Soldiers: 37 thieves to kill up to 37 soldiers
Arson: 750 thieves to burn up to 3 homes
Horses: 0 thieves to release up to 0 horses

The Lady is pleased. It is rarely this easy—a target with no thieves guild sitting on a pot of gold. She clicks the "Thievery" link on the left-hand column of her screen.

Lady Peace & Love but Mostly Love,

Welcome to the Thieves' Guild. Masters of the black arts, your thieves can perform a variety of operations. What would you have them do?

The Lady sets the scroll-down bar to "Rob the Vaults." The screen reads:

This is an offensive action that may affect your honor rating. Which province would you have your thieves perform this action on?

The Lady is not concerned with honor. She sets the drop-down menus to "8" for kingdom, "19" for continent, then scrolls down to "ULULULULU LAND."

Your target has been selected. Your thieves have not been used recently and your current thievery effectiveness is 100%. How many thieves do you wish to send?

The Lady types 589 into the dialog box, then clicks a button that reads, "Send Thieves." The screen comes back with:

Your operation is a stunning success! Your thieves have returned with 35,107gc.

The Lady repeats the process over and over again until she has stolen all the gold coins she can safely steal. She watches as her thievery effectiveness steadily drops: 100%, 95%, 90%, 85%, 80%, 75%, 70%, 65%, 60%, 55%, 50%. Sometimes instead of reading, Your operation is a stunning success, it reads, Your operation is a success, you have lost 9 thieves in the operation, but the attempts are always successful and the money she gains overwhelmingly compensates for the thieves she is losing.

300,000 gold coins in the first 12 hours. The Lady is ecstatic. This is a tremendous start. She immediately pours this money into the Alchemy and Housing Sciences, just as she had planned.

The Lady Peace & Love but Mostly Love has finished with aggressive activities for the day. She wants to know how her kingdom mates are doing. She clicks on a link in the left-hand column of her screen that reads, "The Paper." The hourglass spins and a new page appears:

News for The Boneyard: April, YR1

☠ *DangerZone* (3:23) has captured 24 acres from 666 (12:5).

☠ *Ghost in the Machine* (4:7) has captured 31 acres from *Third Reich* (12:5).

☠ *Permafrost* (10:1) has pillaged the lands of *Third Reich* (12:5).

☠ *Land of BonZ* (12:5) attempted an invasion of *The Bermuda Triangle* (15:15) but was repelled.

☠ *The Bermuda Triangle* (15:15) has captured 28 acres from *Land of BonZ* (12:5).

☠ Our good province *Nevermore* (12:5) has captured 43 acres from *crackheads* (48:5).

☠ *Red Dragon* (9:19) attempted an invasion of *jekshtwdw* (12:5) but was repelled.

☠ *School You* (36:18) has captured 20 acres from *GurGle* (12:5).

*********************************** *End of News************************************

One successful attack for and 5 against is not a good sign of things to come. The Lady decides to check the kingdom rankings page to see how she is doing in comparison to the rest of her kingdom mates. Another list appears:

The Kingdom of The Boneyard (12:5)

	Race	Acres	Net Worth	Rank
1. Nevermore	Avian	260	18,239	Knight
2. The Strangely Peaceful Citadel of Blue Orcs	Orc	260	18,120	Lady
3. sKyLaR's PlEaSuRe PaLaCe	Faery	275	18,004	Knight
4. Ali Baba	Halfling	262	17,947	Knight
5. Wonderwizzies	Elf	256	17,734	Knight
6. Sleep Deprivation	Elf	240	17,631	Knight
7. War Place	Dwarf	250	17,624	Knight
8. One Hundred Happy Acres	Faery	290	17,612	Lady
9. Land of BonZ	Undead	272	15,210	King
10. ronald's homeland	Human	240	14,999	Knight
11. 666	Orc	216	13,873	Knight
12. Swallows	Avian	200	13,742	Lady
13. burgermeister meisterburger	Dwarf	240	13,741	Knight
14. The Frozen Wastes	Undead	240	13,249	Knight
15. Dandy Lion	Human	220	13,281	Knight

		Race	Acres	Net Worth	Rank
16.	penisbreath	Human	200	12,193	Knight
17.	Land of Hell	Orc	200	11,291	Knight
18.	Third Reich	Undead	219	11,192	Knight
19.	GurGle	Orc	180	8,210	Knight
20.	jekshtwdw	Human	200	8,000	Knight

The kingdom list is more promising. There seems to be a core group of good players within the kingdom. They are staying quiet like her, reserving their resources for less volatile times. The exception seems to be Raven. He is already flexing his muscles, showing everyone who is boss.

She prepares a message for him:

Dear Raven,

It appears that you are doing quite well. Nice attack on those crackheads *chuckle.* I look forward to joining forces against our mutual enemies in the future.

Signed, Lady Peace & Love but Mostly Love

Before she hits the "Send Message" button, something on the corner of the screen catches her eye, NEW MSG. She clicks on the link. It is another message from King BonZ:

kindom mates ~~ we must retaliate all attacks against our kindom! we will divide into 3 groups to coordinate our attaks. grop leaders will be chosen later on. the groups are ~~

red group: Nevermore, Wonderwizzies, One Hundred Happy Acres, The Frozen Wastes, GurGle, penisbreath, ronald's homeland

green group: Ali Baba, Sleep Deprivation, War Place, 666, Dandy Lion, Land of Hell, jekshtwdw

blue group: Land of BonZ, The Strangely Peaceful Citadel of Blue Orcs, sKyLaR's PlEaSuRe PaLaCe, Swallows, Third Reich, burgermeister meisterburger

post all activity against provinces that have hit us or kindomsthat we are at war
wit on your group's thread in the message boards

King BonZ

King BonZ is nothing if not aggressive. He is dictatorial and tyrannical;
he hasn't consulted anyone to see if they thought this was a good way to do
things. He is encouraging aggression early in the age, a dangerous strategy.
And yet, The Lady admires him for his organizational skills. This will motivate the newer provinces and keep them active. Later on, they will need even
the provinces that are not particularly strong.

Of course, she has no intention of following the king's dictates. She
doesn't check the message boards. She will not retaliate against provinces
that have found the kingdom's weaknesses and exploited them. Not for now.
For now she will remain strangely peaceful. The Lady sends her message to
the province named *Nevermore*, then she logs out of The Realm.

Thank you for your time in The Realm. For bonus gold, be sure to visit our sponsors.

6. KNOW YOUR MATH.

GEK-LIN TROUNG IS SPEAKING with Uncle Charley. She is smoking fiercely, smoking the last cigarette from a pack of illegally obtained Marlboros, the last
cigarette from a pack that she purchased from Uncle Charley a mere three
hours ago, a pack she purchased with the coins she had stolen earlier in the day
from an old woman's satchel. It is 3 A.M. in Bangkok. Gek-Lin is 14. Uncle
Charley is 35. Uncle Charley is not Gek-Lin's uncle, nor the uncle of anyone
else at the Blue Moon Internet Café, an Internet café in a basement underneath the kitchen of a restaurant that serves the troops of international
backpackers who trek through Bangkok at all times of the year, an Internet
café that during the day is filled with these international backpackers writing e-mails about the great cave diving they did last week off the coast of the
Klongs, but during the night is filled with orphans, a cadre of neglected, but
highly intelligent, local 12- to 17-year-olds.

Uncle Charley is the owner of the café. He was, himself, one of these gifted
orphans—the son of an anonymous U.S. serviceman and the Vietnamese

whore who serviced him—so he understands these kids, understands their drive, a drive to live and experience that is far greater than that of the average child. The Blue Moon is a place these kids can go at night, at night when they would otherwise be sleeping under grub-eaten banana leaves in the Bangkok steam, when they would be simultaneously sleeping and contracting infectious disease.

Besides providing the orphans with a place to go at night, Uncle Charley also puts aside for them leftovers scraped off the plates of the Blue Moon's guests: monkfish in coconut curry; calamari in a yellow sauce. The orphans dig into the delicacies with chopsticks that move like the scissors of a sweat-shop seamstress.

He also provides the orphans with showers, showers that he shuffles them into one at a time as they arrive mud-caked and salty from a day pilfering food and hiding in the shade of Bangkok's open-air market. Although the sustenance and hygiene that Uncle Charley provides the orphans is certainly valuable, it is not what draws the orphans to the Blue Moon Internet Café, what draws them are Uncle Charley's 486s and 56k modem connections. What draws them is a nightly twelve-hour escape from reality.

Although Uncle Charley could, and probably should, be considered a kind of Mother Teresa, he understands, as would any orphan who has lived on the streets, that philanthropy comes with a price. He cannot maintain twenty 486s, no matter how unwanted and outdated, and twenty modem connections on the meager income he exacts from the backpackers who need to change their $100 American Express Traveler's Cheques for their .25¢ meals at the Blue Moon. Uncle Charley maintains his café and orphanage through the X2 webcams he has secreted in the showers.

Gek-Lin Troung is angry. Uncle Charley has translated the messages that have appeared on her kingdom's message boards from English to Thai. She does not understand why her provinces are not listening to her, why they are not retaliating for their kingdom mates' losses.

Uncle Charley understands what Gek-Lin's kingdom mates are doing: they are being patient. Gek-Lin, if she were smart, would be doing the same, but she is young and doesn't understand such things.

While Uncle Charley is aware of Gek-Lin's faults, he can't help but respect Gek-Lin's willpower and verve. The fact that she, at age 14, was able to gain the throne of a kingdom in The Realm without being any good at playing the game fascinated him. Gek-Lin used brute force. In the last age, Uncle

Charley had translated the words that she had wanted to say to her king-dom mates. He thought it was ridiculous, Gek-Lin demanding that they make her king so early in the game. But they had done it, and Uncle Charley himself had learned that patience in The Realm is not necessarily a virtue, sometimes it is important to reach up and grab the gold ring as soon as it appears.

This age her strategy is working to a point, but her poor game play is lowering her standing with her kingdom mates.

Gek-Lin slaps the sides of her cheap, putty-colored monitor with the palms of her hands. "Fuck it," she says in the English she has been learning from Uncle Charley and the backpackers upstairs.

"If you damage my property, you will no longer be allowed to play," says Uncle Charley.

Not responding to him, but rather to the drama that is unfolding in front of her, Gek-Lin replies, "Why I bounce?"

Uncle Charley looks at Gek-Lin's screen:

Your troops have been routed. You have lost 150 skeletons and 15 ghouls.

Gek-Lin's thick lips are extended in a pout. Her palms have left the sides of her monitor, and are pressing into her cheeks.

"Why did you make that attack?" Uncle Charley asks.

"I retal," answers Gek-Lin.

"The game is about math, Gek-Lin, you must study your algebra. If you study your algebra you will begin to understand the force you must use to be successful in your attacks."

"Algebra boring!" Gek-Lin shouts.

"If you apply it to your game, you will find that it is not boring. And once you begin to understand algebra many other doors will open to you. Maybe you will even go to America one day."

Gek-Lin turns to Uncle Charley. She crosses her arms in a gesture of frustration. "Show me the algebra then."

"I've shown it to you before."

"Show me again. Now."

"Well, if you take your soldiers and multiply them by—"

"No. Write down."

"We don't have any pa—"

"On the computer. Type into my computer."

"You can't just—"

"If I have question, I ask you."

"There is more than one algebraic equation, Gek-Lin. If I write them all down, you won't understand which formula works for which race of peoples you are attacking, and besides, you need to be able to make the formulas yourselves because the rules change. It's a system in flux."

"I know—*flux*. I read. I study. Write them down, now!"

Uncle Charley reprimands Gek-Lin's incorrect use of the English present, "I *will* read. I *will* study."

Gek-Lin's eyes could assassinate. She says nothing in reply.

Uncle Charley submits, "OK. Scoot over."

"No! On your computer! E-mail to me!"

Uncle Charley adores Gek-Lin's obstinacy. She is, in a way, a born general, but she needs to tame her rashness if she is to succeed, either in The Realm or in Real Life. Of course, Uncle Charley has a soft spot for Gek-Lin. It is nice to be so needed, and although Gek-Lin would never admit it herself, she listens to every word Uncle Charley says. He would sit down and type out every formula he could think of that was applicable to The Realm. Besides, Gek-Lin deserves it. She is Uncle Charley's top-earning child porn star. The way she attacks herself with soap and a sponge in front of the web cams in the shower is the stuff of online legend.

As Uncle Charley got up to return to the café counter, a counter that had on it both an old manual register and Charley's Pentium, the only Pentium in the café, and one of the few real Pentiums in all of Bangkok, Gek-Lin's contemptuous voice stops him, "Wait. You must type me message."

This was a never-ending task that Uncle Charley had unnecessarily taken upon himself, translating each kid's messages from Thai to English. He gave each kid a kind of signature writing style. For example, he had given Gek-Lin's persona, King BonZ, an overbearing voice. He printed her words with misspellings, on purpose, to hint at her impatience. He realizes that this isn't doing Gek-Lin any favors, either in The Realm itself or in Real Life. Gek-Lin will probably misspell English for the rest of her days, but Uncle Charley is a gamer, and gamers like to give their characters personalities.

The other reason Uncle Charley translates the messages is to keep his English writing skills sharp. He has no intention of actually using these skills to better himself; he simply does it to remind himself of what he once was, and what he once had hoped to be.

At Bangkok University, Uncle Charley had been an English scholar, and much admired by both his professors and fellow students. He had memorized a Pocket Oxford English Dictionary. Those who had an inkling of his past were amazed, amazed that an orphan with no formal education was capable of reaching such heights. These same people would have been even more amazed if they had known that one April when he was seventeen, Uncle Charley had mailed his entire savings of $40, a savings he had accumulated by performing fellatio on a few of the surprisingly large number of gay Navy SEALs, to the Standard Academic Testing Corporation in Washington, DC.

Uncle Charley, known not as Uncle Charley at age seventeen but as Charlie Hum, received the reply from the Standard Academic Testing Corporation in the form of an 8x11 manila envelope with a 75¢ Amelia Earhart airmail stamp on it, an airmail stamp that he, to this day, wears in a locket around his neck. He received this reply from his pimp, who was eyeing him with inquisitiveness. The letter inside the envelope instructed him to arrive no later than 8 A.M. on May 1st at the nearest SAT testing facility, which, as he studied the list of locations, happened to be eight hundred miles away in Hong Kong. Although the cost of the passport and bus fare meant he would have to graduate from standard fellatio to more specialized forms of sex-play, Charlie Hum had never felt so elated.

He knew he would do well. His clients had been his teachers. After the dead silence of the sex act, his clients talked. They didn't expect that he would understand, him not knowing English, but he had understood almost every word, and those words that he didn't understand, he looked up in the Pocket OED that he had found at the U.S. Consulate General.

Charley knew math too, had learned it from his pimp, a pimp who took regular trips to Honolulu and Los Angeles, a pimp who said to Charley, "You know calculus, Charley, you know the world." Charley's pimp would do anything for his boys and girls, and since Charley had expressed an interest in math, Charley's pimp had taught him everything he knew, and what he didn't know he showed him in his books, piles and piles of mathematics texts that littered Charley's pimp's floor.

Charley's pimp was an unusual pimp in another way. He encouraged his boys and girls to quit. They were no good to him once they hit seventeen anyway, so when the airmail letter came from the Standard Academic Testing Corporation for Charley he didn't flip out and accuse him of disloyalty, nor did he flip out when Charley disappeared for a week, nor did he flip out when a much fatter envelope from the Standard Academic Testing Corporation showed up a couple of months later with Charley's scores. In fact, when Charley's pimp opened the letter, opened it before showing it to Charley, opened it before showing it to Charley not out of spite, but out of pride and curiosity, when Charley's pimp opened the letter and read MATH: 740; VERBAL: 720, when Charley's pimp realized that these scores were quite possibly the highest ever attained by a Thai citizen, and certainly the highest ever by a Thai child sex slave, he wept like any caring mother or father or pimp would.

Almost as surprising as young Charley's rise to academic heights was his fall from it. He had just obtained a scholarship to Oxford's Business School, a scholarship that he was sure to accept, since it meant leaving Vietnam to go to England, the country where Charley's beloved language was the native tongue. He had also recently become engaged, a fact that, given his troubled past, was perhaps more surprising than his academic success.

To Charley, becoming engaged was the final step, the thing that pushed him from the masses in the red into the few in the black. His fiancé was the kind of person who rode in a tuk-tuk; not someone, like he had been, who dodged them. He was now amongst the users rather than the used.

Of course, once he became a user he didn't like it. And, of course, he fell in love with someone other than his fiancé, a fellow street urchin, a few years younger than himself, just a girl, just a girl working for yen. And that girl—she was just a girl—she met a john with whom she smoked a bit too much opium, a john who had a fascination with razors, a john who had a fascination with razors and what they could do to just a girl.

And of course, one morning he woke up, woke up in a bed (he had a bed!), woke up to the phone (he had a phone!), woke up next to his bride to be (he had a bride to be!), woke up to the voice of his pimp (his pimp?), woke up to the voice of his pimp saying, "The police think I did it, Charley. They'll listen to you, Charley. You're respectable. You know I wouldn't do it, Charley. I loved you all," woke up to the voice of himself saying, "Who? What? Where?" woke up to the voice of Charley's pimp saying, "No one. It was just a girl. She's at the station. Can you come?" woke up to his own voice saying, "Yes. I will come," woke up to his bride-to-be saying, "Who? What? Where?"

Charley Hum left his phone, his bed, and his bride-to-be, to exonerate a pimp and identify a girl. He identified a girl lying dead in an interrogation room with cracking, pea green walls. He identified a girl lying dead under the remnants of a greasy, cardboard box, a box cut into thirds with a razor, just a girl lying dead cut up with a razor, thin ribbons of epidermis exposed with a razor, just a girl—his girl—having bled to death, cut up with a razor.

That morning, Charley Hum left his phone, his bed, his bride-to-be, his dead lover, his scholarship to Oxford, his bright future safe and warm and in the black, and left Vietnam for Thailand. He thought to himself—*nevermore*.

★ ★ ★

Uncle Charley begins to type the note that Gek-Lin dictates. He types:

kindom mates ~~ we must retaliate all attacks against our kindom! we will divide into 3 groups to coordinate our attaks. grop leaders will be chosen later on. the groups are ~~

7. YOUR SUCCESS IS DETERMINED VERY EARLY IN THE AGE.

OUTSIDE THERE ARE RUMBLINGS. Days have passed since the poetry slam incident and still he fails to understand. His concern is for her, when his concern should be for himself. She must send him another message, must bring him, somehow, back to the present.

There are rumblings. Gabriella is looking out the window of her apartment while Bubba, the neighbor's one-year-old, eats popcorn bits off the orange shag carpet. The first thunderstorms of Northern Arizona's monsoon season are rolling in. The clouds are black and flat-topped and flat-bottomed like anvils, like the anvils that The Coyote used to throw over the edge of sheer cliffs in order to crush the Road Runner, like anvils attached to a thick rope attached to the ankle of The Coyote, like anvils that would cause The Coyote to sail downward, rapidly accelerating, to a sure death at the bottom of a cliff, where he would land face-first in a giant cactus, completely flattened, full of thorns, birds flying around his head to represent a concussion, and yet alive.

The sky is big and booming outside of Gabriella's window and she decides to take Bubba for a hike. She pulls a white T-shirt over his head and tries to pull it over his belly, but it is too small and it crops back up so that his outie is exposed. Bubba is wearing the too-small T-shirt and a diaper and that is all.

Gabriella places Bubba in the car seat that she has temporarily buckled into the back seat of her blue Ford Escort. Bubba is sucking down the liquid in his plastic bottle. He has advanced past formula and now drinks whole milk, gallons of it. Bubba has more than the average share of baby fat.

Gabriella buckles Bubba into his car seat then walks around the car into the driver's side. The storm clouds are spreading thick above Gabriella's head like the whites of an egg on a skillet. She gets into the Escort and drives past the Planned Parenthood building, then onto Main Street. She drives a mile or so until Main Street becomes a winding two-laner called Granite Tower Road. The air is charged and Gabriella can feel the charge. Today is that day. Every day is that day for Gabriella.

Looking up, Gabriella sees the familiar shape of Granite Tower, one of the three Rest Stop landmarks that are plastered on postcards in the tourist shops: Granite Tower, Whiskey Row, The Old Courthouse. Granite Tower looks like a thumb sticking up into the gray sky, looks like it wants to hitch a ride and go somewhere else, somewhere big and sprawling like Phoenix or big and mysterious like North Dakota, anywhere but little, middle-of-the-road Rest Stop.

Gabriella's thought today is *SHE must die so that HE might live.* Xerxes is being stifled, prevented from being his true self, because of her. He would leave Rest Stop, return to San Francisco, pick up the pieces; be Xerxes Meticula, FOUNDER; be the smiling, thick-lipped, slightly orange-tinted boy regularly featured on CNN, a spitting image of herself, only masculine, not feminine; be her better half, the half that lived inside the world while she lived outside it. He would be all these things, but she was preventing him from doing it.

Now the world was off-center. They were both spinning around outside of it. They were like two electrons floating around an empty nucleus: H^{--}. They were leaving the world with an extremely negative charge.

A raindrop hits Gabriella's windshield like the first splatter of a Pollock painting. A lightning stream, not a bolt or a flash, but a stream, a stream that must be hitting a power source somewhere and shutting down a grid, flows lava-like behind Granite Tower.

Gabriella drives the windy two miles down Granite Tower Road. She drives past the ranger station. She flashes her ALL PARKS pass at a bored ranger who nods and tips his thin-brimmed ranger hat. She turns to the left, then parks her car in front of the Granite Tower trailhead. She gets out of the car and pulls Bubba out of his car seat. She doesn't have a backpack for Bubba, or a BabyBjörn, instead she carries him in her arms. She cradles him as she begins her climb up the Granite Tower trail. The clouds above the tower are growing as ominously and quickly as the clouds above Devil's Tower in *Close Encounters of the Third Kind*.

When Gabriella and Xerxes were young, and they were sitting in the living room of their house in Plano, Texas, the living room with the cozy, zebra-striped couch; and the weatherman on TV was showing radar screens with big red splotches, their mother Melissa would tell them that the low-pitched sounds they were hearing was God moving the furniture upstairs, or, alternatively, the angels bowling. Gabriella believed these things. She agreed with her mother and said things like, "that must have been the sofa," or "strike." Xerxes would just roll his eyes and say derisively, "Mom," and then go out to the porch where he would watch the yellow-tinted sky swirl. The weatherman would say, "Thunderstorm Warnings for Dallas, Tarrant and Denton Counties until 6 P.M." "Flash Flood Warnings for Dallas and Tarrant Counties until 9 P.M." "Tornado Watch for Dallas, Tarrant and Denton Counties until 6 P.M."

Gabriella would grab her mother's hand, pleading with her to bring her to the laundry room where it was safe. Meanwhile, Melissa would yell, "Xerxes, get inside!" and Gabriella would yell, "Come on, Xerxes," but Xerxes wouldn't come.

What it was that had erased Gabriella's fears was unclear. She had been a shy, easily frightened child. She was a bed wetter. She hid under her covers from monsters, the Cookie Monster, the big burly blue Cookie Monster with bulging black eyes. But now she was like the girl in the Neutral Milk Hotel song who had escaped the Nazis:

> Now she's a little boy in Spain
> Playing piano in the flames.

There was no fear anymore. She had become comfortably numb. Maybe it was what had happened to her in Nepal; or maybe it was what Xerxes had done to her when they were kids; or maybe it was what the doctors said, "a chemical imbalance;" or maybe it was the evil, money-grubbing, out-for-a-game-of-golf doctors themselves, doctors who live under that sick code of distance from their patients, that code that the AMA trains all of them to believe, against their own better judgment, *keep a safe distance*, doctors who add Red Dye #40 and stick you on a Petri dish; or maybe it was the chemicals meant to balance the chemical imbalance; or maybe she had been struck like Paul, formerly Saul, while riding her donkey down a path one day, maybe she had been chosen, chosen by God, or better yet, chosen by Shiva, the Indian goddess of destruction. It was so hard to tell. So hard to analyze. So confusing, What had happened to her? What was real and what was unreal? What was *the disease*? Why did they call it *a disease*? What was *the cause*? Why did they need *a cause*?

It really didn't matter. Today would be the day: the day of sacrifice. Gabriella's boots slog through a stream of water that cascades down a thin ribbon of concrete. She is not in good shape, her thighs tremble in rhythm with the thunder. She overheard Melissa on the phone with one of the Buena Vista girls yesterday: *and she used to be such a pretty girl, it's such a shame*. She stops in the rain. She shifts Bubba from her right arm to her left. She tries to light a Liggett but it is soggy and splits. Bubba's eyes are ice blue and Gabriella's eyes are emerald green and the tips of the blue spruce that line the Granite Tower path, the perfectly shaped blue spruce that make perfect Christmas trees, are ice blue. She starts up again, moving forward, moving upward, mummy-like, a mummy with a big sack of potatoes. Mummy and child. Lightning flashes. *One one-thousand, two one-thousand*, boom. The storm center is two miles away and closing. Gabriella's face is frozen, unrippling, an ice-covered lake.

★ ★ ★

Xerxes has seen the storm front too. At first, his back is to it. His back, slightly hunched, hunched slightly to the left from a mild case of childhood scoliosis—his back faces the blind-covered windows of the downstairs living room which looks over the Mingus Mountains towards the storm, while his face studies The Realm strategy sites on the laptop in front of him, studies the strategy sites until his digital clock hits the hour, at which time he logs back into The Realm. Each time he logs into The Realm he finds that his net worth has risen astronomically. The Lady is now first in net worth in the kingdom—first, in fact, on the continent, and ninth in the entire Realm. The thieving + defense strategy is working. No one has even tried to hit her. There isn't even a:

So-and-so has attempted a thievery operation on our province and failed.

Or a:

Our mystics sense that so-and-so has attempted to cast an evil spell upon our lands.

Xerxes has never tasted this level of success in The Realm before and he is at a loss as to what he should do. His thieves and magicians are all spent, and he has chosen to keep his soldiers idle.

Xerxes walks to the kitchen, which he doesn't use as a kitchen, but rather as a place to store maps, paperwork, and a couple of two-liter bottles of Coke. He walks to the kitchen countertop where all these things are strewn about and unrolls a topographical map that reads REST STOP, GROOM CREEK, POTATO PATCH. He unrolls this and marks the trails he plans to take with a yellow highlighter.

Despite the potential for rain, Xerxes is not concerned about getting struck by lightning. Like a car, a bicycle is one of the safest places to be in a thunderstorm: rubber does not conduct electricity, so as long as you're on your bike and your tires are on the ground, you're safe. There's some danger of being killed from the residual heat of a nearby tree getting hit, but this is a risk that Xerxes is willing to take. He imagines himself muddy from head to toe. Yes, it will be good to leave The Realm for a while. It will be good to feel the elements.

★ ★ ★

Xerxes was 12. Gabriella was 12. Xerxes would construct a "fortress" in the family room out of a worn gold blanket. He would secure one corner to the pool table using billiard balls, another corner he would drape around a chair and secure with the foot of the chair, another he would throw over a lamp. He would put a pool stick in the middle to hold the whole structure up. The pool stick would often fall down and interrupt whatever was happening inside the fortress.

Xerxes would invite the neighborhood kids over to play Dungeons & Dragons and they would all crawl into Xerxes's fortress to play. Jason was a fighter, he was too dumb to be anything else. Tyler, a neighbor, was pretty dense too. He had to be a fighter as well. Peter, the other neighbor, was smarter and got to be a wizard. Gabriella was always stuck being the cleric. "But I don't wanna be a stupid cleric." Gabriella would say. To which Xerxes would reply, "But your party needs a cleric."

Clerics were boring because they fought with maces and maces were big clunky balls with spikes connected by a chain to a handle. They looked kind of like the wands that the priest would use to sprinkle holy water on the congregation in mass. Everyone else fought with swords and sometimes the swords were magical. It was really hard to find a magical mace. All clerics did was heal the fighters and wizards when they got hurt.

Xerxes was always the Dungeon Master. He would put up a screen that had a gold dragon on it. The gold dragon had a long column of spikes running down its back like shark's teeth and smoke coming out of its nostrils. The dragon was asleep, guarding a sea of gold that it had stolen from humans in fits of rage. The dragon was asleep, but had a sixth sense. It would always wake up to defend its treasure.

Xerxes would put up the screen and roll dice behind it. The die were oddly-shaped and opaque like gems. When you bought them at the store you had to take a white crayon and color in the grooves where the numbers were, then scrape off the excess crayon with a penny or a fingernail. You had to do this to make the numbers show. There was the ruby-colored 20-sided die that was the "attack" die. You used this when a character, when Jason or Tyler, took a swing at an orc. For some reason, they were always fighting orcs, going into the orcs' hideaway, a cave in a mountain somewhere, the Mountains of Shadow, and killing orcs. The orcs usually had a big pit in front of their cave covered with branches so that you couldn't see it. If you were smart you used your sword to poke at the ground in front of you as you walked or you had your wizard cast a Detect Traps spell. Most of the time Jason and Tyler would forget to do this and, wham, they'd fall into the pit, trip off the alarm, and all the orcs would come running.

Besides the 20-sided die, there was also a diamond-colored 12-sided die, a rose quartz-colored 10-sided die, a sapphire-colored 8-sided die, an emerald-colored 6-sided die, and an ochre-colored 4-sided die. The 4-sided die was the only die that wasn't opaque. Gabriella had to use the 4-sided die whenever she attacked things with her mace. "But I can never get more than a 4," she would say.

Behind the gold dragon screen, Xerxes would roll the dice. He would pull the dice out of a purple, velvet pouch and roll them idly. Much of the time he would roll the dice without a purpose, to stall while he figured out what to do next. He would roll the dice while he consulted maps that he had drawn out on graph paper with a pencil, maps that he hid behind the screen. He would say, "There is a fork in the cavern here, do you take the right or the left branch?" Sometimes he would roll them to see if Jason, Tyler, Peter, and Gabriella had encountered a wandering monster; giant bats, or rats that crawled down cavern halls and walls. Whatever Xerxes did when he was the Dungeon Master, he was in control, was in control until Jason or Tyler would run out from under the gold blanket yelling, "That's not *fair!*"—their fighters lying dead in a pool of blood at the bottom of a pit, pierced in the gut with orcish spears.

Underneath the gold blanket was also where Xerxes would drag Gabriella. This is the place where he would drag her with his arms underneath her armpits, his hands locked behind her neck, would drag his sister kicking and screaming, would drag her because he was now bigger than she was, because he was the Dungeon Master, because he had the power, because he was the boy and she was the girl.

Underneath the gold blanket is where Xerxes would drag Gabriella to find out what was underneath the bikini tops of the vixens in the *Monster Manual* and the *Player Compendium*, where he would drag her to discover the secrets of the succubus, where he would unmask the medusa.

Underneath the gold blanket, Xerxes would pin his sister down by the wrists, would pull up her shirt while she squirmed beneath him, would unhook her training bra, would unsnap her shorts and pull them down, would pull down the white cotton Target panties, would look at the small, pointed rises and the W-shaped creases below, would look at these and then let her go, tears welling in the corners of her emerald-colored eyes.

★ ★ ★

Xerxes is climbing up the last rise of Rubrick's Mine Road and Granite Tower Trail Connector. His asthma is acting up and he takes in oxygen in rapid, shallow breaths. His legs are on their last legs, have gone rubber, are shaky. He has fallen once, hard, while on the Groom Creek Horse Loop. His front wheel had slipped on a slanted slab of granite and then wedged in a small crack. The bike had gone end-over-end and Xerxes had landed first on his wrists, then on his head, then gone end-over-end himself. When he got up, he didn't see birds like the Coyote, but small blue dots in his peripheral vision with tails like comets. He sat there for a moment in a bed of pine needles, looking at his cut-up hands, taking off his helmet and staring at the baseball-sized gash in it, toying with the brakes on his Cannondale that had been bent backward. He sat there and calculated whether it would be faster to climb back up Spruce Mountain and go back to his parents' house or whether it would be best to stick to the trails that he had mapped out. 10 miles with a hard 1,000-foot climb back. 8 miles with a more moderate 800-foot climb ahead. Xerxes chose to continue on.

Xerxes is climbing the last rise and he is questioning his sanity. Rain is coming down in sheets. It's like he wanted it to be—he's covered in mud—only now he's not so sure it was a good idea.

Xerxes is climbing the last rise in his third gear, the third gear out of twenty-four. He is barely moving. His back tire slips in the mud, and he steers the front tire rapidly to the right, then to the left, in order to keep his balance. The storm behind Xerxes is closing rapidly. He thought he could beat it to the top, but the wind has risen and it's picking up speed. A stream of water is now coming down the path and the mud is too thick for Xerxes to continue on wheels. Xerxes gets off the bike. Turns. Turns to see it.

Cumulonimbus: The Mother of All Storm Clouds. A black hole. A vortex. An upside-down sombrero. A spinning, swirling center that sucks up moisture and a flat horizontal periphery that spits it back out. In the Midwest, the center would mean tornado, but here, in Arizona, it means electricity, electricity that you see in every issue of *Arizona Highways*, electricity against a purple backdrop and the black shadows of saguaros. The center will hit him just as he reaches the top of Granite Tower. Xerxes turns back and then falls in the mud. Falls a second time. Gets back up. Limps from where his kneecap hit a pointed rock. Moves forward up the slippery slope. Logic has given way. There is no reason not to go back down where it's safer. No reason at all. *An object in motion tends to stay in motion.*

Lightning flashes. *One one-thou*— Boom. Half a mile. Maybe a third.

* * *

Gabriella will sacrifice Isaac. She will be just like Abraham. It will be Biblical. She is at the top of Granite Tower. Not actually at the top of the tower, but at the base of its final reaches, for the tower is a monolith, unclimbable without a rope and some leads. The tower is home to peregrines and rock climbers.

Gabriella is at the base of the tower. She is on her knees in the gravel. She is retching, dry-heaving. She holds herself up with one arm, while with the other she holds Bubba to her chest. While she heaves, Bubba drools. The drool mixes with the huge puddle that Gabriella kneels in. The detox makes her do this. Makes her dry heave when she exercises. And also, she is exhausted, exhausted from hauling Bubba up a mile-long trail in the rain.

Lightning flashes. *One one-thou—* Boom.

It is almost here. It is almost time.

Gabriella stands up. Some of the gravel drops off her legs and leaves indents in her skin; some of it stays there, imbedded. Gabriella sees the cumulonimbus cloud, too, but she doesn't see it as cumulonimbus. She sees a chariot and six white horses. She thinks: *This is how it must end. I am to be taken. I will be taken and so shall this innocent one.*

It is not suicide, what she is doing. It is being taken. Allowing the elements to do with her what they will.

The cloud rushes towards Gabriella, low enough to embrace her in its mist. One-third of a mile. One-fourth. One-eighth. One-sixteenth. The wind screams like the phantoms that Indiana Jones released when he opened the Ark of the Covenant. She holds Bubba above her head. As she holds him above her head, sleet comes and stings him like a hundred hornets, but he just smiles, arms outstretched, as happy and content as the fat baby in a tire in a Michelin commercial. Gabriella opens her lungs. Shouts at the tempest, "Strike us oh powers that be and take us down."

And then she sees him, sees him pedaling furiously up the connector trail. It is Satan. Satan on a Cannondale.

* * *

Something strikes Xerxes and knocks him off his bike. He falls for the third time. It is not rain that hits him. It is not sleet. It is not lightning, although in the split-second before he loses consciousness, he thinks it is. What sends Xerxes sprawling off his seat and down a 20-foot ledge into the spiky, waiting arms of a century plant is a baby.

A baby falls from the sky and knocks Xerxes to the ground.

8. WEATHER THE FIRST STORMS. REBUILD QUICKLY.

IT WAS SO KEANU in *The Matrix* to do what he had done next: *Follow the white rabbit.*

Xerxes stood on the glass-topped desk with the halogen lamp looking up at the coaxial cables and T1 lines thinking, *I must escape.* He had never had this thought before. In 31 years, his life had followed a linear, escalating path, and suddenly he didn't want it anymore. For the first time, he was listening to his own bullshit, the bullshit that he had fed to his employees—*think outside the box*—and realizing that he had never really done that himself. Sure, his outward appearance was unusual, and his mannerisms as well. He had spent a lot of time fostering these things. But was his eccentricity a façade? What had he ever done that wasn't simply following the path laid out for him?

To exit the machine, you must first enter it. Xerxes looked up at the circular cover of the air duct above him. It was funny, really. Hysterical. Either he would enter the intestines of the beast itself and be shat out on the other side, unscathed, cleansed even, either he would enter the dark night of the soul and emerge enlightened, or he would be another outlandish entry for screwed-company.com. Xerxes removed the cover of the air duct.

Tomorrow, Xerxes thought, the headline would read:

Just when you thought it couldn't get worse for maximuminventory.com, it did!

On Friday morning, the morning after the Bimbo's incident, a maximuminventory.com employee thought she heard rats in the air conditioning vents and promptly called A1 Exterminators, the first extermination company listed in the book. A1 Exterminators, proud of their designation as the Bay Area's fastest acting extermination outfit, and also happening to occupy a small unit in the basement of 2050 Folsom St., just downstairs from the offices of maximuminventory.com, responded in an uncharacteristically quick, even for them, five minutes.

Entering the building with giant, pill-shaped tanks of rat poison strapped to their backs, holding in their hands spray-devices armed and ready to dispense large quantities of toxins with a single twitch of the index finger and thumb, and wearing gas masks that made them look, alarmingly, like giant rats themselves, A1 Exterminators crawled up into the air conditioning ducts. What they discovered there was Xerxes Meticula, the company's founder.

Thomas Stench, the good man from A1 Exterminators who had responded to the call, pulled Mr. Meticula out of the duct by his Chuck Taylors, threw him over his shoulder, and carried him down the ladder.

"Here's the rat," he exclaimed.

Mr. Meticula declined to be interviewed for this article, and a motive for his foray into the company air conditioning system is unclear. Speculation that Mr. Meticula may have been attempting a clean escape from the maximuminventory.com premises due to its impending bankruptcy does not seem unfounded.

Or worse than getting caught, maybe he'd get stuck. Maybe someone would detect a horrible smell. Maybe Kristin Yellner, the receptionist, would be tending one of her bonsai plants, be contemplating how a snip here or there would effect the bonsai's shape five years down the road, when she would say to John, "What is that horrible smell?"

John Drake, the graphic designer, wouldn't hear her. His headphones were always on. But he would turn, having smelled it himself, crinkling his nose and looking up at her quizzically.

"Dude," he would say, too loudly, speaking to drown out the music in his ears. He would take out his earphones, one at a time, still speaking too loudly, "What *is* that?"

John and Kristin would sniff around boxes; boxes that are a constant fixture in any Internet company's office; boxes that lay around marking the exit of one employee and the entrance of another; boxes marking the movement of one employee to the cubicle of another; boxes that symbolize the lack of stick-it-to-ive-ness of an Internet company, its state of constant change, its *waste*. John and Kristin would poke around the boxes and then look up. "It's coming from the ceiling," John would say.

John, being the take-charge type, would pull a conference table out of the K2 Conference Room and a chair out of his cubicle, would stack the chair on the conference table, would stand on the chair and lift up a rectangular ceiling tile, would lift the tile and be overwhelmed with the stench of piss and shit and decay. In a moment of true enlightenment, John would say, "My God, it's *human*."

Of course, what if this didn't happen; what if he got away with it? It made perfect sense. Escape through the machine. He had studied the blueprints, knew exactly the path he would take, knew the width of the ducts and the danger points. It shouldn't be that hard, he thought, and he could avoid being above most of the common areas. He would simply stay over the conference rooms that weren't being used that morning. The difficult part would be the 20-foot vertical shaft that led to the roof, but it shouldn't be too bad, he should be able to wedge himself in the metal walls and climb. It would be just like climbing a chimney. And how much fun. How much adventure. What a superhero.

Xerxes hoisted himself into the 18" hole. As he disappeared into the circulatory system of 2050 Folsom St., the soles of his shoes read: *Converse All Star*.

★　★　★

When Xerxes regains consciousness, he has two immediate and conflicting concerns. The first concern enters his brain from the lower regions of his central nervous system. It is pain. Something, something very sharp, has entered his skin just millimeters from the 2nd vertebrae in the lumbar region of his spine, has entered his skin and is still there. The second concern enters his brain from up top, from his cerebrum. It is a thirst for knowledge, a need to know *what the fuck just happened*.

The second concern confronts Xerxes first, confronts Xerxes in the shape of his disheveled sister, wild-eyed and wailing at him,

"Do you know what it's like? Do you know what it's like to be medicated all the time? Do you know what it does to you? It makes you crazy. I'm crazy, Xerxes. CRAAAAAAAAAAAAAZZY. Crazy. You killed him, Xerxes. YEEEEEEEEEEEW. You did it. It's your fault."

Gabriella's voice rambles on, is like an elixir. Xerxes wants to sleep, but he can't. He must know. And there is pain. Pain. He opens his eyes, first one and then the other.

Gabriella is hovering over him, her voice has gone from its hysterical pitch to a much more frightening monotone. She has noticed that Xerxes is alive. She's mimicking Bones from *Star Trek*.

"He's dead, Jim. He's dead, Jim. He's dead, Jim. He's dead—"

Xerxes hears himself speak. He speaks in a commanding groan, like a creature from the grave. "Put the baby down," he says.

Only after Xerxes speaks, does he know why he has said it. Gabriella is hovering over him and holding out the neighbor's baby—Jack. She is holding him out and shaking him. His head is bobbling like a bobble doll.

"He's dead, Jim. He's dead—"

"Put the baby down," Xerxes says again, "He's not dead. Help me up. I need you to put the baby down and help me up. There's something in my back."

Thunder, like a jaguar that once roamed these mountains and is now nearly extinct, barely making a go of it in Mexico's Copper Canyon, a jaguar seeking revenge on the human race, growls and answers Xerxes. Xerxes remembers the storm. He still hasn't put the pieces together.

He thinks, *maybe lightning struck me and I am dead, maybe lightning struck and yes, I am in hell. Surely, I am in hell and I will be impaled like this for eternity, impaled with my twin sister screaming at me, accusing me of all this loss, accusing me for all eternity.*

Xerxes is thinking this and stretching out his fingers. They move and Xerxes has no idea how miraculous this is, how close he came to a severed spine, how, if it were not for a childhood disease, a childhood disease that caused a minor curvature, a miniscule parenthesis in his back, he would be paralyzed, would not be stretching out his fingers now. Xerxes holds out his hairy arm and Gabriella holds out her puffy arm and their fingers meet, their fingers meet and Gabriella pulls. Gabriella pulls Xerxes cleanly off the 2-inch stem of the century plant that had impaled him, the century plant that spent more than 25 years (but not the 100 you would expect) storing the nutrients that it would take to shoot a 15-foot stalk into the sky, a stalk that grew at an unheard of rate of 2½ inches per day, a stalk then when Xerxes snapped it, 14 ⅞ feet of it crashing amongst the boulders, ⅛ of it entering Xerxes's back, dispensed over 60,000 seeds into the fertile, rain-soaked red clay around the base of Granite

Tower. For the century plant, Xerxes's accident could not have happened at a more opportune time.

When Gabriella's and Xerxes's fingers touch it is the most electric thing that has happened all day.

Wondertwin powers activate.

Lightning crashes. *One one-thousand, two one-thousand, three.* The vortex slips down a valley and up another ridge. The storm has passed.

* * *

Xerxes's emergence from the circulatory system of the maximuminventory.com offices on 2050 Folsom Street onto a windswept, gravel rooftop had been dishearteningly anticlimactic. He had left the cool confines of a SOMA office building only to arrive on frozen tundra.

I'm on a plain. I can't complain.

The 20-foot vertical shaft that he had been concerned about had actually had a ladder in it. It had taken a mere 2 minutes for him to crawl through the horizontal tubing before making the easy climb up the vertical shaft. His journey had seemed preternaturally noiseless, as if time had magically stopped for him to make a clean getaway.

When he emerged, lint blew out of his tussled hair then vanished into a river of flowing fog. He was reminded for a minute of his two-week-long trek to Machu Picchu. There was the timeless feeling of having arrived in a dreamland. That two-week long trek to Machu Picchu had been the one comma in an otherwise unpunctuated work life.

Xerxes walked to the edge of the roof, past the aluminum of electric fans and their cages. He walked to the ladder that lead from the roof down three floors to Folsom Street. He placed his hands and sneakers on the clammy rungs and climbed down. The possibility that Xerxes would run into a stray smoker were high, but this did not happen. Xerxes placed his Chuck Taylors on the solid pavement of Folsom Street, turned, and, as if by destiny, was immediately illuminated by the headlights of a Yellow Cab, a Yellow Cab with black letters that designated it as Number 267, a Yellow Cab that was slowly cruising the fog-saturated streets of SOMA looking for someone exactly like him, a young Internet tycoon who was too absent-minded to have the office secretary call the cab company for him. Young Internet tycoons, the best tippers the world has ever known.

Xerxes opened the front door of the cab, realized that the front seat wasn't where passengers sit in a cab, closed the front door, opened the back one, and then scooted in. The cabbie thought, *yep, Internet tycoon, as bubble-headed as they come—10 buck tip on a 10 dollar fare.* The cabbie turned around and stared at Xerxes. He was the silent-type, his brown Arabic eyes said *where to.*

Where to? Where do you go when you have just abandoned the only life you have ever known? Where do you go when it's very likely that your girlfriend, the girlfriend that you were living with, was fucking your best friend next to the martini glasses on the black and white-tiled kitchen counter of your very swank, very modern, live/work studio? Where do you go when screwedcompany.com has stated, quite bluntly, in its brutally truthful way, that you're "totally screwed"?

Xerxes's eyes were crossed in front of him as if a bee were perched on his nose. His circuits were busy with an influx of too much newness, too much change. Cartoonlike, as if he weren't a real taxi driver, but only a made-for-TV one, the cabbie said, "Listen, Mac, I ain't got all day."

"Fort Point." Xerxes said, still looking at the tip of his nose, his voice a baritone B flat.

Fort Point? At 10 A.M. on a Friday morning? A rendezvous with a lover, with an exotic dancer from The Lusty Lady who just got off her shift? No, the loser got laid off. So much for the 10 dollar tip. The cabbie stepped on the gas.

Eight cylinders voiced their disapproval and Xerxes was jerked out of his trance. As they drove away, Xerxes contemplated the powder blue and white logo installed on the red brick façade of 2050 Folsom Street: a powder blue and white logo that John, his ingenious graphic artist, his visual guru, had designed; a powder blue and white logo that Zahn and he had approved, had nodded in unison over, arm-in-fucking-arm; a powder blue and white logo, the colors of the Tarheels; a powder blue and white logo designed '50s-style as if it were an old relic of Route 66; a powder blue and white logo with maximuminventory.com in a heavy, slanted script and a man on it, a man that mimics the man on the Community Chest card of the *Monopoly* board game, the man to whom you have to pay a $15 poor tax. The man had the same quizzical expression on the logo as he had on the Community Chest card.

His pockets were turned inside out just like on the Community Chest card but instead of being empty the pockets have piles of coins coming out of them. It was as if the man is saying, *how did all this money get here?*

Xerxes, previously emotionless, previously just sort of stunned, looked at his arms, arms that were covered with an odd aluminum powder, and was filled with an unspeakable dismay.

*   *   *

The situation at the top of Granite Tower is still dire: Xerxes, in excruciating pain; Gabriella, mad as a hatter; Bubba, exposed to the elements. Xerxes, despite the fact that his back, having come unstoppered, has leaked a good quarter pint of blood down the backs of his legs, performs a careful, step-by-step analysis of the state of affairs and concludes the following:

1) The short-term goals:
    a) Stop the blood flow
    b) Calm Gabriella down
    c) Get himself, Gabriella, a baby, and his bike off the tower

2) The long-term goals:
    a) Get Gabriella to the St. Francis Sanitarium and back on her medications
    b) Get home and log onto The Realm

Gabriella, having lifted Xerxes off the stem of the century plant, is still repeating the words of the engineer from *Star Trek*, though she is saying the words faster, though her voice has gotten smaller, is less desperate and more melancholy.

"He's dead, Jim. He's dead, Jim. He's dead—"

Xerxes is still holding Gabriella's hand. He lifts the underside of the other to Bubba's lips. He feels the baby's warm, wet breath.

"No, Gabby, feel this, he's just sleeping."

Gabriella drops to one knee, still holding Xerxes's hand as if genuflecting to him, she lays Bubba flat on a pile of pebbles. "He's sleeping, Jim. . . . He's sleeping. . . ." She looks up at Xerxes, her eyes glowing green like grass that has just been watered. "Thank you for taking this cup from my hands."

In a calm voice, with an almost imperceptible quiver, Xerxes says, "It's OK now. Everything is OK. Watch Jack. I'll be right here. I just need to take care of something. I'm going to let go of your hand. You're going to be OK. Everything is OK. Bubba is OK."

Xerxes lets go of Gabriella's hand and it drops limply to the ground. Her face starts to convulse. She begins a round of tearless sobs. Her eyes stay glued to Xerxes. "You've saved me once again. You knew, didn't you? You knew."

Xerxes bends over his bike. It looks remarkably intact: Cannondale, solid American-made frames; Shimano, ingeniously flexible Japanese-made components. As he bends over, pain shoots up his spine like a flame shooting down a wax-less wick. The blue comets return. They move sperm-like to the center of his vision, their tails wiggling in his vision's edges. *Don't lose consciousness now. We can't have an unconscious adult, a lunatic, and a baby on top of a mountain.*

Xerxes unzips the pouch of the Cannondale Emergency Repair System underneath his bike's seat. From the bottom of the pouch he removes a first aid kit. Carefully, ignoring the sperm growing to tadpoles in his vision, Xerxes pulls out gauze and a bandage. Xerxes takes off his shirt and stuffs it into the waistband in the side of his shorts. He puts the bandage over the wound on his back, wraps the bandage tightly around his midriff, and secures the gauze with two tiny metal clips. He looks down at the blood staining the reddish brown soil beneath his feet a slightly deeper red.

Xerxes grits his teeth. He knows he has to take one for the team, pretend that everything is OK so that he can get the three of them, four if you count the Cannondale, off the mountain. He feels like Luke in that scene in *Cool Hand Luke* where his prison mates have tied him to a bench and are stuffing his mouth with hard-boiled eggs, are counting 97, 98, 99 as they stuff his mouth with hard-boiled eggs so that he can win a bet he made to the warden, a bet that would allow his prison mates to get extended smoking privileges, a bet that he could eat a hundred hard-boiled eggs. They are stuffing Cool Hand Luke's mouth with hard-boiled eggs, his eyes are rolling into the back of his head, his arms are splayed out like Jesus on the cross, he is slipping in and out of consciousness, but he is still swallowing them, swallowing the hard-boiled eggs whole. Ninety-nine gets stuck in his mouth for a minute, then, somehow, miraculously, slips down his throat. His pupils are in the back of his head, and his eyes, look, well, like hard-boiled eggs. After he swallows 99, seemingly unconscious, Cool Hand Luke extends a finger, his index finger, *one more.*

Xerxes winces. Bites his lip. Pauses for a moment. Then he turns back around to face Gabriella. Gone is the wince. On his face is a shit-eating grin: a transformational, disarming, all-encompassing, shit-eating grin. He pats his belly with his hand, a hand with blood in the fingernails and in-between the fingers. He pats his belly, smiles, and says, "All better."

Gabriella, who still has one knee to the ground, who is still genuflecting, who has been staring disconsolately at Xerxes while Bubba / Jack lays unconscious on the ground, recognizes the shift in tone. She is distracted. She stops her mantralike mumblings. She joins Xerxes. Joins Xerxes in the fun. She knows that Xerxes is playing now. She knows that when Xerxes is playing, everything really is all right. She gets up from the ground, steps over the baby, rubs Xerxes's belly like he had rubbed it, and says in a childlike voice, "Xerxes all better now."

As Gabriella is rubbing Xerxes's belly a baby's head laying on cold, wet, hard gravel turns rapidly blue, then purple. A baby's mouth opens wide in an O the size of Jupiter and a baby's tonsils begin to vibrate. A baby named Bubba clears his throat in the miraculous way that baby's do. Bubba howls a howl—a fierce, wolf-like howl that echoes down the sides of the two ridges on either side of Granite Tower.

Down below, somewhere amidst a carpet of wet pines swaying in the after-storm breeze, somewhere in the land of milk and honey, somewhere in America, a coyote howls a response.

9. RELY ON YOUR KINGDOM MATES.

XERXES METICULA gave the cab driver the $14.70 fare + his customary 20% tip rounded to the nearest dollar: $18. He got out of the cab and walked along the blacktopped pedestrian path that lead to Fort Point. To his right, the pavement ended at the ocean, chunks of it, from erosion, forming a concrete beach. Through a fog even thicker here than on the SOMA rooftop, Xerxes could see surfers that looked like shadows on the waves. The surfers at Fort Point were what they called gray whales, 50+ year-old surfers with long gray hair tied back in ponytails and oversized guts that loomed large in their black wetsuits. A gray whale on an old-school 10-foot balsa-wood board danced to the front of his board, and then to the back. He navigated the face of the wave like a mariner of old.

Xerxes watched the surfers and wondered how they did it, how they lived such a purposeless existence. There was no ladder here. They surfed, and the surfing got them nowhere. They finished their ride and fought their way back to the line-up. They ended up right back where they started; they didn't seem to care.

Xerxes had been doing something that he thought would change the world. Zahn and he were the Dynamic Duo. There were other founders, other founders of bigger companies, companies with Web sites that had web traffic running into the hundred of millions, but man, the media had loved them. They were the Ben and Jerry of the Internet world, spreading good cheer on every news program of every major network.

No one seemed to even care what maximuminventory.com did. They just wanted Zahn, the symbol of the pull-yourself-up-by-the-bootstrap 2nd generation American, with his slick-backed and moussed hair, they just wanted Zahn in his pure, sly, Mexican-American way, to tell them how maximuminventory.com would mean less waste, would mean that a farmer in Iowa could make supply meet demand with magical accuracy. There would be no grain rotting in the silos. There would be more room for parks: national parks and national forests. People in third world countries would stop starving. Maximuminventory.com, when implemented on a global scale, would maximize the efficiency of the entire planet. It would change the world.

And then there was Xerxes, the genius. An interviewer would ask Xerxes a question about how it all worked, and Xerxes's wide mouth would start moving, would start telling her exactly how it worked, would start spouting out the formulas, would start scribbling reams of data on a white board. Xerxes Meticula—America's new Einstein, the man building the bomb.

The truth was, what he had done, it *was* genius. But no one really wanted to know how it worked, or even that it could work. They just wanted to *look* at a genius. To see him on a wide-screen TV and know that he existed, that he was moving forward America's corporate agenda, that he was continuing to advance America's world dominance, its Number 1-edness.

Of course, not all of this was the world's fault. He, Xerxes Meticula, was not an idealist. Even though the words coming out of Zahn's mouth suggested that their product could change the world, even though Xerxes had planted those words there, even though his product and the numbers it produced, could, if carefully implemented, help to maximize the efficiency of the planet, this was not at all what he wanted to do with it.

What he had wanted to do was to sell maximuminventory.com's product to *Fortune 500* businesses at high cost, make a yearly income just over the $10,000,000 mark, and receive the respect of all the old boys at Stanford. What he had wanted was to be thought of as a visionary, a budding Ted Turner without all the weird philanthropy stuff, someone who went against the grain, who had a unique business angle that worked, someone who didn't do business in a starched white tie or even khaki pants but who nonetheless got the job done. He had wanted it and he had achieved it. He was successful, as full of success as a 31-year-old could be. He supposed that it had made him happy. He supposed this, but looking back on it, it all seemed a fog.

And it had been a fog, a fog of Xanax and Valium and the occasional line of cocaine when he needed to be alert. He had never been more than 50% there, more than 50% in the present. While he stood up at the weekly board meeting, and told the board members about the weekly organizational re-structuring; while he drew squares on a dry-erase board and filled names in the boxes; while he placed his name at the top, Xerxes Meticula, technology side, placed Zahn's name next to his, Zahn Mendoza, business side; while he did this he would be buried in his maxims and numbers: *how to deal with loss during distribution, e.g. if you move your product from Memphis to Seattle there is an inherent loss of your product due to fragileness and perishability. I need to incor-porate a perishability factor in the 2.0 release that is based on a) product type b) the method of transportation c) the physical distance between the product's departure point and its destination.*

Living in this fog did something strange to him. It seemed to make time pass at an alarming rate. Days disappeared and could not be accounted for. Friends, good friends, he would not see for months. He would not call his sis-ter, his dear twin sister who needed him, for weeks. His aging rate seemed to substantiate this perception. He didn't look a day over 25. It was as if some-one were tearing days out of his calendar.

Xerxes, in a physical fog, contemplating a mental fog, walked past Fort Point, a fort that was built in 1853 to protect the San Francisco Bay from intrud-ers, intruders who might come to steal the stockpiles of gold that were collect-ing in its ports from the Gold Rush. Xerxes walked right past the fort, didn't see its Please Pay Here sign. He walked past the fort and underneath the bridge, a bridge that was built with an arch underneath it to accommodate the fort that was built to deny intruders. He walked beneath the Golden Gate Bridge.

The Golden Gate Bridge. The end of the earth. You could, I suppose, go farther west. West being the direction that you go to follow the sun to the end. You could go farther west before it becomes east, before you cross the arbitrary International Date Line that separates east from west; you could go to Alaska or Hawaii and be farther west. But Alaska, everyone knows, is more north than west, and Hawaii doesn't count because of the water, because you can't just get to Hawaii by walking across a great continent, you have to fly or take a Princess Cruise. No, California is the end. The last place you can come before you have to start over. And the Golden Gate Bridge, bathed in eerie orangeness, topped with lofty towers, is the end of the end.

There was this book that a woman, Xerxes's and Gabriella's babysitter when they were 8 or 9, an odd nervous woman who Xerxes always suspected knew some secret that no one else knew, who when she wrote 7's wrote them with a line through them as if she were Celtic, used to read to them. It was called *Hope for the Flowers*. *Hope for the Flowers* had thousands and thousands of caterpillars in it who were all climbing up caterpillar pillars. The caterpillars spent their whole lives shoving and clawing and biting their way up to the top of the caterpillar pillars. When they got to the top of a caterpillar pillar they realized that there was nothing there, that there was nothing at the top of the caterpillar pillar but categorically mean caterpillars, that the caterpillar pillar was in fact, nothing but a pillar of caterpillars. Despite their horrendous and painfully obtained knowledge, the caterpillars, once they got to the top of the caterpillar pillar, had no choice but to fight to stay on the caterpillar pillar. And so they would, the caterpillars at the top of the caterpillar pillar would stay there as long as they could, hurling other caterpillars from the top of the pillar, hurling them until they got hurled off the caterpillar pillar themselves. The caterpillar pillars were tall, tall pillars and a fall from a caterpillar pillar meant sure death. The caterpillars at the top had themselves become categorically mean.

Xerxes was reminded of a song, a song titled "Plateau" written by the Meat Puppets:

> *Nothing at the top*
> *But a bucket and a mop*
> *And an illustrated book about birds.*

Xerxes cannot see the towers of the Golden Gate Bridge from his vantage point. He was below the bridge and it was foggy. He could barely see its underbelly. He couldn't see much of the bridge but he could hear it, could hear cars crossing its span. The cars sounded like roller coaster cars. The beauty of the bridge, what makes it the most famous bridge in the world, is that its designers designed it with whimsy, designed it with the same eye for fantasy that the designers of Disneyland designed Disney. The Golden Gate Bridge is a toy.

Xerxes saw the bridge, or rather heard it, and he knew what he would do. He would be number 1103. He would not have wanted to be number 1000, such a round number, so common. Number 1000 had been met with much press in the *San Francisco Chronicle*, had prompted a big discussion about railings, railings to prevent the jumpers from jumping. Someone, someone with some poetic sense, squelched the talk. The Golden Gate Bridge after all, represented the end. How horrible, how horrible even at the end, to be faced with yet one more barrier, one last societal grasp. Big brother did not want you to die.

* * *

Gabriella knows what Xerxes has to do. She knows that he will take her to the hospital even though neither he nor she wants him to do it. She is re- signed to this. Her fury is spent. She walks silently, obediently pushing the Cannondale beside her. Her poor brother, he does not know how to stop driving so hard, how to be in unity with his surroundings instead of trying to conquer them. Her poor brother hears voices too, but ignores them, ignor- ing them being just as dangerous as listening to them. Her poor brother, she must consult her tarot cards soon. She must help him find some answers.

Xerxes and Gabriella reach Gabriella's Ford Escort. Xerxes asks Gabriella for the keys and she gives them to him, wordlessly. Mechanically, over the sound of Bubba's howling, Xerxes says to Gabriella, "I think I should take you to the hospital. I just want you to chill out for a while. I don't know what else to do."

Gabriella nods to Xerxes, mimics his matter-of-fact tone, "I understand."

Xerxes continues, "You can't tell anyone about the baby. We'll say that you dropped him in the kitchen, while you were microwaving a bottle of milk, and that you called me and didn't know what to do. When they ask why you're at the hospital, just tell them that your brother thought you should go and that you're having suicidal thoughts."

"I'm not going to tell them that."

"What are you going to tell them?"

"The truth."

"The truth that you climbed to the top of a mountain and threw a baby at me?"

"No, the truth that I was called to the top of that mountain and that what I did was my destiny."

"That's not the truth at all."

"Then what is the truth?"

"That you climbed to the top of a mountain in a thunderstorm and threw a baby at me."

"I'm just going to tell them that my brother dropped me off here and that I have no idea why and he's the one that's crazy."

Xerxes had placed Bubba—who had finally fallen silent, who Xerxes had stuffed with a pacifier—into the baby seat, had started the ignition, and began the drive down from Granite Tower Road. "You know why."

"I didn't try to commit suicide. And I didn't try to kill Bubba. I just went to the top of the mountain. I was called to the top of the mountain and then what happened on the top of the mountain happened. You're the one who tried to do it, Xerxes. You're the one who should be committed. You're the one who had to be talked off a bridge."

Xerxes keeps up his cool façade, goes thin-lipped, and takes the turnoff to St. Francis. *How does she know? She doesn't actually know does she, she is just guessing, acting like she's a goddamn psychic. This is her, flashing that all-knowing smile like she can see things that no one else can.*

* * *

Xerxes walked up the paved path from Fort Point to the foot of the bridge and began to walk across its span. The bridge is rainbow-shaped, is at an upward angle to start, levels out, and then a downward angle by the time it reaches the other side. If you can find the exact point at which the bridge reaches an exact level, then you know you are at the exact midpoint of the bridge. If you find the exact midpoint of the bridge then you know you have reached the place at which you have achieved maximum distance between you and the water below. Although you will have achieved terminal velocity long before you hit the water, the additional distance between you and the surface increases the chance that you will be blown awkward by the wind tunnel that is formed by the rocky cliffs that guard the entrance of the San Francisco Bay, a wind tunnel that is blowing fiercely, blowing an icy wind at

Xerxes right now. If you are blown awkward you will not hit the water feet first, which will be your inclination, when you are in midair and are flapping about, but will land head-first, or back-first, or stomach-first, and will be killed instantly. If you land feet-first there is a chance that you will live, that your natural survival instinct will kick in and despite the fact that you are fully clothed, are 50 feet under the surface of the sea, have broken every bone in both feet, a tibia, and blown the ligaments in your knees, despite the fact that when not long after you surface the news will surface and you will be ridiculed mercilessly by screwedcompany.com, despite all this your natural instinct will kick in and you will frantically swim to the surface to be rescued by a passing trawler.

If he was going to do this he had to do it right. He had lived his life with precision and now he was going to meet his death with precision. He would not fail. Xerxes passed the 3rd of the 8 red Crisis Hotline phones. The phone stared at him like those antismoking billboards with an old, wrinkled woman on them who is smoking a cigarette through a hole in her throat, those billboards that he used to stare back at after all-nighters; used to stare back at while a mean early-morning sun drilled itself into his skull; used to stare back while he defiantly smoked a cigarette, smoked his brand of cigarettes—American Spirit. Xerxes passed the 3rd of the 8 red Crisis Hotline phones and said out loud, "Fuck you."

What was strange about Xerxes, what was strange about him as he walked through a fog on The Golden Gate Bridge that was so thick that he could only see 10 feet in front of him, 10 feet behind him, 10 feet to the right where lay empty air and a fall into nothingness, 10 feet to the left where other agents of death zoomed by at 50 miles per hour, 10 feet above him where a proud engineer designed an invisible turret, what was strange about him as he stared below him at Chuck Taylors that were 6 feet below him and blurry, was that he thought this was about the vagaries of success and failure, he thought that he was choosing to end his life because he was tired of the constant and neverending work that was required of the gods of capitalism, at least those gods of capitalism who truly believed, those rare gods who were truly working instead of committing white-collar crimes.

Xerxes doesn't realize that what this was about, that what was really bothering him, was that he had been betrayed in cold blood, that capitalism had betrayed him, that all the dreamers—Zahn, his V.C.'s—all those who acted like this was magic, acted like the Internet industry didn't follow the normal rules, acted while he pored over numbers that they had given him, numbers that didn't make sense, had betrayed him; that, most importantly, his friends and family had betrayed him, that when the chips were down Zahn started snorting Ziploc bags full of cocaine, Dixie jumped ship, Mike Meticula changed his tune, Melissa Meticula started talking to God, and Gabriella Meticula became something that he could not comprehend. He had never had time for a lot of friends. He was a busy, ambitious man. So he had had a few. And none of them had ever stuck. And now he was alone. Xerxes was alone.

Xerxes stopped walking. His back was to the bridge traffic and his face was turned towards nothingness. He had made it, had made it to the center of the span. Shadows passed by him, holding hands, chatting. A foghorn blew. The Golden Gate Bridge—death; tolls.

Gabriella had called him just yesterday. It was late and he was on the computer at home while Dixie was "out." He sort-of grunted into the phone while Gabriella was talking to him. He said "uh-huh," "uh-huh," "uh-huh," at regular intervals—keeping a conversation alive that he had wanted to die. Gabriella was egging him on; she had out her deck of tarot cards and had wanted to pull out a card to determine Xerxes's immediate future.

Gabriella said, "Xerxes, tell me when to stop shuffling."

Xerxes, still not paying attention, replied, "I've got work to do. I don't have time for a game." (When, in fact, what he was really doing was playing a game, was on the computer in The Realm.)

Gabriella, either unaware that Xerxes was ignoring her, or not caring, had shot back, "You don't have time to discover your true destiny?"

Xerxes, capitulating, had closed his eyes as if Gabriella could see him through the phone cord and said, "OK, OK, pick that card."

There had been a silence on the phone. Xerxes took his eyes off the screen.

Finally, she spoke, "You picked the Tower card, Xerxes."

"The Tower card?"

"Yeah, the Tower card."

"What's the Tower card?"

"It's the most powerful card in the deck."

Xerxes was annoyed with Gabriella's drama, her insistence that there was power in things like a deck of cards. "Why do you do this?"

"The Tower card means death and destruction. Things are going to change for you, Xerxes. They're going to change quickly. I picked the Death card for myself. We need to be careful the next couple of days. Very careful. It's weird, Xerxes, I've never picked the Tower card for you before. You're not a Tower card person."

Xerxes was thinking about the conversation that he had had with Gabriella and was leaning over the railing. This was the perfect ending really. A reporter would ask Xerxes's crazy twin sister why he had done it and she would say, "Because it was written in the cards." Most people when they did this left a note, some hint for the world to make sense out of a senseless act, but Xerxes didn't see the need. The reasons for his suicide were obvious: dot-com founder achieves success beyond his wildest dreams, dot-com founder falters, dot-com founder goes bankrupt, dot-com founder jumps off bridge. It would make a great story. The *Chronicle* and the *Examiner* would tear at each other like vultures for it. He might even go national. Still be on CNN even after he was dead. Why complicate their story by trying to make it sound deeper? Suicide notes were written by romanticists who didn't see the shallowness of their own lives. Xerxes saw the puddle he lived in. There was no need to pretend it was an ocean.

It was important to do this right. The fog was so thick that it was doubtful that anyone could see him, but he needed to take precautions to prevent himself from having any last-minute second thoughts. He didn't want some stranger finding him hanging on to the back of the railing for dear life. He designed a process, take 10 giant steps forward, turn right, put right leg on the first bar of the railing, swing left leg over the top of the railing, follow with the right, lower self down onto a 2-foot-wide metal grate that runs the length of the bridge, bend like a diver on a diving board, jump. He imagined it in marker on his dry-erase board. He saw a Xerxes's stick figure jumping off a hastily drawn replica of the bridge.

Xerxes flipped his switches: *emotions—off, thoughts—off, mechanical legs— in motion*. He read to himself, "Xerxes Meticula, you have been sentenced to death by a jury of your own peers and a judge in good standing . . ." Xerxes took his first step, then a second, then a third. He shut off all systems.

An object in motion tends to stay in motion.

There was only one thing that could have stopped Xerxes at that moment, and that one thing, that thing with the million to one odds, happened.

Xerxes felt a vibration just centimeters from his pelvis. He stopped in mid-fourth-step. *How ironic.*

He wondered if he was the first human being to have been interrupted in the middle of a suicide attempt by a cell phone in vibrate mode.

Xerxes wondered which V.C. this was. He pulled the phone out of his front pocket and checked the Caller ID. The LCD read: Gabriella Meticula.

*   *   *

When you imagine an insane asylum, when you envision it in your mind's eye, you think of a castle on a hill, a castle on a hill with ivy creeping up the sides and the hint of a storm in the air, a castle on a hill surrounded by razor wire. If you are more practical, more practical and have grown up in a big city, you see the insane asylum as a floor, the 13th floor of a clean building with shatter-proof windows, the 13th floor of a hospital where crisply-dressed nurses in white administer sedatives to drooling idiots clothed in blue and white hospital gowns. The St. Francis Sanitarium is nothing like this. The St. Francis Sanitarium is zoned commercial. The St. Francis Sanitarium is sandwiched in a strip mall between Safeway and Oreck vacuum cleaners. The St. Francis Sanitarium has automatic doors and a card that says OPEN on one side and CLOSED on the other, a card that gets turned to OPEN once around noontime and once again in the evening to indicate the hospital's visiting hours. It is kind of like a strip-mall romper room, kind of like the Gymboree, from outside you can look in the window and see giant-sized Legos on the floor. Being in a strip mall, the St. Francis Sanitarium has a strip mall attitude—get in, get what you need, get out.

Xerxes is walking in front of Gabriella, looking determined and important. He is ready to take charge. He steps on the mat that triggers the electric doors to open. He has been here before, was here the first time that this happened. A woman with hair that has been dyed that shade of maroon that seems to be in fashion here in Rest Stop in the summer of 2000, a woman with a name tag that says Rene, smiles a fast-foodlike smile at Xerxes, and says in a pleasant voice that can never actually sound pleasant but will always sound fake, "Can I help you?"

As Xerxes prepares his answer, as he thinks to himself, *I'll have a #2, hold the pickles, fries and a chocolate shake*; as he prepares to exert his influence on Rene; prepares to speak with just a hint of a Southern accent to denote authority, he hears Gabriella behind him starting to sob.

The heels of Gabriella's palms dig into her eyes and the waterworks start. "I dropped the baby. I dropped the baby. I dropped the baby."

Xerxes is not sure whether these are real sobs or practiced sobs. The idea that they may be practiced troubles him. He had never thought of this before, never imagined that she could have any control, that his sister was anything more than a victim.

Either way, she is making this easy for him. His words come out robotically, "My sister Gabriella was here a couple of weeks ago. She called me an hour ago from the house where she was babysitting. I think the baby accidentally fell from the counter. She hasn't been able to stop crying about it since. I'm worried about her. I think she needs her medication adjusted."

Rene's smile does not swerve. It remains unchanged, as if her lips have received a Botox injection. "OK, well just sit down over there and fill out this intake form. Make yourselves comfortable."

As Rene hands Xerxes a clipboard, a clipboard with a two-sided sheet of paper on it that includes the question, *Have you ever been a victim of incest, molestation, or rape?* a question that must be answered by checking either a box that reads YES or a box that reads NO, as Rene hands Xerxes the clipboard and Xerxes turns wordlessly to Gabriella and in turn hands her the clipboard, as Rene is doing this, a man walks in the room, walks through a swinging door painted a cheery, cherry red, walks through a metal swinging door with a one foot by one foot window crosshatched with wire, the kind of window that inmates look through to see the loved ones who visit them.

The man is about 6'6". The man has fiery red hair. The man has a butterfly bandage covering up 9 stitches that have recently been sewn into a cut above his left eyelid. After he walks through the swinging doors, he holds his arms straight out and lets his wrists dangle; he stares straight ahead, stares straight through the plate glass windows of St. Francis Sanitarium into the glare of the sun reflecting off hundreds of SUVs. The man says, "I am Frankenstein."

Simultaneously, in two completely different tones, Rene and Gabriella speak. Rene's reply is stern, "Leonard?" Gabriella's reply is querulous, "Carrot Top?" They both turn towards the man. The man's eyes stay level, stay straight ahead. He turns back around, does a complete 180°, returns to the cheery, cherry swinging door, his arms are still out; his motions do not seem to acknowledge the presence of anyone else in the room. He says, "I am not Frankenstein. I am the monster. I am the invention. You are Frankenstein."

He walks back through the swinging door. As it swings back, swings towards shut, his voice rings out, "Gabriella Meticula returns to the homeland!"

Rene and Xerxes both lift an eyebrow.

⋆　⋆　⋆

When Xerxes had stopped in the mid-fourth out of ten steps that he had designated as the number of steps he was going to take before he mounted, then slipped over the orange railing that was the only physical object keeping him from the great beyond, when Xerxes had stopped his personal process of elimination on the Golden Gate Bridge and looked at the LCD screen of his cell phone that read Gabriella Meticula in digital letters, he hadn't really expected to be interrupted by a greater circumstance, perhaps the only circumstance that would have prevented him from restarting his fourth step and continuing his 10-step life-ending leap.

It was Gabriella. An eerily calm Gabriella. A Gabriella who at that very moment was standing in a long hallway with cheery, cherry red walls. A Gabriella who at that very moment was standing in a long hallway holding the very scratched and battered black plastic receiver of a telephone, a black plastic receiver that has pink bunny stickers stuck on it, pink bunny stickers with bunnies on them that have even-pinker little bunny noses and pearly white bunny smiles. A Gabriella who seemed unusually lucid, unusually put-together. A Gabriella whose voice contained a faint quiver, the quiver of the overcaffeinated, and also the quiver of the person who is holding back emotion, the quiver of a police officer who has seen a body, a body lying on the side of the road with two missing ears, a police officer who says simply into his walkie-talkie, "D.O.A."

A Gabriella who was saying to Xerxes, "I swallowed them all. They were aqua. Like in Kurt's song. The last song on the last album. The live one. *Aqua seafoam shame*. They were aqua and triangular and they were in the palm of my hand. They were aqua but the water in the glass wasn't aqua it was greenish, greenish because the glass was greenish. And then the water was gone and the aqua was gone. The gems of aqua were gone. The gems that contained within them the ocean, the sea primordial, the oneness, the wholeness, the soup from which all life began. The gems were inside me and soon I would be there, be there with the everything, be one with the all. The gems were inside me and I could already feel the warm fuzzy pinkness of the all rising up from my stomach juices, jumping up my esophagus like the flesh-eating bacteria. The warm fuzzy pinkness—Xerxes, do you know what it reminded me of, do you know what the end reminded me of? Do you know what heaven, or hell, or probably purgatory—that's where I would end up, purgatory—do you know what purgatory looked like? Do you know what the afterlife looked like? Because not only could I see it, but I could feel it, I could feel it numbing me and taking me over. The afterlife was exactly the color and consistency of Pepto-Bismol, Xerxes. There's no heaven or hell or purgatory. The afterlife is Pepto-Bismol."

Xerxes's left hand was clutching the railing of the bridge; the knuckles of this hand were white. Xerxes's right hand was clutching his metallic and modern-looking Sprint PCS cell phone, which was simultaneously clutched to his right ear; the knuckles of this hand were also white. The phone had little pinpricks of moisture on it from the fog.

Xerxes realized that he was cold. It was a strange sensation. It was the first physical sensation he could remember having felt all day. Xerxes looked down. He knew the ocean was there even though he couldn't see it. He knew the ocean was choppy today with intermittent whitecaps.

Gabriella continued her monologue, "No. No. It's not Pepto-Bismol. It's Calamine lotion. The afterlife is calamine lotion. Remember when we were seven, Xerxes? We were seven and Mom filled the whole bath with calamine lotion. She dumped bottle after bottle of calamine lotion into the bath, banging the bottles against the porcelain until she got every last drop out. Do you remember that? We were seven and we had the chicken pox. We were scared and couldn't stop scratching. She would yell at us if we scratched but we still couldn't stop. Mom grabbed us both from under the armpits and stuck us one by one, you first then me, into the pool of pink in the bathtub. I think she was mad at us. Or maybe mad at her fate. She was ranting or mumbling, mumbling or ranting. I can't remember which. And I can't remember her words. But I remember thinking that this was what she was saying. I remember this very distinctly. I remember thinking she was saying this, 'Why two? Why not one? I didn't want any kids at all. I wanted trips to Europe, trips to Italy, to Rome and Venice in the spring and fall when the tourists were gone. I didn't fucking want any. But no. *Contraception is against the Will of God. A marriage has not been consummated in the eyes of the Church until a child has been born.* And so I agreed. I agreed to have one and then I would go on the pill. And you stewed. You stewed about this and said *we'll see.* You stewed and thought *while we were all dying in Vietnam.* You stewed and thought *I married a good Catholic woman who is now telling me that she doesn't want children, that she wants to have one at the most. I should divorce her but I can't divorce her because that is a mortal sin, a mortal sin to break one of God's sacred seven sacraments. I won't divorce her and now we will see, we will see what God's will is.*

"'Oh and we had, we had seen God's will, we had gone to see your friend Dr. Taylor, your friend in college who had gone on to medical school while you studied law, we had gone to his office for a sonogram. It was experimental then, the sonogram, was only to be used when the doctor thought there might be complications, but Dr. Taylor said it was perfectly safe. Your friend Dr. Taylor, my acquaintance in college, a man who I had incidentally slept with one night when I was a junior, one night after a few too many dry martinis, something you never knew about, Dr. Taylor asked me to strip naked and lay on the thin mattress of a hospital bed. He asked me to strip naked and I obeyed. I lay on the thin mattress and Dr. Taylor put on gloves and rubbed something sticky and yellow on my belly, my distended belly that was bigger than it should have been at five months, much bigger. Dr. Taylor rubbed something sticky and yellow on my belly and I didn't want to think this but I couldn't help it. The something sticky and yellow reminded me of come. While Dr. Taylor did this you stood there watching, watching and talking to Dr. Taylor about technology, about how wonderful the new technology was.

"'Dr. Taylor, who you called Fred, pushed the mattress into the machine. It looked like a giant egg, this machine. Fred put me in the machine and took pictures of me naked, took pictures of my internal parts, pictures of parts of me that no one had ever seen. He took pictures of my womb. When I came out on the other side of the machine there was no one there. There was no one in the room. I was alone and naked and strapped to a thin mattress with a comelike jelly on my stomach. Alone and naked and bathed in the cold, blue light of an X-ray reader. I was naked and strapped down and I could smell cigar smoke and hear the voices of two men chuckling behind a closed door. Two men, a one-night-stand and my husband. Two men, Fred Taylor and Mike Meticula. I could hear voices and one man saying, Fred saying, *Mike, you're going to have to buy two of EVERYTHING.*'"

Gabriella went on, Xerxes pressed the cell phone closer to keep the wind-created static out of his ear. "That's what she was thinking, Xerxes. I know that's what she was thinking. I couldn't have made all that up, Xerxes. That's the thing about me that nobody understands. I know things. When that happened I wanted her to drown me. When I knew that about her, I wanted her to drown me. She wanted to. She wanted to drown me, Xerxes, she wanted to drown me in that pool of calamine lotion. And it would have been perfect. A perfect death. The calamine lotion was so soothing, so cool and calming. It was the cure-all. Both of us stopped screaming and itching. I wish she would have done it. I wish she would have done it then. I should never have been born, Xerxes. It was a mistake. It should have been just you in there. I should never have been born."

Xerxes had been silent up to this point. Had been physically and emotionally frozen. He couldn't feel the railing or the cell phone anymore. He spoke, "That didn't happen, Gabby."

"So, it could have happened. It might have happened. The calamine lotion happened."

"How many did you take, Gabby?"

"What?"

"How many gems did you take?"

"The whole bottle."

"How many is that?"

"A hundred."

"A hundred of what?"

"I don't know, Zoloft or lithium or whatever they gave me."

"50 or 100 milligrams?"

"A hundred."

Xerxes did the numbers like he always did. This time he thought out loud. "A hundred times a hundred. That's 10,000."

"Xerxes?"

"Huh?"

"Are you all right, Xerxes?"

"Am *I* all right? You just took 10,000 milligrams of Zoloft or lithium or whatever."

"Where are you, Xerxes?"

"The bridge."

"What bridge?"

"The Golden Gate Bridge."

"What are you doing on the bridge?"

"I'm on the phone with my goddamned sister."

"You know why I stopped Xerxes? Do you know why, when I could feel the calamine lotion leaving my digestive system and entering my central nervous system, when I could feel the cool, calm, salmon-colored afterlife taking over my brain, do you know why I panicked? Do you know why I panicked and screamed so that they would know what I had done? I panicked because I saw you, Xerxes. You were floating, Xerxes. You were big and bloated and orangish like a grapefruit. And you were chewing some bad gum. You were chewing some bad gum like that girl in *Willy Wonka and the Chocolate Factory*, like that girl who turned into a giant floating blueberry. You were chewing bad gum even though you knew it was poisonous. You kept chewing the gum even though it was making you bigger and more bloated. You kept chewing the gum even though it didn't taste good anymore. You were going to explode if you didn't spit out the gum, Xerxes, and there was no one there to tell you to spit it out. So I wanted to live, Xerxes. I wanted to live so I could tell you to spit out the gum."

"I'm not a grapefruit."

"No, but you are eating some bad gum."

"Where are you now? Did they pump your stomach?"

"I'm in the hospital. I was asleep for 48 hours. I just woke up."

"Where's Mom and Dad? Why didn't they call me?"

"I don't know."

"Look, I'm going to come out, Gabriella. You need help. You need someone to be there. I'm going to take a vacation from my company. I'll just take a week off. Did they pump your stomach?"

"They don't pump your stomach anymore. They give you an injection of some countersubstance that neutralizes everything. It's weird. It's just like in the movies."

"So you're OK."

"They used the word, 'stabilized.' I'm stabilized."

"What's the name of the hospital?"

"It's the St. Francis Sanitarium."

"What's the address?"

"I don't know. It's in a strip mall. It's in the Rest Stop Shopping District strip mall."

"OK. Tell the folks that I'm coming."

"They won't be happy."

"I don't care."

"Yes you do."

"Look Gabriella, you tried to commit suicide. You need help. I'll come and help. We'll figure this out. You need your own apartment. You shouldn't be living with your parents anymore, you're too old."

"You're not really doing this for me."

"Gabriella, I'm going to go. I'm going to hang up the phone. You're OK, right?"

"I'm stabilized."

Xerxes was cold. Never in his life had he felt so cold. "Hey, Gabriella, will you listen to me? Really listen to me for a minute." Xerxes paused. "I love you, Gabriella. I love you and you're right about me. I'm fucked up and I need you. I'm a goddamn blueberry or grapefruit or whatever that's about to explode and I need you to help me spit out the bad gum. All right? Is that what you wanted to hear? I gotta go. You'll be at the hospital, right? The St. Francis Sanitarium in the Rest Stop Shopping District strip mall."

"Yeah, that's where I am."

"I'm going to hang up the phone, Gabriella, OK?"

There was a brief pause. It was not a pregnant pause. It was more like an aborted pause.

"OK, Xerxes."

"Bye, Gabriella"

"Bye, Xerx."

Xerxes looked down at his phone. The LCD screen read **20:26**, then **20:27**, then **20:28**. He pressed the END button and the numbers stopped at **20:28**. After a few seconds the **20:28** changed to read 11:58 A.M. Xerxes thought: *time of death 11:58 A.M.* He clapped the talk end of the cell phone shut. He clapped it together so that it was smooth on both sides, a large silver bullet, a silver grenade. Xerxes imagined this, that the cell phone was a silver grenade. He pulled the antennae out, pulled it out as if he had popped a pin. He leaned back like a pitcher, his left knee going up and his right arm going back. And Xerxes threw his cell phone, threw it as far as he could into the swirling nothingness, into the sphere of fog that surrounded him. He saw the words SPRINT PCS, the lettering on the back of the phone, spin and spin and then disappear. He waited but he didn't hear it. The wind was howling on the bridge and he didn't hear the splash, didn't hear the splash or the kaboom.

Xerxes retraced his steps and began his long walk off the bridge. He passed a sign that read: THROWING OBJECTS OFF THE BRIDGE IS A MISDE-MEANOR OFFENSE PUNISHABLE BY A $5,000 FINE.

BOOK II: THE PLAYERS

RL TIME: LAST DAYS OF JUNE/FIRST DAYS OF JULY, 2000
REALM TIME: END OF YR 1/YR 2

Catching signals that sound in the dark
Catching signals that sound in the dark

—NEUTRAL MILK HOTEL, "TWO-HEADED BOY"

10. YOU'LL NEED A RELIABLE MAGE.

sKyLaR; REAL NAME: DIETRICH BJÖRNSON; Real Sex: Male; Real Age: 25; Place
of Birth: Stockholm, Sweden; Permanent Address: 285 Ave. D #12, NY, NY
01022, USA; Current Latitude: 90°S; Current Longitude: ∞; earlier today
married Caitlin Williams on the continent of Antarctica. Dietrich and Caitlin
were only the second couple to marry on this particular continent, and the
first to do so during this continent's winter. It is safe to say, although difficult
to confirm, that Dietrich and Caitlin's wedding was the coldest wedding ever
performed, the temperature at their particular latitude and longitude on the
continent of Antarctica being −55°F,−45°C, and a mere 204 kelvin. It is also
safe to say that this wedding was both the first, and the last, in which the
wedding ceremony involved the married couple drinking a fifth of Jack
Daniels, stripping down to nothing, running, the woman's nipples hard, the
man's penis microscopic, across a flat and featureless hundred-yard expanse
of ice, an expanse that extended for hundreds of miles in every direction, an
expanse that was lit up with spouts of blue flames from high-pressure hydrogen tanks, an expanse that if it were not for the blue flames would be completely dark, completely dark even though it was nearly noon. It is safe to say
that this wedding was the first and last in which the married couple ran
across a flat and featureless hundred-yard expanse of ice, hand in hand,

naked except for wool socks, running shoes, mouth pieces, and headphones; safe to say that it was the first in which the couple listened to the wedding march on their headphones, touched a 15-inch-high orange pylon that marked the South Pole, said "I do" into their mouthpieces, lowered their mouthpieces, pressed their lips together, lips rendered dry and unfreezable with a thick application of zinc oxide, embraced briefly, body parts touching body parts numbly, ran back towards the hangar-like entrance of the research station, the man's headphones tuned to blips and loops of his favorite Autechre song, the woman's headphones tuned to the crooning of her beloved Johnny Cash, ran back to a crowd of grizzly, huddling, cheering men, men with icicles hanging from their beards, men armed with blankets, whiskey, and a couple of bottles of cheap, though not easily procured, champagne that froze completely when it was opened, champagne that formed giant champagne snow cones on the tops of the bottles, ran back to a crowd of grizzly men who dogpiled them with love and affection and warm blankets the minute they made it back to the safe haven of the station.

Dietrich Björnson never dreamed that this would happen; not the being naked and nearly frozen for his wedding ceremony, this wouldn't have surprised him at all, but the part of the wedding ceremony that involved actually getting married.

Dietrich had been the biggest player in the East Village. He looked the typical East Village-type: preternaturally skinny, big chops, sculpted goatee. He wore a Buffalo Bills stocking cap, T-shirts in various '70s colors, a tight jean jacket, and dirty black jeans. His shoes were also black, black with bulky rubber heels, heels that added another two inches to his already tall 6′ 2″ frame. But Dietrich had a slight edge over the everyday Alphabet City hipster in that he wasn't so cool that he was actually cold. In fact, his cool exterior masked a rather warm and mischievous spirit. His blasé attire, upon closer inspection, masked a nervous, but somehow charming, twitch. The coolness got Dietrich the ladies' attention, and the warmth drew them closer.

Plus, he smiled. Plus, he remembered. While the rest of the young men walked past the souvenir shops on 12th turning their heads at young women wearing long jackets with big, furry collars—turning their heads with sneers or feigned ambivalence, turning their heads and looking at their jackets, collars, or breasts—Dietrich smiled, looked every single one of them in the eye, and took a mental snapshot of their face. And these women, invariably, if they saw Dietrich days, or even weeks later, if they saw him eating vegan food and drinking a Guinness at the Life Cafe, or dancing in his whirling dervish way on a boat turned dance club, would catch Dietrich's eye again, and Dietrich would smile again, and Dietrich would remember exactly where he saw them last and what they were doing, *Hey, you were eating dinner at Angelica's Kitchen the other night weren't you? You had the portabella mushroom fettuccine. That's my favorite. I saw you through the plate glass windows*, and this would knock them out, absolutely floor them, and if they lived in the Village they would talk about veganism, or clubbing, or vinyl for a while and then give Dietrich their numbers, and if they didn't live in the Village, if they were expats from France, or Portugal, or Pakistan, and they didn't have anything to do, because they were on holiday, Dietrich would give them a tour, would show them bars in subways, clothing shops in cellars, artist's spaces in old warehouses, would show them the wonders of The City that the tourists don't get to see, and then he would invite them up to his studio, his studio with the two burners, the half refrigerator, the T-shirts and dirty jeans and old leather jackets hanging from the curtain rods, the walls covered with inks from various underground shows, the clanky, steam-generated radiator keeping things warm, his studio with one piece of furniture—a bed, a comfortable queen-size bed complete with box springs and flannel sheets.

Dietrich would take the expat from France, or Portugal, or Pakistan to his studio; he would take the expat's coat, the one with the furry collar; he would put the coat on a hanger and hang it next to his leather jackets on the curtain rod; he would invite the expat to lounge on his one piece of furniture; he would turn on his burners, boil some water with Thai noodles over one, stir-fry bok choy, snap peas, bean sprouts in a wok over the other; he would add spices: ginger and ginseng and chili; he would serve the dinner on thrift store plates and then eat the dinner, in bed, with the expat; they would smile and eat and then Dietrich would throw on some peppermint tea and the kettle would whistle. Dietrich would talk and smile and they would sip the tea, reclining in bed, facing each other, heads propped up with elbows, until the tea was gone; and then Dietrich would remove the tea cups and the plates and return to where he was reclining, and now there would be nothing between them: no plates or tea cups or words.

And there would be nothing to do but kiss. And after they had kissed, Dietrich would undress the woman, and then undress himself, and he would lie there with her, still reclining, heads still propped up with elbows, and Dietrich wouldn't make his move, like most men, no, instead he would just smile, and now, for once, his eyes would come unglued from her eyes and he would look at the rest of her and take another mental snapshot, would take a mental snapshot and add it to the collage in his head, would add her to his pLeAsUrE pAlAcE.

Sometimes Dietrich never made his move. He would just lie and play with the expat's hair and fall asleep, fall asleep to the slow drone of Aphex Twin's *Selected Ambient Works Vol. 1 & 2*. Sometimes he would make his move. Or she would. And then they would make love like that, side-by-side, a leg lifted, crooked and wrapped around, movement muffled, lips on noses and chins. Either way, it would be the start of a week or month-long love affair, a love affair that invariably ended the day the expat's visa expired, a day that seldom ended in tears on either side, but rather an unlikely mutual understanding, an understanding that there had been a time and a place. So Dietrich would take a cab with the girl over the Triborough Bridge, would walk her to her gate at the international terminal at JFK—a terminal he knew as if he'd built it—would blow the girl a kiss and then return via cab and bridge to the souvenir shops on 12th Street, a smile—a genuine, unperturbed Dietrich smile—on his face.

Dietrich's reasons for leaving this idyllic life in Manhattan for the misery and monotony of Antarctica were vague. Dietrich had been sitting cross-legged smoking a hookah in a vegetarian cafe off of 8th, a typical East Village dive called Kopi that had a huge message board with desperate notes from desperate travelers attached—*Seeking CHEAP room for month of June. Please HELP. Myrna, meet me in Philly for the 4th! Artist needs Village digs under $600*—when an acquaintance, hoping for a free puff, sat down next to him on his couch.

The acquaintance was talking to Dietrich, and Dietrich was ignoring him for the most part, just letting him take free puffs from the hookah. The acquaintance was complaining about tourists. He was saying, "These yuppie tourists go everywhere. And they say snobbish things like 'I was in Tikal for the full moon with this Israeli couple. They carried wine and some soft cheese all the way to the top of Temple V, and I sat with them and we all passed around a joint, It was so beautiful.' or 'I don't know whether I'm going to go to Amsterdam or Cairo this year for New Year's Eve. Where are you going?' They say things like this while ignoring the beggar kneeling before them with a hand held out for a nickel. Man, look at these people, they miss everything."

Dietrich nodded. He'd heard this argument before, the obliviousness of the tourist, and he agreed to a certain degree, but he found that the people who made these arguments tended to be less generous than the ones passing around the wine and cheese and joints. The man continued, "They should send all these people to Antarctica, man. There's nothing to do there but get along with your fellow man. You can't ignore anyone in Antarctica, man, because you need whatever skill they have for your survival. Antarctica is a closed system: there's no homeless, they'd die off in a second; you gotta love everyone in Antarctica, even the guy with bad hygiene who masturbates loudly in the bunk above you every night."

This "closed system" resonated with Dietrich; the one thing that bothered him about Manhattan was that he couldn't know everyone there, that there were people walking around who he would never meet. "Do you know anyone in Antarctica?" Dietrich asked.

"No, there was that woman who got cancer and they had to drop her chemotherapy from a helicopter in the middle of a blizzard, but I don't know her."

"Just your fellow man," said Dietrich dreamily, leaning back on the couch and filling his lungs with smoke from the hookah that he had just filled with apple-flavored tobacco.

"Yeah, sounds wonderful. Freezing your balls off for three months and not getting any play."

"I'd do it," Dietrich said, catching a buzz as the nicotine, a drug he indulged in only rarely, hit his bloodstream.

"Shit, go uptown to Columbia and talk to the head of the mechanical engineering department. They're one of the universities doing research for the ASF. They need welders to maintain the heating systems. It's slave labor, and it's all volunteer-based, and you'll be fucking miserable 'cuz there aren't any ladies, but show 'em some of your engine block sculptures and they'd hire you in a second."

And that was that. Dietrich took the 1 Line uptown to Morningside that afternoon and after a year's worth of interviews and psychological examinations he found himself huddled with twenty-two men and one woman in the cargo hold of a transport plane that was depositing three months of food and the winter grunts onto the permanently iced-over Antarctic tundra at the Scott-Amundsen Base one hundred yards from the South Pole.

Dietrich was not unhappy in Antarctica. It had taken some adjusting, adjusting from a life amongst women to a life amongst men. He wasn't the most masculine of men and he had spent a good portion of his first two weeks at the pole vomiting the dried beef (he had been a vegetarian) and copious amounts of whiskey (he hadn't been a drinker) that were the standard Antarctic diet. He often passed out in his bunk after his daily 8-hour shift in the boiler room, but after his stomach adjusted and his lanky frame gained some bulk, Dietrich, true to his nature, became the Antarctic Minister of Camaraderie.

Dietrich started such events as Tuesday night's *Stupid Penguin Tricks*, Saturday's *Ice Croquet under the Stars*, and the ever-popular daily round of *Ring Around the South Pole*. Dietrich's playfulness pulled several a depressed citizen of the Scott-Amundsen Dome out of bouts of Seasonal Stress Disorder, and even the most serious Russian scientist in Dormblock D spit out his Tang when Dietrich convinced the new group of rookie researchers that penguins were turning yellow from over-exposure to cosmic rays, a sign of the debilitating effects of the ozone hole, when in fact, Dietrich was secretly putting Yellow Dye #5 into the penguins' bowls of anchovies every morning.

Dietrich was becoming a man's man, and the transformation had not gone unnoticed by the one woman who lived in the Scott-Amundsen Dome who might notice. Caitlin Williams, a sandy-haired, unexemplary-looking woman born and raised along the banks of the Cuyahoga just outside of Cleveland, Ohio; a woman with a predisposition to the solitary life, a woman who loved nature; a woman who worked with her mother for years, her mother who was head of the government committee that organized the 10-year clean-up of the Cuyahoga after it had caught fire—one of America's darker environmental moments—a woman who, like Dietrich, had an inexplicable affinity for welding, a woman who pulled car parts out of America's most polluted river, pulled them out of the Cuyahoga, the sewer of the Iron Belt, welded them into odd, precariously balanced sculptures, and arranged them in her and her mother's organic garden; Caitlin Williams noticed Dietrich, and he was the first man, since she had arrived and immediately intuited the nature of things, that she had allowed herself to notice.

Caitlin worked on the same five-man, one-woman welding crew as Dietrich, the crew that maintained all of the base's heating systems during the Antarctic winter. Caitlin had learned to act democratically around the men at the base, she was the only eligible woman there this winter (besides her there was a lesbian couple, and a married geophysicist who was unpopular and kept to herself), and because of this, men tended to get extremely friendly around her after their evening nips. By befriending her crewmembers and the other men who she interacted with on the base in an equal manner, she maintained an effective safety net around herself, so that the men policed each other around her. A man in a parka standing over another man in a parka saying, "leave Caitlin alone" was the standard signal that the evening's carousing was over in Scott-Amundsen's cramped bar, The Great White Plain.

Showering any extra attention on any one man would end the peaceful equilibrium that Caitlin had been able to precariously maintain, but somehow, now that Dietrich seemed to be gaining status as court jester/leader of the pack, she sensed that perhaps she could make a play.

Dietrich, for his part, was also very aware of Caitlin and her role on the base. He didn't consistently flash her his trademark smile like he would have back in The Village. He did keep an eye on her, but it usually went undetected behind their welding visors.

Dietrich was often one of the men in parkas standing over the man in a parka who had just put an arm around Caitlin at The Great White Plain. He tended to take a more jokey approach to the affair, "Hey, Stanley, you gettin' some?" he would say, loud enough so the whole bar would hear, and the guy, a fellow welder or one of the electricians or a scientist from the East Wing, whose name was never actually Stanley, since there was no one named Stanley on the base, would pick up his cue, slightly embarrassed, and slur, "Hanley, I'd be gettin' me some if there weren't so many stags around here." And Dietrich would pick the guy up from his stool, drag him over to the cheap linoleum booth where the rest of the guys were playing 7-card stud, turn his head to Caitlin and say, "you better join Stanley and me over here, Ms. Williams, it's getting awfully hot on that end of the bar."

Dietrich's feelings towards Caitlin were unusual for him. His love, and after a while he did recognize it as love, didn't come on fast and automatic like it usually did, like a gas-operated fireplace in a suburban home, it came on more slowly, a spark that took a few minutes to set off the kindling that took a few minutes to set off much larger branches. It was natural. Before this, Dietrich had never realized that his other relationships had been unnatural, that it was unnatural to be able to shut off flames with the flip of a switch, but now that he had met Caitlin, had met her and not become involved with her right away, but had watched his feelings for her develop over time, he recognized that he could never go back, that all future flings would seem superfluous and shallow, and that his one desire, his reason for traveling to the God-forsaken bottom of the earth, was to have this revelation, and if at all possible, to act on it.

This revelation was, of course, not quite as conscious as this. Dietrich was not one to sit and contemplate the dynamics of love. It took the encouragement of the other men on the base to seal the deal. For although every man on the base had a crush on Caitlin, they all also had a crush on Dietrich. It may have been a brotherly love kind of crush, but it was a crush just the same.

And so it was decided one night, one night when Dietrich seemed to be getting stuck with a lot of ace highs that weren't panning out, one night when Dietrich was losing and was therefore being forced to drink more shots than usual, that it was time for Dietrich to make his move.

One of the other welders, a guy who had just pulled off a heart flush, said to Dietrich, "Hey, Hanley, looks like Stanley's at it again," and Dietrich had replied, "Yep, I'd better go retrieve Ms. Williams," and Dietrich's fellow welder had said, "Hanley, maybe you should get rid of Stanley and keep Ms. Williams company yourself for change," and one of the other card players had said, "Yeah, Hanley, might as well go over there. If you drink any more we're going to have to mop you up off the floor anyway."

So there had been collusion, a tacit understanding between Dietrich and the other men. And why not. Somebody should be getting some, and Dietrich wouldn't rub it in anyone's face.

So when Hanley had disposed of the current Stanley, and instead of asking Ms. Williams to join the rest of the group as was the custom, had plopped down on the stool next to Ms. Williams, and when the room slowly and purposefully cleared, Dietrich finally flashed his Dietrich smile, a slightly drunker version, but a Dietrich smile nonetheless, and after the smile Caitlin opened up and talked about her sculptures, and her clapboard house in Ohio, and the simple beauty of her eventless childhood in the Midwest, and Dietrich, who was used to discussing the superiority of French-made wines with the daughters of foreign-born aristocrats, felt in that moment that he had found his hearth and home, his moral center, and he knew that he had been reborn.

Or so he had thought. For although he had married the lovely Caitlin Williams just that day, Dietrich Björnson had a midnight secret. In his free time, late at night when his crew members were snoring and silently masturbating in their bunks, just to feel a part of things, just to separate himself from the daily repetitions of building a heating system, drinking whiskey, playing poker, and discussing the names of his future children with his wife-to-be, Dietrich Björnson became sKyLaR: a wizard, a trickster, and a guy who couldn't help but flirt a little.

sKyLaR is viewing the blue group message boards. Largely, he's been ignoring the dictates of Lord BonZ and instead been sending flirtatious messages to someone named Lady Swallows. He decides, though, that it would be best to attend to some duty. He enters his wizard's guild. He types in some numbers:

Your wizards have cast a fireball into Pepper Daisy. They were successful. You have killed 410 peasants.

Your wizards have cast a fireball into Pepper Daisy. They were successful. You have killed 410 peasants.

Your wizards have sent meteors into Pepper Daisy. They were successful. You have destroyed 12 buildings.

II. STAY ACTIVE IN YOUR KINGDOM'S DISCUSSIONS.

SINCE RETURNING TO THE RANCH from the St. Francis Sanitarium, Xerxes Meticula has been unaware of his surroundings. He doesn't notice the sun setting, or the sun rising the following morning. He doesn't notice that the weather outside is unusually oppressive and humid for Arizona, that the dryness the retirees have come to expect, a dryness that wrinkles the skin and yet preserves it, is not there. He doesn't notice that the retirees in The Ranch have skipped their walks and left their dogs to sulk. Layers of stratus paint the horizon wet and sticky like slug tracks.

Xerxes has been in The Realm for 15 straight hours now. He has been in The Realm ever since visiting hours at the St. Francis Sanitarium ended, has been there ever since hearing the electric doors of the St. Francis Sanitarium shut automatically behind him, with finality, by some ugly, under-the-mat magic. Xerxes has been in his room lying on top of his Native American–print sheets. He is dowsed in sweat. The humidity has given his normally crisp and dry sheets a soggy and feverish life. Xerxes has locked the two doors to his bedroom, the door to the hall and the door to the bathroom. There is no ventilation, no oxygen entry into the room. The air has the yellow smell of the terminally ill.

Xerxes is naked. Naked except for a white patch on his back that covers a near-circular wound in his back, a wound that looks astoundingly like a bullet wound. He is naked and lying on his stomach. His knees and elbows are pressed into the mattress. His hands hold up his head. His face and eyes are bathed in a blue light. Occasionally he shifts, lays on one side or the other. He is uncomfortable. He can feel the splinters of the century plant in his back, the splinters that he wasn't able to remove when he sat on the bathroom counter, turned his head around 120 degrees and gingerly picked with tweezers. Sometimes when he turns, a splinter grazes his spine and he feels a metallic twinge, like a loose filling biting into ice cream.

The thought, *I should open the window and let in some fresh air*, never enters Xerxes's mind. Xerxes is not Xerxes. He is not here. He has achieved his subconscious desire, the desire of any junkie or chemical-dependent or soap opera mother or teenage Nintendo addict. He is somewhere else, has achieved disconnect, disconnect from RL—Real Life. Xerxes has plugged the cable line into the wall, the cable modem to the cable line, the USB cable to the cable modem, the laptop to the USB cable.

The Realm is a unique addiction. It has confines. You cannot wander beyond them. There is no mushroom-induced tripping—no danger of mind expansion. It does the same things over and over and over again. The guild-master says, what would you have me do, and never anything else. There is comfort in this, the world on a definitive 13-inch screen.

It is difficult to say whether Xerxes is aware that he spends half his life in a limited world, aware that he has traveled to a hard-wired womb. For an instant, when he presses a thumb to the active matrix screen, it looks like a pregnant woman's bellybutton.

And yet The Realm is more than that. It would be too easy to simplify it as mere escapism or avoidance, too easy to say that Xerxes was there in The Realm, on that eerie, late June night and morning in which the crickets and cicadas were silent, because he didn't want to think about his sister, Gabriella, doped up, drugged, and under suicide watch at the St. Francis Sanitarium, because he didn't want to think about his own loss, the loss of his dreams, the loss of his idyllic dot-com existence. It would be too easy to say that Xerxes's endless mathematical mechanizations were the product of a tough few days, days in which he saw his twin sister attempt some sort of symbolic suicide three times, three times in which he caught her in that very act, three times in which, if he had not been there, his sister may very well have been dead: burned or asphyxiated or electrocuted.

Xerxes is searching for something. The Realm, the world on a two-dimensional screen, is 100% man-made. It contains no impurities. It is not like the earth, designed by forces unknown and unseen, marred only by a thin film of human formation and detritus. The Realm is "our" creation, manufactured solely by the people of the Planet Earth for the people of the Planet Earth—no one else built it for us. We can't fuck up The Realm. The Realm is ours and ours alone.

And because of this The Realm is an unclouded mirror into the human mind and soul.

*　*　*

On the *Blue Group* message board the Lady Peace & Love reads this string:

blue groop ~ post all your successful military, theef, and magic attaks her

King BonZ

———

Someone keeps stealing all my land. I will @#*W# them. Hitler will be revenged. It is time for the white race to stand tall. It has been written that those who have the strength have the power. Join me my kingdom mate to avenge my losses.

Sir Hitler's Revenge

———

sKyLaR dOn'T kNoW aBoUt ThIs HiTlEr StUfF. sKyLaR wOnDeR wHaT LaDy SwAlLoWs SwAlLoWs.

Sir sKyLaR

———

who avenge these loss? one must get them back! who do?

King BonZ

———

i'll bet you would, sKyLaR. private IM @ 9 P.M.

Lady Swallows

———

sKyLaR dOn'T kNoW aBoUt PrIvAtE iM. sKyLaR make gOoD mUsIc. CoMe To sKyLaR's PlEaSuRe PaLaCe FoR dRiNk AnD mUcH PlEaSuRe. sKyLaR pLaY the SyNtHeSiZeR.

Sir sKyLaR

———

Are you from Germany, Skylar?

Sir Hitler's Revenge

———

I make good music, too, Skylar. I'm a snake charmer;)

Lady Swallows

———

blue groop ~ this message boar din fro serious discussion adnd attack posts only!!!!! There is a taverhn for chahtting. choose a grop leader for coordinating atTaks. i hit Hitler aggressor 4 now.

King BonZ

————

Damn it, why the fuck is everyone attacking me?

Sir Hitler's Revenge

————

Please do not use profanities on your kingdom's message boards. Continued abuse will result in deletion.

The Lords of The Realm

————

since this groop has not chosen a leeder i will be leeder. all groop members shod be active int he mrsage boards. Who is the leeder of the stangely pwace-ful citadel of orcs? We must retaliate now against carrot flower. I try to hit but no good, now you attack.

King BonZ

————

sKyLaR tHiNkS tAvErN sMeLlS bAd. CoMe To sKyLaR's Pleasure PaLaCe FoR fOoD aNd DrInK aNd PlEaSuRe. sKyLaR cOmEs FrOm SwEdEn. HiS fAtHeR wAs A vIkInG. sKyLaR hAs SeNt HiS mErRy MaGiCiAnS tO mAkE mErRy In ThE kInGdOm Of CaRrOt FlOwErS. sKyLaR hOpEs KiNg BonZ hApPy. sKyLaR lIkEs HaPpY.

Your wizards have cast a fireball into Pepper Daisy. They were successful. You have killed 410 peasants.

Your wizards have cast a fireball into Pepper Daisy. They were successful. You have killed 410 peasants.

Your wizards have sent meteors into Pepper Daisy. They were successful. You have destroyed 12 buildings.

Sir sKyLaR

————

sKyLaR wOuLd LiKe ThE lAdY oF tHe StRaNgElY pEaCeFuL cItAdEl Of bLuE OrCs To CoMe MaKe MeRrY iN hIs PlEaSuRe PaLaCe. ShE iS bIg AnD pOwErFuL aNd ShE cOuLd UsE tHe HeLp Of sKyLaR's MeRrY mAgIcIaNs. sKyLaR pLaYs ThE sYnThEsIzEr.

Sir sKyLaR

12. SILENCE CAN BE USEFUL.

LEONARD B. WALKER WALKS. That is what he does. That is the only thing he does. It sounds funny, a guy named Leonard B. Walker who walks, but Leonard B. Walker doesn't think it's funny at all.

It started out as a mean joke. Leonard's family was from Duluth. It was 1976 and the automobile industry was in the midst of a recession. In Detroit, the Ford Motor Company was laying off people in droves and production was down 30 percent. Because production was down in Detroit, the shipping industry in Duluth had also taken a big hit, and Leonard's Dad had been laid off. Because Leonard's Dad had been laid off, and because his Dad's 1955 Ford truck was in ill repair, and because Duluth's busing system did not extend down Minnesota's R.R. #3954A, and also because Leonard's Dad was a soft-spoken man who would not be caught dead in a PTA meeting, his son Leonard, a scrawny, redheaded fifth grader at Weehaket Elementary in Duluth, had to walk six and a half miles home from school five days a week in the cold and dark of a Minnesota winter.

Despite the hardship that this placed on Leonard, this was not the mean joke. The mean joke began because Leonard, being scrawny, being the only redhead in Duluth, being poor, being soft-spoken, being befreckled, being a bit skittish, being prone to outbursts when pushed, was the kid that everyone picked on at Weehaket Elementary, and not only at Weehaket, but also at neighboring Mesaba Junior High, and even extending into the freshmen and sophomore ranks of Duluth Central two blocks down.

Leonard—or Laney, as the other fifth grade boys called him, called him in conjunction with "is a girl," as in "Laney is a gur-url! Laney is a gur-url!" called him while standing on tiptoes, as if they were wearing high heels, and holding their hands under their chests, palms up, mocking breasts—encountered a constant barrage of insults.

In gym class, Leonard was a favorite target in murder ball, a crueler hybrid of the much more common but similar game of dodgeball. In dodgeball, two equally divided teams stood in a small court divided by a single line. Players on one side of the court would throw a large rubber ball at players on the other side of the court. If a player was hit with the ball, a ball that stung like a horse crop when thrown at high velocity, a velocity that most of the dockworker sons in Duluth were able to attain, the player was called "out" and left the game. The game continued until all players from one side were called "out."

Murder ball used the same dreaded large, bouncy red ball and followed the same rules as dodgeball with one notable exception: there was no line. The players of murder ball were given jerseys, either blue or red, jerseys that, incidentally, sat at the bottom of a storm shelter for most of the summer and never seemed to get washed, so that they smelled, at least they smelled to the twelve-year-old Leonard, like a lethal combination of old people and roach killer. Because there is no line in murder ball, the players run around pell-mell and hit each other with the red ball at point-blank range.

This, children hitting children with a large rubber ball at point-blank range, is not as bad as it first sounds. Because the players are running after each other, and because the players don't have time to make concentrated, hard-thrown strikes, the ball, generally, does not get thrown as hard as in dodgeball, so that there are less raised welts on most children after a game of murder ball than after a game of dodgeball.

Unfortunately for Leonard, the game of murder ball was not as benign to him as it was to most children. Since the game of murder ball had no lines, what inevitably happened to him, since he was the boy at Weehaket that everyone picked on, was that the boys in red jerseys, or the boys in blue jerseys, depending on what particular jersey Leonard had been given that day, would team up on him. Two of the boys would grab his arms, one arm per boy, and they would pin him to the stone wall of the court, a third boy would then stand about twenty feet away, far enough so that the ball he was about to throw could gain some speed, but close enough so that it had a good chance of hitting him, and aim the ball at Leonard's genitals. This scene, though thoroughly embarrassing and terrifying to Leonard, was a source of neverending, daily amusement to both the boys in red and blue jerseys and the gaggle of girls who would inevitably postpone their four-square games to watch Leonard's humiliation.

As the boy aimed the ball at Leonard's genitals, Leonard, his face turning the color of his hair, would stare the boy throwing the ball in the eye, his eyes wide with fright, and in a high-pitched, crackling pre-pubescent voice would shout, "Don't! Don't! Don't!" On the third "don't" the boy would throw the ball. What Leonard would do, in order to avoid a direct hit, was to jut one of his hips forward, like a female model executing a turn on a runway. This little dance that Leonard would do, unfortunately, was what made the whole thing funny, and whether the ball missed him altogether, hit him on the hip and caused him minimal pain, or, did, in fact, find its target, didn't matter to the other fifth graders. The boys and girls of Weehaket Elementary just wanted to watch Laney dance.

Although this certainly qualifies as a mean joke, it still was not the mean joke that caused Leonard B. Walker to become a walker. Nor was the watch-Leonard-pass-out joke, a joke which involved Tony, the largest boy in fifth grade, coming up behind Leonard some time during recess, wrapping his arms around him, pressing his fists just under his diaphragm and picking him up off the ground for fifteen or twenty seconds until he passed out. After he laid him out, Tony would call to the other fifth graders to come watch Leonard, whose eyelids sometimes fluttered in the couple of minutes that he lay unconscious. When Leonard woke up, one of the other students would ask him what the last thing he remembered was, and he would look at him dazedly, not comprehending, and say, "I–I was playing soccer."

This was still not the mean joke. The mean joke that drove Leonard to his calling in life was played on him one evening late in February. The temperature that evening was, as usual, hovering around the 10°F mark, and Leonard was, as usual, shivering helplessly on his walk home. In order to stay out of the deep, dirty, almost black snow that had been bulldozed off the streets into huge 8-foot-high walls, Leonard had to choose between walking down the middle of the road or through people's yards. Leonard preferred the yards to the roads; instead of an icy tunnel that looked like an urban drainage, an icy tunnel whose walls echoed with the ching ching ching of tire chains on Suburbans, the yards offered views of wood-slatted houses, which, though gray, were at least pleasantly lit and offered protection from the carbon monoxide of the roadways.

It was while Leonard was walking along through someone's yard, crossing over a driveway, that Ben White, one of Leonard's fifth grade classmates, one of the boys wearing red jerseys who had that very day held Leonard's right arm against the murder ball court wall; that Ben White, a fifth grader who was riding in the passenger seat of his brother's gold '68 Camaro, spotted him, and said to his brother, "Look, it's Laney Walker."

Dan White, having just gotten from his father the keys to this Camaro and wanting to see what the super-wide white-walled back tires could do, glanced at his brother Ben and said, "What do you say we spray the walker?" And Ben had smiled and said, "Yeah."

So Leonard was minding his own business while walking through the crunchy snow in someone's yard, not enjoying the cold walk home, but looking at the warm lamplight in front of the gray houses and not hating it either, when suddenly there was a screech and a tidal wave of black snow; when suddenly he was buried in gritty, rock hard snow; and when suddenly, adding insult to injury, he saw the tailpipe and spinning rear wheels of a Camaro showering him with chunks of ice and gravel as it tore off down the half-pipe. Leonard stood there, frozen, both literally and figuratively. It was bad; bad enduring seven periods, a recess, a gym class, and a lunch break full of pranks, but now even his torturous, but at least peaceful, long walk home wasn't sacred.

It was while standing chest deep in snow as he drove off, listening to his classmate's brother, Dan White, shout, "Look at the walker now!" that Leonard made his life-altering decision. His first instinct was to yell, to yell at the Camaro. His second instinct was to sob, to stand there and sob until his face formed icicles. But Leonard followed neither instinct; that day Leonard chose to follow a third instinct, an instinct which had laid dormant until that day. That day Leonard's third instinct was to just keep walking.

★　★　★

Gabriella Meticula is sitting on a neon green plastic picnic table bench in a dining room with cheery, cherry red paint—the cheery, cherry red paint that covers every wall of every room at the St. Francis Sanitarium. She is using the blunt end of a black crayon to draw a picture of the Grim Reaper on a bicycle. Leonard B. Walker is pacing the floor behind her, his arms extended like Frankenstein. Sara Bronstein, a young volunteer who is trying to complete her hours so she can get her counseling degree and start working with some normal people, is trying to get through the last twenty minutes of the anger management seminar that she runs weekly at St. Francis.

Sara is angry. She has, for the eighth time, politely told Leonard to sit down and Leonard has, for the eighth time, completely ignored her. She has read the chart on Leonard, the one that says, "extremely intelligent; extremely stubborn." She had thought that she would be able to get through to him, that with a careful and gentle tone he would settle down and sit, but it hadn't worked and she is angry. What's more, Gabriella, who she swore had given her the evil eye earlier, had interrupted her this last time, and in a challenging tone, and this time not giving her the eye at all but rather adding the scythe to her drawing of the Grim Reaper, had said, "Why don't you just leave him alone? Could you pass the red?"

And when Sara had replied, "He needs to be a participant in the group," and Gabriella had retorted, "He is a participant in the group. He's doing what he does best," and then added a flourish of red lipstick to the Grim Reaper, and this time definitely given her the evil eye, bedlam had broken out and the forty-something heroin addict named Joanna, who had fallen on and off the wagon some thirty plus times and was currently on methadone—and therefore very surly—looked up at her and stuttered, "ck–ck–ck–cunt," and mentally retarded Eric had started snapping crayons in half, and Helen, the shopping-cart lady, who had been drawing a very pleasant scene of a sailboat on a lake, grabbed Gabriella's black crayon and defaced the entire drawing.

While bedlam broke out, while she prepared the proper tone to control Eric and ask Helen why she was desecrating the sailboat, and while she prepared to ignore Joanna, and while she was figuring out what she needed to say to Gabriella, who was challenging her and who, maybe, she needed to defer to, even though she wanted to slap the bitch, in the millisecond that Sara gave to thought, Gabriella made things worse by saying, "Why don't *you* join the group? You're the one that's angry."

Of course she was angry. She just needed a hundred more hours to get her goddamned degree, but the only work she could find, the only work she could find in this God-forsaken hick town that she should have never come to, a hick town that was so different from her beloved New York City (oh God the Big Apple, the *lights*), the only work she could find (and she was working for *free* goddamn it) was a weekly anger management workshop at a psychiatric hospital in the middle of a fucking strip mall, a weekly anger management workshop that only gave her an hour a week. At this rate it would be another fucking *two years* before she got her degree. And with this in mind she had forgotten herself, and replied to Gabriella, "I am *not* angry," in a tone that she had intended to sound hard, but came out childlike, a tone totally different from her usual fake gaiety which, of course, conveyed just how angry she was.

She had blown it, and she knew it. Her face flushed. When her face flushed, Leonard, a Leonard whose eyes were always pointed forward and who never seemed to observe anything, laughed, not an out-of-character laugh, but a good-old-fashioned Frankenstein *mua-ha-ha*. And Gabriella glanced up at her, grinned, took the black crayon back from Helen, and drew dark curls on the Grim Reaper, a Grim Reaper who was beginning to look a bit like Sara.

Sara feels defeated. She is sitting on a plastic neon green bench attached to a plastic neon green picnic table that was built for children to sit on, not adults. She is sitting in a child's room, a room with cherry red walls. She hadn't known what else to do, so she had composed herself and said "OK, I will join you," and had sat down, and now she is drawing a picture, drawing anger, a picture of five people sitting down at a neon green picnic table, a picture of five people sitting down and one standing. A woman standing, a woman standing with her arms crossed and thick, black smoke coming out of her ears.

Sara is drawing a picture, and while Sara is drawing, a woman, Rene, the receptionist at St. Francis, steps into the room. She looks at Sara funny. She says "Ms. Bronstein, it's time for the patients' lunch." Sara looks up, looks up at a clock that reads ten past twelve. Sara has never done this before, her sessions always end exactly on the hour, precisely at the point when the red not-moving-quickly-enough hand meets the hardly-moving long black hand and the imperceptibly-moving short black hand at the top of the clock. Another line has been crossed. She has made another error. If a patient sees that you will go over, then they will think that you are always willing to go over.

Sara stands up abruptly and says, "Sorry, everyone, I lost track of the time. We'll have to discuss our drawings next week." She walks behind Gabriella and notices that Gabriella is gazing blankly at Sara's drawing, a drawing that she now realizes that she drew in a sort of trance, a trance that caused her to draw something that went way beyond the unprofessional behavior that she had already exhibited. It was obvious, even to a drugged, borderline-affective-schizophrenic-with-suicidal-tendencies nutcase like Gabriella, what the drawing was. It was obvious to Gabriella that Sara was drawing them, and that Sara was angry at them, and that Sara hated being there.

Gabriella, still staring blankly at Sara's drawing, says, "I drew you and you drew me," and Sara says, "Yes, isn't that funny," and Gabriella says, "It sure is," and Sara says, "I'll be back next week," and Gabriella says, "Cool."

13. YOUR ENEMY IS HUMAN.

TRES RAWLINGS IS RAIL THIN: his muscles have fully atrophied; leftover flesh spills over the sides of his chair. He is nearly blind from Web surfing: he wears thick, rounded, black-rimmed glasses that make it look as if a pair of binoculars have been permanently attached to his head.

You might describe Tres as looking like a typical computer geek, although his disability would keep you from saying that. What Tres really is, is someone who has completely disowned his physical existence, a man who lives outside his body. Edward Calvin Rawlings III, a former world-class downhill skier, has disowned his former self, a former self of lithe body and powerful musculature, a former self of joy in the corporeal. E.C.R. III does not move these days. E.C.R. III lives through a computer screen.

Tres has multiple monitors in his bedroom. They hang from the ceiling and are angled down at him. He can control these monitors with the lilt of an eyebrow. On one of those monitors Tres is preparing an attack. He puts in numbers under archers, under knights, under war horses. He clicks the "Send" button. An hourglass spins. His screen reads:

Your troops have fought a brave battle and won. You have appropriated 98 acres of land from The Strangely Peaceful Citadel of Blue Orcs (12:5). Your army will return from the battlefield in 16 days. Be sure to visit cardscards-cards.com for 24-hour Texas Hold 'Em Action.

★   ★   ★

Xerxes is nearing the end of his all-night and all-morning clicking. He is still lying there, naked, sweaty, on top of his sheets. He is looking at the kingdom page of Island 47, Continent 50—the kingdom of *Carrot Flowers*. He is looking because he is concerned about what King BonZ and Sir sKyLaR have done, concerned that their attacks and spells will draw the kingdom's ire.

Xerxes does a double take at both the name of the kingdom and the name of the province of its king. The name is the title of a song he knows. It is the title of a song by an Athens, Georgia-based indie rock band called Neutral Milk Hotel, a rock band whose lead singer is amazingly, uncontrollably, and invariably off-key, off-key in such a way that his words seem like they must be tremendously important. The song is a ballad, it has a trumpet in the background that makes it sound like a national anthem. The song's lyrics, when you take the time to listen to them, aren't as deep and meaningful as the lead singer makes them seem like they should be, but they are catchy:

> When you were young,
> You were the King of Carrot Flowers
> And how you built a tower tumbling through the trees
> And holy rattlesnakes fell all round your feet.

Xerxes is looking at the kingdom page of *Carrot Flowers* when something startles him. The numbers on the header of his screen have suddenly changed. His acreage is lower. His net worth is lower. Xerxes quickly pulls up the main page. On the bottom is the following news:

Your lands have been invaded. You have lost 98 acres, 225 trolls, and 24 spearthrowers. The attack came from the province named King of Carrot Flowers, Kingdom 47, Continent 50.

A metallic twinge shoots up Xerxes's spine. It is not possible. He has the strongest defense at this time of anyone in The Realm.

Xerxes is The Lady and The Lady is angry, has gone red in the face. She checks her ranking—she's been knocked clear off the charts. *Someone must pay*, she thinks. The Lady is familiar with this feeling. It is not what is missing—your land, your troops—it is the feeling of invasion, that something that was once yours, something that you worked long and hard for, is now someone else's and that that someone else, that Two-Headed Boy, is out there, somewhere, laughing at you. Or worse yet, is out there, completely ambivalent.

This feeling, however induced by a false reality, is not unlike, in its magnitude, any other moment of Real Life horror. It is not unlike the feeling of hearing on the radio that the Japanese have attacked Pearl Harbor, or watching live as a terrorist flies an airplane into Tower #2. It is a feeling of sorrow colored by hatred and rage.

This is not an exaggeration. Game players' feelings towards the provinces they have spent hours building up are strong and are intertwined with their egos. Players measure their intellect by their ability to prevent this from happening, by their ability to keep other provinces from robbing, casting spells on, or attacking them. Xerxes cannot help but feel that he has missed something, that he has committed some indiscretion to allow such a breach.

It is, in a way, this feeling of being besieged that players play the game for. Perhaps their lives are missing some excitement; or perhaps it is something else, perhaps they are trying to forget some Real Life event with a similar quality, perhaps they are trying to forget their loss of a lover, a friend, a business, or a twin sister.

The Lady, however, is not contemplating her raison d'etat. What happened to her, happens often. You cannot retaliate immediately. This is what your enemy wants. Your enemy wants you to blindly gather all your spear throwers while you are weak, and try to hit him. If you do this, your enemy will come back and steal your lands from you again and again.

No, you must be strategic. You must make decisions. What do you have to gain through retaliation? Can you get some of your land back?

Is your enemy too small? If your enemy is too small you tell your smaller kingdom mates about him—let them hit him if they can. Is your enemy too big? If your enemy is too big you concentrate on your own growth, you grow your army strong and wait for the day when you can retaliate. If your enemy is your size, and you have something to gain, then you retaliate. And you never, ever, do it without help.

The Lady is contemplating this. She reaches over the edge of the bed, takes a swig out of a 2-liter bottle of Coke. She sees the Valium, the little Valium tablets with the V-shaped donut holes, she sees them lying in a pile on the lamp stand like a pile of turquoise stones in an Indian rock shop. She knows she should take them but it is the pain that has been keeping her awake. The colon on the digital clock by the lamp stand is blinking and the clock reads 11:57 A.M.

What to do? The Lady gingerly gets up from the bed and opens the blinds. For the first time she notices the clouds, the thin stratus clouds that have been oddly humidifying the Arizona air for the last few days.

The Lady opens a window and there is a slight movement of air, but the movement of air is out the window not in, hot air moving out into slightly less hot air. The Lady looks back to the bed where she had lain, her imprint on the bed in sweat. She runs her fingers through her hair. The Two-Headed Boy found a chink in her armor and she must simultaneously patch up that chink and find a chink in his. *What to do?*

The Lady is thinking this when another something new appears on her header bar: NEW MSG. The Lady clicks. The Lady reads:

Once upon a midnight dreary, while I pondered, weak and weary,
Over many a quaint and curious volume of forgotten lore—
While I nodded, nearly napping, suddenly there came a tapping,
As of some one gently rapping, rapping at my chamber door.

Signed, Sir Raven of Nevermore

Raven's message is archaic, could mean anything. It has been an odd morning—how and why is it getting so weird? On a whim, The Lady prepares her own message, hands it to a messenger, sends it off:

'Tis some visitor,' I muttered, 'tapping at my chamber door—
Only this, and nothing more.'

Signed, Lady Peace & Love but Mostly Love

The reply is swift:

My dear Lenore, (may I call you that?) If I read things right, you have been up all night, deep into that darkness peering. (Your online color has been red since 10 yesterday evening) Why don't you get some sleep? When you wake the Raven will still be sitting, sitting never flitting, on the pallid bust of Pallis just above your chamber door. Good ol sKyLaR and I have some plans for Two-Headed Boy. That palace of his isn't all pLeAsUrE. You just steal yourself some more gold and rest your little head. We need you big.

Signed, Sir Raven of Nevermore

The Lady smiles. She has back-up. And Raven is right—she needs sleep. The Lady reaches over to her lamp stand and removes two Valiums, pops them in her mouth, grabs the nearly empty 2-liter bottle of Coke from the edge of the bed and takes another a swig. She prepares one last message for Raven,

I will quaff, will quaff, this kind nepenthe
And forget this lost Lenore.
Good night, my Raven from Nevermore.

Signed, Lady Peace & Love but Mostly Love

★   ★   ★

Tres is surprised by what he sees on his screen:

Your lands have been invaded. You have lost 124 acres, 225 archers, and 24 knights. The attack came from the province named Nevermore, Kingdom 12, Continent 5.

He did not think them organized enough for retaliation. He is grudgingly impressed.

Tres switches to another monitor. This monitor is his Rolodex. It is what he uses to keep track of his online friends. Every screen of this Rolodex looks like an oversized ID card—vital information on the left, a photograph on the right. The profiles start with a name of some sort, a chat room handle or in the case of The Realm, the name of a province and a persona.

Tres has hundreds of entries in his Rolodex. He enters #994 now. He is entering The Lady Peace & Love but Mostly Love into the persona field, *The Strangely Peaceful Citadel of Blue Orcs* into the province field, and *The Boneyard* (12:5) in the kingdom field. There are other fields too: real name, real age, real sex, e-mail address, IM aliases. Tres leaves these fields blank. Underneath the photograph are fields for eye color, height, weight, hair color. In addition to this assortment of fields are links to subfields. Links that read facial contours, body shape, skin color, hands, legs, feet.

It is the subfield Facial Contour of File #994 of Monitor #4 that Tres is monkeying with now. He is giving The Lady Peace & Love but Mostly Love a face. Or rather he is giving Xerxes Meticula, a man who he thinks is a woman, a man whose name he does not know, a face. He chooses Sex: Female. He shifts her cheekbones up a notch and watches as this morphs the photograph on the main ID screen. He adds some thickness to her lips, makes them lush with a womanly cleft in the middle. He gives her a thin, sculpted nose. He makes her up with lipstick, a reddish violet, the color of gladiolas, a bold, bright, brazen choice. He adds some rouge, a pinkish color, the kind of color that a child would choose, a color that hints at recklessness, a recklessness that in The Lady is a façade, for The Lady only acts in cool calculation. Tres gives The Lady blond curls, girlish but sinister, superfluous curls that mask practicality and deceit.

Tres gives The Lady all the qualities that he desires in a woman.

*   *   *

The digital clock's colon blinks at Xerxes. Xerxes is trying to figure out where he is, what all has happened. He is in his bed. His clock says 6. 6? 6 in the morning? No, it is 6 in the evening. It is May 13th, Year 1 in The Realm. It is May 13th in The Realm and he had been attacked this morning by the Two-Headed Boy. Or rather 9 days before. 9 days before in Realm time. Nine days before the Raven had visited him and called him Lenore; 9 hours ago in real time. In real time it is 6 P.M. Sunday, June 25, 2000. In real time the visiting hours at St. Francis Hospital have just begun. The visiting hours in Ward B of the St. Francis Sanitarium were from noon to 2 and 6 to 8. He had promised that he would be there, that he would walk through the metal detector at 6 o'clock and greet her in a hallway that had cherry red walls. But he was not there. And because he was not there she might be having a fit. And because she was having a fit she was probably in restraints and foaming at the mouth.

Xerxes is worried about his sister but he is also worried about them, about his peasants. Xerxes leans over the side of his bed, hauls in his laptop, logs into The Realm. He goes, quickly, to the kingdom's news page:

News for The Boneyard: May, YR1

💀 The King of Carrot Flowers (47:50) has captured 98 acres from The Strangely Peaceful Citadel of Blue Orcs (12:5).

🐾 *sKyLaR's pLeAsUrE PaLaCe* (12:5) has kidnapped 235 peasants from *The King of Carrot Flowers* (47:50).

🐾 *sKyLaR's pLeAsUrE PaLaCe* (12:5) has kidnapped 235 peasants from *The King of Carrot Flowers* (47:50).

🐾 *sKyLaR's pLeAsUrE PaLaCe* (12:5) has kidnapped 235 peasants from *The King of Carrot Flowers* (47:50).

🐾 *sKyLaR's pLeAsUrE PaLaCe* (12:5) has kidnapped 235 peasants from *The King of Carrot Flowers* (47:50).

🐾 *sKyLaR's pLeAsUrE PaLaCe* (12:5) has infected 60 soldiers from *The King of Carrot Flowers* (47:50) with nightmares. They have deserted.

🐾 *sKyLaR's pLeAsUrE PaLaCe* (12:5) has infected 59 soldiers from *The King of Carrot Flowers* (47:50) with nightmares. They have deserted.

🐾 *sKyLaR's pLeAsUrE PaLaCe* (12:5) has infected 58 soldiers from *The King of Carrot Flowers* (47:50) with nightmares. They have deserted.

🐾 *Nevermore* (12:5) has captured 124 acres from *The King of Carrot Flowers* (47:50).

💀 *Pepper Daisy* (47:50) has captured 62 acres from *Raven* (12:5).

💀 *Tomato Rose* (47:50) has captured 41 acres from *Raven* (12:5).

💀 *Broccoli Bluebonnets* (47:50) has captured 19 acres from *Land of BonZ* (12:5).

💀 *Okra Orchids* (47:50) has captured 13 acres from *Land of BonZ* (12:5).

🐾 *Land of BonZ* (12:5) has attempted an invasion of *Broccoli Bluebonnets* (47:50) but failed.

💀 *Squash Lillies* (47:50) has captured 49 acres from *Land of BonZ* (12:5).

💀 *Venus Fly Trap* (47:50) has captured 26 acres from *Third Reich* (12:5).

*********************************** *End of News* ***********************************

Raven has paid dearly for his indiscretion, but he has done it, he has knocked Two-Headed Boy clear off the Top 100 rankings. sKyLaR weakened him with magic, and Raven polished him off. The Lady's loss has been avenged.

The Lady wants to do something, wants to do something that you simply don't do in The Realm. She wants to send the enemy a message. The Realm is not a place where this is done. You don't acknowledge your enemy—he attacks you and you attack him back, and then it is over. You move on. The smarter players know this. You never allow it to get personal. The minute that emotions get involved you start to do things that are stupid—you send out too many troops and leave yourself wide open for counterattack, you start using your thieves for operations that harm the enemy but do not help you, you bring others into the conflict and so do they. Eventually, both of you slink off the leaderboards and respect is lost. You will now be everyone's victim.

But she is drawn in. She is drawn into the screen that says, *your messengers await your commands,* the screen that has a nymph-like man outlined in neon-purple, a nymph-like man outlined in neon-purple like the man in *Tron*, a nymph-like man with wings on his feet and a scroll in his hands that delivers messages instantly, that can carry language to the ends of The Realm *instantaneously.* The inhabitants of The Realm have their very own Hermes.

She must take a jab. Take a jab at the Two-Headed Boy. What he had done was an affront. There was no need for him to do it. They could have shared the top, fought it out by building up their troops and thieves and attacking lesser targets. You just don't do it. You protect your net worth at all costs. But the Two-Headed Boy had struck *her.* Number 1 had attacked number 2. It was a disturbance in the time space continuum that could not simply be ignored. And both of them knew it. The Two-Headed Boy, whoever he was, wherever he was, had done something that he knew he shouldn't have done.

The Lady has to send him a message, has to let him know that she knows that what he has done is a mistake. The message she wants to send Two-Headed Boy is this: Overconfidence is your greatest weakness.

The message is a mistake. It will appear that she is taunting him and he will team up with his powerful kingdom mates to steal more land. But she can't help it. There is something about the Two-Headed Boy. She feels he will understand. The Lady clicks her mouse:

Lady Peace & Love but Mostly Love,

A courier has been sent with a communication for The King of Carrot Flowers. Please remember that inappropriate messages may be cause for removal from The Realm.

The Lady logs off. There is still time. She transforms herself back to him. She gets in #8 and heads down The Ranch's serpentine drive.

———

Edward Calvin Rawlings III is gazing at the text on his monitor:

Overconfidence is your biggest weakness.

This is just a message, one of the hundred that cross his computer screen an hour. His monitors are awash with boxes, boxes of streaming text in red and blue. He arranges the boxes on his monitor like one of those number puzzles where you're trying to get all the numbers arranged in order—

1	2	3	4	5
6	7	8	9	10
11	12	13	14	15
16	17	18	19	20
21	22	23	24	

Tres does not have the usual barriers to rapid digital correspondence, so he is able to reply to all these messages with amazing alacrity. It is not his fingers that do his communicating for him. Tres communicates with his computer through his eyes. He simply looks at one of his monitors and a red laser dot, one of those red laser dots that annoying teenagers are always pointing at movie screens, appears like a cursor at the spot on the monitor where he is looking. To choose something on his screen all Tres has to do is blink. Tres can blink a click.

Overconfidence is your greatest weakness. It is a simple statement, not particularly cutting or mean, and yet there is so much in it, so much irony in the fact that it has crossed Tres's screen at this point, in this time. First of all, overconfidence is your greatest weakness, is a line from a movie. It is what Luke Skywalker said to The Emperor in *Star Wars*. Although Tres bears no resemblance to The Emperor, he does, with his head gear, look a lot like The Emperor's prodigy, Darth Vader.

Secondly, overconfidence *is* Tres's greatest weakness. Tres has never been frightened of anything. As a teenager he had raced down vertical slopes at breakneck speeds without a thought to caution. It had never occurred to him what could happen, that one day a minor adjustment at the wrong time, just as his edge hit a rut, could cause this.

It also appears, appears now that the Lady Peace & Love but Mostly Love's kingdom mates have managed to disable and then attack him, as a minor, but aggressive province called Nevermore has invaded and robbed him of a good portion of his land, that he *has* been overconfident. This is his twelfth age. In the last age his kingdom had finished first and he had been the most powerful province in The Realm. He was accustomed to being #1.

In this age, things had been going along swimmingly. He had easily gained prominence. His kingdom mates were well-known friends, people he had worked with for five ages or more. They sent him everything he needed: extra gold, extra soldiers, they even cast spells on him to increase his land mass. He, in turn, protected them by his sheer size. Other kingdoms were afraid of both him and his kingdom mates. He had not been attacked since Age 10 when he was still learning the game and building up his network.

And now this is happening. He had thought he had her. Yes, she was the #2 province in The Realm, but she had seemed a rogue province, a stand-alone target. She had built no offense—there was no way she could attack him back, and he didn't think anyone in her kingdom would have the where-withal to come back at him. Furthermore, her kingdom seemed to have no organization. Although she was the largest province in her kingdom, she wasn't even the leader of it. She was just a Lady. She was not a Queen. Their King made stupid decisions, didn't know how to make a proper attack. Their province names were pell-mell. They obviously had never played together before.

All systems were go and so he had gone. And now he is surprised. The retaliation had been swift. There seems to be a triumvirate at the top of The Boneyard: the Lady is the defense, she draws attacks to her; sKyLaR is the set-up man, he weakens the enemy with spells, and Nevermore is the offense, he waits for the unsuspecting to attack his Lady and then he strikes back with force.

Yes, they are disorganized, but they seem to know their roles. It reminded the Two-Headed Boy of when his kingdom too was young, when it was Age 11 and he was *Mask of Silver*. He remembered when he had first met Lady Ling of *Ling's Many Fingers*. Lady Ling who is now Pepper Daisy; Lady Ling, a Japanese woman who works for the Fujimoto Bank in Real Life, who flies between Hong Kong and Tokyo on a regular basis, who has a Palm Pilot with a software program called Blackberry on it, who has a software program called Blackberry on it so she can log onto The Realm the minute she deplanes. Lady Ling had said she liked gold and would get it at any cost. She would be a thief. And so she was. He liked this—a Japanese banker in Real Life, a thief in The Realm who sent her extra money to the King, to *The Mask of Silver*, to him, to her paralytic hero. He imagined her: a powerful Asian businesswoman with long red fingernails, a woman who would not bend. They had started it, he and Ling. They had pulled the rest in: Manuel, a Brazilian; Ice from Minnesota; Demon in Texas; Asif in Pakistan; Njera from Sierra Leone. They had pulled a bunch of strangers, a bunch of people who had never seen each other in Real Life, together to spend countless hours focusing on becoming the best at a game. It had taken four ages to reach the top, to reach the pinnacle of success. And they had done it. They had been the best.

The Lady's kingdom reminds Tres of his kingdom when they began. It is exciting: strangers getting to know each other's strengths and weaknesses; strangers aching to reach the top; strangers whose only hope in doing so is their trust in each other. The Lady's kingdom reminds Tres of his kingdom and the Lady reminds Tres of Tres. She seems a mirror of his own mind. She, too, knows her weaknesses. It is the only reason she would have sent him that message. She knows that Tres has to play the Evil Emperor, that he has no choice but to respond: Your faith in your friends is yours.

A red laser skitters about on a visual keyboard. Words appear on his screen. Tres sends them off.

14. USE DIPLOMACY.

GABRIELLA INTRODUCES her fellow St. Francis patients to Xerxes as her friends. They are having a Thanksgiving dinner, even though it is June. They are eating turkey, turkey that has been boiled and not roasted; Uncle Ben's instant potatoes; green beans that came from a case of aluminum cans that were donated by a woman named Patsy who had been storing them for years in her cellar in case of a nuclear attack; and cranberry sauce, also canned.

Xerxes ignores Gabriella's "friends" and asks her questions. He asks her how she is doing, how they are treating her, how she feels. He asks her about her medication, whether it's doing her any good. Gabriella shovels canned green beans into her mouth.

Although Xerxes is trying hard to ignore Gabriella's friends, Leonard is hard to ignore. He is standing behind Xerxes, all 78 inches of him, with his arms outstretched and his right foot tapping the tile floor with a speed metal beat. Xerxes doesn't know this, because he doesn't know about Leonard's walking, but Leonard is exercising amazing restraint. Leonard is actually standing still, and Leonard *never* stands still. Xerxes also doesn't know that the reason Leonard is standing still is out of respect. Leonard is meeting someone famous, he is meeting the much-discussed Xerxes Meticula, Gabriella's twin brother, the founder of an Internet company and a man who frequently appeared on CNN, and not only this but a man who understood two sides, a man who understood both business and queerness, both what is considered a success and what is considered a failure.

This is what Gabriella had said. She had said that he understood her. And if he could understand Gabriella then he could understand Leonard. A businessman, a man of the world, could understand Leonard. And if he could understand Leonard then maybe they could go on a walk together. Maybe Leonard and the beloved Gabriella and the beloved Xerxes would someday walk in a beeline across Death Valley, a beeline across the flattest place imaginable, a walk with no boundaries but your own, a walk across a limitless two-dimensional space with no obstacles, not even the occasional patch of creosote.

Leonard had done this walk before while making his way southwest from Duluth. It was a walk which had very nearly ended in his death: a very pure and perfect death, a very beautiful and shriveled and waterless death, a death to be pulled apart by vultures and shat back out on the sand. Not carrying any water and at the point of hallucination, Leonard had imagined that his hair was fire: his fiery red hair on his head was fire; and his reddish arm hair was fire; and his chest hair was fire; and the hair on the top of his feet was fire; and yes, his red curly pubic hair was fire. He had imagined that he was fire, a Leonard-sized fireball moving slowly through the desert, and he tingled and the sweat, the last remaining moisture on his body, had evaporated, and he was much bigger than Leonard-sized he was sun-sized, he was all hydrogen and helium and flares and he was dying because he had no water in him. Only he wasn't dying, because he was the sun.

Leonard had imagined this and when he woke up he was in yet another institution but this feeling and this knowledge was now his. Perfection was his, and no matter his humiliation, no matter his low life, no matter that he had no other form of communication than to walk and to make the occasional bizarre quip about being Frankenstein, no matter that fear, on almost every level, ruled him. He knew perfection. He had seen it in the desert.

Xerxes turns and says, "Hi, Leonard," and holds out his hand. Leonard does not shake hands, he hugs, but he wishes that at that moment he could break free from his set ways and shake Xerxes's hand, or, even more strongly, he wishes that Xerxes would understand him well enough to hug him. Leonard doesn't move and Xerxes turns back around to face Gabriella and her Thanksgiving dinner.

Gabriella says, "You have to hug him."

Xerxes says, "That turkey looks tender."

Gabriella repeats what she just said, "You have to hug Leonard."

"I'm not going to hug him."

"You're being rude. Leonard isn't stupid, he knows what you're saying."

Xerxes turns to look at Leonard, whose eyes are looking straight ahead at the wall. "I'm not going to hug him."

"Why are you being so rude?"

"Why do you have to make everything a challenge? And why on earth do you think he wants me to hug him?"

"Because that's how he says hello."

Xerxes is silent. His patience is running thin.

"Right, Leonard?" asks Gabriella.

Leonard stares at the wall. Leonard says, "I am Frankenstein."

"I suppose that means yes."

"It does."

"OK, Miss Mind Reader."

"OK, Mr. Closed-Minded. . . . Leonard is my boyfriend. You should be nice to him."

"Oh, he's your boyfriend? I didn't know that. Well, Leonard, let's get together and have a good old-fashioned, twin-brother-meets-twin-sister's-zombie-boyfriend hug."

"That was uncalled for."

"That was uncalled for? This isn't second-grade playtime. *You have to hug Leonard. Leonard is my boyfriend.* You're acting like a child. And you're not a child, Gabriella. You can get out of this if you try. You're talented and smart and if you would just take your medicine and chill out and not live every day like the apocalypse is here, you wouldn't be in this situation."

"The apocalypse *is* here."

"Stop it."

"Stop what?"

"Stop acting like a goddamned psychic."

"You don't *know*, Xerxes. You can't see. You need to stop and listen. The world is—"

"I'm not going to listen to this, Gabriella. You need to stop thinking like this. You can't worry about the world. You need to just figure out your thing, and do it, and once you're doing your thing, you're not going to be standing on a mountain in the middle of a thunderstorm throwing a baby at your brother. You've got to stop trying to do something big and dramatic and just do something small. Just get your own apartment, and see your doctors twice a week, and do some volunteer work, and get a part-time job until you're feeling stable, and then you can teach kindergarten or write poetry. Think small. Small is OK."

"You don't understand. I'm called."

"Called to do what? Kill neighbors' babies?"

"The baby isn't dead."

"He would be if I hadn't broke his fall."

"But you did."

"And I suppose I'm going to magically show up every time you throw a baby."

Gabriella wishes that Xerxes would have just a little faith.

Xerxes keeps going, "Do you know that you nearly killed me too? I had a two-inch chunk of century plant in my back."

"You needed to be nearly killed."

"Oh?"

"You need to wake up, Xerxes."

"Well, it worked. You woke me up. I'm up every night well past three with a sharp, metallic pain in my spine."

"You know what I mean."

"No, I don't know what you mean, Gabby. What do you mean?"

"You want it to end, too, Xerxes."

That day on the bridge, the day when Xerxes had almost jumped, the things that Gabriella had said made sense to him, but Gabriella was always saying things, was always hinting at things that were bigger. And you just can't live like that. You can't always be thinking about matters of life and death. Why couldn't she talk about something light? *Hey Gabby it's cold today. Yep, Xerx, it's colder than Antarctica in June.*

"No, actually, I don't want it to end. I want it to go on and on like that terrible Dustin Hoffman movie *Ishtar*. Did you see that movie? My God. That's what happens when an actor tries to direct. What a nightmare."

"Why can't you be serious?"

"Why can't you not be serious? Why can't you just focus on your turkey dinner? Look you have a turkey dinner and it's not even Thanksgiving. How cool is that? You know what I had for dinner? You know what I stopped for on the way over here? Two bean burritos, an order of nachos, and a medium Coke. 69¢ times 3 plus 99¢ for the soda times the 8.25 percent Arizona state sales tax. They made a complete dinner for me that cost $3.31. 12 people worked in assembly-line precision, at a breakneck pace, and made me a lunch this cheap. Can you believe it? And look at you—a free Thanksgiving dinner, and it's not even Thanksgiving. And you're sitting here complaining and trying to figure out what it means to live? Why, Gabriella? We live in America. We have everything."

"The turkey sucks."

"Yeah, it looks like they cut it up into chunks and boiled it."

"I think you're right. It tastes like water. The mashed potatoes are bad too. I think they're instant."

"And the cranberry sauce?"

"Canned."

"See this is good. We're focused on the present. We're having this conversation and it's just about food. It's like two normal people in a restaurant. One orders filet mignon and the other orders eggplant parmesan. It's probably the guy that orders the filet mignon and he probably gets a baked potato too, with butter and extra sour cream, and chopped green onions, and bacon bits. And the girl, she orders a side salad, or maybe she gets up and goes to the salad bar. Yeah. That's it. The girl gets up and goes to the salad bar and while she's there the guy has time to reflect on the girl who's eating the eggplant parmesan, and he is contemplating her beauty, and how golden her hair is, and he doesn't think, boy, that must be fake, but thinks that she has the most natural Goldilocks–like hair, a head of girlish blond hair that miraculously survived adulthood. But here's the catch. When she comes back to the table, he doesn't say what you would say, he doesn't freak her out and say

'My God, you have the most beautiful hair.' He doesn't hold his heart out to her like that, he doesn't hold his slab of meat out, his filet mignon, and say, 'look, this is my heart and I want to give it to you.' He would be insane to do that, and you, since that's what you would do, you'd never get the girl, she'd be scared, and she'd never return the messages that you left on her answering machine. No, what he says, even though he's smitten with her hair, what he says is, 'How was the salad bar?' "

"I don't want that, Xerxes, I don't want a girl with fake blond hair to talk to about the salad bar. I want . . ."

"OK, so it's a guy, and his hair is long and dirty blond and not dyed or anything. And you're not at a restaurant but outside the corner store. And he's kind of the hippie type like you. And he's gone into the corner store to get Power Bars and trail mix for a hike that the two of you are going on for your first date. You like him, of course; he's your type. But you still don't look at him right away and say, 'your eyes are like diamonds,' you can do this later, when you're sitting at the vista point that you've hiked to, and you've smoked a bowl, but you don't freak him out and leave him speechless in front of the corner store, you just ask him what he bought, Chocolate Banana or Peanut Butter."

"I still don't want it."

"Gabby, it's a dance. You need to learn to dance the dance. It's fun once you get the hang of it, and there are variations. There's salsa and merengue and the tango. It's not as dull as you think it is."

"I don't want to be fake, Xerxes. I don't want to be thinking your eyes look like diamonds and say, what did you buy Chocolate Banana or Peanut Butter? Why should I? I want to be taken at face value, right away, right from the start. I want the boy with the long, dirty blond hair to hold my face in his hands and say 'your eyes look like diamonds too.' Why do things have to start cold and then work to warm? Why can't people just be warm, right from the start?"

"It's a trust thing, Gabby. What if the boy with the long, dirty blond hair turns out to be a psycho killer and because you've said his eyes look like diamonds he knows that you're going to be an easy target to tie up between some rocks and leave half-dead on the side of a mountain."

"I don't care. I don't want to live cold like that."

"It's not cold once you get to know someone."

"Oh yeah, and where are your warm friends."

"I've got warm friends, I just have work to do."

"You know what I'm saying. You've spent years with people and you still don't trust them."

Xerxes is sitting in a psych ward in a strip mall talking to a mental patient and he knows the mental patient is right. He hates this about his sister. She is always right. But right is not easy. Right is painful and wrong.

"Well, this has been fun, Gabby. Anything else to say? Glad to see you, Xerx, thanks for visiting?"

"That's not nice."

"I'm sorry. I just want you to be happy and when you're so unhappy it makes me grumpy."

"I'm not unhappy. You're unhappy. This is where I'm happiest. Here with Leonard."

Xerxes looks back at Leonard. Leonard's face is still to the wall, but it is now contorted in a grimace. Leonard is thinking, *he doesn't get it, he doesn't understand*. His grimace is the grimace of disappointment. Doesn't he know? Doesn't he know that Dylan song, doesn't he know that wail from the North Country—from his, from Leonard's country—doesn't he understand the reason for the Leonards and the Gabbys and the Bobs in the world: *when you ain't got nothing, you've got nothing to lose*.

★   ★   ★

When he returned from St. Francis there had been much to do. Repairing the damage that the Two-Headed Boy had caused wasn't easy, and it could only be done if he convinced him to lay off, a task that was easier said than done.

The Lady had taken heart in the Two-Headed Boy's response, though: Your faith in your friends is yours. It meant that the Two-Headed Boy was willing to play, that he didn't take the attacks personally. She composed a more diplomatic communiqué to send to the Two-Headed Boy and sent it off. It read:

To My Worthy Foe, Two-Headed Boy,

As you know, the force that was used against your province by our kingdom was a direct result of an unprovoked attack against my province. The Boneyard sees no need to continue this conflict as we feel the appropriate retaliatory measures have been taken. I will speak to my kingdom mates and ask that they discontinue reciprocal attacks effective immediately.

We do not want war with your kingdom, as such a war at this early stage would sap the strength of both parties. Your kingdom is, admittedly, more powerful than ours, but we are strong enough to pull you down a good ways with us. Please ask your kingdom mates to discontinue their aggressive actions against us.

Signed, The Lady Peace & Love but Mostly Love

The message had been responded to within the hour. The Lady was pleased, because the Two-Headed Boy was someone who could be reasoned with, but she was also troubled by the note's implications:

To my Equally Worthy Foe, The Lady Peace & Love but Mostly Love,

It was understood, that the aggression that you and your fellow provinces took against my province followed common rules of engagement in The Realm, and was not taken personally. We, too, have taken retaliatory measures and feel that the original score has been settled.

Despite this, our kingdom is carefully monitoring yours as a target for war. Many of your provinces have made some loosely planned attacks on our provinces and left themselves exposed for a good deal of land grabbing. We are tempted.

In addition, your king has sent threatening (when intelligible) notes to some of my provinces. Although I do not take him too seriously, and although his threats have been met with a great deal of glee by my provinces who have, in turn, robbed him of most of his lands; he does make the rest of you look dumb for having given him the monarchy.

I will carefully consider your request for peace, but I must ask you why your kingdom has accepted such weak leadership.

Signed, Two-Headed Boy

It was true what the Two-Headed Boy was saying—King BonZ was a liability—but she couldn't exactly steal the monarchy. She would need the votes, and it would be difficult to get those votes in a short amount of time. There was also the problem of hurt feelings, she had to do this without causing Lord BonZ to be discouraged and leave the game. She needed the coup to be bloodless.

If BonZ were to leave, the net worth that his province had obtained would suddenly be gone, and the kingdom would be left without 5% of its wealth. This was the greatest act of revenge available to those in The Realm: simply closing your account, or worse yet, just failing to log on. There is nothing to keep you from doing it either, from growing bored, or getting angry and just calling it quits. The people who are your partners in The Realm, your lifeline, are nothing to you in Real Life. They are phantoms. A player may feel some latent guilt for quitting, but there are no repercussions; in fact, there is often relief, because suddenly they have more time, more time for girlfriends, or wives, or work, or exercise, or fresh air. But no one in The Realm wants you to think about that, because if one of your provinces quits, one of the provinces that has taken weeks, sometimes months to develop, the strength of your kingdom is greatly diminished. And so the people behind the provinces in The Realm work hard to build the delusion that they have no Real Lives, and that what Real Lives they have will not in any way interfere with their dedication to The Realm, because if they show this weakness to the other people in their kingdom, the other people in the kingdom will start to think about it too, and before you know it you have provinces dropping like flies.

And so The Lady must make it clear to BonZ and to the rest of the provinces that have been following him that the game will continue to be fun, and that she is dedicated to them, more dedicated in fact than she is to anything in her Real Life, and that with her as a leader they can achieve greatness.

Xerxes looks at his screen. This is how it happens. This is how one gets sucked in. This is his folly. It is so much easier to play a bit part.

Most people could accept mediocrity in their work lives. You put in a minimal amount of effort, the minimal amount of effort you can get away with to keep your job. For Xerxes, work wasn't like this. It wasn't simply a means, but an end. Work was play. Work was everything. And because of this, Xerxes became a natural leader, and not only a natural leader but a workaholic. Xerxes bought into the Ayn Rand philosophy that was so despised by his contemporaries: that work gave your life meaning; that work, was, in fact, life; that it wasn't the forty-hour-a-week blackness that the average employee considered it.

Ironically, it was his love of work, his desire to achieve, that drew him to something that on first glance appeared to be anti-work, something that appeared to be play. The Realm is a place where leadership, dedication, hard work, diplomacy, and intellect show immediate and quantifiable rewards.

In The Realm, there was no hiding a flawed province behind a powerful brand name, there was no hiding poor management under a veil of rhetoric, there was no speculation. Your numbers were there, posted right in front of both you and everyone else, easily quantifiable. Any bum in Real Life could win the lottery, or sue someone, or catch an historic home run, and suddenly be a millionaire. Real Life operated on the chaos theory: it was a game of chance. It offered no real intellectual challenge. But in The Realm, the score was clear.

What the hell, Xerxes thinks. Why not? So it is an imaginary world, so it isn't *real*. What is *real*? And in The Realm, as limited a world as it is, at least you know who your friends are.

Xerxes knows what The Lady must do. She must write some poetry. She begins composing a message to Raven. She writes:

Dear Raven,

Lo! Death has reared himself a throne
In a far, far land made out of bone
Within The Realm, ne'er East nor West,
Where the good and the bad and the worst and the best
May soon go to eternal rest.

Signed, The Lady Peace & Love but Mostly Love

15. A MONARCH NEEDS HER COURT.

UNCLE CHARLEY HAS NEVER found himself in this position before. Considering the random generation of the kingdoms, what had happened was very unlikely; there were, after all, 3,000 kingdoms in The Realm. But through a twist of fate, his protégé, Gek-Lin, has ended up in the same kingdom as he.

Because he has this insider knowledge, he knows with certainty what the

Lady Peace & Love but Mostly Love can only guess at: King BonZ is not fit for the monarchy. Uncle Charley decrypts the Lady's poetry. He is enjoying this banter between them. She is able, just as easily as he, to communicate through poetry. What she is saying—that with King BonZ as its leader their kingdom, The Boneyard, is in danger—is undoubtedly true.

Uncle Charley thoroughly agrees, and he will say as much. The problem will come later. The problem will come when he needs to convince Gek-Lin that she should step down.

Raven summons his messengers. He sends off his reply. The reply is followed by a reply from her, her reply followed by a reply from him, and so on, and so on. Uncle Charley is Raven, and the Raven spends his day here, below the ground, in one of the world's many self-made tombs.

Dear Lenore,

Ah but Lenore! Nigh it has to be!
A brighter dwelling-place, I yet can see
And fresh green pastures 'stead of fields of bones
And bright young maidens ensconced on thrones
One constant star to light our way.

Signed, Sir Raven

————

Dear Raven,

Oh the light! From King to Queen too much to say!
With gilded tongue and troubled tooth,
I fear my words not ones to sooth
That Death be the stillborn son we sire
Fresh green pastures soon to fire.

Signed, The Lady Peace & Love but Mostly Love

————

Lenore,

Ah fear! Lower your starry voice!
Best to birth a messenger
To gather afresh and to concur.
To raze the field of bone and begin anew,
We need a quiet bloodless coup.

Signed, Sir Raven

————

Raven,

True words spoken, feathered friend
Perhaps we need not fear the end.
I leave you with your ink-stained quill
Companions to gather and death to still.
Of silence will know I.

Signed, The Lady Peace & Love but Mostly Love

————

Lenore,

I'll talk to sKyLaR. You'll be queen in no time!

Signed, Sir Raven

*   *   *

Dietrich thinks that this place where he is standing, where he stands weighed down by twenty-five pounds of fleece and down, is the single most beautiful place on Earth. He thinks this not because the sky is rippling with the eerie green hues of the aurora australis, and not because there is a full moon at about 20° to the horizon, encircled with quadruple concentric rings, rings caused by dust-like particles of H_2O; he thinks this not because of the color and the light but because this strange place where a barbershop pole sticks straight up out of the Earth, this place surrounded by the flags of 44 nations, the ceremonial bottom of the world, Antarctica, symbolizes what Dietrich thinks is man's greatest achievement—Antarctica is the only stateless land mass in the world.

Dietrich, from his days as the unofficial good sex ambassador to New York City, to his current role as the equally unofficial Antarctic Minister of Camaraderie, has always been a sort of natural peacemaker, the kind of person whose bubbling enthusiasm and silly scheming makes serious rifts between parties seem like childish disputes, but he is rarely, as he is on this evening of sub-sub-zero temperatures, so acutely aware of his own feelings about these things.

Perhaps the reason that Dietrich is so aware this evening of who he is and what his role is in the greater scheme of things, is because he feels that the good fortune that has seemed to follow him wherever he has gone is finally leaving him, that he is finally, after all these years of living on the lighter side of the karmic divide, going to have to deal with darkness.

*   *   *

Dietrich and Caitlin did not have much of a honeymoon. Five hours into what was supposed to have been two days of peace and solitude, peace and solitude being a rare commodity in the overcrowded quarters of The Dome, they were forced to leave their love nest in the private bedroom of the doctor living in Biomed, the only private bedroom on the base, because the doctor who had offered them the bedroom, a kind, older gentleman from England named Peter Walls, who was affectionately, and at times not-so-affectionately, dubbed Doctor Jekyll by the Polies, had turned "Hyde." Dr. Walls had stood before them enraged, his face a disturbing shade of red, a pure red that only a very white Englishman whose face had not seen the light of day for five months could achieve, and stammered "Get . . . out . . . of . . . MY . . . bed!"

Dietrich and Caitlin, who were, as Doctor Jekyll looked down at them, wrapped in nothing but flannel sheets and a goose-down comforter, and who also were in a rather compromising position, seeing as Dietrich's Tab A was currently inserted into Caitlin's Slot B, did the only thing that was sensible to do, since running naked out of Biomed into the pure darkness and killing cold outside wasn't an option, which was to try to switch Hyde back to Jekyll. Dietrich decided to go for the direct approach. He said, "Peter, I think you've become Hyde."

Peter Walls was aware that the other Polies referred to him as Dr. Jekyll, and he was grateful, in a way, that they dealt with his character flaw, his bouts of uncontrollable anger and memory loss, in a humorous manner, since in the outside world, as an E.R. attendant, his temper had not been dealt with in this way, and he had been transferred many a time because of it; but he was not, at least yet, able to reverse the anger. Despite the sudden realization that he had told them that they could use his bedroom for two days, he still insisted that they return to their bunks in the commons.

This, in and of it itself, would not have done much to dampen either Dietrich's or Caitlin's spirits; in fact, if anything, it was a welcome new chapter in the growing archives of insider lore that the Polies, whose only entertainment in their insular world was the eccentricities of their fellow inhabitants; but it was notable, in its way, because it was the first in a series of cascading events that began to wedge Dietrich and Caitlin apart.

A few days after the Dr. Jekyll incident, Dietrich was in the cold and cavernous incomplete garage of the new Scott-Amundsen dome, soldering together aluminum brackets. He was taking great care to get it right, as the difficulty in getting labor and materials to the Pole meant that any error could cause the NSF millions of dollars, not to mention month-long delays in the project, and so didn't notice Caitlin slipping behind him. Caitlin got Dietrich's attention with a gentle rap on his shoulder. When Dietrich switched off the blue flame of the torch and turned around, he was shocked at what he saw.

Caitlin, the most-together woman he had ever met, the incorrigible, stable sure-thing he had married, was standing before him on a floor of ice, barefoot. The garage was heated to a survivable temperature, ten degrees Fahrenheit, but it was certainly no place to stand as unprotected as Caitlin was. What was more, one of Caitlin's eyelids was frozen shut from crying, and the other frozen open. This, combined with her caked-together hair and her bare, rapidly bluing feet, made Caitlin look like a creature straight out of *Poltergeist*, rather than the woman he had married.

Dietrich wrapped Caitlin up in a blanket as fast as he could and paged Dr. Jekyll with a potential case of frostbite. Caitlin was lucky, Dr. Jekyll arrived quickly, toting Biomed's outdated, but amazingly effectual foot whirlpool, and got the blood flowing in her feet before there was any damage, but Dietrich was more worried about his new bride's mental condition than her physical one.

Caitlin had been exhibiting symptoms of chronic hypoxia—spaciness and short-term memory loss—throughout the winter. In the construction garage where they worked, she would put bolts down right next to her and then ask Dietrich where the bolts were, forgetting that just a moment ago they were sitting in her hand. This kind of behavior was considered par for the course for those who lived at the Pole (as was, for that matter, the irrational irritability that was eating at Dr. Jekyll), and Dietrich hadn't thought much of it.

As Dietrich stood in front of her in Biomed, he couldn't help but wonder if perhaps she was getting worse. It was late in the Antarctic winter—temperatures were at their lowest, howling winds created a disheartening drone, and supplies were dwindling. In addition, the effects of hypoxia were worse due to the extremely low barometric pressure; the South Pole was already at 9,000 feet, and with the barometric pressure hovering just over 27 the effective altitude was well over 13,000. To make matters even worse, a tinge of color began to appear in the sky, a sort of false dawn that, although it produced hope, also seemed to produce a sort of short-timers disease: the workers frequently made mistakes and the frostbite cases in Dr. Jekyll's Biomed had doubled in the last few weeks.

Thinking this must be the problem, Dietrich said so to Caitlin. Caitlin, who was sitting in a chair shivering, her feet invisible under the bubbles of the whirlpool, shook her head. Instead of saying anything, she pointed to the computer that sat on Dr. Jekyll's desk.

Dietrich walked over to it. This is what he read:

TO: Caitlin@nsfantarctica.org
FROM: lswilliams@earthlink.net

Caitlin,

Hey. It's Mom. I saw the photographs from the wedding. (Once I figured out what an "attachment" was. Thank God Trudy is here to show me. A 10-year-old teaching a 68-year-old *how to work a computer. Imagine!) Well, at least I saw the photos that you would show me. With that Dietrich you're marrying I'm sure there were some pictures I missed. What drove you to marry such a clown? (You know I'm teasing. It sounds like he adores you. I want to meet him SO badly!)*

Anyway. I wish I didn't have to tell you this, especially since there's so little you can do, (I know what you're going to try to do, but, please, please don't. You are doing something important down there.) but I've been diagnosed with breast cancer. The doctors say that it's quite advanced, but that in some cases women respond quickly to chemo, and since this is a new case, there is still plenty of hope. (This must be so much to swallow. I'm so sorry, honey!)

I'm having a mastectomy next Thursday. Quick, I know. (I'm thinking positive. What's a breast when you're 68? Lord knows, I'm through trying to attract men. Gets in the way when I'm gardening anyway. Both the breasts and the man.) ;)

(Learned the emoticons from Trudy.)

Love, Mom

P.S. Really. DON'T WORRY!

⋆   ⋆   ⋆

Dietrich turns to go back, negative eighty degrees is much too cold to stand around in contemplation. Jerri Nelson, the doctor who herself had managed to develop cancer on The Ice two years ago, and who had had something akin to a religious experience beating it while wintering over, had said in her e-mails to her parents that the experience of wintering over at the Pole was either that of a monk who had found the true meaning of life, or that of a POW who went mad. What Jerri didn't mention to her parents was how difficult it is on the monks at the Pole to keep the POWs sane enough to survive.

Flashlight in hand, Dietrich follows a string of poles that have been topped with green flags to indicate the route from the Ceremonial South Pole to the Dome. He has brought a few extra, to replace the flags that have been torn, and he stops at a pole, clumsily tying on a green flag without removing his thick sealskin gloves. Dietrich too has been affected by hypoxia, but his symptoms are of the opposite sort. Rather than experiencing the usual listlessness, easy irritability, and short-term memory problems, Dietrich has become an insomniac.

Dietrich, forever the optimist, did not lament this loss of sleep. Instead, it had given him the opportunity to play an on-line game, one that connected him with the citizens of a much warmer world than the one he lived in. The wee hours of the morning were the perfect time for Dietrich to do this, as the satellites that allowed the Dome its internet connection were above the horizon, and the number of users during those hours negligible.

Dietrich enjoyed his time in The Realm, but the one thing he didn't like about it was how businesslike and unfriendly it could be. He didn't like the fact that these people who you spent countless hours with in fruitless number crunching were so unwilling to talk about nongame-related things.

Especially now that things were getting rough. After discovering the cause of the "running around barefoot" incident, Dr. Jekyll, concerned with Caitlin's mental condition, decided to confine her to Biomed for a few days, which quickly, as Caitlin became more and more listless, turned to weeks. Losing a welder meant that the rest of the construction crew had to do extra time in the shop. Dietrich himself didn't so much mind the extra work, but the rest of the crew, in their light-deprived irritability, did, and they were all letting Dietrich know it. A couple of Russians and an Argentinean began complaining openly about women being allowed on the construction crew. More enlightened members, people who Dietrich considered friends who would have previously come quickly to Caitlin's defense, were now nodding with them in agreement. What was more, all the events that Dietrich planned—poker nights, ice croquet under the stars, stupid penguin tricks—had gone from heavily attended, to sparsely attended, to Dietrich feeling alone and abandoned at the Great White Plain. His fellow Polies excused themselves by claiming that the extra work was giving them less time for leisure, but Dietrich knew the truth— Dietrich's wife was perceived as a drag on the community, and they were going to take it out on him.

Dietrich found it hard not to take any of this personally. All the Polies were toasted, so it wasn't surprising that a sort of communal pettiness was coming over them, but still, these were people who he'd thrived on entertaining for the last four months, and now they had turned on him.

Dietrich has finished tying on the flag and is approaching the tunnel that leads into the Dome. The entrance to the Dome reads:

THE UNITED STATES OF AMERICA WELCOMES YOU TO THE SCOTT-AMUNDSEN BASE.

If the Polies don't want Dietrich's company then he will find some people who do. It is late—two in the morning—but to Dietrich it could just as well be two in the afternoon. Time has no impact on him. Before the great silence, he measured time by the number of people that were awake on the base with whom he could interact. In a place where the sun was no help, this was the only way. Daytime was when he communicated with people, evenings were when this communication became more intimate, and the dead of night was when the silence came.

But now, with everyone on the base purposefully avoiding him, there is only the silence, and Dietrich has lost his means for telling time. Dietrich needs this anchor, his people time. Without it, every moment feels like it is happening in the dead of the night. Dietrich can't take a 24-hour graveyard shift. He needs daylight hours. He goes looking for friends to give him this daylight.

Dear sKyLaR,

Hey dude! I just messaged Lady Peace & Love but Mostly Love. She wants to be queen. We need to get her in without pissing off BonZ and the rest of the kingdom. Since BonZ thinks I'm a bad ass and listens to me, I'm going to send a message to him saying that we want her to be Queen. Could you do me a favor and message all the other provinces asking them what they think about making her the queen? I don't want it to look like the three of us are ganging up on him, so it would be good if some of the other provinces started registering dissent in the forums.

Signed, Sir Raven

———

Dear rAvEn,

dO yOu ThInK sHe'S a ReAl GiRl?

Signed, Sir sKyLaR

————

Dear sKyLaR,

I don't know but she sure sounds sexy.

Signed, Sir Raven

————

Dear rAvEn,

LoL. I'lL sEnD mEsSaGeS tO aLl ThE pRoVINcEs.

Signed, Sir sKyLaR

16. CROWN YOUR STRONGEST PROVINCE.

IT IS STRANGE, OF COURSE, to be doing it this way, to be communicating with a person sitting ten feet away from you via computer rather than simply talking to them, and yet it is not at all uncommon. In the cubicles of America this happens all the time. Uncle Charley's reasons for doing this are different than the reasons people do this in cubicles. It doesn't have to do with gossiping, flirting, or disseminating porn. Instead, Uncle Charley knows that Gek-Lin might listen to his on-line personality, but that there is no way she will listen to his Real Life one.

He composes a message to her. He writes it in an English she will understand. He has spoken to the Lady Peace & Love and received from her a concession for Gek-Lin. She will receive a position in the kingdom's court. Uncle Charley speaks to Gek-Lin's ego. He tells her that she is a strong fighter, and that she would be better off sticking to fighting rather than having to spend all her time organizing the kingdom. He writes:

King BonZ,

You have been a strong fighter and are always defending the kingdom. The other players don't understand and want the Lady Peace & Love to be queen because she is the biggest. I think you should step down and lead the attacker's guild. Then you don't have to worry about the whole kingdom and you can do your job.

Signed, Sir Raven

* * *

Gek-Lin has received the message from Raven. The Raven is someone she respects. He is an attacker; he knows how to defend his kingdom's honor. Unlike this Lady Peace & Love, who only explores, who grows big but does not protect her kingdom mates, the Raven understands The Realm. Because he suggested it, Gek-Lin decides that she will give up the throne. She goes to her Election screen. She goes to a pull-down menu. She changes her vote.

* * *

Xerxes's mind is a blank. He has forgotten the fruitless conversations that he had with his sister. He is lying on top of the Indian-print comforter of his bed. He is waiting for the hour to pass. When the hour passes the results will appear on his screen.

After sKyLaR sent messages to all the provinces discussing their intentions, and Raven delicately informed King BonZ that he may be dethroned, sKyLaR had called for the election.

The Lady Peace & Love but Mostly Love is not concerned about the results. She will, at the moment the digital clock strikes the hour, be the new queen. The number of votes that each province receives is weighted heavily in favor of those provinces with a high net worth. Her, sKyLaR, and Raven's votes alone are almost enough to put her over the top. What Lady Peace & Love but Mostly Love is most concerned about is attrition. If the weaker provinces are disgruntled, they might quit or become disinterested, and if they quit or become disinterested the strength of the kingdom will be greatly compromised. The Lady Peace & Love but Mostly Love is concerned about unity. And so she anticipates the hour, and when her digital clock reads **12:00 PST 07/02/00** and these results cross her screen, she is overwhelmed:

Election Results for The Boneyard

Province	Votes For	# of Votes
The Strangely Peaceful Citadel of Blue Orcs	The Strangely Peaceful Citadel of Blue Orcs	6
sKyLaR's PlEaSuRe PaLaCe	The Strangely Peaceful Citadel of Blue Orcs	5
Nevermore	The Strangely Peaceful Citadel of Blue Orcs	5
All Baba	The Strangely Peaceful Citadel of Blue Orcs	3
Wonderwizzies	The Strangely Peaceful Citadel of Blue Orcs	3
Sleep Deprivation	The Strangely Peaceful Citadel of Blue Orcs	2
War Place	The Strangely Peaceful Citadel of Blue Orcs	2
One Hundred Happy Acres	The Strangely Peaceful Citadel of Blue Orcs	2
Land of BonZ	The Strangely Peaceful Citadel of Blue Orcs	1
ronald's homeland	The Strangely Peaceful Citadel of Blue Orcs	1
666	The Strangely Peaceful Citadel of Blue Orcs	1
Swallows	The Strangely Peaceful Citadel of Blue Orcs	1
burgermeister melsterburger	The Strangely Peaceful Citadel of Blue Orcs	1
The Frozen Wastes	The Strangely Peaceful Citadel of Blue Orcs	1
Dandy Lion	The Strangely Peaceful Citadel of Blue Orcs	1
penisbreath	The Strangely Peaceful Citadel of Blue Orcs	1
Land of Hell	The Strangely Peaceful Citadel of Blue Orcs	1
Third Reich	The Strangely Peaceful Citadel of Blue Orcs	1
GurGle	The Strangely Peaceful Citadel of Blue Orcs	1
jekshtwdw	The Strangely Peaceful Citadel of Blue Orcs	1
Total Vote Count:		
The Strangely Peaceful Citadel of Blue Orcs		40

!!

Winner of the Election: The Strangely Peaceful Citadel of Blue Orcs

★　★　★

In an Internet café in Bangkok, Uncle Charley is pestering Gek-Lin. She does not want to tell him what she has done. Finally he says, "You stepped down from the throne didn't you? I am proud of you. You did the right thing. You are a warrior. You lost a battle but you will not lose the war. When I am in The Realm, I am a warrior too. You have learned a valuable lesson today, Gek-Lin."

Gek-Lin bristles. She did it for Raven, not for this fool, not for Uncle Charley. She wonders why Uncle Charley cares so much.

★   ★   ★

In the room where he spent his childhood, underneath his windows to the world, Tres Rawlings, about to declare war on The Boneyard, notices that the kingdom has a new leader, a woman who he is rather fond of, and changes his position. The Two-Headed Boy sends off messages to all his provinces:

Cease your attacks on The Boneyard. They have dethroned their leader. I expect the new queen will be more cooperative.

★   ★   ★

In separate sleeping quarters at the St. Francis Sanitarium, Leonard B. Walker and Gabriella Meticula both dream of the desert. In the dream they are naked and standing still, their arms stretched towards the sun.

BOOK III: THE PLAGUE

RL TIME: AUGUST/EARLY SEPTEMBER, 2000
REALM TIME: YR 7-YR 12

It's amazing what devices you can sympathize.

—R.E.M., "WORLD LEADER PRETEND"

17. NEVER BOUNCE.

XERXES WAKES UP AS HE OFTEN DOES, halfway dressed, halfway under his sheets, Chuck Taylors permanently attached to his feet. This morning, for reasons unclear to him, he is also halfway hopeful.

Xerxes throws on his mustard yellow *We've Come This Far by Faith* T-shirt. The Queen has, over the course of the last month, accomplished a great deal. She has completely revamped the organizational structure of the kingdom. There is now a Ministry of Subversive Activities, a grouping of provinces specializing in thievery, otherwise known as the M.S.A., of which she is the head; the Red Crown, a non-profit that helps provinces in need, run by Raven; the Department of Practical Jokes, open to any province adept at wizardry, also called the PJs, led by sKyLaR; and the all-important Performers of Aggressive Acts, the P-double-As, headed by the dethroned King BonZ, demoted to Lord BonZ, with Raven appointed as special advisor.

She has also renamed the kingdom, changing *The Boneyard*, an unfortunate kingdom name that implied that they would all soon be in the graveyard, to *Paradigm Shift*, a kingdom name which the Queen thought represented well their new power.

Once she had delegated leadership roles to the stronger provinces, the kingdom took off. Under the Queen's tutelage, *Paradigm Shift's* economy boomed. The Queen taught all the provinces involved in the M.S.A. her thieving techniques and before long Raven's Red Crown was overflowing with gold coins.

Although the Queen's band of rogues were infrequently caught thieving, drawing the ire of the provinces they had attempted to steal from, sKy-LaR's tricksters were so adept at casting protection spells that no one was able to counterattack, and when they did, they often failed miserably, leaving the P-double-A to clean up.

Lord BonZ was the biggest surprise. Raven had talked the Queen into letting Lord BonZ run the military arm of the kingdom, an important post that she didn't think he was up to, given his past failures. But out of nowhere, he had proven amazingly adept at finding easy targets, and the kingdom's armies were making off with large amounts of land. On top of this, Lord BonZ's attacks were suddenly fail safe, his armies were now succeeding in conquering an average of 4 opponents in a week, without being hit himself, and he was reestablishing himself as one of the stronger provinces. The Queen had sent him a message of congratulations and Lord BonZ had returned with an explanation that made her laugh: I lernt my algebra.

With the kingdom rolling in dough, the Queen had instructed all the provinces to train military elites, expensive but deadly forces, and after a week of economic and military expansion, she deemed the kingdom ready to perform the most dangerous, but potentially lucrative, act available to kingdoms in The Realm. This evening, Queen Peace & Love but Mostly Love will start a war.

Although the primary cause of Xerxes's joie de vivre is the anticipation that his alter ego will soon be engaged in battle, Xerxes is also halfway hopeful about his sister. Xerxes, for the most part, doesn't trust the psychiatrists at the St. Francis Sanitarium, but a new doctor has taken an interest in Gabriella, a doctor named Sara Bronstein, a short, petite, woman with a Bettie Page haircut and jet black hair who has kindly offered to take on Gabriella as a sort of special project.

Sara had pulled Xerxes aside a few days ago during visiting hours and asked him a surprisingly subjective question, "So do you think your sister is really crazy?"

Xerxes, taken aback, had answered, "I'm not a doctor. I don't diagnose."

"But you're her twin brother. You know her better than anybody. You must have an opinion."

"I think according to the classification system of the *DSM IV*, my sister would be defined a borderline affective schizophrenic."

"So, you've read her charts."

"Yes, I've read her charts and they seem quite accurate. Why don't you tell me your opinion, Doc?"

"I don't know, I'm not a doctor either."

"So what are you?"

"I'm a student. When I complete my hours I become a doctor."

There was something about her that drove Xerxes to sarcasm, "Oh. I'm sorry. What is your opinion then, Ms. Bronstein, as a student of the fine art of psychiatry, of my sister's condition?"

She seemed to take his attitude in stride, and to even match its tone, "As a student of psychiatry I agree with your unprofessional but astute diagnosis, Mr. Meticula, that your sister is a borderline affective schizophrenic. As a human being, I sense that your sister is simply a rebel."

"Like in *Girl, Interrupted*."

"No, not like that at all."

"Right. She doesn't have big brown eyes and short black hair, and she isn't Winona Ryder in real life."

"I'm being serious, Mr. Meticula."

"Don't call me Mr. Meticula."

"Then don't call me Ms. Bronstein."

"OK, Doc."

"Listen, Mr. Meticula, you are probably right. Your sister probably is a borderline affective schizophrenic, as defined by the DSM IV. But you and I both know that this method of classifying mental disorders has only been in existence for twenty-two years, and that methods of classification only explain so much. Your sister sees things, Xerxes. She knows what's going on with people in a way that's disturbing. Disturbing to both the people around her and herself. And when she intuits things she can't ignore them, so she acts on what she sees. She's kind of like a prophet, Xerxes. If she were an Aztec, they'd worship her like a goddess. If she were a Pilgrim, they'd string her from a tree."

"Great."

"What?"

"Great. So, she's a witch in an age without magic. So what is she supposed to do? What are we supposed to do?"

"Let her go."

"Oh, that's brilliant. Let her and Leonard run off until they get arrested or shot for trespassing because they've been communing with some cattle rancher's cows."

"I mean let her mind go. I mean stop drugging her and trying to 'stabilize' her. Let her have her flights of fancy and see where they lead. Just organize her a good support network, so that she has something to fall back on, and then let her be."

"Yes, let's organize her a support network. A fine idea, Doc."

"I'm sorry, the psych terms are a habit."

"That's all right, the sarcasm's a habit too."

"What would you say if I suggested that they taper her off her medicine?"

"Sara, I've gone through this a million times. I'd rather have a muted version of my twin sister than no twin sister at all. The medicine keeps her, not to mention the neighbor's children, alive."

"Sure, you want her to be safe and secure, but what does she want? It's not all black and white, Xerxes, is it? And we can't control other people's lives, not even our own faltering twin sisters."

Xerxes ignored Sara. "It's better to burn out, ba, ba, ba, ba, ba, ba, bah," he sang, "than to fade away."

"Is that in reference to Neil Young, Def Leppard, or Kurt Cobain's suicide note?"

"Kurt wrote that in his suicide note?"

"Yeah," said Sara.

"Shit," said Xerxes.

"So you were referring to Def Leppard then?" asked Sara.

"Yeah, you know, no serenade, no fire brigade, just pyromania."

"I know the lyrics," said Sara.

"Sara Bronstein knows the lyrics to Pyromania?" asked Xerxes.

"It was the early '80s."

"You didn't happen to have pink hair back then, did you?"

"Yep," said Sara, "and a mohawk."

After that conversation Xerxes had trusted Sara Bronstein, not because he agreed that Gabriella should be tapered off her medicine, but because he knew that Sara knew that there were no right answers, that there was no proper means for caring for a patient, that there was only trial and error, then more trial, then more error. He also trusted Sara Bronstein because she had once had a mohawk.

While he is thinking these thoughts about Sara, Xerxes is placing his laptop on his bed.

You are the Queen Peace & Love but Mostly Love. It is January 1st, YR 7. Welcome back to The Realm.

* * *

Gek-Lin feels a bit uncomfortable. It is her first visit to the Blue Moon Internet Café during the day and gone are her fellow orphans; gone is Uncle Charley with his slicked-back hair and spectacles; gone are the paper plates full of the day's leftovers.

Replacing these are a large group of Australians carrying denominations of Thai bills that Gek-Lin, who herself is Thai, has never before seen. Gek-Lin walks past them and sits down at a computer terminal. She has brought with her a stuffed animal. Gek-Lin is not sentimental. She isn't a cute girl contenting herself with a dolly. But still, she brought with her a secret fetish, a talisman—Psyduck, one of the most mysterious and unusual of the race of Pokémon; Psyduck, a very slow Pokémon who says nothing but 'Psy, Psy, Psy' over and over again; Psyduck, the Pokémon who the other Pokémon sit with and watch sunsets, days of sunrises and sunsets, sitting with the Psyduck waiting for the answers that always come when you sit with the Psyduck for hours on end; Psyduck, the Pokémon Buddha.

Gek-Lin, age fourteen, does not make the connection that the Psyduck is teaching her the patience that she both needs and desires, that she is metaphorically sucking up the psionic energy of the Psyduck and slowly getting smarter, that Psyduck is a powerful symbol. Gek-Lin is an orphan and she rarely has an opportunity to watch television or play with Pokémon cards. Gek-Lin likes Psyduck because he is big and yellow and looks charming with his large, slightly crossed eyes and his orange bill, and because he was easy to steal from the market when the young saleswoman ran off to get some change for a tourist.

With Psyduck standing guard, Gek-Lin goes through the motions. She has never done this before, not without Uncle Charley close by. She types in www.thisistherealm.com. Then, geklin. Then, BonZ.

The battle plan had been Lord BonZs's idea. The Queen had given them the target kingdom, a kingdom called *Amphibious*, but everything else had been up to him. He is going to go on a suicide run. He's going to hit a very powerful province, The Serpent, the Queen of the *Amphibious* kingdom. Lord BonZ's battle plan is to commit the majority of his troops to this attack, causing a chain reaction that will certainly weaken him, but will allow the rest of the provinces to make great gains.

It had been his idea, the Queen Peace & Love but Mostly Love had said it was brilliant, though a little rough around the edges. Although she agreed with the idea of having Lord BonZ attack *Amphibious's* strongest province, the Queen thought it was both unfair and counterproductive to have one province take the brunt of the retaliation, since *Amphibious* would surely counterattack Lord BonZ when all Lord BonZ's troops were out fighting.

What the Queen Peace & Love but Mostly Love proposed was a three-pronged defense of Lord BonZ's land. First, the other members of the P-double-A, immediately after his assault, would each send him a phalanx of soldiers to use in defense. Second, Raven would have the Red Crown prepare a large shipment of money to send so that he might retrain these soldiers into defensive specialists. And third, sKyLaR's PJs would immediately draw protective circles around Lord BonZ's lands, making it more difficult for *Amphibious* to ascertain the strength of Lord BonZ's province until it was too late.

The end result of all this maneuvering was to be, according to the Queen, that *Amphibious* would have no idea how many troops to send after Lord BonZ, and that one of two things would happen: either *Amphibious* would overcommit their troops when attacking Lord BonZ, effectively subsuming a large portion of Lord BonZ's land, but exposing themselves to a retaliation that would rapidly turn into a rout; or they would undercommit, leaving Lord BonZ with all the land he had just stolen from The Serpent.

The Queen's strategy was sound, with only one potential flaw, and that potential flaw was BonZ. If he bounced, then all the reinforcements would be wasted, and *Amphibious* would swoop down on *Paradigm Shift* from on high.

Gek-Lin puts Psyduck on her lap, then reaches down under her seat for her lunch pail, a lunch pail on which a crowned, green-suited elephant named Babar holds court. She pops a silver latch. The lunch pail opens and inside are scraps of paper—shredded napkins, receipts, squares of toilet paper. Gek-Lin sifts through the scraps. She pulls one out. Written on it is a complex pattern of Thai characters. If these Thai characters were translated into English, they would say:

Algebraic Formula for the Slaying of an Amphibian by an Undead Warrior

$$(((a1 * 1) + (b1 * 3) + (c1 * 5)) * s1) * 20\%^1 = ((((((a2 * (1 + 1^2)) + (b2 * (3 + 1^2)) + (c2 * (6 + 1^2))) * s2) * 10\%^3) * (5\% + g2))$$

[1] *the additional 20% here takes into account the randomness factor and the possibility that protection spells have been cast on the target.*
[2] *the 1 here should only be added if the attacker has a death horse to match each attacking unit.*
[3] *bonus for declaration of war*

where:
a1 = Target's total basic soldiers. (Note: Target's total soldiers can be lowered by successful assassination attempts by thieves.)
b1 = Target's total lava lizards.
c1 = Target's total giant crocs.
s1 = Target's war studies percentage.
a2* = Number of basic soldiers that attacker wishes to send.
b2* = Number of skeletons that attacker wishes to send.
c2* = Number of ghouls that attacker wishes to send.
s2 = Attacker's war studies percentage.
g2 = Attacker's number of generals.

* Note: Attacker should use skeletons (since reapers have no defensive value) before ghouls, and ghouls before basic soldiers (since soldiers are weak attackers and can be trained later as either reapers or ghouls).

Gek-Lin arrived at the Slaying-of-an-Amphibian formula herself. She had refused the help of Uncle Charley, who said he would check it for her. She was confident that it was correct; she had fact-checked it many times. She only needed the variables to be filled in. And true to their word, sKyLaR and the trusty PJs had supplied them for her. A message came across Lord BonZ's screen:

sKyLaR's pLeAsuRaBlE sCoUtInG rEpOrT oN tHe SoOn tO bE vErY dEaD pRoViNcE oF tHe MoSt UnWiSe SeRpEnT

bAsIcLy DeAd SoLdieRs: 500
IAvA lIzArDs FoR lUnCh: 34
cRoCk Of S*** cRoCs: 3429

---

sKyLaR's eVeN mOrE pLeAsuRaBlE sCoUtInG rEpOrT aFtEr ThE M.s.A's vErY sUcCeSsFuL aSsAsSINaTiOn AtTeMpTs oN tHe MoSt UnWiSe SeRpEnT

bAsIcLy DeAd SoLdIeRs: 10!!!
IAvA lIzArDs FoR lUnCh: 34
cRoCk Of S*** cRoCs: 3429

---

tHe Pj'S InVaSiOn oF tHe SeRpEnT's lIbRaRiEs DoNe iN gReAt SeCrEcY bY tHe VeRy SnEaKy aLi BaBa

wAr StUdIeS: 9%

Eyeing the numbers makes Gek-Lin angry. She doesn't want to do the math. She wants to *win*! She doesn't want Uncle Charley to be right. She wants to *win*! But algebra is the only way. And she can do the algebra. No matter that she has to sit here next to these Australians who look at her like a 14-year-old Thai girl, like a 14-year-old Thai orphan girl who they could have in Bangkok, a 14-year-old Thai orphan girl who for some reason it was OK to have in Bangkok, even though it wouldn't be OK to have her in Sydney, a 14-year-old Thai orphan girl who could spit Ping Pong balls out her watusi.

She can *do* it. Even though she wants to run. Run up the stairs and out the door into the streets. Run out and steal a jackfruit and eat it on the garbage-strewn shore on the klongs. She *can* do it.

Gek-Lin fills in the variables. On the left side of the equation she enters: $(((10 \times 1) + (34 \times 3) + (3429 \times 5)) \times 9\%) \times 20\%)$. This becomes: $((10 + 102 + 17,145) \times 9\%) \times 20\%)$. Turns into: 22,572. On the right-side of the equation, Gek-Lin begins to try out her numbers. If she sends all her troops she would have: $((((((1000 \times (1)) + ((274 \times (3)) + (226 \times (4)) + (2500 \times (7))) \times 20\%) \times 10\%) \times (5\% + 4))$.

Gek-Lin's face is flushing. She wants to *attack*. She feels dizzy. But the numbers are there and she has to do them. $((((1000+822+904+17500)\times 20\%)\times 10\%)\times 20\%)$. And then: 27720. She has more than enough to win. But she can't send them all. She had promised the Queen that she would send the minimum. Who cares, though? Why does she care? Because she wants to *win*. Take out the soldiers, Gek-Lin. Take out the soldiers and some of the elites: $((((822+904+(2000\times(7)))\times 20\%)\times 10\%)\times 20\%)$. Equals: 24923.

This is good. Good enough for Gek-Lin. Gek-Lin begins filling in the fields on her screen with numbers. Gek-Lin will *win*. And then Gek-Lin looks down at Psyduck and Psyduck stares empty-eyed at Gek-Lin, and Gek-Lin knows that she doesn't have it yet, that she has not achieved perfection yet, and that perfection is *winning*, and that perfection in this case, in the case of numbers, is indeed achievable.

Psyduck is staring at Gek-Lin and Psyduck is saying this: There is one variable left, Gek-Lin. $a1$, $b1$, $c1$, $s1$, $s2$, and $g2$ are constants; $a2$ and $b2$ you can make constants. When there is one variable left in an equation you can find out with exactitude what that variable should be. You can find out with exactitude the number of ghouls to send that will give you a 100% certainty in your attack without sending excess troops. This number is perfection, Gek-Lin. And to achieve perfection is to win.

And so, Gek-Lin, despite a burning impatience, and despite something else that is happening, something else that she knows is different and unspeakable, something that would happen again and again but never again for the first time, moves numbers to the left side of the equation, moves all the numbers to the left side of the equation until there are only numbers on the left side of the equation and a single variable on the right, moves numbers until she discovers the value of this variable. She then enters the numbers into the fields: 0 soldiers, 500 skeletons, 1,523 ghouls. She clicks the "Send Troops" button.

Lord BonZ, your troops have fought a brave battle and won. You have appropriated 125 acres of land from The Serpent. Your army will return from the battlefield in 18 days. Be sure to visit our sponsor sites for additional Realm bonuses.

When Gek-Lin is finished she reaches underneath her seat cushion. Gek-Lin does not have a mother to tell her what this is. She doesn't have a sister who has experienced this before. She doesn't even have a father to explain things awkwardly and ask the counterperson for, um, something, um, for my daughter. Gek-Lin is sitting in a room where she is a sex object, a room full of men traveling from locations all over the globe for many reasons—for adventure, to see the sights, to live freely and cheaply in a foreign land, to be somewhere where the social constructs are a little less constrained. They come for many reasons but usually with one thing somewhere on their unwritten list of things to do: Bangkok's Pan Pong District.

Gek-Lin does not have anyone to tell her what this is, but she knows, instinctively, what this is. She knows that today she is a woman.

Gek-Lin gets up. She does not look down at the chair. Gek-Lin gets up and walks with dignity past rows of 486s. She walks up the stairs and into the streets. She holds Psyduck by a webbed foot at her back. Eyes burn behind her but they don't see a thing.

18. A GREAT DEAL CAN HAPPEN WHILE YOU ARE ASLEEP.

TRES RAWLINGS IS VIEWING ANOTHER MONITOR, a monitor which we have not yet discussed. The monitor displays a bed, a bed with an aquamarine-colored comforter with prints of The Little Mermaid. The bed belongs to a woman, a goth girl around the age of twenty, a goth girl with a head that is shaved bald except for a long purple tuft that hangs over her eyes in the front, a goth girl with the tattoo of a serpent covering the whole of her back, a serpent facing downward, a serpent whose tail wraps around her neck and whose tongue flickers at the space between her legs.

Two years ago Tres had met someone with the handle *Slash246* in a forum titled Varied Interests. Slash bragged about how he had installed a hidden camera in the light fixture above his girlfriend's bed, and had offered the Web feed to anyone who wanted to watch him and his girlfriend having sex. Slash even scheduled times when he would be going over to his girlfriend's house to "go at it" with her. Slash called the girl The Serpent, and appropriately so.

Tres had seen this sort of thing before, over the years he had become an on-line sex connoisseur. Slash and The Serpent didn't do anything extraordinary. In fact, what they did was kind of annoying. Slash would lay on the bed facing the old chandelier above them with a cunning, but somehow stupid, grin on his face, his hands underneath his head and his elbows out in a self-satisfied posture. Slash had a mustache, one of those adolescent mustaches that has no density, and between the mustache and the self-satisfied grin, and Slash just laying there while his girlfriend rode his prick like the devil, Tres had had a hard time watching.

Tres watched them twice before he forgot about the Web feed, but one day, a month or so later, the URL of the Web feed had popped up in the address field of his browser, and he had idly blinked a click on it, without remembering what it was. When the Web feed came up, The Serpent, who he had forgotten about, who apparently Slash had forgotten about, who still had that hidden camera attached to her chandelier, who now had a bright orange fluorescent tuft instead of a purple one, was there on her bed naked. She was sitting at the head of her bed, her back against the wall, her legs splayed in a V over the Little Mermaid comforter. She had big, beautiful mocha-colored eyes, eyes that he hadn't seen before when he was watching her and Slash fuck, eyes that were staring straight up at the light fixture immobile and expressionless. She wore thick mascara, smeared both over and under her eyelids. The mascara had dripped from her eyes onto her breasts, apparently from crying, so that the top of her breasts looked like they were dotted with candle wax drippings.

The scene was somehow more pornographic than anything else Tres had seen before. It was an invasion of privacy. And it was exactly this that kept Tres tuned in, that caused Tres to dedicate a monitor to her exclusively.

Tres witnessed a parade of Slashes (that's what Tres called them, although their names were ostensibly something like Ian or Darren or Eric), and became a sort of invisible chronicler of her sex life. There was Slash #247, Slash #248, Slash #249, Slash #250, Slash #251, Slash #252, Slash #253, Slashes #254 & #255, Slash #256, Slashette #257, and finally Slash #258. She had no preference in partners in terms of race, size, or even sex, although she did have a predilection for tattoos and body piercings.

Tres witnessed all kinds of perversions while spying on her, and it was the kind of stuff that you'd never see watching your standard porn: it was awkward and unpracticed and real. There were fights, real fights that ended in sex. There were broken diaphragms and screaming. There were sincere stop-that's and ignored no's. There was a lot of stuff that people would pay thousands of dollars to see, and if Tres had wanted to he could have easily started a racket, but Tres never really liked it when she was with her Slashes. Tres liked his alone time with her, he liked to watch her in the wee hours of the morning when the Slash of the moment had been deposited on the street, when she leaned against the wall staring glazed-eyed at the light fixture, naked and empty and oozing semen on her Little Mermaid comforter.

When Tres watched her like this he felt like God; like that version of God where He just sets things in motion and then watches them, not interfering in any way with His creations, but just kicking back on High and sending down beams of love. Tres felt like the one man in her life who had persisted, the one person—and it didn't matter that she didn't know this—who was always there. Tres felt like he was protecting her, as if in some way, with him watching, her series of Slashes could never really hurt her. Tres liked this role reversal with him as the protector and her as the protected.

Tres's only wish is that he could send her a signal, some sign that with him there she is safe.

*　*　*

Mary Lynn Klavich does not know who she is. It's not amnesia—having amnesia implies that you did, at some point, know who you were. It's that Mary Lynn Klavich has never known who she was.

To compensate, she's always become the person others have wanted her to be. When she was younger, this was easy. Her mother was a single mother, and her mother wanted her to be a sweet little girl who played with dolls in her own room, very quietly, and read books and watched cartoons. This is what she did and this is who she was. But then, after her mother passed away, when there wasn't anyone to whom the role of telling her who she was naturally fell upon, things began to get difficult.

If there is one group of people you can count on to tell you who you should be, those people are men. Mary Lynn Klavich did not have a father, that she knew of, so she was not aware of this trait in men. And, unfortunately, her mother had never told her to be wary of it. When her mother died, she discovered them, men, and their habit of telling you what you should do, and once she'd discovered them, she couldn't get enough. She needed them to tell her who she was.

It started with Dalton. He was the first. Dalton was into kinky sex, so she was into kinky sex. Dalton was into tattoos, so she was into tattoos. Dalton was goth, so she was goth. Dalton did heroin, so she did heroin. Dalton was into computers and fantasy, so she was into computers and fantasy. She was good at this, becoming what someone else wanted her to be; she was a quick study. When she was told to be into kinky sex, she very quickly learned the many ways to be kinky. When she was told to be into tattoos, she had every ability to find very good tattoo artists and get very good tattoos. When she was told to do heroin, she found very good dealers. When she was told to go goth, she found black clothing, good hairdressers and hair dye. When she was told to be into computers and fantasy, she found very good games; she discovered The Realm.

The problem was that in the end Dalton didn't like this. She had done everything that he had told her to do, but what Dalton really wanted was an untainted girl who had spent her early years alone with her mother playing with dolls. This wasn't conscious, to Dalton; it was just that after he'd corrupted her he no longer found her interesting.

When Dalton left, Mary Lynn was crushed. It wasn't that she loved Dalton; it was that she hated being left without someone to tell her who she was. It was like being an actress without a script.

Mary Lynn was determined, at this point, to never be left in this situation again, so she found two things, two things she could do so that she would never be caught alone again. She chose two things because it was best to be redundant; you just never knew. Something could always go awry.

The first thing was The Realm. She'd discovered The Realm through Dalton. The Realm was perfect for her because it never ended, it was a game that was always on and that repeated itself ad infinitum. She would always know who she was in The Realm.

She was good at it, too. Just as she was good at everything she'd been told to be good at. She'd ended up a leader, a Queen, which seems strange for a person who could be only what she was told to be, but Mary Lynn was a good leader. The Realm, its unspoken dictate, that the person who is the best leads was in and of itself a voice telling her who she was supposed to be.

The other thing she discovered was Casual Encounters. Casual Encounters was an on-line ad listing for people who wanted to have anonymous sex with strangers. The nice thing about Casual Encounters, for Mary Lynn, was that there was always someone there to have a casual encounter with. The ads never ended. It was more of a sure thing than monogamy. There was always the possibility when arranging a casual encounter, that the casual encounter wouldn't show up, but then, well, you just ordered another casual encounter.

Mary Lynn didn't really enjoy the casual encounters, they just seemed necessary to who she was, or rather to who she wasn't, or something like that. When she encountered this casual encounter, she was able to be who she wasn't, she was able to conform herself to whatever role that casual encounter wanted her to conform to. She was good at this; she was good at being what she wasn't. She wouldn't go so far as to say she liked it; it was just that it was necessary, so that she wouldn't ever be left alone, not knowing who she should be.

It should be noted here that Mary Lynn never used her real name in these interactions. She always called herself The Serpent. It was her moniker in both The Realm and in Real Life. No one knew she was Mary Lynn. She did this not because she was trying to be anonymous, which is why most people would do it, but because she didn't know who Mary Lynn was. She knew, however, who The Serpent was. The Serpent was a goth girl with a tattoo of a serpent down her back.

It felt safe for her; having her identity so nicely delineated. There's something else, though, about Mary Lynn, something that went against the theory that Mary Lynn didn't at all know who she was. Mary Lynn liked to sleep alone. Despite all her casual encounters, and the necessity of them, for making her feel like she was somebody, what she really liked was sleep, and she liked that sleep to be completely undisturbed. She made sure her casual encounters left before sleep overcame them. That was her one rule, the one thing she could be sure about herself—she was a person who liked to sleep alone.

At this moment, though, Mary Lynn is not asleep. She is, instead, awake and logged on to The Realm. She is looking at the soldiers she's lost, the lands of hers that have been invaded. She sees in front of her a bold declaration of war. Mary Lynn knows what she must do. She has received her assignment. Another person, another man, someone named Lord BonZ, has come, and she must struggle with him, must fight with him, must find out what it is he wants.

*   *   *

Sara Bronstein's instincts tell her that something is wrong. It's not just the sister. It's the brother, too.

The sister is animated. Her emotions are always there on display. She acts out, and although the way she acts out is sometimes dangerous, both to herself and to society, her actions are consistent with someone who is frustrated, frustrated with an inability to find a place for herself in the world.

The brother is the opposite. He is somewhat robotic. His emotions are buried under the weight of layers and layers of sarcasm. He is, in this sense, a modern man. He seems a functional adult, fully capable of a normal existence within the boundaries of society. But he must be frustrated too: as frustrated, if not more frustrated, than his sister.

Here is a man who was once successful, who brought a childhood dream to fruition, and then watched it all come crashing down. This once-successful man, this multimillionaire, moves into his parents' basement, moves away from everything he once knew to a small town in Arizona under the auspices of helping out his sister who is a mental patient. Here's a man who must have had a PalmPilot packed to the last megabyte with friends and associates, who suddenly disappears and shows up in Rest Stop, Arizona, acting as if everything is OK, acting as if he's super busy, riding his mountain bike every day, visiting his sister (when he can, he says), looking disheveled and preoccupied.

Something doesn't fit. When Xerxes comes for his visits he looks like he's still at his job, like he's been in front of a computer screen coding.

Sara writes in the chart that she has open on her bed: *Ask brother what he does during the day.* She knows it's none of her business, that there is no legitimate benefit for the sister in obtaining this information, that therefore this is a breach of trust, but she is curious, and she suspects that these breaches, the breaches that she allows herself in these doctor/client relationships, are the very holes that need filling in. She is starting to trust her intuition. She is starting to be a psychiatrist. And besides that, it's not like there is someone here to watch her, it's not like there's some professor behind a one-way window, whispering into a receiver in her ear: *Ms. Bronstein, that is an inappropriate question.*

Sara looks around at her cabin. This is so not her. An old cabin made with pine wood permanently darkened with soot. An old cabin that sometimes housed miners, sometimes housed prostitutes, sometimes housed both. Here she is, a Banana Republic girl from the city, a girl who six months ago was taking evening psychology classes at NYU for her counseling degree while working as a product manager for marthastewart.com during the day, a busy girl with a jam-packed social schedule, a busy girl with friends fighting for a chance to share a Friday happy hour with her, living in a log cabin with a phone that never rings and a pile of books for company.

It is so Walden, which would have been nice, if she were fifty, independently wealthy, and some sort of poet. It had seemed so romantic from New

York. She'd imagined herself driving an SUV over miles of red-tinged dirt roads, a cute, well-dressed lass in a Ford Explorer, going from reservation to reservation counseling Indians on the dangers of alcohol addiction, racking up hours so she could go back and open an office on the Upper West Side where she'd become the counselor of Wall Street brokers and their society wives, where she'd graduate from Banana Republic to designer labels.

That had been the plan until she got here and found that Rest Stop wasn't in the desert, but in the woods; that there weren't any Indians, only screwed-up white people; and that there wasn't more work, but only the two hours that the St. Francis Sanitarium had promised her.

Now she was in trouble. She couldn't go back to New York. She couldn't afford it. Martha Stewart wouldn't take her back, and there wasn't a single tech company left that didn't have a hiring freeze. And she couldn't stay here. At the rate she was going she wouldn't complete her counseling hours until 2010.

For some reason, though, she couldn't motivate herself to do anything about it. She couldn't even head over to the local library to send an e-mail to her advisor at NYU. She couldn't herself seek the help that counselors advise their patients to seek. Instead, she sat silently in a cabin, burning logs in the fireplace even though it was summer, reading Sue Grafton mysteries (she was at *F is for Fugitive*), and obsessing about this weird pair of twins.

Sara's thoughts come back to them. They were born under the sign of Gemini, and though she is a scientist, though she doesn't believe in astrology, she can't help but feel that their coming to her at this stage in her life portends something. She isn't sure what, though. She feels as if they are the key to something she is missing, something larger.

Last week, she had made a suggestion to the staff at the St. Francis Sanitarium. She had suggested that the relationship between Gabriella and Leonard that they were trying to deter might actually be healthy. She argued that Gabriella's depression was not entirely the result of a chemical imbalance caused by her borderline schizophrenia. Instead, Sarah posited, Gabriella was depressed because she was an intelligent and driven person who wanted nothing more nor less than to be successful and productive and good at something, but because of the disruptive nature of her schizophrenia, she was unable to. Gabriella's Myers-Briggs scores indicated that identity was essential to her, and that her schizophrenia was keeping her from obtaining a satisfactory identity. Thus, her suicidal tendencies.

Leonard, contrary to Gabriella, had achieved an identity. Although it was a somewhat self-destructive identity, although his identity was that of "a walker," it was, nonetheless, an identity. Gabriella had subconsciously latched onto Leonard because she was impressed by the single-minded way in which he pursued his chosen occupation. Perhaps Gabriella had something to learn from Leonard, perhaps she too could find a hobby that she could focus her energy on, perhaps that hobby would help alleviate her depressive symptoms.

Why not let them spend more time together, under supervision, outside the confines of the hospital, while Leonard was doing what Leonard does best—walk—and see what developed. The staff had told Sara she was overthinking this, which she was. They had asked her who was going to supervise, and they had suggested that the Meticula family would never approve it.

Sara, seeing where this was leading, told the staff that she would take on the responsibility. The director of the program gave her permission, but said, "we can't pay you and we can't give you any hours" (what a bitch!), so Sara had talked to Xerxes, and told him her idea, that they take Gabriella and Leonard out of the hospital and chaperone them on a hike, and Xerxes had said he thought it was an "OK idea." He had looked at her quizzically, as if he wanted to say, "Why the hell do you care?"

Sara wasn't getting any help from anybody. But it didn't make much difference. This afternoon, Xerxes and Gabriella Meticula, Sara Bronstein, and Leonard B. Walker are going to take a walk.

19. SPREAD THE DISEASE.

GEK-LIN AND SEVERAL OF HER FELLOW ORPHANS are crowded together on a thin sliver of sidewalk against a whitewashed wall in a side alley in Patpong. Tuktuks zoom down the alley, coming within inches of their backs. Pedestrians squeeze by them, avoiding eye contact. Oblivious to the tuk-tuks and the pedestrians—as well as the grit, the carbon monoxide, the noise pollution, and the general disdain hurled in their direction—the orphans play games. Most are huddled around a pair of dice being thrown against the wall. They play a game called Seven, Fourteen, Twenty-one that is played by adults in local beer bars. Gek-Lin, meanwhile, is absentmindedly playing Connect Four, a game which she likes because she has recognized all its patterns and is able to win consistently without much effort. She plays now with a small boy about two years her junior. He does not seem to mind that he consistently loses; he only watches Gek-Lin with his heavily lashed eyes.

Gek-Lin Troung has seen them often, lined up along the wall across the street as they are now, but has never really taken the time to figure out what they are doing. She watches them now, intently, while dropping her red checkers into the slots. She already has this game, will win in eight moves unless the boy does something really foolish.

There are nine of them. They have numbers attached to them with safety pins. #47, #9, #103, #49, #92, #30, #24, #83, #99. They stand there smiling; their lips are rouged the red of Coke cans. They shift their weights from long-standing, each placing a leg behind them against the wall for support. In their short skirts they look like a row of storks in a zoo. They stand on the sunny side of the street. The sun and the humidity are causing their makeup to run. The china white drips off their faces, leaving white splats on the pavement, not unlike the splats left over from the careless application of white milk paint to the wall behind them.

Next to the nine figures is a man Gek-Lin has seen here before. The women are usually different, but the man standing here with the girl line-up is always the same. She has heard the women speak of him. They call him Papa-san, and sometimes, amongst each other, but never to his face: Kin-Dong.

The man is speaking to two other men. Their crisp white shirts; red paisleyed ties, and black, pleated trousers seem inappropriate for the climate. They both have sweat circles under their armpits. Gek-Lin identifies them as foreigners. Their eyes have the downslant common amongst the Chinese. Gek-Lin's playmate drops another black checker into a slot—just one more move towards his ultimate demise.

The two men appear to be friends, or at least, business associates. They whisper to each other, and then point to the girls. They stagger a bit, indicating that they've had too much to drink, and their faces are flushed beet red, that unique red common to Asian alcoholics.

Kin-Dong regards these two dourly while they laugh and joke. He hands them each some sort of ticket and a pen, then barks something at them, something that stops them from their whisperings and gets them quickly to write on their tickets. The men hand their tickets to Kin-Dong. Accompanying the tickets, if Gek-Lin is reading this correctly, is also money, a great deal of money if gauged by the thickness of the wads. After counting the money, and looking the men over, as if dressing them up, Kin-Dong snaps his fingers. He says, "Number one-oh-three; number twenty-four." The women with these numbers then sashay over, as if they've won a beauty pageant; then they smile at the men they've won, say something to them with their cavernous mouths, take them by the arm, and lead them away.

Gek-Lin drops a final red into a slot. "Connect Four," she says.

Once the winners have gone, the losers shift their weights, putting one leg down and shifting the other up the wall behind them. Their smiles never leave their faces; to do so would be to admit defeat, and increase the chances that they will lose the next time. All the losers do this, in unison; that is, all the losers except for Number 9.

Number 9, instead, makes a noise that sounds something like "Bah!", throws a feathered boa over her shoulder, and crosses the street towards Gek-Lin. The man named Kin-Dong yells something which gets lost in the high-pitched drone of a three-wheeler going by. Number 9 yells back, "Write me up a bar fine," and then adds, in English, and in an unusually deep voice, "you fuck!"

Number 9 yelling this makes Gek-Lin laugh. She places her hand over mouth to suppress it, but it still comes out—loud and throaty. Sammy has started another game. Gek-Lin drops a red checker on top of Sammy's black one.

"What are you laughing at?" says Number 9 to Gek-Lin.

Gek-Lin, a bit intimidated by the woman with red stilettos, a short skirt, a feathered boa, and an unusually deep voice, who is now standing within kicking range of her, does not answer this question. To Gek-Lin's horror, the woman appears to know her.

"Well, if it isn't Miss High and Mighty Gek-Lin Troung from the Blue Moon Pre-Slut Program checking out the action ahead of time. Don't you need to go back to your Uncle Charley and take a show . . . er."

Gek-Lin hears the click of another of Sammy's checkers dropping. C1, she's pretty sure. She cranes her neck around to look into the woman's face. *Who? It's not. It is.* "Huy?" Huy had been an orphan at the Blue Moon until about six months ago, when he had disappeared. Uncle Charley explained it off as he always did: *he's found a happy home.* There was a lot of this at the Blue Moon, 14- to 15-year-olds suddenly finding happy homes. The younger orphans looked upon this as something to look forward to, like Jewish kids looking forward to Bar Mitzvah, but the older orphans had their doubts: work camps, or Malaysians, or prostitution were often mentioned. The orphans were too young to know what these terms signified, but the terms swirled with menace, and it was implied that the happy homes Charley talked about weren't as happy as he promised.

"Not Huy, Belle d'Jour," says Number 9, jutting out a bony hip, "And when are *you* going to be joining us Miss Gek-Lin Troung? Old enough to bleed, old enough to breed."

Gek-Lin is trying to put two and two together. Sammy, normally patient, is prompting her to play, "Gek-Lin, your turn." She doesn't even look. E1. What does all this mean? She'd seen Thai men dressed as women before. It was something often joked about. But she'd never known a person who had become one of these; these Katoeys, as they were called. Despite the sharpness of the stilettos, Gek-Lin wants to get to the bottom of this, and one of the things Huy, or Belle d' Jour, or Number 9, or whatever her true name was, had just said had hit a nerve: *old enough to bleed.* . . .

"Bleed?" Gek-Lin asks.

Huy's haughty expression suddenly turns compassionate. He had always liked Gek-Lin. In a way, he had modeled his impetuousness after her. She was an unusual Thai girl, not as submissive as most. He had observed the effect this had on Uncle Charley, the way that it had earned her his grudging respect. Huy grabs Gek-Lin beneath the armpit and picks her up off the sidewalk.

"What?" Gek-Lin tries to protest. The Connect Four grid spills over sideways, red and black checkers rolling into the street.

"Just follow me," Huy says.

Gek-Lin lets him lead her. Where is this going?

"Are you bleeding?" Huy asks.

"Yes." Gek-Lin replies.

"You tell Charley?"

"No."

"You have feminine pads?"

Gek-Lin doesn't know what feminine pads are. She'd been cleaning herself from scraps of paper she'd gathered together during the day. "No."

"OK. We will buy you these. Have you left anything with blood on it around for Charley to see?"

She hadn't. She'd thrown the scraps back out onto the street and washed her clothes in the dead of the night in the city's fountains. "I don't think so."

"Good. You must not let Charley know. Don't leave the dirty pads or the wrappers anywhere for Charley to see, OK? Also, no showering while you're bleeding, OK? In fact, stay away from the orphanage when you're having your period. The bleeding, it's called that—your period. It happens once a month or so. Do you know this? God, what do you know? This will prolong things. I don't need any more competition out there. You having your period right now?"

"No. It ended yesterday."

Huy and Gek-Lin enter a small corner market. Huy purchases a box of tampons and some tamarind sweets. "OK. Hide the tampons in your backpack, then go back to the sidewalk with your friends. If they ask you where you've been, give them the candy. Take care now, Gek-Lin." And with that Huy walks out the store, flings her hand in the air, flags down a tuk-tuk, and disappears in a flash of feathers.

Gek-Lin isn't sure what all this is about. She returns to Sammy, who is now sitting cross-legged against the whitewashed wall absentmindedly flipping a checker.

★   ★   ★

The Serpent runs her kingdom differently than the Queen Peace & Love but Mostly Love. The Serpent sends out orders, and her kingdom mates follow. They are assigned targets and they execute their attacks. *Paradigm Shift* has declared war, and now she will counter. It is a simple equation.

The Serpent watches her news screen fill up with the first wave of counterattacks against Lord BonZ, then she logs off. It is time to figure out who she will have for the night. They are there, lined up, all the m4f's. She sorts out all the cons and freaks from the potentials. She probes, sending an e-mail here, an e-mail there. She gets pictures; she sends them. She is a goth and she needs a goth in return. No pudgy, pink-faced business-types will do. Sometimes she goes f4f or even f4fm if she can't find the right m4f. Eventually, she finds her man.

★   ★   ★

Xerxes drives the four of them to the 510A trailhead in #8. He had checked the forecast before setting out, and the sky is cloudless, but early August in

Northern Arizona is unpredictable, and you never know when a washer will whip through. Sara Bronstein's hips are pressed against his in the small cab of the truck, with Gabriella's next to hers, and Leonard's against the door. He has to reach between Sara's legs to shift gears.

Xerxes has the window rolled down. As #8 passes by mesquite trees, he hears cicadas drone. Xerxes is silent. He is thinking of The Realm; he is thinking of war.

Sara sits sandwiched between the two twins. She wonders what the silence in the truck means. She looks in front of her as Xerxes maneuvers them over dips in the road. A wrist on top of the steering wheel shifts in time with the curves. Sara breaks the silence, "So what did you bring for our picnic?"

Xerxes's facial expression doesn't change, even though he's making a joke, "Turkey and Swiss for the adults. Peanut butter and jelly for the kids."

"And we have plenty of water, right?"

Xerxes is aware of Sara's bare leg pressed against his. She is wearing khaki shorts, a white T-shirt that says *Run For The Cure*, and a pair of Rockport hiking boots that he can tell she's never worn. This is not Sara's normal attire. She probably thrifted the T-shirt and shorts. Bought the hiking boots yesterday at Copeland's. She's not much of a hiker, Xerxes thinks. The pale leg next to him looks somehow obscene not covered in its standard black stockings.

"We have 1 gallon per person—2 liters in my Camelback and the rest in plastic bottles. 1 gallon per person for 3 hours should be plenty."

"Great," Sara says, trying to drum up some enthusiasm in the uncomfortably cramped and sullen confines of the truck. Gabriella and Leonard haven't said a word and Xerxes's mind seems elsewhere. "This will be exciting, won't it?"

No one responds. Xerxes pulls #8 into a dirt turnout a couple miles up the road. "We'll park here and walk the rest of the way to the trail, that way we won't have to pay the entrance fee," he says.

The group exits the truck, walks to the trail ahead, and makes its way along the path. Xerxes has chosen a rather innocuous route—a 6-mile loop that winds along a dry creek bed amongst low alligator pines. It is more of a stroll than a hike.

Sara, who had wanted to take this opportunity to analyze her patient, and to find out more about her patient's mysterious brother, soon loses herself in the unspoken, mutually agreed-upon silence. Her eyes hunt for sparrows singing from the depths of thick bush, spy a woodpecker atop a spruce, catch the tail of a kitty hawk sailing high in the breeze. They walk for a mile or two in silence. She is enjoying herself, the rise and fall of her brand-new hiking boots on the red clay and granite chunks. She can see why people do this, why they leave the city and go granola. She can even for a moment understand environmentalists—people who read Edward Abbey books and try to burn down billboards. It is so quiet here. There are no sirens, no cabs, no rumbling and whoosh of subway cars jetting around the space below.

It is so quiet. It is so quiet that she can't even hear the footsteps of her companions on the trail. It is so quiet, that when Sara Bronstein stops and looks both in front of her and behind her, it takes her a good while to realize that one of the reasons it seems so quiet is that she is walking through the thick pines alone.

*   *   *

Xerxes has climbed a couple of switchbacks that take him up out of the creek bed. The Queen Peace & Love but Mostly Love left something out when she spoke with Lord BonZ. Lord BonZ's race is undead, and as an undead, Lord BonZ is a carrier of the plague. If *Amphibious* responds to Lord BonZ en masse, which Xerxes expects they will, then a great many of them will be infected by the plague, which will weaken their troops and make them more susceptible to attack. The Queen, when she returns from her RL outing, will then order a counterattack against these weak provinces. *Paradigm Shift* will make out with a lot of land. Things will get more difficult after this. She must end the war at a point where her kingdom mates have achieved a maximum amount of land, without it appearing this way to the other side.

At a bend in the trail, Xerxes hops onto a human-sized rock, one of those strange Southwestern rocks that isn't halfway in the ground, like a normal rock, but 100 percent out of the ground, like it's been dropped where it is from a plane, or, if you believe in such things, placed there by a god. Xerxes hops onto the rock. He wonders how far he has walked, how far behind they are. He looks at his watch. It's been 24 minutes since he last saw Sara.

"Sara! Leonard! Gabby!" Xerxes shouts. Where has his head been?

*   *   *

Leonard's arm has shot across Gabriella's chest, stopping her midstride. "Shhhhh," Leonard says. Leonard and Gabriella stop in the middle of the trail and watch Xerxes and Sara fade off into the distance: Xerxes walking straight ahead at a woodsman's pace; Sara zigzagging the width of the path, looking absentmindedly at tree and sky.

"They're cute," Leonard says while Gabriella giggles. "Now we go west."

Leonard cuts through the thorny bushes to the right of the path and begins to climb up the slope out of the creek bed. Gabriella isn't worried about Xerxes, he is walking down the trail thinking his brilliant brother thoughts, he will be OK without her, better in fact; but she is a little worried about Sara, she likes her, and she doesn't want her to lose her job.

Leonard, his head a constant compass, insists on keeping as straight a line on due west as possible. Rather than make his way safely around the boulders that block his way, he climbs over them. Gabriella follows, awkwardly; she tries to follow him, but the adamantine grit of the rock that Leonard is climbing cuts a slit in her index finger. "Ouch," she cries.

Leonard is not used to someone following him. He is used to solitary walks. He turns and looks down to where Gabriella is standing, at the base of the slab, her index finger in her mouth, sucking at blood. Leonard is about twenty feet above her. His bare hands and worn Puma tennis shoes stick to the granite like a superhero's. He is gifted in this regard, his long arms are perfect for hanging onto edges and cracks, his bulging calf muscles perfect for smearing against walls. He has no problem climbing these rocks of granite and quartz, these rock walls like coarse sandpaper, but Gabriella standing at the base below him does have a problem, and this presents a dilemma. Can Leonard B. Walker bend the rules?

Leonard buries his fingers deep into a finger hold and then leans back to look at Gabriella. He scratches his head with his free hand. His long red hair dangles behind him. Perhaps, he could pull her up. Perhaps, he could grab one of her hands and with her feet she could get enough leverage to make it to where he is. But as Leonard thinks this, he knows that there might be problems in the future, that if he allows someone to follow him, that if he takes responsibility for someone, that he will have to make allowances, that there will be times when he can go due west and she cannot.

This is a crucial juncture, he can either go on alone, in which case she would scramble her way around for a while trying to keep up, until he lost her, or until she lost interest in following, it not being particularly fun to travel with someone when they won't stop and wait for you.

Since he left Duluth ten years ago, there has never been anyone in his life who simply wanted to follow him. People, whenever they had any interest in him at all, wanted to stop him. When he walked, in his unvarying pattern of spending an entire day walking due west, followed by spending an entire day walking due south; when he left Duluth that fateful April two days after his sixteenth birthday with the imagined intent of reaching Los Angeles, the city that he assumed would stop his walking, a sort of urban elixir that would cure him of his compulsion, or where, he supposed, he would simply walk into the ocean, the undertow sweeping him off his cracked and calloused feet, pulling him to his ultimate doom; when he walked someone always stopped him: the highway patrol fining him for strolling along I-80; an assistant sheriff in Cheyenne, Wyoming arresting him; the feds busting him in Nevada for breaking into the Naval Testing Grounds; and the last stoppage, where he passed out in the middle of a salt flat in Death Valley National Park, where he was spotted by a park ranger face down in the salt, where he was revived, driven to Bishop, and eventually released into the hands of the St. Francis Sanitarium, the nearest psych ward that would take him in.

The simple walk that, at age 16, he had estimated would take at the most 6 months, had now lengthened to more than 10 years, and included long stays in penitentiaries and psychiatric homes. There was rarely any grounds for them to hold him, the private landowners on whose land he trespassed never pressed charges, but as the years went by, as the nineties extended to the naughts, bureaucracy in the courts seemed to have increased tenfold, and with it lengthened jail time and longer psychiatric stays before he was even evaluated, so that it was often found that he was being held "without grounds" or deemed "non-threatening" some six months after he was initially held without grounds and thought to be threatening.

As you watch Leonard B. Walker, perched precariously on his slanted slab, a slab with a rounded top that protrudes from the earth like a fallen tombstone, you have to wonder if what he is doing is just an eccentric's political statement, some disaffected Ted Kaczynski thing; if he is actually capable, mentally, of ending his tortured touring, if he is just trying to get across a message, a single statement, that America has become completely subdued.

Whatever mental gymnastics Leonard's hard-coded head is performing seems to have encountered a glitch in Gabriella. He stands poised for a full minute in the position he has assumed, fingers in crack, arm extended, hand scratching head, calves taut and twitching, head turned and gazing into Gabby's emerald eyes. Leonard's circuitry is caught in an infinite loop. Come off the rock, go down to Gabriella, grab her hand, go around the boulder, pronounce two syllables, "fol-low." NO. Continue west, alone. NO. Come off the rock, go down to Gabriella. NO. Continue west. NO. Come . . .

For her part, Gabriella is standing at the foot of the slanted slab watching. There is a man above her. The sun is above the man, so that most of what she can see of him is in silhouette. The man is frozen in position. It seems that he will stay forever in that place, that he will stay there and slowly rust, like an anchor bolted into rock. Gabriella feels Leonard's purpose, she waits below for the message to be delivered.

One wonders how long they would both have stood there immobile, if a hornet, a hornet who made his nest deep within a crack of granite, hadn't desperately wanted to go on a pollen run, hadn't encountered a surprise obstacle, hadn't, in its frustration, buried a stinger in that obstacle, as far and deep as the stinger could go.

*   *   *

Xerxes sees him falling. It is sickly comical, all this falling. Tech stocks, cell phones, babies, Xerxes, and now Leonard—all of them yanked out of the stratosphere by gravity's cruel tug. It's a little like the Tower of Babel. Xerxes wonders if there is anything left that could fall.

A low-toned *"aaaaaarrrggg"* is coming from the direction of Leonard, a Leonard who is falling from the sky about a quarter of a mile back in the direction from which Xerxes came. Other than the *"aaaaaarrrggg,"* Leonard does not fit the image of a flailing falling man. Leonard is stiff. His arms are extended like the first time Xerxes saw him, like when he held his arms out like Frankenstein. His legs are extended too, and his feet pointed. He looks like a cheerleader doing a "C." The way Leonard is falling his heels will hit the earth first, then his buttocks, then his shoulders, and then the back of his head, with a slam.

*   *   *

Sara doesn't panic. She had thought that they were all in front of her so she had power-walked ahead, figuring that she would eventually catch up with them at her blistering pace. She hears Xerxes's voice, ahead, querulous, calling her name. She is relieved to hear her name, but she is also filled with a certain dread, since he is not only calling her name, but also calling the names of Gabriella and Leonard, which means they are not with him.

Sara doesn't panic, although at this point she does break into a slow jog. Then she hears an *"aaaaaarrrggg,"* followed by the crack of tree branches, followed by a rustle, a rustle that sounds like a bear emerging from its hiding place in the bush. Sara Bronstein panics.

★   ★   ★

Leonard's fall is merciful, perhaps even miraculous. Twenty-five feet, four body lengths, is a long way to fall without serious injury, but Leonard's body seemed, and this was odd, to have almost been propelled off the slab, so that rather than bouncing off the rock backwards and landing on his head, Leonard hit the ends of a couple of tree branches that were leaning towards the rock, breaking his fall, before he hit a much larger branch that struck him underneath the knees, twisted him into a somersault, then spun him around so that he landed stomach and hands first into a prickly juniper bush.

Gabriella is standing only a few feet away from this particular bush. Having watched the whole thing, and having thought that Leonard's act was an amazing act of trickery, she breaks into applause, shouting, "Leon-ard. Monkey. Wwwwwal-ker."

Leonard himself is still suspended a couple of feet off the ground, stuck in the juniper bush. As you would expect, he is a bit dazed. He tells Gabriella, "I got stung." He holds up his finger to show Gabriella.

Gabriella shortens the distance between herself and Leonard, she looks at Leonard's finger. It is hardly a scratch. "I got stung too," Gabriella says. "Mine's worse."

Leonard looks at Gabriella's finger. It is amazing. Matching wounds. Leonard knows what he will say to Gabriella next time. He knows that he will tell her to follow. He knows that he is not doomed to walk alone.

Leonard also knows that he won't be doing much walking until someone resets his leg.

★   ★   ★

Xerxes reacts to the emergency quickly, decisively, mechanically. Xerxes was a Boy Scout; he had advanced one step below Eagle before he decided that he'd

157

rather spend his time with a pencil and graph paper planning out dungeons to kill off his junior high friends. Because of this he has all the tools available to an almost-Eagle Scout: an acute sense of direction, a full knowledge of all things first aid, and most importantly an innate ability to be prepared. Besides the Camelback and sandwiches, Xerxes has a Swiss Army Knife, a first-aid kit, a compass, a top, and a GPS device in his waist pack, all of which come in handy.

Yet despite all his readiness, Xerxes moves more sluggishly than usual. It just seems too surreal. Too much has happened to him. It is impossible, absolutely impossible, that he could be faced with yet another crisis situation. He feels as if he is a character in a novel who wakes up to discover that the reason so much has happened to him in so short an amount of time is that he isn't real, is that he is only a character in a novel.

Because of this he finds himself loping. Not running, but loping. Taking giant steps like he is on the moon. He runs like this down the switchbacks, consciously sucking in big lungfuls of air to counteract his asthma; he hits the dry creek bed, lined with low pines and bushes, yucca and prickly pear. Still loping, Xerxes is surprised by the approaching figure of Sara Bronstein, who is not loping at all, but rather galloping, galloping with the gait of a gazelle, a Sara Bronstein who yells to Xerxes, "Bear! Bear! Bear!" as she passes him and leaves him in a cloud of dust.

When Sara passes him, Xerxes uncharacteristically breaks all rules of engagement. She is galloping and he is loping and Leonard is falling and everything has become so surreal. Xerxes stops in his tracks; he expects to see timepieces dangling from trees, liquid watches melting and dripping onto the sandy soil. His plan for rescuing Leonard was already in full motion; he had pulled out his compass, memorized the contours of the boulder Leonard had fallen from, and approximated about where he would need to leave the trail and head up the ridge.

But now here Sara is, ricocheting up the trail in the wrong direction— Xerxes can make nothing out of her but a dust cloud and a pair of ghost white legs, and his instinct is to chase her down, to growl like a grizzly in her tracks until she realizes that there isn't a bear, that there hasn't in fact been a bear sighting in this forest since 1928, and even when there were bears, they were koala-like black bears, bears that were kind of goofy and stupid and rarely dangerous.

Xerxes turns around. He abandons the hapless Leonard, who, unbeknownst to Xerxes, is wounded but perfectly all right. He heads back up the trail. He runs in no particular hurry; he can still see the dust cloud that is Sara. He continues his lope, an antelope lope, only now his arms are outstretched and he growls.

⋆   ⋆   ⋆

Her casual encounter, it hadn't gone well. There had been an argument, an argument about condoms. She had wanted to use hers; he his. They were there, at that point, when it had happened. They were naked and he was on top of her, holding down her wrists. It had really been quite pleasant, until this point; he had let her grind, given her a little fingering, but then he had gone to his back pocket to pull out his condom, and she had gone over to her bedside drawer to pull out hers, and she had said, no, use this one, and he had said, fuck, no, how do I know you're not trying to get pregnant or something, like maybe you put a hole in it or something?

The way he said that, it sent a brief note of worry through her mind. It would have been easy to be cool about it: *sorry, babe, I prefer my brand* or *I need something sensitive* or *that one just won't fit*. But he hadn't been cool about it; he'd gotten kind of weird.

Suddenly, very suddenly, she wasn't in the mood. "Forget it," she said. "Forget what," he said, still holding one of her wrists down with one hand, unrolling the condom onto his cock with the other. "I don't want to do this anymore," she said. He'd smirked when she said that; he'd said, "yes you do," and had inserted his cock.

He never put the condom on. The nice grinding ended and he banged her hard. She stared up at her chandelier, the moonlight refracting a galaxy upon her ceiling. She was this tonight: a lifeless blow-up doll. She supposed she could have resisted more, but really, why? This is what he wanted, and this is what she would give him. At least it was a role, albeit a tragic one.

When he had finished, he got up, put his clothes back on, and left. When he was gone she was glad. Now she could sleep. She stared back up at her chandelier. She fell asleep quickly, as she often did when she finally found herself alone.

It is now the next morning and she is up. She is logged onto The Realm and she is surveying the damage. Her kingdom screen reads:

News for Amphibious: January, YR7

☠ Land of BonZ (12:5) has captured 125 acres from The Serpent (23:34).

♦ Our good province Tree Frogs (23:34) has captured 63 acres from Land of BonZ (12:5).

☠ Tree Frogs (23:34) was infected with the plague!

♦ Our good province Mudpuppy (23:34) has burned 8 buildings in Land of BonZ (12:5)

♦ Our good province Mudpuppy (23:34) has burned 8 buildings in Land of BonZ (12:5)

♦ Our good province Mudpuppy (23:34) has burned 7 buildings in Land of BonZ (12:5)

☠ Mudpuppy (23:34) was infected with the plague!

♦ Our good province Sal A. Mander (23:34) has captured 42 acres from Land of BonZ (12:5).

☠ Sal A. Mander (23:34) was infected with the plague!

♦ Cottonmouth (23:34) attempted an invasion of Land of BonZ (12:5) but was repelled.

♦ Our good province Snapping Turtle (23:34) has charmed 85 soldiers from Land of BonZ (12:5). These troops will be ineffective for 20 days.

♦ Our good province Snapping Turtle (23:34) has charmed 70 soldiers from Land of BonZ (12:5). These troops will be ineffective for 20 days.

☠ Snapping Turtle (23:34) was infected with the plague!

☠ sKyLaR's pleAsUrE PaLaCe (12:5) has infected 116 soldiers from The Serpent (23:34) with nightmares. They have deserted.

☠ sKyLaR's pleasure PaLaCe (12:5) has infected 95 soldiers from The Serpent (23:34) with nightmares. They have deserted.

☠ Nevermore (12:5) has captured 145 acres from The Serpent (23:34).

☠ sKyLaR's pleAsUrE PaLaCe (12:5) has infected 103 soldiers from Mudpuppy (23:34) with nightmares. They have deserted.

☠ sKyLaR's pleAsUrE PaLaCe (12:5) has infected 76 soldiers from Mudpuppy (23:34) with nightmares. They have deserted.

☠ The Strangely Peaceful Citadel of Blue Orcs (12:5) has captured 99 acres from Mudpuppy (23:34).

☠ Wonderwizzies (12:5) has infected 65 soldiers from Snapping Turtle (23:34) with nightmares. They have deserted.

☠ Wonderwizzies (12:5) has infected 54 soldiers from Snapping Turtle (23:34) with nightmares. They have deserted.

💀 GurGle (12:5) has captured 62 acres from Snapping Turtle (23:34).

💀 Sleep Deprivation (12:5) has captured 66 acres from Sal A. Mander (23:34).

💀 War Place (12:5) has captured 53 acres from Tree Frogs (23:34).

*********************************** *End of News*************************************

20. YOU ARE BEING WATCHED.

GEK-LIN TROUNG IS DOING SOME INSPECTING. She has her right eye against one of the purple tiles of the Blue Moon Internet Café's basement shower installment. It is odd the work Uncle Charley has put into this shower. It is not what is normally done, especially in shower installments constructed for orphans.

Most shower installments in nonluxury Thailand are constructed with cheap concrete. But Uncle Charley's shower is constructed with expensive ceramic tiles imported from Hong Kong. The shower walls are mostly made of white tiles. The white tiles each have a Cantonese character on them. Translated into English, this character would mean "love" or, in certain contexts, "lust." There are also purple tiles interspersed randomly amongst the white. The purple tiles were even stranger. Gek-Lin had never noticed this before, but if you stick an eye right against them, the purple tiles are see-through, are made of some sort of weird tinted glass. When you don't stick your eyes against them, they seem more silvery, and are reflective, like mirrors.

Besides the odd tiles, the shower also has an always-polished chrome showerhead, a frequently desuded chrome soap holder, and a small chrome rack with various lotions on it. Etched into the soap holder, Gek-Lin had once read: Chillicothe, Ohio. The chrome fixings were all from America.

These are not the kind of things one can simply purchase during a stroll through the Bangkok bazaar. Uncle Charley would have had to special order them and he would need a small fortune to buy them, a small fortune that Uncle Charley might have, but that Gek-Lin couldn't see him spending unless there was some practical explanation for being extravagant. He had even bought a water heater. Only the fine hotels bought water heaters, everyone else simply used these mechanical devices that you hooked to the shower head to heat the water, devices that never got the water very hot, that frequently caused fuses to blow, and that were known to cause anywhere from a mild to a somewhat severe shock if one did not have a rubber mat on the floor of the shower.

The whole setup was unusual for Uncle Charley. He was miserly to a fault. He kept a sharp eye on his cash register at all times, always suspecting one or another of the orphans of having stolen a few of the bhats that the café food and Internet usage fees brought in every day. The daily specials that Uncle Charley tried to push on the Blue Moon's patrons were based on the rise and fall of the prices of the catfish, squid, cuttlefish, and shrimp at the local market. Whatever he could get the cheapest he would buy in large quantities, and then try to pawn this off to the tourists as being the most "fresh."

Although the clues are all here, Gek-Lin does not make the connection right away, does not suspect Uncle Charley of any wrongdoing. She does not suspect that there are men watching her shower, at this very moment, in tens, if not hundreds of different countries; that there is, in fact, one man who sees just now a close-up of Gek-Lin's iris and pupil, the iris a deep brown that is rarely penetrable, that is only penetrable at this close a range, the pupil a pinpoint that is slowly enlarging, adjusting to the darkness behind the purple tile she looks through.

Gek-Lin does not suspect anything just yet. But she is the type of girl who wants answers, and who wants answers now. There is something all together wrong with the rounded, mechanical, bug-eyed things that move and vibrate behind the purple tiles.

She turns the trussed-up, four-finger, hot and cold knobs until they tighten and the water shuts off. She grabs a clean white towel that says Bangkok Hilton on it from the towel rack and wraps it around her, tucking it in just above her breasts so that it won't become unraveled. She does not put on her red short-shorts or *Girl Power* T-shirt in the changing room. She wants to know now. She walks out of the changing room into the dark basement with the 486s. The other orphans peek out from under the blue lights of their computer screens at Gek-Lin wearing nothing but her towel. Some snicker. Others gawk. She knocks on Uncle Charley's door.

* * *

At first, she had really thought it was a bear, but then when she passed Xerxes, and he had sort of just kept going right past her in the other direction, she had figured out that even if it was a bear, it probably wasn't still chasing her. She glances around, still running. She can see a good fifty yards back, and there is no indication of a bear bounding behind her. Sara knows now that there was no bear, probably had never been a bear, but still she runs.

It feels incredibly liberating for Sara to run. She is not doing the controlled type of running that one does in Central Park, with your head lifted and your eyes pointed straight ahead, snubbing the panhandlers sitting on benches, but the out-of-control sprinting that one can only do during a pure panic, when a wild boar or rapist comes charging out of a bush.

Sara runs up the switchbacks that Xerxes had gone up earlier. The incline eventually gets to her. She slows. Not long after she slows, Xerxes catches up. She looks at him and he looks at her.

"Growl," he says.

"Shut up," she says.

* * *

Charley is cleaning himself up when she knocks. He has a piece of toilet paper wrapped around his wrist and is using it to wipe the come from off his stomach. He knows it is her, she is the only one precocious enough to ignore the Do Not Disturb sign posted on the door. "Do not disturb," he shouts grumpily, as if she couldn't read the sign.

"There is something wrong with the shower," Gek-Lin shouts back.

Charley knows that there is nothing wrong with the shower, that Gek-Lin has probably found the cameras. He is not sure how to play this, except that he must do some damage control, must make sure that this is something that stays between him and Gek-Lin. He pulls up the trousers that were pooled around his ankles, grabs a plain white T-shirt from off his desk and puts it on. "Come in!" he says. He'll have to wash up later.

Gek-Lin doesn't come in. "The problem is in the shower," she says.

"Come in and we can discuss it," Uncle Charley says.

"I don't want to discuss it," Gek-Lin says. "I want to show you."

Charley doesn't want this to become a scene, he doesn't want the other children to wonder at what is going on, but Gek-Lin is going to push him. If he were smart, he would sell her out right now. It would take just one phone call to his business associate. He'd make a good two hundred dollars. She'd end up with the rest of the prostitutes with a number around her neck. He is going to have to do it in six months anyway. She is too valuable of a commodity to escape Kin-Dong's greedy clutches for long, and although Charley will try to keep her for as long as possible, both because she is so essential to his kiddie porn business and because by being obstinate he could get a better price for her, he will eventually have to give her up, before the strong arm of the Thai Mafia marks him as "noncooperative," and the protection that he enjoys suddenly disappears.

Charley gets up and unlatches the door. He delivers the lecture. He has to. "When the sign says Do Not Disturb, it means do not disturb for any reason, you understa-a-and?" Uncle Charley stutters for a minute; he didn't expect Gek-Lin to be undressed, to be wearing nothing but a towel. The image of her massaging her breasts with the peppermint liquid soap that he had placed in the shower specifically because it has a tendency to make one's nipples hard was fresh in his head. Gek-Lin's nipples were amazing. They stuck up like a light switch in the "on" position.

Uncle Charley is staring at the contrast between the white of the terry-cloth towel and her olive skin, "I am doing important things. *Important*. I have to keep the books so that you parasites can stay here eating my food and playing my games. And what are you doing in that towel? Do not come out here dressed like this. You are a lady now, not a girl. Ladies get dressed before they stand before a man. Now, what is wrong with the shower?"

With Uncle Charley's words, Gek-Lin gets it. She is a woman. And Uncle Charley is a man. Gek-Lin is not a star pupil who Charley is training in the wonders of math, but a future prostitute, a number on a Bangkok wall. She had watched his eyes graze her chest, seen the lingering hard-on in his trousers. Gek-Lin is a nice catch, an 80-pound catfish to be auctioned off by some Mekong fisherman. She must escape. She isn't sure how she is going to do that, but she must. If there is one thing she has learned though, it is that she cannot be rash. She has learned some things in The Realm. Calculate and then act with authority. She will bide her time and then sting when the poison is ready.

"I'm sorry," Gek-Lin says, willing her face to flush in that submissive way that good Asian women's faces are trained to flush, a submissive flush with a trace of naughtiness. "I will get dressed before knocking on Uncle Charley's door from now on."

★   ★   ★

Xerxes and Sara reunite at the rock. Sara is out of breath. Her hands are on her knees. Xerxes is a bit winded too.

"Why were you running?" Xerxes asks.

"I don't know," Sara says.

"He fell," Xerxes says.

"Who fell?" Sara replies.

"Leonard," Xerxes says.

"Oh," Sara answers.

"Do we care?" Xerxes asks.

"I don't know," Sara says. "Is he all right?"

"I don't know," Xerxes says.

"What do you do, Xerxes?" Sara asks.

"What do you mean?" asks Xerxes.

"I mean, you're this smart guy who founded this Internet company, and now you're here in Arizona chasing your sister and her demented boyfriend through the woods."

Xerxes looks at Sara; the ludicrous nature of this discussion, the fact that it is happening right now, right after he has seen his twin sister's sanitarium bunkmate tumble off a very treacherous-looking geologic formation to what, at the very least, has to be a serious injury demanding immediate medical attention, the fact that instead of acting on this knowledge he is standing there with the pair's supposed guardian exchanging niceties and making small talk, makes it easy to answer this question in a truthful manner, a truthful manner that for professional and personal reasons he would otherwise never intimate.

"I'm a gamer," Xerxes says.

"A gamer?" Sara asks.

"Yeah. I play this on-line game. I lead a kingdom. It's called *Paradigm Shift*. There are 19 other people in my kingdom. I meet them on-line every day and together we plan attacks on other kingdoms. It's complicated."

"Fascinating," Sara says.

"Do you know what happened?" Xerxes asks.

Sara wonders what happened to Xerxes, what happened to lead him to this escapism. "What?" Sara asks carelessly.

Xerxes points towards Leonard's slanted slab. "Leonard fell off that rock over there."

"What?" Sara asks again, this time with urgency.

"Leonard fell off that rock over there and he's probably dead and my sister is probably standing over him panicked," Xerxes says.

"Why are we just standing here?"

"I don't know."

"I thought only kids played those things," says Sara.

* * *

"What is that?" Gek-Lin is asking Uncle Charley. She has her hand on one of the specially designed purple tiles with a PVC-coated antisteam surface and a one-way mirror that Uncle Charley had installed in the shower. The tiles cost him $200 apiece, plus the interest on the loan he'd needed to purchase them.

Uncle Charley is debating what and how much to tell her, just like normal parents debate the most appropriate time to tell their children about the birds and the bees. He feels suddenly uncomfortable, as if what he tells her will mutate her sexuality forever.

Gek-Lin hates when Charley gets like this. She has no patience for a man who stares blankly at shower stall walls. "What are those mechanical things behind the tiles?"

Charley coughs. The sound echoes off the walls like the first note of a trombone in a symphony orchestra. He becomes acutely aware of the possibilities of the situation—an adult male standing fully clothed in a shower stall with a 14-year-old girl dressed only in a white towel. It is like the opening salvo of a porn video: the girl invites the plumber standing in the doorway to fix a leaky faucet; she is dressed only in a bathrobe. Once he's in the room the plumber, who at first seemed so innocent, undoes the knot on the bathrobe, and views the appliance that needs plumbing.

There are excuses he could make for anything that he does here. It is economically astute. The web cams are on. He could treat the pay-per-view patrons of www.wetthailolitas.com to a very special live event. He could charge them a whopping $49.99 to view the rape of Persephone. (Persephone was Gek-Lin's screen name.) He could undo the towel knot, shove her back against the tiles, hold her wrists against the wall. He could lift her feet off the floor. He could force himself into her. He could suppress her screams as best he could and bang her head against the wall until she is quiet, until she submits, until the girl who always refused to submit, submits. He could break her coolly and calmly with his own hands. He could do it himself, not like the Pontius Pilate he was, not like the man who passed lambs onto the slaughter.

He could break her like he had been broken, without warning. At a time when she finally had some hope of escape. The rape would be like getting a phone call and having to identify your dead lover in the middle of the night.

Gek-Lin's voice was mocking him. "Earth to Uncle Charley. Come in Uncle Charley. What are those things?" He could really do it. The orphans would hear her screams and think she had it coming to her. He was their master, their guardian, and you listen to your guardian. No one would question him. They would be colder around him, less trusting, but none would question his authority, his right to do whatever it was that he had done. The local authorities allowed certain discretions to men of commerce, and a man of commerce he was. And the men behind their computers, the men who witnessed it all, he had nothing to worry about from them. To them it was all entertainment, all a set-up, all an act. And even if a part of them wondered, wondered if it wasn't just an act, they buried that quiver of a question quickly, and logged off.

The contempt rises up in Charley, contempt for what he is, contempt for what the world is. Before him, wrapped in a towel, is a choice. He can act with hatred or he can act with nobility, or if not with nobility, then at least with a shred of respect. But then again, as he looks at her, he doesn't really have a choice, whatever spunk or spark he once had died the day he had lost his first orphan, his first love. Now his only choice is to act by the rules, with minor bending due to a lingering sense of compassion. It isn't nobility at all.

"They're cameras," Uncle Charley says.

*　*　*

Gabriella keeps waiting for Xerxes to burst through the bushes, a big *M* on his chest. *Here he comes to save the day, Mighty Mouse.* This doesn't happen. Instead, it is just her and Leonard, a remarkably silent Leonard who has managed to roll out of the juniper bush into the sand at the base of the slab he had fallen from. Leonard is probably in shock. He is sitting upright with his legs extended, an obviously alien bump protruding upwards about two inches below his kneecap, just barely not breaking the skin.

Gabriella sits right next to Leonard, watching the sun dip behind the rock. The shade is nice, considering the way the sun at high altitude can drill into your skull, but if it gets any later in the day it might start getting cold, and it is dangerous, Gabriella thinks, for someone in shock to be so exposed. Still, Gabriella doesn't move. She watches ants instead. It is strange what the ants are doing. There are two ants in the middle of a circle of other ants. The two ants are fighting. One of the ants grabs the other by the neck with its mandibles, turns him over, body slams him. The body slammed ant quickly rolls over, marches back over to the first ant, pokes him in the eye. The fight goes on endlessly, mandibles bumping and knocking together like swords.

What Gabriella finds fascinating about this is the way the ants on the outside just stand around, the way they simply watch the warrior ants' dance of death. She doesn't understand why they have left the fighting up to these two, why they aren't participating. Most of all she can't figure out why the other ants don't *help*.

It's her medication that makes her like this: *Extreme emotions brought on by illusionary circumstance. In real crises, the patient often affects no emotion at all* reads her report in the St. Francis files. It's her medication that keeps her sedated. If she wasn't medicated she would be motivated, motivated to do what Xerxes would do in this situation. She is sure that he would have a roll of gauze in his backpack, inserted into an amazingly well-organized first aid kit. She is sure that he would look around and find wood to use as a splint—two pieces of wood, exactly the size of Leonard's shin—and that he would take these pieces of wood, place one on either side of the leg, and wrap the gauze around the contraption. She knows her twin. She has seen him in action. She knows that if he were here he would take one look at Leonard's leg, then look at Gabriella with a glint in his eye; he would rub his hands together and show them to Gabriella, as if he were about to perform a magic trick, as if to prove to her that there was nothing hidden in them; then he would bend over Leonard, ask him if he was ready, and wait for Leonard's nod. When Leonard nodded, Xerxes would place one hand on Leonard's calf pressing up and the other on his knee pressing down, and there would be a snap and the bump in Leonard's leg would be gone.

Gabriella knows what Xerxes would do and the coming cold makes her shiver. She hates the ants. She sifts her hand through the sand, erasing the ants who have formed the circle around the pair of warrior ants; some are buried, some run away in anger, some sting the invading hand. The two ants in the center of the circle stop fighting. They stand there, bewildered. There is no reason to fight once their audience is gone.

* * *

Gek-Lin is not jai yen. She does not have that "cool heart" so famous amongst the Thai. She does not possess the qualities that the Thai people are so famous for: an intolerance for the raised voice, a smiling face that never shows irritation, an abhorrence of confrontation. Gek-Lin is not eager to please, does not insist on keeping up the appearance that everyone is having a fun time.

She does, however, possess one quality that the Thai are often accused of possessing. She does place a high value on money. She is, in a way, a sort of human calculator. And so when leering, tongue-tied Uncle Charley finally spills the beans, she holds back the rising tide of anger ready to burst forth from her fourteen-year-old lips. If she is careful, perhaps there will be something in this for her.

She looks Charley dead in the eye, "What are the cameras for?"

Uncle Charley looks dreamy, is staring at nothing in particular. He seems resigned to tell all, to give it all away, like so many of those would-be conquerors—Arabs, Australians, Americans—who walk into the half-light of the Grace Hotel in Pan Pong, uncertain and waiting to be led by shy, smiling girls into back rooms for the ubiquitous Bangkok body massage. Before they enter the back room they will ask the proprietor if the girl is pretty, clean, and safe. When they ask the proprietor these questions, the answer is always, as the answer is to every question asked by foreigners in Thailand: yes, yes, yes. The foreigners somehow miss the significance of the STD clinics franchised like 7–Elevens on every corner.

Charley is standing in front of Gek-Lin and he wants to confess all: wants to confess his past as a boy toy in Bangkok; wants to confess his countless relations with U.S. Navy SEALs; wants to confess his desire to leave this region, to escape; wants to confess how close he came to that. He wants to tell Gek-Lin what he was just thinking, how badly he wants her. "They are Web cameras. I broadcast streaming media images of you taking showers to men who pay a subscription fee to watch it. You are one of their favorites, Gek-Lin. I make a great deal of money off of you."

Gek-Lin, her hair still dripping, doesn't understand streaming media. She doesn't understand subscription fees. "How much money?"

"Enough to run the orphanage. Enough to keep you all here."

"How much money, just me?"

"I don't know. I don't keep individual records."

Gek-Lin can smell a lie like she can smell durians at the market—the smell is sickly sweet with a hint of manure—But she lets this pass. She talks dumb, purposely, like a look-look girl. "Maybe some for Gek-Lin?"

It is an obvious solution, a bribe for silence; but Uncle Charley cannot just give her the money. In his heart, he does not want her to be just another girl, another petite thing holding hands with an overweight foreigner, showing up at the Hilton eating expensive meals, exchanging sex for a Nintendo X-Box. This is the way it starts. The first compromise. She will hoard away money in her Babar lunchbox imagining an escape while getting deeper and deeper into the life that will make it impossible. He would be her first sugar daddy, the first in a string of elusive sugar daddies that promise everything then leave without a trace. They speak lies that each party understands are lies, lies that make the possibility of ever obtaining truth impossible.

"I cannot give you money, Gek-Lin. Maybe there is something else you want."

Gek-Lin is fourteen and she knows what she wants. She wants to go to America. Here there is no future for her but that of a sex worker or a kept wife.

Maybe Gek-Lin wouldn't have been able to articulate it this way. Maybe it was more of a sixth sense, a sense that her thoughts and deeds were not those of a Thai girl, but those of an American girl, that she belonged mixed up in that surreal stew of driven dreamers, amongst those people whose reputation for hard individualism is both their strength and demise. Whatever her true thoughts, the words that come out of Gek-Lin's mouth do not come out as a question but a command, an order to Uncle Charley that he cannot help but understand as such.

"You will bribe the embassy and get me a visa to America," she says.

"I don't know," says Uncle Charley.

"I will keep posing for your cameras. I will make you lots of money. You will get me to America."

Take me to your country. Give me your life—the communal cry of thousands of Thai whores as September's high tides and hammering monsoons flood the streets of Bangkok, forcing Johns and their concubines to abandon visits to the Buddha for bedrooms. Under crisp, sterile sheets, promises are expected to be given and promises are expected to be broken. You will take me to your country. Yes. You will marry me. Yes. There was never a question as to when this would happen; neither party was willing to breach the lie.

Gek-Lin's cry to Uncle Charley, though, is a subtle variation on the Thai whores' oft-repeated theme. It is not: take me to your country; give me your life. It is: give me that country; I will take charge of my own life. And the thing is, when Uncle Charley hears Gek-Lin's cry, he can't help but find it compelling; it is, after all, so similar to the cry of his own youth, his desire to go to England and become an English scholar. It is a cry of a victor not a victim. It is a cry that he had all but forgotten.

Gek-Lin's cry expands from one small spot on his brain to the outer reaches of his being like an earthquake expanding from an epicenter. It shakes him up. It makes him remember who he was, who he had been, who he had wanted to be. He recalled his desire to be unique, to be the orphan who had escaped. It was too late for him. He was tied to this life like any mafioso. You couldn't get out. Either you were in or you were dead. But he could get Gek-Lin out, and if he did, if he were able to break that cycle, then his life had been worth living, then he had ultimately accomplished something.

Uncle Charley shakes these thoughts off. No, it is impossible. Hope is squandered; death presides. She'll never make it out of here.

Uncle Charley decides to use this against her: he will continue to broadcast her washing in the shower, he'll hook her up with Kin-Dong, and then he'll sell her out to prostitution. It's his job; it's his unfortunate destiny.

"I tell you what Gek-Lin. I will try to get you to America."

Gek-Lin doesn't trust Uncle Charley. She smiles, plays it sly. She will lie low, like a scorpion beneath a bed pad.

21. WHEN YOU'RE LEFT WITHOUT A MONARCH, YOU'LL HAVE TO RELY ON YOUR OWN RESOURCES.

XERXES AND SARA are walking back down the zigzags. They realize that they should be running. But something precludes this. Xerxes and Sara are simply walking and talking. It is as if they are already preparing their court case, their explanation for how the crazies got away and then killed themselves. It is as if they already know Gabriella and Leonard's fate, as if they have been preparing for it for years.

Sara, well-trained through her hours of practice counseling at NYU, is adept at drawing out a confession. She is leading the witness. "When did you have your first inkling of Gabby's illness?"

Xerxes, not at all well-trained in being on the stand, is providing the answers, and whether from the high altitude, the heat, his previous loping, or from the directness of Sara's questioning, he is sweating a little. He is not used to this kind of honesty, so he watches his feet, talking as if it were only to himself, "It was, I guess, 1990. Gabriella was at Mills in Oakland, and I was at Stanford. We were only a car drive across the San Mateo Bridge from each other but we rarely saw each other. I was focused on what I wanted. I was studying computer engineering and I had a friend, Zahn Mendoza, the guy who became the co-founder of our company . . .

"Anyway, I had stopped talking to my family. This wasn't out of any sort of contempt, although, now that I think about it, it might have been contempt, but more out of this feeling that in order to succeed I had to stay on task, that any break from my studies would somehow keep Zahn and me from owning a business together.

"Gabriella would call me every once in a while. Usually it was late at night, while my eyes were glued to a computer screen. I would only half-listen. Mills has a reputation amongst Stanford students as being a kind of quasi-school, something for young ladies—at the undergraduate level it's an all-women's school—to do while their male peers at Cal and Stanford study something serious. Gabriella would ramble. She would tell me about all the knowledge she was gaining, how she was learning to be more open, more free. She has a girlfriend. She'd emphasize this, *a girlfriend*. I'm *a lesbian*, she would say. No, no, I'm *a bisexual*. She'd tell me about Harbin, the nudist camp with the hot baths up in wine country, and how someone had given her a watsu, an underwater massage, and how freeing that was. She'd tell me how she dropped acid, while picking strawberries with her friends, and how she had talked to the migrant farm workers, and how she'd let one of them touch her, and how that had been such a good thing. She had learned something. She would tell me that she was seeing a counselor, and that the counselor had helped her to discover what had happened to her when we were kids, how badly she had been mistreated, and how terrible our parents were.

"I only half-listened to her. I didn't want to know about her sex life or talk about the past. I ignored her and just brushed everything off as a phase that young women go through. So when her words got weirder, I didn't notice that some line was being crossed. It didn't occur to me to be worried that her truths were getting mixed up with her lies, that she could no longer distinguish between events that had happened and events that hadn't happened at all. You see, it didn't happen. Most of the stuff she was talking about didn't happen. She claimed that my father had molested her. She accused him of that. And a couple of friends had raped her. And it started spiraling. There was no way to tell what was truth and what was a lie.

"And, well, I felt guilty about the whole thing, because, I had . . . well . . . played with her, when we were kids . . . even though it never went too far, I mean . . . I would drag her under a blanket that I used as a tent and I would undress her. She hated it. She would kick and scream. . . . I mean . . . I was a kid, Sara, not a monster. Kids—they do things."

Xerxes kicked the pine needles carpeting the red dust of the path. He'd never told anyone about this before. He didn't dare look at Sara, to see the judgment on her face. "My mom called me one morning. It was on the answering machine when I came back from class. The message was trite. 'Hey, it's your mom. I have bad news. Your sister's in the hospital.'

"I called her back. She and my father were packing their bags to make the trip out to California. She said that Gabby had shown up at the house of some acquaintances at four in the morning. Even though it was college, it was still strange for someone to show up at someone else's house at four in the morning, and even stranger for that person to spout off uninvited tales of incest and rape, interrupted by long spells of wailing and rage. The girls were frightened. They didn't know how to get rid of my sister, didn't feel it was appropriate to simply ask her to leave. They were worried about her, so they called a resident assistant that they knew in one of the dorms, and the R.A., no doubt bleary-eyed and pissed off and expecting to encounter another drunk bunch of coeds, came over, and, even with her limited amount of training, after a half an hour of listening to Gabby, determined that the girl in front of her was experiencing a serious mental break.

"So the R.A. called the resident director, and the resident director called a 24-hour crisis hotline, and by 6 a.m. she had been admitted."

Xerxes was expecting some emotion from Sara, or at least a quiet *I'm sorry, that sucks,* but Sara was in analysis mode, and her next questions were clinical, "That was your first inkling? When she had already been admitted to a psychiatric hospital? There were no earlier signs?"

Xerxes answered her as if hypnotized. "I don't know, hindsight is twenty/twenty. I guess you could say she was sensitive. I mean that's the stereotype of the schizophrenic, right? As children they cry more than the average child. They're more needy of parental support. In school they get picked on because they're so easy to rattle. But I always thought she was simply more aware of her surroundings. I thought she had a gift. I mean, my dad would take us to Arlington Stadium, to see a Major League Baseball game, and my head would be buried in the program, memorizing on-base percentages and strike out/base-on-balls ratios, and Gabby would look at the right fielder, the way he had his hands on his hips, and she'd say, 'he's not happy,' and sure enough, the guy would go 0-for-22 over the next week, and get demoted to the minors. It was uncanny, the way she could see through people. The things she would say seemed kooky, but in the end she always turned out to be right."

Sara went in for the kill, "Do you think it's your fault?"

"Huh?"

"Do you feel that if you hadn't exploited her weaknesses as a child, she'd be a different person than she is today."

Xerxes started to answer, "I . . ." then stopped and looked up at a turkey vulture circling in the sky.

"It's not your fault, Xerxes."

The vulture banked, as if a hot wind had risen up below it. "That's the shrink in you talking, Sara. How do we know that for sure? Why shouldn't I feel guilty? Why shouldn't I keep trying to fix things? We're twins, Sara. I don't know if I can change her, but I know when I am around we give each other energy. That sounds kind of hippy, like Gabby's talking; I don't know how to explain it in rational terms, but it's true. Gabby's more sane when I'm around, and I'm more . . . emotional. We're like each other's crutch."

"Schizophrenia is a chemical imbalance, Xerxes. It's nature not nurture. It has to do with misplaced genes, not corrupted childhoods. She had a predisposition for this, and what you did or did not do, as a child, isn't particularly abnormal for children that age to do."

"That's bullshit, Sara."

"Why do you think it's bullshit?

"Because it is. Because it's psychobabble. I mean you said it yourself. She had a *predisposition*. Predisposition isn't the same thing as trigger. What was the trigger, Sara? Was I the trigger? I'll never know. But there is that distinct possibility. There's no denying that."

"So the reason you left your company, and moved out here to Arizona, was to save your sister?"

The vulture was flying east; back in the direction from which Xerxes and Sara had started the walk.

"Where are they?"

"Where's who?

"Gabby and Leonard."

"I have no idea."

★   ★   ★

Gabriella snaps the leg back into place. She isn't herself when she does it. She is her brother. She simply becomes *him* for a moment. It is neither as easy nor as hard as she expected it to be. It had taken several tries, with Leonard grimacing, sucking air in through his teeth, biting his tongue, then telling her "harder" each time she had tried. She hadn't expected it to be like this, so imperfect, so human. Either, she thought, she wouldn't have been able to touch him, or she would grab the leg, snap it into place, and that would be that. But it had been a struggle; she had wrestled with the leg, pulled it in different angles, been made to stop while Leonard dealt with the pain, and then, after several tries, after being convinced that this was a horrible idea, and that she should stop before she killed him, after Leonard had told her to try again, each time, "a different way," she had looked at his leg, as if with X-ray vision, seen the angle at which it appeared it needed to be bent, yanked the leg hard, and it had snapped into place, just like that, as if she had been an orthopedic surgeon for years.

As she looks into Leonard's eyes, it comes to her how her brother does it. He doesn't think about it. He doesn't take the time to contemplate the intricacies of success. To do so is, itself, a failure. One must act, quickly, decisively, the best one knows how. One must go forward, into the universe, looking as closely as one can at the moment at hand. A leg must go back in place; a leg must be straightened, bound, and held in position. The owner of the leg must be brought to a hospital to be cared for by a professional. The human aspect of the situation must be ignored until the emergency is taken care of. And what Xerxes had done, in order to survive, in order to ignore all the philosophical questions, was to make the world one giant E.R. His cell phone rang and rang and rang for years on end with one important client or investor that needed to be placated, or bought from, or sold to, after another. And this is how he went on, how he became successful, how he became an American hero. He simply never stopped to answer the larger questions. One thing led to another and he never asked himself why.

This is Gabriella's big revelation. It is the lightning bolt that finally strikes her like Saul, that guy in the Bible who changed his name to Paul. But unlike Paul-formerly-Saul, Gabriella isn't converted.

She walks around the oversized boulders that surround her and Leonard, finds a branch that is thick enough to support weight but thin enough to break; she breaks this branch over her knee, breaks it into two pieces the size of Leonard's shin; she comes back to Leonard, takes off her T-shirt, then places the wood on either side of Leonard's leg and binds them together with the shirt. She does it like she knows her brother would. The color returns to Leonard's face and when she asks him if he can get up and walk he says that he can. She gets on the side of him with the wounded leg and helps him up, supporting his weight. She does all this, but she still isn't converted.

She could find a way to deal with the day-to-day like everyone; she could make small gains until the grand total equaled something worthwhile. But even as she manages this once to perform a great deed, she knows that this is not her calling. Gabriella's job is to be a recorder of emotion, a poet, a journal keeper, a photo album maker, a philosopher. While the rest of the world moves at its blinding pace—businesses, buildings, and human beings born and erased in an instant, forgotten by all but those closest to them—Gabriella will watch and take notes. She will remember and record that before the Bellagio there was Circus Circus, that before the Lexus there was The Flamingo. She will take a pen and write down the essentials. She will make sure her pen is permanent.

Gabriella will not pour her soul into a microchip, code it into HTML, watch it be replaced in a new release. She is determined to keep things solid. And a person who keeps things solid cannot function in today's world. They want to go to a bank, hand their money to a teller, watch the teller put the money in the vault, come back a week later and get that same money, identical serial numbers and all. It bothers them that wealth is dispensed by something called an ATM, by an Automated Teller Machine.

Gabriella won't accept the clean and dirty reality that while the planet grows warmer its people grow colder. She wants, desperately, to stop on the corner and talk with the homeless guy, con artist or no. She wants to cut short her trip to the Laundromat, or the dentist, or McDonald's, and talk to the guy, for hours if need be. She wants to throw away the whole day and listen to his story and tell him hers and hand him her purse and wallet. She wants to give the homeless guy all her money and her three credit cards. She wants to tell him her birth date, her mother's maiden name, and her Social Security number. She wants to pull him into her blue Ford Escort, which is parked across the street, and make love to him, his smell be damned.

Gabriella Meticula wants to do this. And on occasion she does do this. She talks to the homeless guy for hours and takes him into her arms in the back of a Ford Escort. She stands on the street corner and because of the length and animated nature of the conversation she has with this homeless person, this street person, she turns into a homeless person herself, a bag lady in the eyes of the world; and when the cops come through and do their sweeps they pick her up, and briefly put her in a cell, and put out an A.P.B., and they find out that her family is looking for her, that she has been missing; and so when they are called, her parents come, or her brother comes, and all of them, they want to save her from herself, and really who can blame them, they don't want her to be conned and taken advantage of, but the thing she wants to tell them is that she really doesn't mind being conned. Yes, there are the horrible things that the man might do, but to her nothing the man can do is more horrible than the horror of the man being ignored, the man hanging out on a street corner doing nothing while the rest of the world goes to the Laundromat, or the dentist, or McDonald's.

★　★　★

When Xerxes and Sara finally run into them at dusk, having spent hours looking for them, both Xerxes and Sara with looks in their eyes saying they thought they'd seen everything, eyes saying that at this juncture they had pretty much given up hope and never imagined they'd see Gabriella and Leonard strolling in perfectly all right, Gabriella lies and tells Xerxes that Leonard constructed the splint himself.

Leonard, not being the talkative sort, sees no reason to dispute Gabriella's claim. And Xerxes takes Gabby's statement at face value, and nothing more is said about the matter.

Gabriella does change that day, for when she sees Xerxes with Sara, when she sees him and realizes that today, he failed, that he is not infallible, that he couldn't and didn't save her, that Xerxes is as capable, if not more capable, of making mistakes as she is, she becomes, well, warmer—like the Grinch, Gabriella's heart suddenly grows three times warmer.

She will still be found on occasion in her blue Ford Escort, stopped at a stoplight, stopped at a stoplight whose light is green. She will still be honked at, flipped the bird, while she stares at the light, while she asks, *why, why does green mean go?* while she asks, *why, why does red mean stop?* She will still be accosted by the assistant sheriffs of small towns. She will still ask the assistant sheriff, *why should I show you my I.D.? what does I.D. mean? why isn't it I.C., identification card, instead of I.D.? what does the D stand for? what does the D stand for, Dan, assistant sheriff Dan?*

She will still do these things, but she will no longer do them because she is bitter, because the people in the world have something that she cannot have. Gabriella will go on being inquisitive, she will go on philosophizing, she will continue to ask questions about what is normal and in doing so do inappropriate things, but she will no longer be angry about it.

Gabriella no longer feels like the evil twin. She has simply made a choice. She will be she. She will exist on the fringes, in the subspace. She will exist where she has chosen to exist, where she has been called.

The sky above them is hot pink. A coyote, deep in the forest, a step ahead of the new zoning laws, once again howls.

22. THE MORE FRIENDS YOU HAVE, THE STRONGER YOU ARE.

XERXES DRIVES NUMBER 8 TO THE ST. AGNES MEDICAL CENTER of Rest Stop. He goes in with Leonard, and since Leonard has no medical insurance, agrees to pay for the bill himself. The fracture is a simple one, and since Leonard's leg has already been snapped back into place, it only takes a bit of plaster of paris and a short but costly consultation with a doctor before Sara, Xerxes, Gabriella, and Leonard are on their way back to the St. Francis Sanitarium.

While Xerxes had handled the medical aspect of the situation, Sara was on the pay phone with her superior. Though she was red-faced and flustered, her voice on the telephone was strong and confident. She explained the accident quickly, in medical terms, leaving out the hows and whys. The ploy worked. She was learning something from Xerxes's maximuminventory.com handbook.

All is good. Though Sara is no farther along in her quest for hours or compensation, at least she has not killed a patient today. Before Xerxes drops the three of them off at the Sanitarium, he asks Sara a question. "I'd like to talk to you, in private, about what we discussed earlier today. Could I have your phone number?"

Sara says sure. Maybe she is getting somewhere.

★   ★   ★

Another one has left his mark. She has it now, permanently: Herpes Simplex Type II. Men, why do they feel the need to piss on fire hydrants? She's fevered, she's sick, and worst of all she knows that someone has done this to her on purpose.

Mary Lynn Klavich does not know where to turn. She loved being The Serpent, but her ability to change keeps getting diminished. Not long ago, she could be anybody, but now, well, now she was pigeon-holed, forever marked with her tattoos and a venereal disease. How could she be a changeling now?

Men, she was so tired of men; this is what they loved: the surprise attack, the drive-by shooting, the bomb dropped from the sky—destroy and run, this was their game. She had given herself to them and this is what they had done, they had ruined her. They were good at destruction; but creation—well, they really sucked at that.

In times like these, Mary Lynn might turn to The Realm; it was there that she might seek solace, but even there she is being picked apart, infected. Her message box is filled with the angry concerns of her kingdom mates:

Help! As soon as I attacked I got the plague, and then they started hammering me with spells and attacks. Can someone cast an NB on me?

Sir Ribbit Ribbit

———

Me, too. Help!

Lord Sneaky Slithery

———

This strategy bad idea. Why we all attack the undead? Now we are all weak.

Lady Comes from Water

———

I agree Comes from Water. If we choose our own targets then none of this would have happened I'm going to attack that Nevermore guy now, 'cuz if we keep attacking Land of BonZ the whole kingdom will have the plague too. I say we do whatever we want from now on because tihs was a bad idea and the queen she has too much control over our actons. I say everyone thinks for themselves because even though she has been right before this time things turned out really bad and I just don't hting we shoudl do it this way anymore.

Sir Sal

———

There is no comfort here either. There is always someone wanting her to surrender to them. Even now, from the kingdom that had, out of nowhere, declared war on her, there is a message:

Dear Serpent,

mAnY aPoLoGiEs FoR tHe InDeScReTiOnS cOmMiTtEd AgAiNsT yOuR kInG-dOm. LeT mE aSsUrE yOu ThAt NoNe Of It Is PeRsOnAl. If YoU cHoOsE tO sUrReNdEr ThE qUeEn WiLl EnD tHe WaR qUiCkLy. FiNd Me At tHe MaIn PaR-lOr On IrC aNd We CaN cHaT aBoUt It AnD oThEr ThInGs

Sir sKyLaR of Paradigm Shift

———

Even as they do you damage they want to chat, they act like it's all noth-ing. Even so, The Serpent cannot help but give in. It is in her nature. She'll talk to him; she'll flirt with him; she'll show him her body. After she's done with that, she will sleep. This sleep, she's beginning to want it to last forever.

* * *

Unlike most of The Realm's denizens, Dietrich does not measure friends and enemies by those who are in his kingdom and those who are allied with his kingdom versus those who are outside his kingdom, and have warred with, thieved from, or land-grabbed his kingdom mates. To Dietrich, these are meaningless distinctions. In fact, if anything, the warring that his kingdom does is just an additional opportunity to make friends.

Dietrich is using that opportunity now. He's on the IRC with The Serpent. He wants to know what she's like in Real Life. Dietrich finds the war humorous, and he's looking to get away, to escape the depression that's overcome his wife and the other inhabitants of The Dome. They've already discussed the terms of the armistice, so Dietrich moves on to other things:

sKyLaR: *sO wHy Do YoU cAll yOuRsElF tHe SeRpEnT?*

Serpent: *Because serpents are stealthy. They can blend in. And because of that they can be whatever you want them to be. Where are you from Skylar?*

sKyLaR: *i'M sTaTiOnEd iN aNtArCtiCa RiGhT nOw.*

Serpent: *Really? I live in San Francisco.*

sKyLaR: *aRe YoU a ReAl GiRl?*

** **Serpent** blushes*

Serpent: *Of course. Want to see a picture?*

sKyLaR: *sUrE*

Serpent: *P0000012.jpg*

sKyLaR: *:O iS tHaT rEalLy YoU? yOu DiDn'T nEeD tO sEnD mE a NuDiE sHoT.*

181

Serpent: *do you like?*

sKyLaR: *... i'M a MaRrIeD mAn.*

Serpent: *LOL. That's too bad. Well, good night my good married man skylar from Antarctica.*

sKyLaR: *sWeEt DrEaMs, SeRpEnT, sWeEt DrEaMs*

Dietrich does not stop his carousing with The Serpent, he moves on to other players. Like Tres Rawlings, he opens one private chat after another. Although Dietrich would deny that this communication is any way an act of unfaithfulness to his wife, The Realm players that he attempts to contact are generally women (or, at least players with the designation "Lady" or "Queen") and the innuendo that he writes into his messages is flirtatious in nature, if not downright sexual.

He is, in a virtual way, reverting back to his bachelor days in Manhattan. But Dietrich is not really aware of this. To him, this is not cheating on his wife, it's simply survival: survival when locked in a dome with a bunch of people who hate his guts and a wife who's losing her mind.

23. IF IT'S ETHICALLY DUBIOUS, IT'S PROBABLY A GOOD IDEA.

SKYLAR HAS SPOKEN WITH THE SERPENT, and *Amphibious* has agreed to the terms of a surrender. In twelve hours, *Paradigm Shift* will have won the war. This does not prevent *The Strangely Peaceful Citadel of Blue Orcs* from making one last attack. After all, the war is still on, and the purpose of it is to attain as much land as possible.

The Queen has some offense now; the offense is not elite, it's not everything that it can and will be, but nonetheless she can take some acreage. The Queen puts in some numbers, an hourglass spins, the results come back:

Queen Peace & Love but Mostly Love, your troops have fought a brave battle and won. You have appropriated 91 acres of land from Sal A. Mander (23:34). Your army will return from the battlefield in 14 days.

★ ★ ★

Xerxes shuts off his computer. The kingdom is performing well, and Xerxes decides he has the time to make the phone call. It is the first phone call he has made in over two months. As he punches Sara's digits into the telephone he feels childish, like a teenage boy calling a teenage girl for the first time.

When the phone rings, Sara Bronstein is lying in a hammock that she has strung up between two spruce trees behind the miner's cabin. She has been reading the National Edition of *The New York Times*. On Sundays like today, she smokes a joint, a habit that she only recently picked up in an effort to alleviate the boredom of her weekends, and reads the paper section by section all the way to the end.

As the phone rings, Sara had just hit the Classifieds Section, was reading through Women Seeking Men. Imagine the calls, she is thinking; an attractive 20-something woman could rack up 30, 40, 50 messages a day from attractive men. She could go to Yankee Stadium in the Bronx, get taken to Joe's Shanghai in midtown. She could have her evenings filled seven days a week, or just five if she wanted a night to recant, drinks with the girls to update them on the latest gossip. How much opportunity there is, there in NYC, and yet she is here in Rest Stop, Arizona, surrounded by an unfeeling forest, smoking dope, and reading Classified ads from people she's too far away from to date.

The phone rings, and the sound is so foreign to Sara that she doesn't recognize it as a phone, it hasn't rung in so long. She doesn't move from her hammock until the answering machine begins projecting the disembodied voice of Xerxes Meticula through her screen door. Xerxes says, "Hello, Sara? This is Xerxes Meticula calling, Gabriella's brother. Listen, we talked, briefly, while we were out on the trail the other day about some things and I thought, well, you seem very good at what you do, and—"

Sara picks up the phone. "Hello?"

"Oh, hey."

"Sorry about that, I was out back."

Xerxes feels tongue-tied, there is no schematic for this, no Visio program to draw up his feelings and line them up on a flow chart. "I was just saying to your answering machine, I mean to you on your answering machine, that, well, we had that talk, and I was wondering if you do private counseling."

Sara doesn't want to talk to Xerxes right now. She hates talking to people when she's stoned. "I'd love to but I can't, I'm not licensed yet."

"I know, but we could do it under the table."

Sara's mind wanders elsewhere when he says "do it under the table." She suppresses a giggle. "I can't do that, it's not legal."

"Of course. I'm sorry."

These slips, Fruedian or not, are making Sara's mind wander. She realizes that it had been there, had been hovering before her like the phosphor of an angler fish, small and seemingly inconsequential, but all-important to her sustenance. There is potential here. She's lonely. Maybe he's lonely too. She's a sophisticated urban girl who's managed to get herself stuck in a cabin in Arizona. He's an entrepreneurial urban boy who's managed to get himself stuck in his parents' house in Arizona. She's attractive. He's attractive. It's as if she were a woman crossing a desert without any water who sees an oasis in the distance and assumes it's a mirage. It was an opportunity so obvious that she had overlooked it. A man down on his luck who was once up on his luck just needs a small push forward to be up on his luck once again. She doesn't want to counsel him in the formal sense. The counselor/client relationship is a one-way relationship. Sara wants to counsel Xerxes, but she wants to seek his counsel in return. And she wants other things, too. "What are you doing today?"

The question takes Xerxes aback. *What is he doing today?* He was going to carb up on Power Bars once he got off the phone and then hightail it up some fire road. He was going to count the revolutions on his speedometer/odometer/altimeter, over 10,000 on a good ride. "Nothing, really. Why?"

"There's an art fair at the plaza downtown and I was thinking of checking it out this afternoon. It'll be mostly crap—cowboy and Indian art—but maybe we'll get lucky and find something worthwhile."

When has Xerxes last considered art? In the heyday, before the gaming addiction kicked in, Dixie and he would go to art openings together. He remembered a Calder exhibit, the intricate way the different parts of Calder's mobiles balanced and counterbalanced each other. He'd stood under one for a great deal of time, examining its physics. "I used to contribute to the MOMA back in San Francisco."

Xerxes voice sounds wooden to Sara. She is wondering about her flash of inspiration. He seems so boring, "Really?"

"I used to go to all the openings. Great wine and cheese."

Xerxes is slipping into his familiar sarcasm, defusing any chance at making this fun. Sara decides to try another tactic, "You know art is used quite frequently in therapy; that's what I teach at St. Francis, art. Your sister, by the way, is quite the artist."

Oh, I get it. You'll counsel me but you won't call it counseling. "Maybe you're right, Sara, maybe I do need to look at some art today."

"Do you want to meet me at the gazebo around three?"

Xerxes thinks he can swing a couple hours away from The Realm. "Sure. The gazebo at three."

"Great, see you then."

"Ciao."

"Bye."

Sara, who found her way back to the hammock while talking to Xerxes on her cordless, presses the "End" button. A breeze lifts the front page of *The Times* off the table next to her hammock. It rolls like a tumbleweed along the ground until it gets caught in a blackberry bush. The breeze is cooler than usual. Sara peeks through the spruce and pine towards Granite Mountain. At the top, aspens are beginning to show a flash of yellow. Autumn is coming to Rest Stop, Arizona. The season is turning.

24. YOU WON'T LIKE ALL OF YOUR KINGDOM MATES. GET OVER IT.

SKYLAR'S MESSAGE ARRIVES in their in-boxes, their header bars simultaneously announcing: NEW MSG

The Queen clicks on hers and reads:

Dear Queen Peace & Love but Mostly Love,

tHiS mEsSaGe HaS bEeN sEnT tO tHe EnTiRe KiNgDoM. tHe WaR aGaInSt ThE uNfOrTuNaTe KiNgDoM aMpHiBiOuS HaS bEeN mOsT sUcCeSsFuL. tO cElE-bRaTe OuR aChIeVeMeNt, eSpEcIaLlY tHe BrAvErY oF lOrD bOnZ AnD hIs Un-CaNnY aBiLiTy To AdMiNiStEr ThE pLaGuE, I wOuLd LiKe To InViTe YoU aLl To ViSiT mY pLeAsUrE pAlAcE fOr A pArTy, tO bE hElD oN dAy 16, MoNtH jAnU-aRy, Yr 12, ReAlM tImE. hAvE yOuR iRc On AnD i WiLl CoNfErEnCe YoU iN.

Signed, Sir sKyLaR

185

Team unity is, of course, a vital part of success in The Realm and The Queen is in complete support of sKyLaR's proposed soirée. The on-line chat will serve to keep players focused, as success in The Realm often leads to lulls. It is nice to have someone else there to propose things like this, so that the other players don't feel that they are being dragged along by an overly ambitious leader. The Queen copies and pastes a message. Then sends it to all the provinces in the kingdom one-by-one:

Dear _____

sKyLaR's proposed meeting is a good idea. I look forward to seeing you all there.

The Queen Peace & Love but Mostly Love

Gek-Lin picks the tail of a squid off a piece of wax paper. She has learned to sift through scraps to find the choicest cuts. She is a Dumpster gourmet. She places the squid tail on her tongue and sucks it down.

Since the shower incident, Gek-Lin has been a good girl. She has continued to take her daily shower for Uncle Charley, scrubbing herself with gusto, lingering a bit longer at her budding breasts than she had before. Knowing that she was being watched, Gek-Lin took to behaving coquettishly: turning to profile, lifting her heels, winking at the purple tiles.

Unfortunately, her behavior has not produced the desired results. Her plan was not completely clear, but she had figured doing Uncle Charley's bidding would draw her closer to him. Maybe, she could seduce him. Maybe, he would take her as his lover and fly her to America. Maybe, once there, she would find a champion of industry to take her on, to give her her own office—an office far, far away from the filthy orphans kicking cheap feathered Thai hacky-sacks over her head.

But she wasn't even succeeding in Phase One. In fact, if anything, Charley's interest in her seemed to be waning; he no longer leered at her from his Pentium across the room, his eyes magnified through his bottom-of-a-bottle spectacles. Ignoring her wasn't unusual, but normally Charley shook around her, exhibiting a nervousness that Gek-Lin took, and correctly so, for lust.

Now, this nervousness was gone. He no longer made eye contact with her. He didn't even seem to look at her when she wasn't looking. Whenever

Gek-Lin snuck a glance, she'd find him staring up at the ceiling instead of at her.

Gek-Lin holds Psyduck by a webbed foot. Psyduck stares straight ahead, the black paint that had once given his eyes pupils was now gone, so that his eyes are only whites. They look like hard-boiled eggs. Gek-Lin knows what Psyduck would telepathically communicate, if this were the real Psyduck, the Psyduck on television. Psyduck would communicate that Gek-Lin should not have expected the most obvious solution to have been the correct one. Gek-Lin would have to look deeper and harder to find the right answer. She would have to unearth all the variables before finding her solution.

Gek-Lin doesn't know yet what she has been doing wrong, but Psyduck, as always, is telling her to be patient. She is still in the game.

* * *

Gek-Lin is driving his web traffic down. The customers at www.wetthailolitas.com know a poser when they see one. They are pure voyeurs; they get off on the knowledge that they are watching someone innocent, both of the world and of the fact that they are being watched. It is obvious to them that Persephone is no longer innocent in either way. Customers like this do not complain, they do not expect "customer service," they simply search elsewhere for what they desire. Customers like this simply disappear. They leave no forwarding IP address.

Uncle Charley is aware of this. It is his own fault for revealing the secret of the tiles. Sure, she would have been corrupted anyway, a foreigner with a snazzy briefcase, a Chinese businessman, a cable layer from the coast, a girl her own age showing her the ropes; but to have accelerated the process was shameful.

But this is a feeling he must let go of. Uncle Charley has come to accept loss as a thing that must be submitted to, as something that cannot be fought off. Trying to save Gek-Lin would only lead to heartache. And besides, Gek-Lin is not Gek-Lin anymore, Gek-Lin is no longer the shocking, defiant girl that he fell in love with; Gek-Lin is just another future prostitute.

* * *

It is 3:05 P.M. and Xerxes is late. He had something important to do at work, he will say, although that excuse is thin since Sara knows that he no longer works. No, Sara is his therapist, he will simply tell her that he was playing his game.

People are everywhere. Leather-skinned men wearing tight Wranglers, plaid shirts with snaps instead of buttons, and Stetsons. Leather-skinned women with bleached hair and perms, eggplant-like in their purple blouses with matching purple sweatpants.

As Xerxes walks the three blocks towards Rest Stop's plaza, as he passes antique shops and gunsmiths, he does not see these people. Perhaps, Xerxes is a snob. Perhaps, he is just preoccupied. Perhaps, it is just the state of things. For these people don't see him either, or each other for that matter, they see crystal necklaces and hematite bookends.

By now, Xerxes is half an hour late. He wonders if Sara has gotten bored waiting for him, if she has wandered out into the grid of makeshift booths carefully laid out by Rest Stop's Art Fair officials, each artist given a ten-by-ten-foot plot of land on the manicured lawn in front of the old Rest Stop courthouse.

Xerxes weaves his way through the Minotaur's maze of booths, avoiding necklaces of silver and turquoise. He makes his way towards the gazebo.

When he arrives, he stands beneath it like a suitor. Sara is there, leaning over the white balustrade. She is wearing a black dress and black pumps. She is night amidst a world of day. She is a welcome tragedy in a world of comedy. She is an anomaly in a Monet painting, the one face looking at the painter. Her skin has not been tanned and tamed by the glare of an Arizona sun. It is white and innocent and altogether un-American. For Xerxes, Sara has finally materialized. He pulls a digital camera from out of his backpack. He points. He shoots. She doesn't seem to notice.

Sara, meanwhile, is psychoanalyzing the crowd. She watches an overweight woman bury her mouth in a waffle cone stuffed with a triple scoop of chocolate, chocolate fudge ice cream, while her skinny, younger husband walks with one arm around her. When Xerxes calls to her, she notices that the face beaming at her from below is unusually sunny, but not much else.

"Hi!" she shouts. She sees no need to point out that he is late. The day is cool, yet lazy, and she's still spacey from the lingering effects of her morning joint. "Come on up."

"No, you come down. I'm ready for my art as therapy class."

Sara hopes he's being playful and not serious. "OK," she says. She crosses the gazebo and walks down the steps. When she reaches the bottom, Xerxes takes her hand, mischievously, and presses it to his lips. "Good afternoon, madam," he says.

For some reason this gesture seems natural to Sara, as if this was a game they played all the time, "and good afternoon to you, good sir. To what do I owe the honor of having my hand kissed?"

"You looked so lovely, there, on the gazebo."

"Are you flirting with me, Mr. Meticula?"

"I do believe I was, Ms. Bronstein."

"Answer me something, Mr. Meticula. You seemed reluctant before to meet me here, and now you are flirting with me quite desperately, why the change?"

"Ah but Ms. Bronstein, you misread me; I was not reluctant at all, I was merely a bit preoccupied. You will forgive me?"

"I will let it pass. One more question, Mr. Meticula, why are we speaking in English accents today?"

"I don't know, Ms. Bronstein; this scene today, it strikes me as very English: you, there on the gazebo; the other people, milling about on a manicured lawn. It's very Monet, don't you think?"

Xerxes takes Sara's arm. Xerxes is underdressed in his *Cocoa Puffs* T-shirt, a pair of shorts, and Birkenstocks. Sara is overdressed in a black dress and black pumps. They are an odd pair walking through the makeshift aisles of the Rest Stop Art Fair, arm in arm; they look misplaced, two people yanked out of Greenwich Village and set down in the middle of Arizona. And yet they do the same things the locals do. They eat corn dogs dipped in mustard and pick cotton candy off a paper cone. They enter the booths to look at the paintings and sculptures.

Xerxes and Sara spend the afternoon together, in this manner, walking between aisles, sitting on the courthouse steps. The conversation is light and whimsical. The day turns, the shadows grow longer and the breeze stronger. The artists and vendors begin taking down their flimsy tents. Eventually, they sense that it is time to go. Sara would like to have him over, she'd like to pick up some spinach and pecans and feta cheese and make him a Greek salad. Xerxes is thinking similar thoughts, but he has another date tonight, a date in The Realm. Their English theme has continued throughout the afternoon. Xerxes says, "What a glorious day it has been, Ms. Bronstein!"

"Yes, such a shame to retire so early," says Sara.

"Ah, but the hearth calls. Perhaps another time, Ms. Bronstein?"

Sara is a little surprised that Xerxes didn't pick up the hint. "Perhaps," she replies. "May I be so bold as to ask, Mr. Meticula, what you intend to do with your evening?"

Although he had planned to tell her the truth about how he planned to spend his evening, he is suddenly not as keen to be honest and open. His attitude towards Sara has taken a precipitous turn. Real Life, the killer of many a kingdom and province, is rearing its ugly head. Xerxes has no intention of missing the party that sKyLaR has scheduled for this evening. "Alas, I must work tonight, my dear."

"Work? And what is it that you work on so late into the night? You know that Internet ventures are out of vogue."

Xerxes thinks the accents are getting old. "I'm wrapping up loose ends with financiers," he says, lying. "Here's what I tell them. *No, we don't have any money left. Yes, you heard me right. There's no money.*"

"Sounds painful."

"It is. I like to do it late at night, via e-mail, that way I don't have to deal with them on the phone."

"Well, I'd like to do this again some time if you're interested."

"I would, too. Maybe, next Sunday."

"Sure, next Sunday; you should come over to my place. I've rented out this old miner's cabin. It's very turn-of-the-century."

"Wow, how very *moderne* of you."

"Kind of ironic how the vintage has become so *moderne*, isn't it?"

"Yes, it is Ms. Bronstein. Yes, it is."

"It's a date, then?" She interjects the word "date" on purpose. She wants him to know what is at stake.

Xerxes, on the other hand, stumbles. He manages this, weakly: "Sure, OK, it's a date."

★ ★ ★

Xerxes is back on his laptop, at the appointed hour, in the appointed place. He's waiting for the invitation, waiting for sKyLaR to show up and invite him to a conference room. Though he is physically there, in front of his screen, he is mentally somewhere else. The place he has gone, mentally, is a sofa in some SoHo loft, a place he has never been, a place he isn't likely to ever go. Sara, looking far more streamlined and professional than he has ever seen her, is addressing him: "Before we get started I need to make something clear. You're not my official patient and I'm not your therapist, we're just play-acting. Is this clear?"

"Yes."

"And you can't hold me liable for anything that happens here, because this is not a real therapy session, right."

"OK."

"That would be a yes, correct?"

"Yes."

"OK, so let's start. Why don't you take off your shoes and lay on the couch."

"Really? You actually want me to lay on the couch? I thought that was just something they did in the movies."

"It is, but since this isn't real therapy, since it's fake therapy, we're going to do it the fake way."

"I'll buy that." In his daydream, Xerxes takes off his shoes.

"Are you comfortable now?"

"Yes."

"OK. I want you tell me about your best friend, Zahn."

"Zahn? Aren't you going to give me one of those Rorschachs or something? Or ask me what my first memory is? Or my mother, isn't there some Oedipal complex you're supposed to be looking for? Why start with Zahn?"

"I don't know. I just have a hunch."

"A hunch? What is this, detective work? Aren't there rules to follow? Where's your Freud or Jung or Skinner manual?"

"Do you want to continue?"

"Yeah, Jesus, don't be so touchy. I thought this was supposed to be fake."

"Just because it's fake doesn't mean you get to be an ass. You said you wanted therapy and because I'm your friend and because we both know there isn't anyone out here for you to talk to, I said I'd try this. Now stop with the bullshit and talk to me."

"You're good."

"Seriously, though, let's try to stop with the tone. Let it out. Your business partner, he fucked you over, right? You must be totally pissed off."

"Not really. It's Zahn, I know Zahn, I should have read the signs."

"You should have read that he would leave you in the dark about the finances of your own company and then go off and sleep with your girlfriend?

191

Why is the impetus on you to act? He was the one with the knowledge. You couldn't read his mind."

"Zahn and I communicated nonverbally. We expected that from each other. That's the way our friendship is."

"Why can't you be mad at him?"

"I am mad at him."

"No you're not, you're making excuses for him, acting like it's your fault, instead of his."

"But what good does it do to blame him? I've known the guy's limitations his whole life. All the signs were there. It's like a chess match, all I had to do was look at the board and I would have known exactly what moves he was going to make. But I didn't. I didn't even fucking look at the board."

"But why should you? Why should you have to spend all your time looking at the board?"

"Can I change the subject here? As the patient am I allowed to change the subject?"

"That depends."

"On what?"

"On whether or not your change in subject is going to involve avoidance and sarcasm, or turn to something truthful and revealing."

"Oh it's definitely the latter."

"What then?"

"Well, I'm really turned on."

"I can see that, Mr. Meticula."

"And the way you're being right now, so professional and formal, and the way you pronounce my last name, drawing out every syllable, so that it sounds sort of dark and dangerous, like, like Dracula, it's giving me a raging hard-on."

"There's no need to be so graphic, Mr. Meticula."

"I'm sorry, I thought that was the point of therapy, to let it all out."

"It is."

"So why can't I be graphic?"

"You can."

"So I can go on?"

"Sure."

"Well, I love the Bettie Page hair, the straight, clipped bangs, the jet black dye job. Your hair reminds me of the hair of this woman, Chase, whose pictures are posted all over the bondage newsgroups, whose hands are always tied above her head, and who is always being gagged in some way. Although the tied hands, and the gag, and whatever else is being done to her, is a total turn on, it's not the centerpiece, it's not the crème de la crème, of Chase. The crème de la crème is her pussy. It's beautiful, her pussy; it's been shaved so that it's just a razor-thin patch of fur. In the photographs of Chase, whatever else is being done to her—nipple clamps, electrocution, whatever—her pussy never gets touched, it's always just there, pristine, unblemished, blaring. So yeah, your hair reminds me of this bondage queen, but the rest of you, it doesn't; the wildness is all wound up in this small package, this petite little five-foot-two frame, and it's really hard to get at it, your wildness, because it's so densely compacted, you're like a supernova that hasn't exploded yet, you're—"

"That's good, Mr. Meticula, that's good."

"You want me to stop?"

"No, I mean, it was good, what you did. You're free-associating. That's good."

"So I can go on?"

"Yes."

"Actually, I think I'm going to change gears again. In fact, if you don't mind, I'd like to suggest, since this is fake therapy, that we do a little role reversal, that I ask you some questions, and you answer them."

"OK, if it leads us somewhere."

"Oh, it will."

"Go on."

"Well, since this is fake therapy and not real therapy, and since fantasy is an antonym of fake, I was wondering if we could change this fake therapy session into a fantasy therapy session, where you, Dr. Sara Bronstein, the alluring, young therapist, can no longer contain yourself from the charms of the downtrodden, self-deprecating young patient, and so, in a wild-eyed dash, you fling your glasses across the table, get up out of your high-backed executive chair, throw yourself onto the plush red leather of the therapeutic divan, where you, unabashed, unzip the fly of the young patient, a fly that you have been watching rise for the entire session, a fly that is so big and blatant and tent-like that you've imagined Barnum and Bailey, a circus full of acrobats and animals protected under its length and girth; where you release the beast, let loose the flea beneath the fly, and in a moment too rife with desperation to allow for the removal of clothing, you push aside a moist panty, and allow the elephant within."

*   *   *

Xerxes is startled by the magnitude of it, the fullness of his fantasy; the come jets all the way up to the N on his *Uncle Jeffrey* T-shirt. His daydream had taken an unusual turn; his days of wet dreaming have long since past. This isn't to say that masturbation isn't a normal, perhaps even daily event for Xerxes, but he rarely came to his own fantasies. Like most men, it was the visual that stimulated him—shots of lips, breasts, and vaginas—not some imaginary audiotape playing in his head.

It is hard not to think that vivid daydreams, just like vivid night dreams, symbolize something, and Xerxes knows that his dream is symbolic. The meaning of the dream, to Xerxes, beyond the rather obvious infatuation with Sara, was that until he dealt with his emotional duress he couldn't have the things that he wanted. He wants Sara, but before he can have her, he has to get the monkey off his back.

And what is the monkey? The monkey is this goddamned game. It is the fact that, whenever he thought that now was the time to pick up the phone and call California, or sit down with his parents and unload, or have a heart to heart with Gabriella, or even to share a couple beers and a spleaf with Sara, he instead slunk down into his self-made dungeon, turned on his computer, and entered The Realm.

As Xerxes thinks these downcast thoughts, the first message appears on his screen. He's had the Messenger on for the last fifteen minutes in anticipation of this, but had almost forgotten that it was actually scheduled to happen. The message is:

sKyLaR: *wElCoMe To My PlEaSuRe PaLaCe. YoU aRe MoSt UnFaShIoNaBlY eArLy, YoUr HiGhNeSs. I aM sUrPrIsEd tHaT yOu DiD nOt WaIt To MaKe A mOrE gRaNd ApPeAr-AnCe. PeRhApS yOu WoUlD lIkE tO eNtEr My PrIvAtE cHaMbErS fOr SoMe PrE-pArTy HoRs D'oEuVrEs.*

It is hard to explain exactly what happens to a gamer, how removed from themselves they become. There are wives who can explain this, how nothing, absolutely nothing, can pull them away from that evil, paste-colored box. Simple questions, not to mention demands, are responded to with in-human grunts and growls; gamers defend their monitors like dogs protecting their masters. Xerxes goes into this mode, is in this mode, has already written,

> **Peace_Love:** *Dearest sKyLaR, to be sure, rumors of their queen retiring to the inner chambers of your pleasure palace would cause a riot amongst the peasants. I would, however, quite enjoy a cup of tea in the main parlor, and a pleasant chat about something other than these infernal wars.*

when Mike's voice comes through the house's intercom system. The voice is Godlike and distant, "Xerxes, come up here. Zahn's on the phone."

There are multiple reasons why Xerxes does not want to respond to this: for starters, there is come on his shirt; and for seconds, he doesn't want to deal with the apologizing that Zahn is bound to do and the forgiving that he is bound to follow with; but the main reason that Xerxes doesn't want to get off his bed and talk to Zahn is because he is the Queen, and he's attending a gathering of the Queen's best warlords and wizards, and he does not want to be called off by some Real Life duty.

> **sKyLaR:** *bUt Of CoUrSe, YoU dO hAvE yOuR iMaGe To AtTeNd To. BuT wOn'T yOu At LeAsT iNdUlGe In A tOuCh Of AbSiNtHe? It HaS bEeN fLaVoReD wItH wIsDoM pOwDeR bY tHe FiNeSt AmOnGsT oUr ClErIcS, aNd In ThE mIdSt Of SuCh TrOuBlEd TiMeS, ThE qUeEn CoUlD cErTaInLy UsE a BiT oF aDdED bRaInPoWeR.*

"Are you coming?"

> **Peace_Love:** *Ah well, if your clerics are so good, perhaps you could color your absinthe the sienna of tea, and render it odorless so that those less worldly amongst our ministers would not be awakened to our folly.*

> **sKyLaR:** *aS yOu WiSh, m'LaDy. YoU pLeAsE mE wItH yOuR iNdUlGeNcE. LeT uS tHeN rE-tIrE tO tHe PaRlOr?*

> **Peace_Love:** *Let's.*

———

Mike pushes the lever to his La-Z-Boy down so that he is upright, then reaches over to the TV tray where his cane lies. He tries to get up, his left hand on the arm of the recliner, his right on the handle of the cane. He tries once—fails. He tries again—fails. He tries a third time—succeeds. His joints ache from the exertion and his breathing has increased. "Hold on," he says to Zahn, "I'm going downstairs to get him."

*You have received an invitation to enter the conference room tHe MaIn PaRlOr from **sKy-LaR.** Will you accept? Y/N*

Peace_Love: *Y*

sKyLaR: *hEllo.*

Peace_Love: *Hello.*

sKyLaR: *sHaLl We SpEaK fRaNkLy FoR oNcE?*

Peace_Love: *Sure.*

sKyLaR: *wHeRe ArE yOu FrOm?*

Peace_Love: *Arizona. You?*

sKyLaR: *aNtArCtIcA.*

Peace_Love: *8P*

sKyLaR: *nO rEaLlY. i'M lIvInG iN aNtArCtIcA rIgHt NoW, aT tHe SoUtH pOlE.*

Peace_Love: *Uh-huh.*

sKyLaR: *sErIoUsLy. ChEcK oUt ThE sOuTh PoLe WeBsItE aT wWw.NsF.oRg. I'm ThE gUy ThAt LoOkS lIkE vInCeNt GaLlO iN bUffFaLo 66 WiTh A yElLoW pEnGuIn On My HeAd.*

Peace_Love: *Not good enough.*

sKyLaR: *oK. dO tHiS. lOg On To WwW.nSf.OrG aNd ChEcK oUt My PhOtO uNdEr PeR-sOnNeL pRoFiLeS.*

sKyLaR: *gOt It?*

Peace_Love: *Just a sec.*

Peace_Love: *Got it.*

sKyLaR: *oK. nOw ThErE's A lInK oN tHe LeFt-HaNd MeNu BaR—iT rEaDs WeBcAmS. cllcK oN tHaT.*

Peace_Love: *OK. There.*

sKyLaR: *sEe ThE cHeMiStRy ViAl In ThE uPpEr RiGhT-hAnD cOrNeR. rIgHt NeXt To ThAt Is A lInK tHaT rEaDs BiOmEd. CllcK tHeRe.*

Peace_Love: *All right.*

sKyLaR: *tHaT's Me. I'm MaKiNg BuNnY eArS bEhInD mY hEaD. nOw, I'm FllpPiNg YoU oFf.*

Peace_Love: *Groovy.*

sKyLaR: *bElIeVe Me?*

Peace_Love: *Go get me some snow.*

sKyLaR: *hMmMmMmM . . . iT's NeGaTiVe 93 OuT tHeRe . . . I'lL nEeD tO gEt DrEsSeD . . . wIlL tAkE mE a WhIlE.*

Peace_Love: *Later then. When we're done.*

sKyLaR: *k*

Raven has requested entrance into the conference room: tHe ChAmBeR bEhInD tHe DrAwBrIdGe. Do you give permission to enter? Y/N

sKyLaR: y

Raven: Greetings and salutations

sKyLaR: hEILo.

★   ★   ★

Step by careful step, Mike Meticula makes his way down the stairs.

★   ★   ★

sKyLaR: wElCoMe To My PlEaSuRe PaLaCe, O dArK oNe. MaY oNe Of ThE sErVaNtS tAkE yOuR cOaT?

* **Raven** hands coat to servant, says nothing, looks forlorn.

sKyLaR: tHe QuEeN aWaItS uS iN tHe MaIn PaRlOr

Raven has received an invitation to enter the conference room: tHe MaIn PaRlOr from sKyLaR. Will you accept? Y/N

Lord_BonZ has requested entrance into the conference room: tHe ChAmBeR bEhInD tHe DrAwBrIdGe. Do you give permission to enter? Y/N

sKyLaR: hOlD oN lEt'S wAiT fOr LoRd BoNz

* **Raven** quakes at the coming of death.

Mike makes his way through the game room, past the pool table, past the painting of Xerxes, into the corridor that leads to the back bedrooms.

★   ★   ★

Uncle Charley is surprised to see

Lord BonZ has requested entrance into the conference room: tHe ChAmBeR bEhInD tHe DrAwBrIdGe. Do you give permission to enter? Y/N

on his monitor. Gek-Lin has always relied upon Uncle Charley to do her speaking for her while playing the game. He has enjoyed the misspellings, the creation of Lord BonZ's character. He wonders how Gek-Lin will do this. She's learned a stunted English from an unusual array of sources: Charley's modest collection of English literature; paperback romances filched from tourists; correspondence between players in The Realm; every Web site there is devoted to The Realm; some random Web surfing; emoticon studded and acronym splotched IM messages to God knows who; and, more recently, through her fraternizations with her soon-to-be fellow Thai whores. (And possibly, since Charley has been a little loose on the reins, their Johns.) Uncle Charley wonders what Gek-Lin's IM voice will be.

* * *

sKyLaR: Y

sKyLaR: wElCoMe To My PlEaSuRe PaLaCe, LoRd BoNz, YoU lOoK dEaD bEaT. ;) wHy DoN't YoU rEtIrE wItH rAvEn AnD i To ThE mAiN pArLoR.

Lord_BonZ has received an invitation to enter the conference room: tHe MaIn PaRlOr from sKyLaR. Will you accept? Y/N

Lord_BonZ: ?

Raven: Push the Y button to get in the conference room.

Lord_BonZ: y

* * *

When Mike opens the door his son greets him with a full frontal, his cock at half-mast. Xerxes has one leg in a pair of boxers and is hopping around trying to get the second leg in. "Jesus fucking Christ," Mike says.

Xerxes gets the leg in and pulls his boxers up. "I told you to hold on a minute."

"Well, I didn't think you'd be—"

"Where's the phone?"

"I left it upstairs."

"And you left it upstairs because?"

Mike goes unusually cynical. "I left it upstairs because I thought my lazy ass son could go upstairs and get the phone himself."

"Look, I'll get the phone, just give me a second."

"All right."

★　★　★

Lord_BonZ has entered the conference room: tHe MaIn PaRlOr.

Raven has entered the conference room: tHe MaIn PaRlOr.

Lord_BonZ: hello

Raven: Hello.

sKyLaR pLeAsE mAkE yOuRsElVeS cOmFoRtAbLe In OnE oF mY mOsT pLeAsUraBlE aRmChAiRs. wOuLd EiThEr Of YoU tWo GeNtLeMeN cArE fOr A cOcKtAiL?

Raven: Thank you my dear sKyLaR, but I do not partake of such pleasures.

Lord_BonZ: ?

Raven: I don't think our Lord BonZ is a native English speaker, perhaps we should speak more simply.

sKyLaR r U tHeRe, YoUr HiGhNeSs?

Peace_Love: sec

Peace_Love: I hate RL

Peace_Love: BBIAF

★ ★ ★

Xerxes, still wearing only his boxers, whips past his father, who is resting, for the moment, against the side of the pool table in the family room. He zips up the stairs, taking them two at a time; he runs through the living room, into the kitchen, and picks up the phone, not the one that Mike was using, because this would take some searching, since he didn't bother to ask Mike where he had put the phone down; he returns with the phone, a phone that has a green dot on it, a dot that Melissa has placed on the phone to identify which cradle the phone belongs to, since both her husband and son have a penchant for picking up phones and not returning them to their proper cradles. Xerxes brushes past his father, who is now in the stairwell, taking one stair at a time, in his shuffling, club-footed way; he brushes past his father, wordlessly, takes a leap down to the bottom of the stairwell, sprints across the "family room" into his room and into his own bed, where his laptop, glowing, awaits him.

★ ★ ★

Lord_BonZ: wtf

sKyLaR: iT aPpEaRs ThAt HeR hIgHnEsS hAs BeEn BrEiFlY dEtAiNeD.

sKyLaR: wHeRe ArE u 2 fRoM?

Raven: England

Lord_BonZ: thailand

sKyLaR: BoNz, YoU aRe ReAlLy FrOm ThAiLaNd?

Lord_BonZ: don't understand

sKyLaR: fRoM tHallAnD?

Raven: Skylar, can you stop typing with one letter capitalized and one letter not? I am having trouble reading it.

sKyLaR: sEc

sKyLaR: *k, back to normal. I created a Word macro so I could do that.*

Lord_BonZ: *i LiKe ThIs BeTtEr*

Raven: *Where are you from?*

sKyLaR: *I was born in Norway, but I have dual citizenship in the U.S. I'm living in Antarctica now.*

Lord_BonZ: *?*

Raven: *Antarctica? Really?*

sKyLaR: *Born Norway. Home in U.S. Live in Antarctica. Understand?*

sKyLaR: *Do you want to see me sitting at my desk in Antarctica? I promised the queen I would get her some snow.*

Raven: *Yes*

Lord_BonZ: *y*

sKyLaR: *All right. Go to your browser window and type www.asf.org. That's the South Pole site.*

sKyLaR: *There?*

Raven: *Yes*

Lord_BonZ: *n*

Lord_BonZ: *computer slow*

sKyLaR: *Now?*

Lord_BonZ: *n*

★   ★   ★

Gek-Lin gets up from her table, littered with ancient monitors lighting up or phan faces. She's annoyed. She doesn't understand what they're saying but she wants to be a part of the discussion. She paces the crowded aisles.

★   ★   ★

sKyLaR: *Well, that's no fun, I didn't mean to scare him off.*

Raven: *Go on though, I want to see this.*

sKyLaR: *k*

sKyLaR: *There's a link on the left-hand menu bar—it reads webcams. Click on that. There are links to different webcams on the page that comes up. Click the one that looks like a chemistry vial. Are you with me?*

Raven: *Yes.*

sKyLaR: *OK. Now in 10 seconds*

Peace_Love: *BAK*

sKyLaR: *Perfect timing, I was just going to go out and get your snow.*

Raven: *What does BAK mean?*

Peace_Love: *What happened to the CaPiTaL lEtTeRs, sKyLaR?*

★   ★   ★

"Xerxes, here."
    "Dude."
    "I'm in the middle of something, Zahn, can I call you back?"
    "Uh, no, actually you can't."

★   ★   ★

Peace_Love: Back at keyboard.

sKyLaR: Raven was having trouble reading them.

Peace_Love: I liked It ThOuGh.

★   ★   ★

"Xerx, I know you're pissed."
  "FYI Zahn, I'm not at all pissed. I just want to be left the fuck alone."

★   ★   ★

Raven: I apologize if I have spoiled your fun.

Peace_Love: nbd

sKyLaR: So would you like me to bear to you the gift of snow, your highness?

Peace_Love: Of course. I told you I want proof. Now you have to obey me, otherwise we won't know that you're not just describing something you pre-recorded.

sKyLaR: Fair enough.

★   ★   ★

"There's shit going on, Xerxes."
  "Uh-huh."

★   ★   ★

Peace_Love: k, well why don't you tell us what you're going to do, and then go out and do it.

sKyLaR: all right, here's what you're going to see. I'm going to get up from my keyboard and turn my back to the camera. You'll see my red parka, the one with the South Pole logo on it. The logo is very cool. If you zoom in on it you can see that it reads Canada Snow Goose, Antarctic program. I'll stand there for a minute, just so you can see this and then I'll start walking, and will leave the camera view. I won't be gone long, there's lots of snow out *sKyLaR:* there. When I come back I'm going to have some snow in one of my gloves. It's not going to be a whole lot of snow. The snow out here isn't the wet slushy stuff that we get in New York City. It doesn't stick, so I won't be able to mush it up into a ball. It's dry snow. It's kind of grainy, almost like sand. It's that way because it's so dry out here. You don't think of Antarctica like this, but Antarctica is the world's

★   ★   ★

"Dude, what are you doing? Are you on the computer or something?"

"Uh-huh."

"Look man, I need your full attention. You're like a fucking sixteen-year-old sometimes—can't you get off that thing for a minute?"

"It's an important Web conference. I'm trying to save our business. You remember our business, right?"

"Bullshit. You're not on a fucking Web conference. Look, man. I'm going to tell it like it is for once, all right. You're going to hear this, because you need to hear it. You haven't done a damn thing about the business since the day you fucking vanished into thin air. You're playing one of those games, I can hear your goddamn laptop beeping every five seconds. You're like a hamster in one of those pinwheel things, just spinning around fucking mindlessly. What is it this time, man, Final Fantasy 4 or Quake 6, or goddamn Evercrack 94? Listen to what I'm telling you, dude. Get your head in the real game, all right?"

★   ★   ★

sKyLaR: driest desert. You should see what our skin does out here. If you get a cut or something it doesn't even heal, it just cracks and blisters. It's weird. I think it's the thing that is the most difficult for me. It's not the cold or the absolute dark or the lack of oxygen or the isolation that bothers me when I'm feeling sick of being down here. The worst part is the dryness. My skin feels wrinkled and old, really old. It's tight on my bones, like it's a

sKyLaR: wetsuit instead of my own skin. I feel sometimes like I'm seventy, instead of twenty-six, and that gets me, because it reminds me of my own mortality, how quickly everything passes, how, if I don't do the things I want to do right now, I might never get around to doing them. And out here in Antarctica, despite how romantic it seems to be here. You miss everything. I mean, my wife, my wife who lives out here with me, is missing her own

sKyLaR: mother's death.

* * *

At the words "Evercrack 94" Xerxes had let the phone drop from where he had perched it between his ear and the upper part of his shoulder to the mattress of his bed. He really didn't need to listen to a Zahn rant at this point in time.

With the phone down, Xerxes is reading sKyLaR's words in something akin to rapture. He is reading the words of this strange man from Antarctica, a man who he feels a kinship with. Xerxes knows this feeling, this feeling of losing time that sKyLaR speaks of. It haunts him everyday. It haunts everyone, Xerxes supposes, everyday.

* * *

sKyLaR: Her mother is dying and we're stuck out here on this unending white plain. Shit. I'm sorry. I'm going off on a tangent. It's strange, talking like this to people thousands and thousands of miles away. I feel like I'm in that David Bowie song, Major Tom, like I'm dying out here and no one is listening. You know, "Can you hear me, Major Tom?" "Can you here me, Major Tom?" I'm sorry. I'm just talking. I haven't got much sleep lately. I have insomnia.

sKyLaR: It's a symptom of a syndrome you get out here called chronic hypoxia. It is 3 A.M. right now, in fact, and as far as I can tell, I'm the only person within a 500-mile radius who is awake right now. Do you know how eerie that is? How scary? Hello. Are you all still out there? Enough blogging. You can do this online you know, just speak your mind. There's no danger in it really. I'm going to go away from the keyboard now, show

sKyLaR: you my logo and fade out. Ready?

Raven: Ready.

Peace_Love: And may Godspeed be with you.

* * *

The voice coming out of the receiver is soothing to Xerxes. "You're missing the real game, Xerxes. And you need to get your head in it and figure out what the hell you're going to do. You're not a goddamn victim, dude, you're every bit a part of this as I am." It is a game they've played a million times over. Zahn rants; Xerxes listens. Zahn is just background noise now. Xerxes is more interested in the words coming across his screen than the words coming through the telephone receiver.

* * *

Gek-Lin is standing behind Uncle Charley. She watches snow seep between the fingers of a single, gloved hand. Dietrich holds his hand there, for a moment, in front of the camera, then spreads the fingers of his glove apart. The snow falls from his glove like sand falling through an hourglass.

* * *

"There's something you need to know, Xerxes, and I wish I didn't have to tell you in this way, but I've got to say it before you hang up the phone on me. Dixie, we're, me and her, we're, getting married."

* * *

Uncle Charley, sensing Gek-Lin behind him, exits Dietrich's streaming video. When he does so, a naked boy washing his hair fills his screen.

* * *

sKyLaR: Your snow, m'lady.

* *Peace_Love* has disconnected from the server.

sKyLaR: M'lady?

* *Raven* has disconnected from the server.

sKyLaR: Still there?

sKyLaR: Shit, I'm losing my satellite feed.

* *sKyLaR* has disconnected from the server.

* * *

Uncle Charley presses the power button. His computer immediately flashes to black. He turns to Gek-Lin. "I'm Raven," he says.

★ ★ ★

* **Lord_BonZ** *has disconnected from the server.*

25. EVERY OTHER KINGDOM IS YOUR ENEMY.

THE TWO-HEADED BOY IS QUESTIONING whether he should do what he is about to do. The Queen Peace & Love but Mostly Love, attacking with such unusual methods, is becoming a threat. Her success against *Amphibious* has bumped *Paradigm Shift* to the #2 spot, just a few thousand points of net worth behind *Carrot Flowers*. Should *Paradigm Shift* continue to find kingdoms to attack as hapless as *Amphibious* they could easily usurp the lead.

He can't let this happen. He has to do something about it. And yet, as he looks on his screen at the woman he created, the one with the high cheek-bones, the full lips, the thin nose, the large breasts; as he looks at her, he can't help but feel the betrayal. After all, this is the type of woman who fills his dreams, the potential soul mate who can play the game as well as he, the woman with whom he can wrestle with, eternally, in the mental world that is The Realm.

But one does not keep the #1 spot by being nice. One must be ruthless and forever vigilant of the up-and-comers. One must destroy with brute force when possible, and when impossible, as in this case, one must use other means. Tres must set his emotions aside.

The Two-Headed Boy is clicking his way through his lists: lists of all the provinces and kingdoms he has attacked; lists of all the provinces and kingdoms that have attacked him; lists of which provinces and kingdoms have attacked which other provinces and kingdoms; and lists of alliances, both formal and informal. In addition to this list of connections, the Two-Headed Boy logs all his communications, keeps them all in a database for easy retrieval.

Using his lists and communication logs, the Two-Headed Boy sends out hundreds of messages every day. Quick notes asking questions, probing for information:

Dear King Jax,

How is your war with the Shanghai Barbarians proceeding?

These notes rarely lead to anything useful, but the contact is important, for when the Two-Headed Boy needs something he has plenty of provinces to ask. And this week, he has something to ask.

To attack *Paradigm Shift* head on would be folly, a sure destruction of both parties, but if he could get someone else to fight his battle for him, if he could get a few other provinces to take potshots at them he could lower *Paradigm Shift's* standings on the leaderboards without them even being aware that he was the mastermind.

So this is what the Two-Headed Boy is going to do. He is going to give out free intel. He'll have his wizards run Crystal Balls and Crystal Eye spells on different provinces in *Paradigm Shift*, and pass this info onto other kingdoms.

It is an underhanded plan, and there will be some resistance to the idea from his contacts. After all, what will keep *Paradigm Shift* from attacking them back? But he will remind them that *Paradigm Shift* just fought a war, and that it will be difficult for them to retaliate, since they are land fat after the war with *Amphibious*; that is to say, they haven't had the time to train the troops necessary to defend the land they've obtained. What the Two-Headed Boy is proposing is ethically dubious, even in the chaos of The Realm, but the end of the age is approaching, and the heat is on. The Two-Headed Boy sends messages to the provinces in his kingdom that are wizards. The wizards run their spells. The Two-Headed Boy passes the intel on:

King Jax,

This province GurGle from 12:5 totally suicided on an attack. Check out this intel. There's a lot of land for the taking . . .

Results of Spy On Military for GurGle 12:5

Troops away for 9.63 days.

Troops at Home	Troops Away
0 Goblins	1,212 Goblins
2,293 Trolls	0 Trolls
0 Spearthrowers	2,169 Spearthrowers
263 War Horses	2,037 War Horses

Troops in Training	1	2	3	4	5	6	7	8	9	10
Goblins	0	0	0	0	0	0	0	0	0	0
Trolls	12	11	13	11	12	14	11	12	13	12
Spearthrowers	24	20	19	22	21	20	19	22	19	18

Signed, Two-Headed Boy

★ ★ ★

What bothers him isn't the revelation that his best friend is planning to marry his exgirlfriend, what bothers him is sKyLaR's falling sand—the falling sands of time moving on without him.

He doesn't call first. He simply whisks his keys off a hook by the door, puts on a T-shirt—a different, though equally soiled one than the one he was wearing earlier—a pair of shorts, a pair of white socks, and his Chuck Taylors. He changes his mind about the outfit when he's halfway into the family room, and returns. He opts for something dressier, something that smells of Tide instead of body odor.

Xerxes picks an orange bowling shirt out of his closet. The shirt has a patch over the pocket that says Dean and, on the back, a stitching of a bowling ball hitting pins. The word over the ball and pins reads *STRIKE!* He picks out a pair of pants from his closet, pants a shade darker than khaki, fashionable pants without pleats in the front. He even pulls out a pair of black dress shoes, shoes without laces, with a tall heel that makes him look taller and lankier than he actually is. Xerxes discards the previously worn clothes in a pile at his feet, puts on the new clothes, then makes his way to the bathroom, where he runs his fingers under the tap, then through his hair, tussling it so that it looks like he has a sort of organized bedhead (as opposed to his usual unorganized bedhead).

On the way out he is afraid that he will run into his father, who will surely have questions about what just transpired between him and Zahn. But Xerxes, taking the stairs as he always does, in twos, does not encounter his father, who has turned the volume up on the television, who is listening peaceably to Dan

Rather's discussion of suggested improvements in the safety features of NASCAR vehicles. Xerxes whips past his father's TV room, through the living room, past his mother who is whistling something-Hosanna while Windexing the marble countertops. He is through the garage and then in #8. He rolls down the window and a blast of cool mountain air, blowing out of the northwest, slaps icily against his ear and cheek. Some things change drastically; others not at all.

*   *   *

After leaving Xerxes and the lawn of the courthouse, Sara returns to her Sunday morning thing, although it is by no means still morning. She picks back up the crumpled *Times*, relights her joint, and lies back in her hammock. The sun sets behind a canopy of trees and the weather turns chilly, but Sara remains, lying beneath a flannel blanket and sipping coffee spiced up with a bit of Bailey's Irish Cream. She reads, through a pair of reading glasses, in the half-illumination of her porch light. In the paper, 3 Israelis were killed in a train station, 4 coworkers were killed by a security guard, and another mass grave was found in Serbia.

The night breeze is clean and she's enjoying its pine-wafted scent. As the time gets later, as the midnight hour comes and goes, Sara stays awake, reading less and less and smoking more and more. She has nothing to do until her anger management class next Wednesday, and can't think of any reason not to just lay there and increase her buzz.

It was while enjoying this buzz that Sara has a vision. In the shadows, standing at the makeshift gate leading to her backyard, she sees a figure. The figure standing at the barbed wire gate is dressed like he is heading out for Bowling League night (and the figure is definitely a man; she isn't sure how she knows this, but she is sure of it). He is pretending to knock on the gate. There is nothing to knock on, the makeshift gate being made out of barbed wire, so the figure is knocking on air. The figure then rings a pretend buzzer.

Sara thinks this is a vision, and since she thinks this, she doesn't say anything to Xerxes, who is standing there miming for her amusement. Xerxes takes it as a rebuff. "Hello?" he finally shouts, "Sara? Can I come in?"

Sara hadn't realized just how fat of a joint she had smoked, until she rubbed her eyes, and the figure, whose voice she recognizes as Xerxes's, is still there. She can't talk, so stoned is she, so she giggles.

Xerxes isn't sure how to take this. In his head, there hadn't been these kinds of complications—it was a simple formula: titillate girl; drink with girl; talk with girl; possibly, if he was fortunate, sleep with girl. He walked up to the gate, made Sara laugh, and then was invited in. He would tell Sara what Zahn had told him and be administered some sort of consolation; it would calm him like a sedative, and then he would move past the problem, and onto the more tangible concerns he had for his life in The Realm.

But now she's just sitting there, her head tilted so that she must be look-ing at him, not saying a word. He isn't sure what to do: whether to walk in uninvited or turn around and go home. He decides to walk in uninvited. He undoes each one of the clamps that holds each row of barbed wire to the string of barbed wire on the other side, then slips through the opening.

As Xerxes draws closer, Sara's giggles turn to out-and-out laughter. What's so funny is that she thought she was having a vision, but really Xerxes is real, and getting larger as he moves closer to her. A part of her, somewhere deep inside her non-stoned mind, knows this isn't really funny, but the fact that she is laughing at something that isn't really funny is really funny. This makes her laugh even harder. Her spleen hurts. By the time Xerxes reaches the hammock, the circles of laughter—the laughter on top of the laughter on top of the laugher that is making her spleen hurt—cause her to double up in her hammock. And the doubling up sends her sprawling, sprawling off the hammock into the dirt and pine needles below. Falling out of her hammock into a bed of pine needles is really funny, and it makes Sara laugh so hard that rivers of tears pour out of her eyes. This is funny too—of course.

Xerxes watches all this in something akin to disbelief. The closer he gets to Sara, the more she laughs. It is as if he were surrounded by some sort of magical laughter aura. What a great addition to The Realm, he thinks, a laughter ray that renders an opponent more and more helpless the closer you get to them. "What's so funny?" Xerxes asks.

Sara thinks about what's so funny, the fact that she thought Xerxes wasn't real, then she thinks about trying to explain this to Xerxes. The idea of her try-ing to explain something to Xerxes that isn't really funny is really funny and out comes a fresh burst of laughter. Sara is on her hands and knees below the hammock. She tries to wipe away the tears in her eyes with her hands. Her hands are dirty and she smudges dirt on her cheek. She also knocks off her glasses. The fact that she's wiped dirt on her face and knocked off her glasses, is, you guessed it, really funny.

This isn't the Sara that Xerxes is used to seeing. When he first met her, at

St. Francis, he had thought of her as a sophisticated New York psychiatrist, perhaps a little young and green, but definitely on her way to becoming the sort of all-knowing and slyly sexual shrink made popular in Woody Allen movies. This image of her was only slightly tainted by their encounter in the woods, her running from nonexistent bears. He had thought of this as a sort of glitch in the system, a momentary loss of sanity caused by an unfamiliar situation. But now that he's watching this, Sara wrapped in a flannel blanket underneath her hammock, locked in a fetal position and laughing hysterically, he has to wonder if his image of Sara as a somewhat elitist snob is a little off. "I'm sorry," Xerxes says. "Is this a bad time?"

The question sobers Sara up a little bit, although the image of a Xerxes action figure standing over her in his "Out for Bowling Night" shirt, asking, "Is this a bad time?" sends another half-laugh/half-squeal from her lips. She turns and sits up, then tries to stand. The flannel blanket catches her and she ends up back on her ass. Xerxes holds out a hand to help her up, but her hands are over her eyes, the fall had set her to sobbing, the kind of cry you get after laughing too hard.

"Can I help you up?" Xerxes asks, and this time she pulls herself together enough to hold out her hand, a muddy hand with a few pine needles embedded in it, which meets Xerxes's hand and transfers those items into his. Sara gets up.

"I'm sorry," Sara says, though just talking starts the giggling again.

"That's OK," Xerxes says. "It looks like you're having a good time."

"I think I'm a little stoned," says Sara.

The pieces are starting to fall in place for Xerxes. Why casual drug-users always assume that other people are not casual drug-users is one of humanity's great mysteries. "*That* explains it," says Xerxes. "Funny, I wouldn't have taken you for a stoner."

"I'm not, really, I just smoke a little to pass the time on Sundays."

"Gotcha."

"So, um, dare I ask what's brought you to my neck of the woods?"

"Would you like to go out for a drink?"

"Um, now?"

"Well, yeah."

"It's, like, one in the morning."

"Well, I didn't think we'd actually go out . . ."

"So you just decided to stop by, at one in the morning, and drink some scotch with me in my cabin."

"Well, sort of. I'd like to explain myself, but I think I need that drink before I can."

"Ah-ha. I'm starting to understand the mystery appearance. How 'bout if we just stay outside and smoke a bowl."

Xerxes is a little afraid that if he smokes pot in his mental state he'll end up crying. Alcohol might have the same effect, but he'd be much more numb to it. "Hmm. That's very tempting, but I'm not very communicative when I'm stoned, I'd rather have a drink."

"We can arrange for that, too."

"I'm sorry I just dropped in, I—"

"Hold on, we'll save the explaining until after the second drink."

Sara's fall from the hammock had sent the *Times* flying, and now the breeze is blowing pages of newsprint down the slope at the back of her lot. She unwraps herself from the flannel blanket, infested with scraps of wood that it will take hours to weed out, and throws it on the hammock. Xerxes is running around collecting the pages that had gone the farthest astray. She tries to help, but stoned as she is, she gets drawn into an article about a new restaurant on St. Mark's serving up a fusion of Latino and New American cuisine. She stands there lost and zombielike, reading the word habeñero three times before her brain clicks off *pepper*. Meanwhile, Xerxes scampers about behind her cabin, scratching himself up trying to get to loose scraps. For a moment her mind wanders from the article, considering whether to tell Xerxes that the fence behind the cabin is hard to see in the dark, and that it's electrically charged, but that's just for a moment, soon she's back to the article, *ha-beñ-er-o, ben-yay, Nero, haben*.

When Xerxes returns, his arms full of newspaper, she is still standing there, reading the same word, *habeñero*. It is always so wonderful when you get a first glimpse of a person's neurosis, when you break through their public front. Sara is standing there looking stiff and possessed, a little like in that Stephen King movie, *Carrie*, where Carrie, dripping with pig's blood that was poured on her as a prank, uses her telekinesis to burn down the high school gym at her prom and kill everyone inside.

Sara's black hair, always so gleaming and well-brushed, is stringy and tangled and full of gunk. She is still wearing all-black—except for the day they'd gone hiking it is the only thing he's ever seen her wear—but out in the woods, rather than looking sharp and sophisticated, it makes her look psychotic, like a prophetic Poe heroine awaiting a sure death. It's very Edward

Gorey: Sara standing shock-still, wearing a sleeveless black dress, black stockings, and black shoes with a gaudy silver buckle, holding up one sheet of a newspaper, while a few more sheets lay pooled around her ankles.

Xerxes knows he is getting a real treat today. There isn't anything that could keep him from going inside her cabin.

"You ready to go inside?"

Sara looks over the newspaper at Xerxes. She'd forgotten that he was here. "Yeah," she says, bending over and picking up both her ashtray and the packet of rolling papers scattered beneath the hammock. "Let's get you that drink."

★　★　★

The Two-Headed Boy has put his plan into effect. He's getting all kinds of messages that provinces have cut and pasted from their kingdom newspapers and sent to his mailbox:

King Jax, your troops have fought a brave battle and won. You have appropriated 83 acres of land from GurGle (12:5). Your army will return from the battlefield in 18 days. Earn 10 free acres of land by visiting our partner site, unlimitedfreecoupons.com.

The Two-Headed Boy feels a little guilty after reading all the damage reports, but The Realm is The Realm, and feelings have to be pushed aside. Besides, the natives have been getting restless; his war ministers had wanted to wage an all-out battle, and the only way to appease them was to come up with a plan to keep them on top without affording any losses.

Although his scheme is working—the attacks have knocked *Paradigm Shift* down from #2 to #4—the Two-Headed Boy, sitting below his array of computer monitors, browsing and blinking, can't help but wonder if his kingdom's deviousness wouldn't have some long-term negative effects. Tres tends to trust his intuition, and his intuition rarely went awry. What Tres is afraid of is this: what happens if the Queen finds out who was behind all these attacks, what would she do if she uncovered his conspiracy?

★　★　★

Xerxes is sitting in Sara's one-room cabin observing the odd combinations of furniture placed about her space—an aluminum media storage unit next to an antique possum-belly cabinet, a serving cart made out of galvanized steel next to a wood-burning stove, a round, ultramodern, bright yellow space heater named Max, made out of ABS plastic with chrome-coated zinc legs, next to an unused, terribly sooty, and quite clearly never-named fireplace, made out of rocks pulled out of the earth sometime around 1880.

Xerxes knows how her place got this way without her having to tell it. Sara drove her Ryder-full of Upper East Side furniture to Rest Stop, Arizona, thinking that it would spice up whatever ugly stucco apartment they'd rented her, only to find when she arrived that what they had rented her wasn't an apartment at all, but a semifurnished log cabin. *Oh my God, Gloria*, he could her voice on the phone to a friend back home, *it was built in the 19th century. They didn't have electricity here then. They burnt oil lamps*. He could see her perplexity at the sudden mismatch of ultra-chic and antique. The conclusion of this mismatch is now in front him. Sara had placed her furniture around the cabin like she was playing some sort of game with her surroundings, like through her furniture she was doing a side-by-side analysis of the differences between her past and her present.

However the room came to be, Xerxes likes it. He feels relaxed in it. From the moment he first sat down on her chaise lounge, a strange triangular thing with twisted rebar as backing, the words have been flowing out of him, as smooth and velvety as the whiskey and water in his glass. In other situations with Sara, he had either avoided inquiries into his personal life, or dumped truckloads of information all at once, but sitting here in Sara's strange museum he is able to speak of matters of the heart with the same combination of nonchalance and calculation that he is normally able to speak of matters of the head.

Xerxes sits on that chaise lounge, the upwardly extending ends of its rebar tipped with molded iron tempered to resemble sunflowers, and he tells her what happened, tells her how his best friend, Zahn, stole his girlfriend, Dixie. He delineates his own involvement at crucial junctures, how he missed what was happening, how his world became narrowed to a 10x14-inch computer screen. He states the facts as they occurred. It feels good the way he is saying it.

The room is soothing him. He imagines a fire in the unused, sooty fireplace. He imagines stories of the hunt. He is a little bit drunk and being drunk is loosening his tongue.

Sara, for her part, is just stoned. She is certainly not her usual analytical self, prying the patient with questions, digging deep. Mostly, she just watches Xerxes's gesticulations. He is one of those people who talks with his hands, punctuating sentences with open palms. Every once in a while she tunes back into the Xerxes channel, so she'll get the gist of his story.

The thing she is wondering, murkily, and she would ask him this if she weren't so stoned, is: why had he been so passive-aggressive? Yes, he had gotten screwed, but shouldn't he have done something about it: dumped Dixie on her ass—hell, fired her; lectured Zahn and gotten him back in line. I mean, he was the founder of a company. Aren't these guys supposed to be go-getters? Aren't they supposed to be raving lunatics when they don't get their way?

Sara couldn't figure out how a guy like Xerxes had gotten to the top to begin with. He wasn't one of those 8s on the enneagram, one of those asserters motivated by the need to be self-reliant and strong, men so blindly sure of themselves that they simply march over any of the cowering doubters who lie in their path.

Of course, maybe that was why he had been successful. Back when the whole Internet boom was starting there had been all that talk about how there was a new way of doing business. It had been exciting, and even good. Outsiders like Sara approved. All those crazy Californians were going to start businesses based on smarts rather than bullying.

And Xerxes was that; he was smart. As he sits there on her couch telling her his story she can see that. He could talk at great lengths about how everything had played out, and he was right, of course, his logic was impeccable. But what he didn't see was that while people wanted all those crazy Californians like him to succeed, they also wanted them to work at it, they wanted them to suffer a bit, and when they put on the squeeze, when they said, *no more money, show us some profit*, those Californians fell over faster than lined-up dominoes.

When everything went down, Xerxes had needed, both professionally and personally, to show some backbone. And he hadn't done that; instead he'd flown the coop.

The thing was, Sara really liked Xerxes. He was a rare bird. He had all the mannerisms of an engineer—absentmindedness, a complete lack of fashion sense, an inability to control the nervous twitchings of his hands and feet, colicky hair—and yet he was somehow more aware, less technical than his counterparts. Perhaps it was because he was so willing to point out his faults; Xerxes was one of the most self-deprecating people Sara had ever met. It was this quality that made him lovable. But still, he needed to do something, and until he did something it was never going to work.

It just comes out of her, after a half-hour of silence, in the middle of his rant. She has no idea how it will fit into the conversation. "You're a coward."

Xerxes stops midsentence. "Huh?"

"I said, you're a coward."

"What does that have to do with—"

"Everything that is happening to you is happening because you're a coward."

"Look, I came over here for a drink and a conversation. I—"

"Do you realize that being a coward is your only fault, the only thing standing in your way? Your friends, your family, most likely your employees, even I, and I've only known you for a few weeks, trust your intellect. They know this product that you came up with, and whatever product you might come up with in the future, was and will be very good. They believe in you. They want you succeed. They don't want to screw you over. But you're not giving them anything back. You're not fighting with them. People need to be fought with, convinced of things. You should be outraged at what Zahn and Dixie did to you."

"What do you think I've been sitting here telling you—"

"You're telling me, Xerxes. And even me you're telling the story to in your glib, matter-of-fact way, acting like it's half your fault and probably just fate and doesn't really matter anyway. Tell them, not me."

"I know, but—"

"But, but, but, but, but."

"Look, Zahn knows I'm pissed off. We've—"

"It's not about what Zahn knows; it sounds like everybody knows everything, but he needs to see it, not just know it, but see it."

"I don't give a shit about alleviating Zahn's guilt."

"Of course you don't, and you shouldn't, but you need to let out some of your own righteous anger, otherwise it's going to eat you alive, and you're going to spend all your time either in some fantasy world or boring your friends with unpleasant griping about how everybody's giving you the shaft."

"You're sounding like my shrink, again. I liked you better when you were rolling in the dirt."

Sara grins. She's been sitting in a beanbag, a yellow thing whose color matched the space heater. She'd pulled it out of the storage shed after getting Xerxes his first drink. She gets up from it. "Need a refresh?"

"Yeah."

Sara is deriving pleasure from getting Xerxes all riled up. She feels like some sort of medicine woman administering a terribly tasting tea made with bats' eyes whose dubious health benefits are offset by the nature in which the tea is administered—the medicine woman hands the tea to her victim with a wink and a smile.

Sara crosses the room to the kitchen part of the cabin where the wood-burning stove is. She takes a fresh glass from a shelf, a shelf that is a natural fixture in the cabin and is blackened, ostensibly from the hands of the miners who'd first tainted it. She takes a half-empty bottle of whiskey from the same shelf. She comes back over to Xerxes, placing both the glass and bottle on the end table that serves as a dumping ground for all of Sara's magazines and books, and then sits next to him resting primly on the thin section of the triangular couch. "You have another fault, too," she says.

Xerxes takes the bottle and fills her glass to its brim with whisky. He opts not to respond to the allegation until she explains further, shooting her a querulous look instead.

Sara answers his unspoken question. "You think too much," she says.

Xerxes fills his own glass. "I think too much, do I?"

"Yeah, you do."

Xerxes pours a glass for Sara. He twists the bottle so that the whiskey doesn't drip off the bottle's lip. "Can I kiss you?" he asks, still looking at the bottle, putting the cork on it and setting it back on the table next to his glass.

"Can I or may I?" Sara responds.

"May I."

"You may."

And that was how the evening's events began to cascade: a kiss; followed by full body contact; followed by much tussling of hair; followed by a discussion of how the chaise lounge with its barely padded triangular base and its ironwork was a very uncomfortable place to be doing what they were doing; followed by much embarrassment and giggling about this, that they were doing what they were doing, and that, like a couple of play-by-play announcers, they were discussing what they were doing; followed by the removal of Sara's bed sheets and goose-down comforter from her twin-sized bed; followed by the laying down of these materials on the floor by the unused fireplace; followed by the placement of the whiskey bottle in said fireplace; followed by the placement of twigs and pine cones around the whiskey bottle, as if they planned to burn it; followed by much laughter as to the ludicrousness of their creation; followed by the picking up of the whiskey bottle and the drinking of much whiskey; followed by Xerxes crossing over Sara to place the whiskey bottle back in the fireplace; followed by Sara pulling Xerxes down towards her, kissing his thick, somewhat girlish lips; followed by the unbuttoning of a bowling shirt; followed, eventually, after some confusion and discussion as to how best to accomplish this, by the raising of Sara's black dress up over her head; followed by the even more problematic removal of Sara's black, lacy, front-clipped, B-cup bra; followed by more embarrassment and giggling and play-by-play; followed by a touching moment where Xerxes looked at the body below him, at the black lace contrasting sharply with the white skin, at a milky, thinly muscled bicep over a dress of lycra, and commented on it, on how beautiful he found her; followed by what would, between strangers, be an uncomfortably long period of close eye contact; followed by acquiescence and lovemaking, by lovemaking beneath an odd combination of newly soldered ironwork sunflowers and rough-hewn wood beams; followed, some time in the early morning hours, by sleep—deep, cradled, comforting, sleep.

BOOK IV: THE DRAGON

RL TIME: SEPTEMBER 2000
REALM TIME: YR 13-16

Two-Headed Boy, with pulleys and weights
Creating a radio played just for two
in the parlor with a moon across her face
And through the music he sweetly displays
Silver speakers that sparkle all day
Made for his lover who's floating and choking with her hands across her face

—NEUTRAL MILK HOTEL, "TWO-HEADED BOY"

26. PREPARE TO BE BLINDSIDED.

KIN-DONG, although he has his fingers in many pies, although he's diversified in all the major commodities—Canadian oil, Brazilian timber, Thai women—made most of his money in the midnineties, when a maverick group of cable layers, a group distinctly different from the typical telecommunication suit and ties, a group from some sinister company called Syyntek, came into Bangkok asking just who they needed to talk to in order to lay both some cable and something finer than what was in the brothels they'd seen so far.

Kin-Dong's ears perked up when word made its way from his subordinates up the food chain. These guys were international; and these guys were speaking his language. They weren't pursuing the usual government channels, digging themselves into a grave of expensive favors and red tape. They had money and they didn't want to spend it on Imelda's thousands of shoes.

These guys weren't here to fuck around. They wanted to lay fiber-optic cable. And while they were at it they wanted virgins, or at least girls who should still be virgins, and they wanted to do them in ways that their wives back home would never approve of.

Kin-Dong saw this confluence better than any of his peers. The older guys in the industry, the guys running mah-jongg games and collecting tithes from their whores, worked foreigners at a distance. They didn't engage them, didn't try to figure out a way to merge their business needs with their other needs.

Kin-Dong saw it, and because he saw it he became one of the most powerful, and feared, men in Thailand. The simple exchange of dollars for women was nothing. What Kin-Dong wanted were contracts, contracts for laying this fiber-optic cable that was supposed to change the world.

Kin-Dong, he got these contracts. First, he got a southern route, and then, because they were having so much fun, because Bangkok was such a sex mecca, and because Kin-Dong was the pimp of all pimps, throwing more money at rural Thai farmers to sell out their little girls than they'd ever seen before, years and years worth of grain income; because those maverick cable layers were having so much fun, Kin-Dong talked them into laying a northern route, too. They used words like redundancy to excuse this doubling-up, but what was really happening, what the cable layers really wanted, was another year in the heat and steam, another year in a place more exotic and sensuous and mystic than anything they'd ever seen in The States.

And so they dug it, this glorious information superhighway, and Kin-Dong got all the contracts. He dug an entire, unnecessary, half-circle across the Thai landscape, over mountains instead of plains, bringing out every idiot with a backhoe within a 500-mile radius, every goddamn crane on the subcontinent, and he dropped giant rectangles of concrete into the thick, black Thai soil.

That was how Kin-Dong made his first billion, his first and his second and his third. And afterwards, as most men who are wise enough and soulless enough and geographically fortunate enough to make pocketfuls of cash, Kin-Dong stopped craving the cash for cash's sake. He wanted the power that came with it.

Kin-Dong wanted power, and his source for finding this power, his only means for discovering how one gains it, were movies. On airplanes, and hotel rooms, and the privacy of his own home, an all-white mansion that he had built for himself and his wife and his children and his multiple mistresses on the Strait of Malacca, a mansion that got whitewashed once a week so that it looked like a Mediterranean castle on a Greek isle, Kin-Dong watched movies, American movies. He watched *The Godfather*, and *The Godfather* sequels, and all of *The Godfather* take-offs. Sometimes they were in English, or sometimes they were subtitled, or sometimes they were unprofessionally dubbed into Thai. But either way, Kin-Dong got the gist of it. To gain power,

Kin-Dong needed a family, a family who would give him total loyalty, and in that family he was going to be the *pater noster*, he was going to pull the strings.

Kin-Dong had never been what you would consider a nice person, but after watching all those *Godfather* movies he took a turn for the worse. The Thai people were a people easily coerced, strong-arm methods were rarely necessary, but Kin-Dong knocked off some people anyway, just so folks knew he meant business.

After that the ducks fell into a row. Anyone who wanted to do business in Bangkok, and not just in the sex or narcotics trades, but anyone who wanted to do business period, had to get permission from Kin-Dong, and Kin-Dong, after watching a lot of movies, wanted nothing more than to have an excuse to knock a few more people off. He needed disloyalty so that he could have loyalty later on.

Kin-Dong was also interested in new venues, new twists on old themes. Because of this he'd been keeping his eye on a man named Charley Hum.

At first, Kin-Dong hadn't given the man much thought. He was mild-mannered and well-spoken, not the kind of guy you would finger a criminal mastermind. Kin-Dong knew about Charley's gig, but he hadn't considered the cleverness of it.

Charley had the perfect scam. Thailand was one of the few places in the world where someone could run an internet kiddie porn ring without the Feds busting down the door the very next day. Because of the high risk, there weren't many quality kiddie porn sites, so Charley had a corner on the market, and the demand was much higher than the supply. Charley got his kids from the orphanage, so his overhead on payoffs was nil. He even looked like a good guy because of it; the foreigners who ran the café upstairs thought he was a saint. And then best of all, whenever the orphans reached a certain age, he could dump them off, for free, on Kin-Dong, and then pretend like he was doing him a favor by handing off washed-up porn stars.

Uncle Charley was putting the big screw to Kin-Dong, and smiling as he did it. Kin-Dong was going to put an end to that.

* * *

Things are not well in The Realm: for some reason, an unsually large number of random attacks are coming in. The Queen is nowhere to be found—even when she is silent, you could see her net worth growing, knew she was there, behind the scenes, plotting and planning, but the Queen is showing zero growth, indicating that something is amiss.

Unfortunately, there is not much she can do personally, her troops are still out on a mission. Hapless, Gek-Lin logs off as Lord BonZ and turns to her other role of the evening, that of Persephone.

★ ★ ★

Uncle Charley is not sure what to do. Kin-Dong's "man" had paid him a visit earlier today while he was alone in the basement taking his midmorning nap. The man had picked the lock at the head of the stairs, walked straight down to Charley's office, as if he knew exactly where that office was, broken down the deadbolt with one swift kick, and confronted Charley, who was splayed out on top of his futon in nothing but his skivvies. Charley, startled, sat up quickly in bed, rubbing his eyes. But Kin-Dong's man, a six-foot-three giant (at least, a giant in Thailand, and a good foot taller than Charley), commanded him to "Lay down!" and Charley, browbeaten, obeyed.

The man placed a heavy boot covered in mud on the futon, while Charley lay there below him, prone, on the bed. "Where's the girl?"

Charley wasn't sure what the man was talking about; he hadn't identified himself in any way, shape, or form. "What girl?"

The man tossed a toothpick he'd been gnawing on onto Charley's stomach. "Kin-Dong sent me to pick up the girl. Don't be smart with me, you know the one."

Kin-Dong sent me to pick up the girl? Does he mean Gek-Lin? Charley mused. He knew what the rules were. When the orphans were old enough, he turned them over to Kin-Dong. And with the arrangement that they'd had—Kin-Dong got a relatively cheap supply of prostitutes, while Charley received little in compensation except "protection"—Charley saw no reason why Kin-Dong would ever interfere with his affairs. Of course, it could be argued that Gek-Lin was at that age, and that Kin-Dong felt Charley was holding out on him, but Kin-Dong had never exhibited this eagerness before. Charley still couldn't figure out what this was about. "They are all out. It's daytime. They are only here at night."

The man ground his muddy boots into Charley's bed sheets, grunted, "I'll be back in twelve hours. Kin-Dong knows what you've been doing. We're taking over this operation. You're to stay here and continue to work. But you'll be working for the dragon now." The man pulled a small statuette of a Chinese dragon from his shirt pocket, a fourteen karat gold dragon with bulging eyes made of small green emeralds and a wicked grin. He tossed it on the bed next to Charley, narrowly missing Charley's right ear. "And make sure the girl is here."

Kin-Dong's man did not wait for Charley's reply. He spun around and left the room in a flash. If it weren't for the mud print on his top sheet, and the ominous-looking dragon in his hand, Charley would have sworn the whole thing had just been a bad nightmare.

Charley still has no idea what this is about. He has been an honest businessman, has kept all sides of their unspoken agreement. And yet Charley knows that there will be no discussion, that what the pater noster wants the pater noster gets. Charley is forever an orphan, and an orphan never complains about what parent they have been given. If he has to work for the dragon, so be it.

★   ★   ★

Gek-Lin had once liked these showers. They were such a luxury. Thailand was not a place where one was often alone, and in Charley's shower stall with its lovely porcelain tiles and its polished chrome, Gek-Lin was able to think of something other than the present; she was able to imagine a future, a future where she herself was rich enough to buy herself a shower stall, and install in it tiles and chrome. But she should have known: you can't have luxury without a price. And now she was paying the price.

Gek-Lin steps into the shower and removes her clothing: first shoes, then socks, then a bright orange T-shirt with blue letters that said *POW!* Next comes her bra, recently smuggled from a duty-free gift shop. Then a pair of short shorts, pink, the ones with a white stripe on the side that everyone in America used to wear in the 70s, which she pulls down along with her panties. Once naked, Gek-Lin teases her clients by leaving the shower for a minute, carefully placing her clothes down on a low bench. She is preparing to reenter when there is an unusual knock on the shower door. It is Uncle Charley.

"Gek-Lin?"

"Yes."

"What are you doing?"

"I'm working."

Uncle Charley sounds annoyed, "Come into my room. I need to speak to you."

"I'm taking a shower."

Charley is being unusually commanding and, perhaps—and she'd never seen this from him before—a little scared, "And get all the way dressed this time before you come out."

His tone of voice piques her curiosity. She picks her clothes up off the bench and puts them back on, then goes to his room. Before Charley can begin speaking, she asks for and receives a cigarette, which she smokes as she always does—puffing in through her mouth and exhaling through her nose, making sure she gets maximum nicotine intake with each breath. Charley begins to explain the situation, and as he does, she begins an interrogation. She needs to get the facts, to know who her enemies are and how best to escape them. He's told her, already, that they'll be here in the next few hours. Time is of the essence.

"What the dragon?"

"It's a code name for the PULO."

"The PULO?"

"The Pattani Unification Liberation Organization."

"The Malaysian Muslim movement? You business with them?"

"Not exactly. Kin-Dong does business with them, and I do business with Kin-Dong."

"Kin-Dong?"

"The boss."

"What make him the boss?"

"He protects us. How do you think I keep this orphanage running? Without Kin-Dong all our computer equipment would have been stolen long ago. You need protection in Thailand."

"Why you don't get your own security guards?"

"Because Kin-Dong would just buy them off."

"Kin-Dong not very nice."

"True."

"So the PULO ask for me? What they want with me? I can't fight in jungle."

"It's not the PULO that wants you, it's Kin-Dong. He . . . Gek-Lin, you must know the truth. Orphans like us, we have no options, we have to go where we are told to go. In another life, when we are reincarnated, we . . ."

"Why does Kin-Dong want me, Uncle Charley?"

Uncle Charley turns his head towards his computer screen, absentmindedly fiddling with its mouse. "You will work in a house of ladies."

Gek-Lin knows what he's getting at, but decides to play it stupid. She hates Charley's indirectness so she counters with sarcasm, "A house of ladies? Like monks?"

"Yes, like monks."

How stupid does Charley think she is? "Female monks that sex with lots of foreign businessmen?" she says, mocking him.

Charley sighs. He picks up the mouse and bangs the roller ball against the table. "It is not so bad. The men give you lots of things—jewelry, nice dinners—much nicer than here at the Blue Moon. And you'll get to meet Americans. I know how you feel about America. They'll send you postcards from New York and Chicago. For an orphan, it is far better than working in the rice fields. Kin-Dong will always see that you look nice and are well cared for."

Gek-Lin finally loses her cool. "Kin-Dong not own me like he owns you!" she shouts.

"Sssssh," Charley hisses.

"Sssssh why? So *they* won't hear me? I go out there right now and tell them to run. You sell them all off to slavery. This is fuck up, Charley! Fuck up! For you, Charley, I no tell them. But me, Gek-Lin, nobody own me. I have to die—*die! die! die!*—then I die! I leave Charley—I walk right out now. You want to send Kin or Kim or whatever the fuck Dong after me? Tell him I go to America, and if he wants to send his men after me, he do. I no care!"

With these words Gek-Lin springs from the floor. Charley, in a rare moment of quickness, is able to grab her arm before she goes out the door. "No," he says firmly.

"Let go of my arm."

"Wait," says Uncle Charley.

"*Let go my arm!*" screams Gek-Lin, struggling to get loose from his grasp.

"It takes time, Gek-Lin. You need a sponsor to sign for you, and cash, too."

"I don't care!"

"Gek-Lin—"

"Let go my fucking arm!"

"I love you, Gek-Lin."

Gek-Lin stops struggling. She turns to him and looks him dead in the eyes. Through his thick glasses she can see tear drops magnified to ten times their normal size. She spits on his shoes.

Charley doesn't take the spitting personally. He deserves it. She's absolutely right—he is selling her out. "Patience, Gek-Lin, patience. I'll get you a passport, but you'll have to find your own way out of the country."

"But you say he be here tonight."

"You will have to wait. Maybe many months. Maybe years, Gek-Lin. These things take time."

"Kin-Dong never own me, Charley. Never!"

"But they will not help you at the American Embassy. You have to get a visa—they only give them to businesspeople and students, and even so, they take months to process. Also, you need a sponsor for when you arrive, and money for your trip. You have none of these things, Gek-Lin. They won't even let you through the doors. You have to think these things through, Gek-Lin. How are you going to get all these things?"

"The Realm."

"The Realm?"

"I contact my friends in The Realm. sKyLaR from America. And the Queen, I think she American too."

"They won't help."

"Why not?"

"Because they're not real friends. They might not even be who they say they are. And they certainly won't believe that you are who you say you are. I can't imagine anyone wiring money to some random address in Thailand."

Logic! Logic! Logic! Gek-Lin hates cold, hard logic! "Shut up and get me passport." He is right, of course, it will take time for her to arrange everything, but unlike Charley she believes that she will find a way. She just needs time, and in order to get that time, right now, she needs to get Charley to let go of her arm.

*   *   *

Gek-Lin is getting to Uncle Charley. She inspires passions in him that he had long ago buried, He, too, had once desired escape. He, too, had been determined to escape on his own terms. Deep in a past he can hardly remember living he had turned down a woman of high-standing, a woman who could have gotten him places, in order to marry a young orphan. Gek-Lin reminds Charley of his downfall.

This was why Charley had started the orphanage. He wanted an opportunity to return and be eighteen again. He wanted to run down the alley where his betrothed was being sliced up and rescue her. He wanted to be a hero.

But he knows now that he can't. He is no Raven. It doesn't matter that he is still 18 inside, it doesn't matter that his spiritual growth has been stunted, what matters is how he looks, and he looks even older than his age, he looks 45. This is Charley's tragedy, and he's never been able to let go of it. He's turned into a sort of stone golem: rigid and resentful.

And all that resentment has turned him into what he is today. Charley Hum is just a dirty old man. He's a pathetic, quivering thing that secretly watches prepubescent girls showering behind a closed door.

With Gek-Lin standing before him in all her defiance, Charley is taken back to a time when he still felt that he had some control, a time when he didn't feel cursed and doomed. Perhaps, there is still a choice to be made.

Charley Hum knows where it is. It sits sandwiched between pages 610 and 611 of his dictionary, its front facing page 610, a page whose headers read "enfeeble" and "English." Charley Hum knows that he, too, has a passport, and that his passport is filled with blank pages. Charley Hum knows what the last line of the definition of England reads, knows that it says, "London is the capital and the largest city of both England and the United Kingdom. Population, 46,220,955." Charley Hum can tell, standing in the laser light of Gek-Lin's stare, that change is still possible, that there is nothing stopping him from taking a flight to London but some clever words and an exchange of cash, something that a man of his stature, even as an expatriate, were he only to exude a bit of self-confidence, could easily do.

In London, he could slough them off, he could slough off these twisted twenty-seven years. He has the money.

*　*　*

The old Uncle Charley stare. He does this, forgets where he is and what he is doing. Gek-Lin hopes he will release her arm in his reverie. It is obvious that his mind is traveling somewhere. She isn't sure if it is to a past, or a future—some place he had been, or some place he would never go—but he is obviously traveling. There is something deeper to Charley than his stoic maxims and his not-so-hidden perversions would suggest.

Gek-Lin suddenly has an idea. Out of the blue she asks, "Do you have parents?"

"What?" Charley asks.

"Who are your parents?"

Caught off guard in the midst of his reverie Charley confesses, "I . . . I don't know. My mother died young; she was Vietnamese. My father was an

American serviceman, or so I imagine. He . . . my skin is white and my name is too. I was an orphan just like you. Gek-Lin, I . . . I'm an orphan, just like you."

Uncle Charley is trembling. His need is palpable and disgusting. He takes off his glasses, as if anticipating a kiss.

Gek-Lin sees exactly what she has to do. It is sad, especially given the revelation he has just shared, but really, he hasn't given her much choice. "Kneel down," Gek-Lin says.

Uncle Charley, like a child visited by a fairy godmother who is offering to grant him any wish, can do nothing but obey.

"You have to give me chance, Charley. Just a few days. Maybe you are right, maybe nothing can be done, but you have to give me chance. You will give me some money, not much, just little, just what Gek-Lin deserves for work."

Charley looks up into the eyes of his young charge. What else can he do? He is so resigned, and so hungry, so hungry for Gek-Lin, that even the pull of self-preservation cannot sway him. He gets up from where he is kneeling, pulls his keys from his pocket, opens the front drawer of his desk, opens a drawstring bag, and pulls out 5 bills, 5 one-hundred baht bills. He comes back to where he was kneeling and places the bills in her hand.

Gek-Lin bends over and gives him a quick peck on his unshaven cheek. Before Charley can once again grab her arm, she is gone.

27. INCREASING YOUR KINGDOM'S NET WORTH IS ALL THAT MATTERS, EVERYTHING ELSE IS A MEANS TO AN END.

IN HIS DREAMS, THEY ARE DYING. Beautiful women with heaving bosoms are being held with knives at their throats while their cheap peasant's clothing is shorn from their bodies. The women are being mounted and raped. After the men are finished, the women are being shot in the head with arrows from crossbows at point-blank range.

In his dreams, the men are being slaughtered too. All his strong and brave warriors overwhelmed by a fierce and unexpected attack. The enemy is taking no prisoners. They have lined all the survivors against a wall. The bowmen are taking aim. They are firing.

In his dreams, he is sleeping through all this. He's in some sort of infirmary sweating it out while the sounds of battle outside reach a fever pitch. He is sick, sick with some dreaded medieval disease that is sure to be the death of him, but this is no excuse. He must get up. He must put on his suit of plate mail, shoulder his shield, unsheathe his sword. He opens his eyes and the nuns who have been his nurses say *no, no, you mustn't*, but he pushes them aside and runs to his weapons.

When Xerxes wakes up from his dream he realizes that he has not been dreaming. He *has* been sweating in his sleep and his peasants *are* being slaughtered. The sweat, though, is not being caused by scarlet fever, but rather by the body heat of one Sara Bronstein, whose arms are wrapped around his neck and whose legs are wrapped around his waist. And his peasants aren't real peasants, but rather a number in a game he plays.

Nonetheless, the anxiety and fear that Xerxes feels, even though it is not generated by a true life or death circumstance, doesn't merely go away when Xerxes wakes up to discover its cause. For although Xerxes's feelings are being brought about by a virtual experience, he still feels them, and he still feels driven to act on them.

Night has rendered Sara's one-window cabin very dark. The only light in the room is the glow-in-the-dark green emanating from the hands of Sara's alarm clock, a clock that indicates to Xerxes that it is 5:30 A.M. Xerxes slips his head out from under Sara's arms, then lifts the leg that Sara has wrapped around his waist. Sara stirs, turns over in her sleep.

Xerxes does not want to wake her, so he lays there, dead still but wide awake. He watches the slow progress of the minute hand as it moves a centimeter downward. At 5:35 he makes his move, slinking out of sheets and standing up off the floor.

In the darkness of an unfamiliar cabin, not wanting to wake his sleeping companion, Xerxes tiptoes his way to the chaise lounge where his clothes had been removed, rather briskly, by Sara just hours before. To lessen the chance of disturbing her, he gets on his hands and knees, crawling about until he finds a pair of pants and both his shoes. He decides that these articles are enough to allow him to make his escape.

In their haste yesterday evening to get into bed, Sara and Xerxes had left the sliding glass door that led to the backyard open. Xerxes glides out that door. Once in the yard, a quarter moon makes negotiating his way easier. Xerxes finds the barbed wire gate and makes his way through, then follows the path to where #8 is sitting in a dirt turnout at the side of Ponderosa Pines Road.

Xerxes knows that what he is doing is not exactly a relationship builder.

To sleep with someone, and then leave them at 5:30 in the morning sans ex-planation, was a pretty sure sign that you had been there for the quick screw, and that you didn't want anything beyond that. He supposes that he should say something, but his excuse seems so childish and lame, that he can't bring himself to wake her.

Besides, he's in a hurry. If he gets home before 6 A.M., he can get in some maneuvers before a day in The Realm passed. If he drives straight home, about a twenty-minute jaunt, he'll have a few minutes of play time before the hour passes. Xerxes starts his truck and makes a U-turn onto Ponderosa Pines. He's got that feeling that truck drivers have at this hour, or that drunks get, that he needs to concentrate more than usual in order to keep his eyes open. He rolls down the window even though it's in the 40s and he doesn't have a shirt on.

What happened last night with Sara could not have come at a more op-portune time for Xerxes. When one is dealing with all the losses that Xerxes is dealing with, it is good to be reminded that life goes on, and Sara, and the po-tential that she represents, is such a reminder. But Xerxes does not have time to dwell on his recent accomplishment; he's driving down tangled roads, deserted at this hour; he's heading into the town square, the white marble walls of the courthouse alight with spotlights, the neon of the restored saloons on Whisky Row extinguished for the night; he's crossing town, driving through the Indian reservation, the hastily built rectangular strip malls and casinos and cigarette shops; he's doing this and the fear is rising up in him. He hasn't entered The Realm in nine hours, and before those nine hours he hadn't trained his troops or cast his protection spells or sent out his thieves to obtain more gold. While he was asleep his net worth had not been rising. The Two-Headed Boy would be increasing his lead, other provinces would be catching up, and those other provinces, sensing weakness, might attack or rob or throw fireballs at his peas-ants. What was worse, he had left his kingdom leaderless. For 9 hours they would be wondering what had happened—where had their Queen gone?

Xerxes enters the enclave called The Ranch, passes onyx statues of muscle-flanked fillies, drives the serpentine drive. Suddenly there is a *blump* and then a bump and then a *whir-whir-whir* and Xerxes yells "Damn it!" out the window. He's hit something in the road.

★   ★   ★

This time, when Kin-Dong's man comes to the door, he knocks. Uncle Charley, whose only visitors during the night were orphans, would normally shout, gruffly, "Come in!" but tonight he is expecting company, and because he is expecting this company, he gets up from the desk that houses his Pentium and goes to the door. The orphans, unaccustomed to this, look up.

When Charley answers the door Kin-Dong's man says, "Good evening," as if he were here for a social visit. He was no longer wearing muddy boots, but rather a white tuxedo and a pair of gloves.

"Good evening," replies Uncle Charley.

"I assume everything is in order," says the man.

"Oh, yes," replies Uncle Charley nervously.

The man walks down the stairs with Charley in the lead. He begins to remove his gloves. "And which one is Persephone?"

Charley plays it dumb, "Uh, Persephone? Persephone not here. Charley thought you meant China Jade."

The man stops in the middle of removing his second glove. "That is disappointing," he says. The man is staring at Charley. His eyes are coal black, they smolder. "I suppose you'll have to come instead."

Charley talks, "Yes, of course, give me just a—" but is interrupted by the man, who has grabbed Charley's arm and twisted it high on his back. Charley stutters in pain, "Ah, ah, ah, ah, ah."

The man pushes Charley up the stairs. He looks back into the room. He points to the girl. "You, follow."

Charley, clearly in pain, squeaks rather than speaks, "The rest?"

Kin-Dong's man looks at them in contempt, "Go! Leave!"

The orphans don't move.

Kin-Dong's man takes Charley's head and shoves it into the wall. "Up the stairs, now!"

The orphans, frightened of getting anywhere near Kin-Dong's man, but at the same time terrified of the consequences of not doing what they are told to do, get up from their chairs. The older ones grab the younger ones. They glare at Charley, whose forehead is bleeding, and whose head lolls to one side.

"What are you looking at?" Kin-Dong's man asks. Go!"

The orphans run up the stairs and out the door together, unsure of where it is they are running to.

★　★　★

Xerxes only has ten minutes to get back to his bedroom, start up his laptop, and make his moves in The Realm. He pulls his truck over to the side of the road, takes a flashlight from his glove compartment, gets out of the truck, and quickly finds the source of the problem—the carcass of a coyote, fresh blood oozing from its lips, is wrapped around his rear wheel. Xerxes imagines his Boy Scout Manual, what it would say about wrapping the animal up, taking it to a veterinarian; or at least giving the animal a proper burial.

But Xerxes doesn't have time for the proper burial of an animal; there are more important things on his mind. With his bare hands, Xerxes peels the coyote's carcass off the top part of his wheel. He returns to the truck, backs it up a bit, then gets out again, returning to the flattened coyote. He pulls the coyote to the side of the road, then returns to his truck. He places his hands, sticky with blood, on the steering wheel. He shifts the truck into first, then second, then third. Xerxes will still get home with a few precious minutes to spare.

But a coyote, it will never howl again.

*　*　*

The moon is well-established in Bangkok, and without Charley or the orphans there, the basement of the Blue Moon Internet Café seems a haunted place. Gek-Lin is sitting in front of the single light source that is on in the large room: a computer screen. It casts its blue, flickering light over the banks of computers sitting lonely on their donated conference tables while Gek-Lin's shadow wavers diaphanously in the nether corners of the room.

Everyone is gone. Gek-Lin had watched them stream out of the Blue Moon's basement door from her hiding place behind two trash barrels. She'd watched the orphans scatter along Surawong Road; and Uncle Charley, along with a terrified looking China Jade, shoved into a limousine with the kind of fathomless, tinted windows that indicate inhabitants who have something to hide. That left Gek-Lin, by herself, in the street outside the Blue Moon with only Psyduck to comfort her. The menace apparently gone, she hadn't been able to think of a reason not to reenter the building. Charley, his hands shaking, had locked the door behind him, but Gek-Lin had long since made copies of his keys. Turning to make sure no one was watching her, Gek-Lin had turned the lock and gone down the lonely stairs.

So now, Gek-Lin sits alone in front of a computer screen. Gek-Lin, like most Thais, is not used to this arrangement. This is not a country where people are accustomed to having space. She misses the physical presence of the others, the mere fact of them being there. She finds the hum of silence much harder to tune out than the orphan chatter. She must stay on task; her goal is America.

The good thing about having the run of the place, and really the only justification she can thinking of for ignoring the occasional wrapping and shaking of the Blue Moon's iron gates, signaling the disappointment of some poor orphan who will, because of Uncle Charley's departure, not only be missing an evening of shooting up demons in Diablo III, but also dinner and shelter for the night, was that she could simply grab whatever she wanted. There would be no begging, demanding, stealing, purchasing, or flirting for objects as simple as pens and paper. Gek-Lin simply had to turn the key to Charley's office and take the stuff.

This was how Gek-Lin imagined life was like on the inside of those green-glassed American buildings. They provided workers with buckets full of pens and pencils, sheets and sheets of spotless white paper. One simply had to pull open a drawer and all these jewels were there for the taking—a gift from an appreciative employer. Charley acted as if merely providing food and shelter to his workers—be they unsuspecting ones or not—was fair payment. In America, there was so much more. In America, you were given money, those oh-so-freeing scraps of dirty green paper, for your work, by laws, that were, as far as she could tell, actually upheld, and with that money you could purchase food *of your own choosing*, and shelter *of your own choosing*, and best of all you could choose, if you so desired, not to be at the mercy of dirty old men. Gek-Lin tried not to think about these things. She tried not to dream.

Gek-Lin tears off a few sheets of the green and white lined paper that Charley uses in his dot-matrix printer; she nabs a small black pencil with BROOKHAVEN GOLF CLUB imprinted on it from a desk drawer. She tears the perforation off each of the sheets and spreads them lavishly around her computer, rearranging nearby monitors to make more space.

Gek-Lin goes to her computer. In seconds she ascertains what countless Time Management Seminars and MBA programs fail to teach the average businessperson. Gek-Lin prioritizes. She writes down on the sheet to her left the order in which things needed to be done.

First, The Realm. Before she can ask for favors, Gek-Lin needs to prove that she is a valuable resource, that, were the Queen to provide her with airfare, a work visa, and a desk job, she would be fully capable of performing any task assigned to her, and that the work performed would be of high quality and accomplished in a timely manner.

And so Gek-Lin must attend to matters in The Realm. Her troops have returned and now she must retaliate against the provinces that have attacked them. She makes her calculations. She attacks:

Your troops have fought a brave battle and won. You have appropriated 159 acres of land from Jax Jerx (27:16). Your army will return from the battlefield in 18 days. Be sure to try Fantasy Hockey, the new game from the Lords of The Realm.

Gek-Lin crosses the task off her list. ~~The Realm.~~ Now, there is matter #2 to attend to: aid. If she is to ask for favors from others, she must demonstrate her own willingness to be helpful. She was lucky in the war, she didn't sustain too much damage from evil sorcery, and she still has some gold in her coffers. She doles her extras out to the more unfortunate provinces—these will be her friends now; maybe, someday, she'll be repaid for her kindnesses.

Gek-Lin crosses off the #2 item on her list: ~~aid.~~ She gazes at the last item on the list: IRC with sKyLaR. The thought of attending to this final order of business was perhaps what made Gek-Lin feel the most exposed. It had been one thing, knowing she was being watched while taking showers, but it was another thing to expose herself willingly to someone capable of affecting the outcome of her life.

Gek-Lin feels the risk in revealing herself. Until now, sKyLaR and the Queen thought of her as some guy, a non-native English speaker who was nonetheless feisty and intelligent, a boy who liked to play war games. But to tell them this, that she is a girl, and on top of that some sort of sex slave who was asking them to help her escape—how would they respond?

There is no time, though, for contemplation. sKyLaR's name is bold before her; it is important to contact him as soon as possible. She can't hesitate any longer; there is no telling when another limo would make its rounds, plunging her, too, into its impenetrable darkness.

Lord_BonZ: hello. sKyLaR?

28. INEVITABLY, YOU WILL GET BLOOD ON YOUR HANDS.

The Queen Peace & Love but Mostly Love has blood on her hands. She knows she should wash them before she touches anything, but she simply doesn't have the time. She'll go back she thinks, she'll wash the grill of the truck, clean the brass door knobs, carefully scrub the keys of the keyboard. There is urgency here. There are troops to train. Blood removal, it will have to wait.

She completes her tasks before the hour passes. After doing so, she can relax—but she doesn't. There are unusual things happening:

💀 A thievery attempt has been made on our lands by Pepper Daisy (47:50).
💀 A thievery attempt has been made on our lands by Broccoli Bluebonnets (47:50).
💀 A magic attempt has been made on our lands by Okra Orchids (47:50).
💀 A magic attempt has been made on our lands by Okra Orchids (47:50).
💀 A magic attempt has been made on our lands by Okra Orchids (47:50).

Her first thought is that *Carrot Flowers* has declared war. Was the Two-Headed Boy that confident? Had he seen that she was away and looked to take immediate advantage. She quickly clicks over to her kingdom page and is relieved. They are OK, so far there is no declaration of war.

Her second thought is that the Two-Headed Boy was gearing up for a single attack on her. In fear, she consults her wizards and casts all the protection spells in her arsenal.

After she has done this, the Queen decides to look elsewhere, she wants to know how her kingdom mates are doing. This is where things get strange:

News for Paradigm Shift: June, YR13

💀 *Jax Jerx* (27:16) has captured 83 acres from *GurGle* (12:5).
💀 *Permanent Frost* (33:22) has captured 90 acres from *Wonderwizzies* (12:5).
💀 *I H8 U* (8:6) has captured 65 acres from *War Place* (12:5).
💀 *01000100011100010001* (9:1) has captured 102 acres from *Dandy Lion* (12:5).
💀 *Water Drinkaer* (17:16) has captured 96 acres from *One Hundred Happy Acres* (12:5).
🖤 Our good province *Land of BonZ* (12:5) has captured 154 acres from *Jax Jerx* (23:34).
******************************* *End of News*********************************

What's strange about the news page is the number of random attacks that have taken place. It's not normal. It's also strange that the attacks are so well-timed. The attacks took place almost immediately after they sent out their last wave against *Amphibious*. This seems too organized for it to be a co-incidence.

The Queen considers the evidence, synthesizes the material. She puts her hands to her face, feeling the blood stick there. She knows what's going on: the Two-Headed Boy is feeding them intel.

★ ★ ★

It is early morning in Antarctica, and sKyLaR is still awake—very, very awake. Tonight, the satellites were properly aligned, and his connection has been fast. A list of names appears on his IRC protocol. sKyLaR is talking to the "Realmies." He clicks on a sideways triangle and the triangle turns downward. The names, all 491 of the Realmies he has had communications with, show up in a vertical column in alphabetical order. The names in bold are names of people currently on-line; the names not in bold are not. When sKyLaR wants to speak with someone—someone out there in the much warmer, much wider world— he merely finds the bold name of a person whom he feels like speaking with, someone experiencing a long Norwegian summer, or a persistent Costa Rican rainy season; clicks on it, then begins with his patented sKyLaR: hElLo!

Before he can get started today, though, before he can choose who he wants to talk to, he has an incoming:

Lord_BonZ: *hello, sKyLaR?*

sKyLaR: *gOoD eVeNiNg, LoRd BoNz. I tRuSt YoU aRe AbOuT tO aSk Me aBoU*

Lord_BonZ: *we go pleasure palace?*

sKyLaR: *t AlL tHeSe RaNdOm AtTaCkS. I HoNeStLy*

Lord_BonZ: *meet in pleasure palace*

sKyLaR: *iS sOmEtHiNg DiStUrBiNg YoU lOrD bOnZ tHaT yOu WaNt To DiScUsS iN pRiVaTe? YoU lOoK pAlE toDaY; aLmOsT dEaD. hA. hA.*

*You have received an invitation to enter the conference room sKyLaR's PlEaSuRe PaLaCe from **sKyLaR**. Will you accept? Y/N*

Lord_BonZ: y

sKyLaR: hEllo LoRd BoNz. WhAt'S uP?

Lord_BonZ: many bad thing. raven gone

sKyLaR: wHaT dO yOu MeAn?

Lord_BonZ: they, how you say, kidnap him. now he cannot play. i have play for him

sKyLaR: bAcK uP a LiTtLe CoWbOy. YoU kNoW rAvEn In RI?

Lord_BonZ: bad man kidnap him. now they after me

sKyLaR: hOw DiD yOu TwO eNd Up In ThE sAmE kInGdoM?

Lord_BonZ: i show you video. i have website like you. you show me video in ice dome now i show you. www.wetthailolitas.com

sKyLaR: ArE yOu FuCkInG wItH mE?

Lord_BonZ: i no boy. i girl

sKyLaR: uH . . . i'M sOrRy, LoRd BoNz BuT i'M nOt ReAlLy InTeReStEd

Lord_BonZ: you no understand. not porn. will show. take name and password free. name: unclecharley022657. password: fullaccess

Whatever this is about, Dietrich wants no part of it. Dietrich closes the conference window then he puts a block on Lord BonZ so he can't access him anymore. He goes back to The Realm for a moment, and sends a message to the Queen. He's not sure what's going on, but he's concerned, there's an imposter on the loose. While he's preparing the message, he gets another incoming on his IRC:

Serpent: I hate you guys, you all suck.

sKyLaR: hUh?

Serpent: You and your kingdom mates, you suck. You're just like everybody else. You pretend to be my friend, but then you go ahead and cast spells on me before the surrender. Why did you do it, sKyLaR? What did you get out of it?

sKyLaR: iT iSn'T pErSoNaL. iT's JuSt A gAmE

Serpent: Exactly, it's just a game isn't it. Life, all of life, it's just a game. You do something and then you forget about it, because it's all a game. It doesn't matter what happened to the person you did it too, and if they take it personally, well, they're being stupid because it was all a game. Well, you know what sKyLaR, I'm done with games

sKyLaR: hEy, SlOw DoWn. tHe WaR's OvEr.

Serpent: I don't care, sKyLaR. I just want someone to know. And writing you makes the most sense, since you're in Antarctica and there's nothing you can do about it. I mean, you don't have phones there, right, so you can't stop me.

sKyLaR: wHaT r U tAlKiNg AbOuT?

Serpent: I'm offing myself. I'm laying here on my bed with a needle full of China White, and there's nothing you can do about it. I'm only telling you because you like games, and I figured you'd think this was fun. It's a suicide game. We're all in love with dying aren't we. You could do it too, just take one step outside that dome of yours, and

sKyLaR: tHiS iSn'T cOoL, sErPeNt. ArE yOu BeInG sErIoUs?

Serpent: You don't know, do you? You don't know if I'm fucking with you or not. I mean, you saw me, you saw my picture, you saw my pierced nipples. I'm just a goth girl. This is play. Death play. Death games. You'll never know. I'll log off and you'll never know. Remember that story about that woman in New York who was raped and murdered beneath that tenement building, beneath a building where hundreds, possibly thousands of

Serpent: people lived. There were people who heard it, they looked down and heard the woman screaming, but they dIdn't do anything. They didn't even call the cops. You know what they thought, sKyLaR? I know what they thought. They thought it was a game. They thought she was some drunk who was raising a ruckus because it was fun. They turned out their lights and pretended it wasn't real. I want you to know sKyLaR that you're not the

Serpent: only one who knows about this but will do nothing. I don't want you to think I'm being irrational, that I'm offing myself because of some stupid online game. Here's the real reason. Someone stole my sleep. It was the only thing I had to myself, and someone stole it. I was looking up, at the chandelier in my room, and I realized that this fuck who I used to date put a camera there, in my chandelier. It's been there, on,

Serpent: for I don't know how long. People have been watching me. I don't care that they've been watching me having sex, that's fine, that's always been theirs, what pisses me off is that they've been watching me sleep. You know what's great about death, sKyLaR? When you're dead no one can get their hands on you. I mean, I suppose a grave robber could, but that's not very likely, unless you're King Tut or something.

sKyLaR: sErPeNt, ThIs IsN't CoO

Serpent: It's going to be just like that girl who was raped and murdered beneath the ten-ement building. There's all these people out there, who knows how many, with this web feed of me, and they're going to watch me shoot up, and then they're going to watch me die. They're going to think it's all a game, sKyLaR, they're going to think it's all great fun.

★ ★ ★

When Tres Rawlings sees the needle, he can't move. It isn't momentary paralysis, like a deer caught in the headlights, it is, quite literally, that Tres can't move, but this is the first time since the accident that Tres absolutely has to move, the first time that it is a life or death situation.

Tres Rawlings knows what is happening. He knows that the plunger has gone back too far. Tres Rawlings, the world's greatest voyeur, knows that the dosage is too high, that unless it's really cut she'll O.D. Tres Rawlings has seen the stopper go back before, on a video Web ring where couples watch each other shoot up, that he'd tapped into on occasion so that he would never be in the dark about perversion.

Tres Rawlings also knows that The Serpent doesn't do this, that her room is sacred, drug-free. That in her own room, when it is emptied of the sexual predators she often brings there, she is clean. He knows The Serpent's modus operandi. He knows that when she is in her room alone, she just lies there and sleeps, lies there and sleeps with her big, mocha-colored eyes wide open, staring blankly at the chandelier in the middle of her room. Her room allows her to rejuvenate. Her room is her dragon's lair.

This time everything is wrong. This time a needle is entering a vein in the crook of an elbow. This time there is no blank stare. This time the stare is very directed. This time the stare is accompanied by a middle finger, a middle finger that is pointed right at Tres. This time the stare and the middle finger are accompanied by the moving of lips, lips that are saying *fuck you, whoever you are*.

* * *

The camera was the last straw. Since the time Mary Lynn was 14 they had wanted her and she had given it to them. She had a hungry look, a haunted look, big eyes and high, sharp cheekbones, and men wanted that these days, wanted something that looked sort of sick. She felt it was her duty, her calling, to give them what they wanted. And she had. She had given them everything, her skin for their inks, her veins for their chemicals, her holes for their excretions, her mind for their altering.

She had held one thing for herself. One thing remained pure and intact. And that one thing had been her sleep. And now some fucker had taken that, some fucker had secreted a Web cam into the chandelier and had been watching her.

Well, if that fucker was still there, if he was still tuned in, he was going to get a helluva show. He'd get the Final Resting Place live and in color. This world was all take and little give, and those who did give were few, far between, and ultimately fucked.

Mary Lynn Klavich pushes a needle through her skin at the crook in her elbow, looks straight at the chandelier, says, "Fuck you, whoever you are."

* * *

Xerxes Meticula gets up off the bed. Xerxes Meticula goes to the sink and washes the blood from his hands.

* * *

Tres Rawlings wants to save her. He wants to leap through the monitor. He wants to rip his T-shirt off and wrap it around her arm to cut off her circulation.

But he can't. He is attached to a feeder that pumps a slow drip of glucose and saline through a shunt that is permanently attached to a vein. He is attached to anodes that are attached to his skull that are attached to cables that are attached to the USB port of a computer. He is attached, locked, bound, soldered into place. He is stuck watching a woman die.

Over the months that he had been watching The Serpent, it gradually slipped his mind that what he had been doing was an intrusion. He had felt like a benevolent ghost. When The Serpent had been asleep in her lair, he had talked to her—well, not talked, since talking wasn't possible for Tres, but had performed a sort of Heinlein mind-meld, a grok. In her sleep, Tres whispered nice things to her, called her baby and sweetie and love kitten, whispered things that the men (and occasionally women) in her life would never say, because in their world the words bitch and slut and whore were supposed to mean the same thing, although they never really did.

Tres had wanted to be different. He had wanted to be The Serpent's One Good Thing. But Tres had been wrong. Tres was not The Serpent's One Good Thing. He was The Serpent's Last Straw.

Tres watches the monitor as The Serpent injects the contents of the needle into her vein, as she takes her thumb off the stopper. He watches her carelessly leave the needle there, dangling sideways like a limp member. He watches her assume the position that she always assumed on her Little Mermaid comforter—her head back against a *Sid and Nancy* poster, her legs splayed in a V, her eyes staring at the chandelier.

There were things he could do. He could use the emergency button to contact his parents. They were an hour and a half away watching the football game at his uncle's house. He could contact them and when they entered his room he could steer their eyes to the computer. What they would do when they saw a strange woman sleeping naked with a needle in her arm on his monitor was beyond him. *What's THAT supposed to be, Tres?*

There were other things he could do, as well. He had access to emergency numbers, to 999, the local constable. But none of these things would save her. He would simply be indicting himself, creating a sensational story for *The Star*: Paralyzed Boy Kills Woman Through His Computer!

243

He simply doesn't know where The Serpent lives, and because he doesn't know where she lives he can't save her. Tres watches the slow transformation take place in The Serpent's skin, as its cast turns from slightly rose to slightly lavender. He watches her jaw drop. He watches saliva drip from her lips. He watches the intently staring eyes develop a glaze. There is nothing he can do but watch.

But it is the one thing that Tres has to stop doing, he has to stop watching.

★   ★   ★

Before she falls asleep forever, a song plays through The Serpent's head:

> *I will take you and leave you alone,*
> *Watching spirals of white softly flow*
> *Over your eyelids and all you did*
> *Will wait until the point when you let go*

29. DON'T GET DELETED.

QUEEN PEACE & LOVE BUT MOSTLY LOVE is considering performing an act of retribution which just isn't done, at least amongst the elite kingdoms of The Realm. She is considering creating a dragon.

The creation of dragons is generally done by the thoughtless ones, those who care little for their peasants, their fellow kingdom mates, and the growth of their own net worths. Dragons, once loose upon The Realm, are difficult to control—they may attack one's enemy, but if one's kingdom does not have a powerful enough wizard to control the dragon, the dragon is just as likely to attack some other unfortunate kingdom, or even the creator of the dragon themselves. What's more, if the dragon is not killed by the party which it is unleashed upon, it moves on, wreaking havoc in the next kingdom and then the next. This would not be such a tragedy for the dragon's perpetrator, except that the Lords of The Realm have designed it so that a dragon always bears the marks of its maker; kingdoms always know just whom to exact their revenge upon.

The Queen is well aware of all these things. Dragons are for dummies, for the non-union of The Realm. Those who create dragons are generally those who let pride get in the way, and who fight in a dishonorable fashion.

And yet, as she surveys the damage done by the minions of the Two-Headed Boy, she wonders if perhaps now is the time to disregard this time-worn maxim. There are several good reasons for doing it. For one, there isn't much time left. The age is approaching a close and *Paradigm Shift* has been knocked down to #4. There is no way for them to catch up unless something dreadful happens to #1. The leader board looks like this:

Top 10 Kingdoms in Net Worth, YR12

1. Carrot Flowers		NW 75,932,693
2. Loony Tunes		NW 67,201,821
3. Naked Pop Stars		NW 66,829,302
4. Paradigm Shift		NW 66,742,902
5. Fast Food Franchises		NW 63,839,299
6. Rocky Mountain Oysters		NW 63,392,570
7. Little White Weenies		NW 62,992,482
8. Beer		NW 62,953,028
9. Perfectly Spherical Orbs		NW 62,849,203
10. The Slaughter House 20		NW 62,759,012

The #2, #3, and #4 kingdoms are all very close in net worth and have little to fear from each other; attacking either of the other two would likely only serve to take both out of contention, leaving the #2 slot for the kingdom smart enough to stay out of the conflict. The only kingdom that has the strength to attack any of them successfully is *Carrot Flowers*, but it seems much more likely that *Carrot Flowers* will rest on its laurels until the age is over, figuring it can stay in the lead on the land it has already obtained.

Conventional wisdom in The Realm holds that you only attacked those kingdoms with a lower net worth than yours—the #2, #3, and #4 kingdoms were scanning kingdoms smaller than they as potential targets, hoping they could make up the ground on *Carrot Flowers* through war spoils—but the Queen felt that there wasn't enough time to catch up. So what the Queen was thinking was this: what if the top three kingdoms went against convention and surprised *Carrot Flowers* in the last week of the campaign with a dragon and an all-out assault?

The dynamics seemed perfect. The Lords of The Realm allowed a maximum of three kingdoms to declare war on any one kingdom at a time—this was to prevent what gamers call "gangbanging," unfair teeming up against a single kingdom. Most inhabitants of The Realm felt that three, or even two kingdoms teeming up against a single kingdom was unfair, and so kingdoms that were teamed up against were often able to find allies who would equalize things by joining the fray.

With the current dynamics, though, it seemed that even if *Carrot Flowers* was able to enlist a good number of the #5 and down kingdoms to fight on their side, they would still have problems breaking through the #2 through #4 block. The way the numbers broke down these kingdoms were simply not powerful enough to do much harm. Besides all this, there has always been a sense of poetic justice in Realm politics. There were a lot of kingdoms out there, especially the ones near the top, who were aware of *Carrot Flowers'* backstabbing maneuvers—no one would be upset to see *Carrot Flowers* and the Two-Headed Boy go down.

Whatever the verdict on her proposal, The Queen wants the matter settled quickly. Dragons take resources to create (dragon building is an odd and nonsensical process; dragons are fed two things: gold and mana, mana being a sort of magical dust that wizards like sKyLar use to cast their spells. A dragon is essentially nonexistent until it has been fed a prespecified amount of gold and mana, at which point it appears on the scene, full-sized and ready for action) and there simply isn't much time left for them to get back on top.

She would like the dragon question answered now, and yet the most important provinces—sKyLaR, Raven, and Lord BonZ—have all been behaving strangely lately. The Queen, in the past, has operated under the platitude that wise leadership involves taking in the opinions of her kingdom mates before voicing her own, but now she feels that time is pressing, the dragon project needs to be started today, and once the dragon project gets started, her Real Life persona needs to get some rest.

The Queen has searched all methods of communication to find the best way to contact these three—she has thrown open the doors of the tavern; she has left notes on the kingdom message board; she has looked for their names in bold in her IRC dialog—to no avail. Tired as she is, The Queen types up a thought-out message. She cut and pastes the message three times into three different text boxes, gives each one a separate salutation—Dear sKyLaR, Dear Raven, Dear Lord BonZ. She sends the message off:

Dear _____,

I'm going to begin a dragon project against kingdom of Carrot Flowers. I know this sounds suicidal, but with the age nearing an end and with Carrot Flowers ordering OOW attacks against us, I think some retribution is in order. I also think that strategically using the dragon might help us. My thoughts are as follows:

1) The only way to capture the #1 ranking by the end of the age is for somebody to take out Carrot Flowers.
2) A dragon is the only way to gain an advantage on a kingdom that is bigger than you. Normally, this trick backfires as soon as the other kingdom generates its own dragon, but if we send the dragon at the very end of the age, so that Carrot Flowers runs out of time to retaliate, it may work.
3) I think that we can convince the #2 and #3 kingdoms to join us in the attack. They will all be hungry to catch up with #1, and I think they will see the logic in attacking together.
4) Because of our size, the dragon we fire off might be the most powerful ever seen. Although I admit to not knowing the numbers (the Lords of The Realm are extremely secretive when it comes to dragon control), I would be very surprised if ours didn't do a tremendous amount of damage.
5) It sure would be fun ;)

Signed, Queen Peace & Love but Mostly Love

Xerxes looks at his clock: 12:21 P.M. He is about to miss another set of visiting hours at St. Francis. As he lies on his bed, his eyes red and fatigued from staying up all night, and from staring, for so many hours, at his computer screen, Xerxes finds himself thinking about dungeons—and about the places we become trapped. There is nothing keeping Xerxes from quitting, there is nothing holding him to this insistent logging on, and yet he cannot stop, he has to see the age through. Call it what you will—obsession, addiction, vainglory—he cannot halt his own reward-free progress.

He is aware of all the other things he should be doing. He is aware that he should not have left Sara's log cabin last night, that today he should still be lying in bed, languishing in the joy of a fresh and new love; he is aware that he should not be in Rest Stop, Arizona, at all, that he should still be in San Francisco, putting the pieces of his broken company back together.

Xerxes is aware of what he should be doing, and yet in his distraction, in the difficulty he has in deciding exactly where it is that he should start, Xerxes finds himself back again in the place he feels trapped, back again in The Realm.

★　★　★

There is one last issue for her to attend to. It is not an easy puzzle to solve. The most difficult problem for any monarch to deal with is internal strife. It can rear its ugly head at any time, and it can destroy a kingdom in no time at all. If someone gets angry and quits, all their province's net worth disappears, leaving the kingdom without.

sKyLaR had e-mailed her the entire transcript of the weird conversation that he had with Lord BonZ. So as not to alarm sKyLaR, the Queen played it off as a fluke, some imposter screwing with him, but as she said this she wondered to herself exactly what was going on.

Lord BonZ was obviously somebody else. For one, his game play had improved. At first, the Queen had attributed this success to Lord BonZ's learning curve, but now, with the other changes she saw in Lord BonZ's character, she felt it could only mean that Lord BonZ had a new controller. Secondly, all the misspellings, and extra symbols, and lack of punctuation that were a signature of his postings had been replaced by quick, to-the-point messages characterized by the bad pronoun use and missing articles of a nonnative English speaker (or at least, thought the Queen, someone mimicking one).

None of this would matter, of course, if the Queen weren't concerned that the indiscretion would cause a deletion.

Account swapping—if the original Lord BonZ had given the new Lord BonZ his persona—was considered a big no-no to The Lords of The Realm; deletion being the punishment if an account swap was uncovered. One of the basic tenets of The Realm, something that kept the game fair and fun, was that the players behind the provinces weren't Real Life friends, that they couldn't get together physically and discuss strategy. If players were permitted to trade accounts, the communication challenges, the organizational obstacles, and more importantly, the work involved in training new players whose background is unfamiliar to the other players—all these things that not only provide a level playing field but also make The Realm an unusual and unique place—would be gone.

Of course, it still happened; accounts were still swapped. It was difficult for The Lords of The Realm to prove that players were account swapping—the shift of an IP address might indicate that a different player was controlling an account but it could also mean that they had purchased a new computer, or that they were playing at work, or at school, or on a laptop. Most account swaps were never caught, and it was for this reason that superkingdoms came into being, powerful kingdoms filled with players who were far too familiar with the strengths of their fellow kingdom mates.

If the Queen only suspected Lord BonZ of an account swap then she would keep her suspicions under wraps and not alarm Lord BonZ by bringing up the potential violation. Her loyalty, after all, is not to what was best for The Realm, but to what is best for the kingdom.

It is, however, a potential further violation that was bothering the Queen. Suddenly the Raven, this English bloke who conversed in Edgar Allen Poe poems, was speaking just like Lord BonZ. The only explanation for this, was, of course, that Lord BonZ had either usurped, or been temporarily given, Raven's account. Like account swapping, playing someone else's account, even for short periods of time, was a crime punishable by banishment, but unlike account swapping, playing more than one account was easy to detect. If a person logged in to different accounts from the same computer, the Lords of The Realm could match the IP addresses. It was highly unlikely that two people from the same kingdom could be using the same public computer, so the Lords of The Realm, when IP addresses were matched, simply booted both players from The Realm.

The Queen, of course, has no way to know for sure that this is going on, but Lord BonZ was becoming enough of a rogue element, between the personality changes and the exchange with sKyLaR, that the Queen thinks she should at least broach the subject. As long as she does it off-line; that is, outside the game (so as not to provide evidence to the Lords of The Realm that something was amiss), there is no harm in simply asking him what is going on.

As if conjured, Lord BonZ's name suddenly appears in bold. The Queen does not hesitate. She must do this as diplomatically as possible:

Peace_Love: *Hello.*

Lord_BonZ: *hello*

Peace_Love: *Great work in the war. With you leading I think we still have a chance against Carrot Flowers.*

Lord_BonZ: thx ;)

Peace_Love: sKyLaR said he talked to you today

Lord_BonZ: yes, i talk sKyLaR

Peace_Love: You are from Thailand?

Lord_BonZ: yes, i live thailand

Peace_Love: You are a girl in RL? sKyLaR said you showed him some pictures.

Lord_BonZ: yes, i am girl. you want see me? then you know it me?

Peace_Love: no, i don't want to see you. can i ask why you want to show us these pictures? sKyLaR did not like them.

Lord_BonZ: i not want offend sKyLaR. i want come america. i think maybe sKyLaR see me and help me. can you help? i want work not be porn star. you woman, maybe you understand?

The Queen pauses, she isn't sure exactly how to proceed. Lord BonZ had hinted at these same things to sKyLaR. sKyLaR had thought it might be some weird extortion/money laundering scheme that someone was trying to pull on him. The Queen had hoped that whoever it was that had messaged him had just gotten ahold of Lord BonZ's user name and password temporarily, but it looked like the IRC Lord BonZ was also The Realm Lord BonZ, and that he was sticking to his story.

The Queen decides to put a quick end to Lord BonZ's speculation and maybe get some information from him about her other area of concern—where has Raven gone?

Peace_Love: I can't help Lord BonZ. Where is Raven? Maybe he can help.

Lord_BonZ: raven no help. he live thailand here with me. he my boss

Peace_Love: I thought he said he lived in England. How is he your boss?

Lord_BonZ: *raven lie. he my—how do you say—photomaker. i orphan. he give me food and place to stay. he let me use computer and learn many thing. he good and bad too. he make me shower. his name uncle charley. he speak english real good, this why he say he from england*

Peace_Love: *Are you pulling my leg?*

Lord_BonZ: *what this mean—pull leg?*

Peace_Love: *NM. So is he gone? When you sent me that message before it sounded like you.*

Lord_BonZ: *i don't know*

Peace_Love: *Are you playing his province?*

Lord_BonZ: *yes*

Peace_Love: *This is very dangerous. If the Lords of The Realm find out they will delete both you and Raven's account. You should not play him anymore.*

Lord_BonZ: *yes. i think of this. i use two different computers. i use one for me and one for him. this ok?*

Peace_Love: *It's ok. How did you get in the same kingdom as Raven?*

Lord_BonZ: *don't know. i think very lucky*

Lord_BonZ: *i sorry i make trouble for you. i no want trouble queen. i understand no trust me because no know me. i come america i visit? i want meet queen. maybe you help find job? maybe i stay with you? i no want make trouble. only friend. you still friend?*

Peace_Love: *Sure, I'm still your friend. I just wanted to make sure there wasn't any trouble in the kingdom. I'm glad you are on top of it. I'm sorry that you are having trouble in Thailand.*

Lord_BonZ: *what this mean—on top of it?*

Peace_Love: I meant I am glad that you are running Raven's province from another computer so that we don't lose the game.

Lord_BonZ: oh, yes, i am on top of it;)

Peace_Love: I still live with my parents so if you come to America you can visit but not stay.

Lord_BonZ: ok, visit

Peace_Love: I must go now and attend to the kingdom. bye.

Lord_BonZ: CYA

Gek-Lin has finished her task list. Things did not go as planned, but for some reason she is not disappointed. Perhaps, it is the late hour and she is simply exhausted, or perhaps it is because although she has not accomplished what she set out to accomplish, she has still reached out. On top of that, Gek-Lin feels that she has learned something; she has improved her negotiating skills. She screwed up with sKyLaR, but with the Queen, even though she was not able to filch money or even a place to stay should she be so lucky as to get to America, she did gain a certain level of trust. Gek-Lin had a friend in America. The connection was tenuous, sure, but it was still a connection.

Gek-Lin looks around the quiet, empty room. The flickers, the shadows in the corners that had at first haunted her, beckon to her now. Gek-Lin does not understand America; she does not understand that it is a place where those accustomed to community do not do well. What those who immigrate do not say, what the staunch anti-Castro Cuban-Americans won't tell you about their Cuba, is how much they miss community. You cannot hitch a ride, from any stranger, in America, like you can in Cuba. You cannot stand on the side of any road and hop on any bus. You cannot stroll over to any neighbor's house for butter or eggs or milk. And if you do, you are certainly not invited for a sip of rum and an hour of gossip. Unlike independence, interdependence, in America, is much maligned.

Gek-Lin doesn't realize that she is perfectly suited for this place called America. She does not recognize that the silence and solitude she feels right now, the emptiness of the basement of the Blue Moon, is a preview of the silence and solitude she will be greeted by in America. She does not know yet that some thrive in the coldness of this, that some wither—and that others die. Right now, Gek-Lin hears only the cry of that statue, the copper one gone permanently green: *Give me your tired, your poor, your huddled masses yearning to breathe free.*

Gek-Lin knows only that she is all of these things: poor, tired, huddled, yearning to breathe free—and that America is a place that supposedly desires these things, that invites these qualities to her shores. She does not yet know that she will have to deal with its coolness when she arrives there, that when she sets foot on America's hallowed ground, she will need every ounce of her fierceness, her inner strength, her intellect.

A sense of place and purpose suddenly overwhelms Gek-Lin. Still sitting upright in front of her computer, the girl lays her head on Psyduck and falls helplessly asleep.

30. FEEDING A DRAGON TAKES TIME.

SARA BRONSTEIN EXPECTS WARMTH, but what she finds is coldness. He is not there. She knows enough about his life to know that he has no reason not to be there. She looks on, and under, her bed sheets, for some note, but there is nothing, nothing that is except a bowling shirt, a bowling shirt with somebody else's name on it, someone whose name is Dean.

She wants, very badly, for him to be here. She had felt, last night, as he had poured out his soul to her, and she to him, that they were fortunate, that they had each found each other at a similar point in their lives. They were both standing there at a crossroads, some Des Moines-esque junction of freeways; standing there on I-80 with nothing but their thumbs to guide them, a boy and a girl. How fortunate that was! How opportune! For the one thing that these two otherwise unfortunate people, who had been dropped off on the side of the freeway, had was time. And time, when someone has someone new and exemplary to share it with, is truly a wonderful gift.

She had felt different, last night, than she had ever felt. It wasn't that the way she felt before was bad, it was just that before, her thoughts had always been to the future—if she went to grad school, and then did all her field work, she would one day be what she wanted to be, and then, and only then, would she be able to live in the present. Last night, she had suddenly seen the possibility of now, that right then, at the very moment that Peter the Pee Pee, her alarm/radio with the glow-in-the-dark hands and the night light penis, read 3:14 A.M.; that everything was as it should be. She had felt, as she lay with Xerxes, that everything, from that moment forward, would continue to be that way; that Wednesday, as she taught another anger management course in a psychiatric institute housed in a strip mall, she would be satisfied, knowing that her future would take care of itself, and that she would continue to receive gifts like Xerxes—people dropping out of the universe and into her realm at opportune times—just when she needed it.

But now Xerxes is gone, has left her alone on that freeway in Des Moines sans explanation. Perhaps, he would call; perhaps, he wouldn't. Either way he had already done it, had already left her there. She is back in a now that looked only to the future. She is back in Rest Stop, all alone.

Sara picks up another Sue Grafton novel. She has read them all and is repeating the series. She picks up *C is for Corpse*.

She supposes, given everything that he'd told her that night, given all the ways he'd avoided conflict, that what he'd done was to be expected. She holds out, with some hope, that it is all a mistake, that perhaps he'd woken in the middle of the night with a bad case of explosive diarrhea, and was sick in bed, at home, and would call her any minute now and explain. But the hours go by—3, 6, 9, 12—and she finishes *C is for Corpse* and begins *D is for Deadbeat*, and she realizes she probably won't see him again until she runs into him at St. Francis, in which case he will probably stammer something to her and reverse himself back out the door.

Sara knows what she should do. She knows what would be therapeutic. She knows that she should just drive right up and give him an earful. She doesn't do this. She stays in her hammock. She continues her novel.

★   ★   ★

The windows and doors of Xerxes's room are shut and the unfiltered air, made more fetid from the heat of an Indian summer, has turned sour. Gnats have taken up residence above Xerxes's head, and although at times, like an elephant slapping himself with his tail at a zoo, he takes swats at them, he pays as little heed to them as is humanly possible. Empty 2-liter bottles of Coke lie on top of his clothing, and a spill from one of these has stained the floor, adding a hint of sugar to the sour-smelling air.

In the end, the Queen Peace & Love but Mostly Love had decided that the matter was urgent, and that she didn't need the approval of her ministers. When they returned, from wherever it was they had gone, they would be happy at what she had done. She'd maximized her economy for the feat, been feeding it, almost single-handedly, its needed gold and mana. Some of the smaller provinces were helping, but it was she that was putting in most of it, returning, every hour on the hour, to feed the dragon its due. She had lost some personal ground this way; her own province's net worth had stopped its usual rapid rise, but no matter, it was the kingdom that mattered to her— what would *Paradigm Shift's* final score be?

The Queen looks at her computer screen. The size of the dragon is like nothing she has ever seen before:

PRISMATIC DRAGON (Conjured by Queen Peace & Love but Mostly Love, of the kingdom Paradigm Shift): AC: -9, HP: 50,000, STRENGTH REDUCTION OF TARGET: -35%, EXTRA LAND GAINED BY ATTACKING TARGET: 25%, LOSS OF FOOD PRODUCTION DUE TO RAZED CROPS: 50%, LOSS OF BUILDINGS TO FIRES: 8%, DESERTION OF TROOPS DUE TO FEAR: 5%

*   *   *

The neighbor's dog was the one that had found her. The dog sniffed trouble, pressed its snout underneath The Serpent's door, barked. Its owner thought the dog's behavior was peculiar, since it rarely barked, and then the owner noticed the smell too. The smell was the smell of a refrigerator full of spoiled meat after a prolonged power outage. The dog owner knocked on the door several times to no avail, then shrugged and walked away.

Over the course of the day the smell grew worse, and this time, when the dog owner walked by again, on her way to take the dog out for an evening stroll, she had one of those autonomic responses that says something is wrong: a shiver went up her spine; her hair stood up on end. She contacted the building manager.

The building manager and the dog owner stood in the hallway of The Serpent's flat and conferred. The building manager knew a little of The Serpent's habits. He knew that she had frequent male visitors, at all hours. He thought she was a prostitute. After knocking and shouting The Serpent's name, the building manager opened the door. By now, both the building manager and the dog owner were afraid of what they might find.

They were right to be afraid. For what they found was the naked body of a dead woman, sitting somewhat upright in her bed, her face and torso a ghostly white, drained of blood. Her legs were spread in a V. In the dead woman's arm was a needle. The needle didn't look real. It looked wrong, as if it were being held aloft by an invisible string. But the worst thing they found there, or at least the thing that the dog owner thought was the worst, was her tattoo. The woman had a serpent tattooed on her, a huge serpent that wrapped itself around her. The serpent seemed alive now that the woman was dead. When the dog owner saw the tongue of the serpent tattoo licking at the woman's genitalia, genitalia that had been shaved clean of pubic hair to give the serpent full access to his treasure, she vomited. For the rest of her life, the dog owner had an image in her mind of evil. It was a live serpent licking a dead woman's pussy.

Tres Rawlings, for his part, had been avoiding looking at the monitor, focusing instead on the information coming to him from The Realm. He plotted spy attempts on *Paradigm Shift*, kept his provinces in line, but still, on another monitor, she was there, his love gone cold, and when there was finally movement, her monitor got his full attention.

The dog owner and the building manager left, and were replaced, a short while later, by an old man in a lab coat. The old man hovered over The Serpent's body. Tres had never seen the old man before in her room, and Tres assumed, and assumed correctly, that the old man was another stranger, another stranger there to do something with The Serpent's body: Don't get Tres wrong; he did not suspect the stranger of malintent. The old man stood over her body. He looked genuinely and appropriately disturbed at the sight before him. He did not seem to derive pleasure from the sight.

The old man put two fingers, his middle finger and his index finger, on The Serpent's wrist, shook his head, turned, and said something. Next, the man took The Serpent's head and turned it. He went over the back of her shaved head with his thumb and index finger as if he were checking for ticks. He turned and said something else. Finally, he turned The Serpent's body on its side. Her back was a swirl of blues and purples that the back of a person still alive wouldn't have. The tattoo on her back looked bloated, as if the tattoo had eaten a mouse. The man traced the tattoo with a finger starting from the neck, going down the spine, down to the buttocks. He turned and said more things. Finally, the old man pulled out a metal box with a red cross on the top from a medical bag that he had brought with him. It looked like a first-aid kit. He put the metal box on the bed. The metal box had instruments in it that Tres recognized instantly. Tres knew things about the instruments that Tres shouldn't know, knew because he had a prurient interest in such things, knew because there were Web sites where play nurses and play doctors and play patients used such instruments.

The man pulled a speculum and a vaginal scraper from the metal box and put these beside The Serpent's swollen body on the bed. He rolled The Serpent back over onto her back. He spread apart The Serpent's legs. He inserted the speculum, then turned the thumbscrew.

Before the vaginal scraper went in, a ray of light went through the circuitry of Slash246's long-forgotten chandelier Web cam and into Tres's visual array, so that, when the metal glinted between her legs, it looked to him like the mouth of The Serpent's tattoo was breathing fire. Tres had wished that this were so. He wished that The Serpent and her tattoo were both alive and well and breathing fire.

But she wasn't, The Serpent and her serpent were dead. She was dead and a medical examiner had out the rape kit, was violating her one last time. He inserted the vaginal scraper, pulled it out, placed the contents of her insides on a glass slide. He left her open. He repeated the process. Once, twice, three times.

The medical examiner did not seem disturbed by any of this. Everything seemed routine. Tres Rawlings, however, was disturbed. If he had been capable of puking, he would have. If he had been capable of shouting, he would have. What Tres Rawlings would have shouted, if he could have, was this: *How, how could you do this? How could you give her in death, the same thing she got in life? You are cold. You are metallic. This is worse. Somehow worse. It wasn't like you think. It didn't go down like that. LEAVE HER ALONE. LET HER BE ALONE.*

Next to what he was shouting, though, was something else. It was a question: a question black and bold on a field of fluorescent green like the question mark on the front of The Riddler's costume in *Batman* cartoons. The question was: *Where is The Serpent's family and why don't they stop them?*

When the old man finally finished with The Serpent, when he laid her to rest under an anonymous white hospital sheet, when yet another pair of men entered the room, slid her onto a gurney, then onto a stretcher, when The Serpent was finally gone from the narrow scope of Tres's Web cam forever, leaving him with a view of Little Mermaids swimming in the soiled sea of a stained bedspread, Tres asked himself where they were, where anyone was: overprotective parents, a nosy brother, a girlfriend—anyone.

No one came. His monitor was live for days after the medical examiners had come and gone. He thought for sure someone would show, that someone would enter The Serpent's bedroom downcast and depressed, would linger at her closet door, would look in; that someone would finger their way through her clothing, touch sleeve and pant as if they were caressing an arm or leg; that someone would return to the room and stare long and hard at her *Sid and Nancy* poster, searching the young punk rock faces for some answers.

But no one came. Eventually, two people dressed like exterminators, covered from head to toe in rubber suits—two people of indeterminate age and sex, but presumably, once again, men—came into her bedroom carrying Glad garbage bags. They removed the Little Mermaid bedspread, sheets, and pillowcases, and stuffed them in the bags. They sprayed the mattress and box springs with something green and foamy and carried them out of Tres's sight. Then they got down on their hands and knees and scrubbed the linoleum floor until it obtained an unearthly sheen, a sheen like the sheen on little glass balls left over from nuclear detonations.

After a while, they put a ladder up where the bed had been. One of the exterminators climbed up it. Tres's last view of The Serpent's room had been that of a tinted square visor, a gas mask, and then the total darkness caused by the black palm of a gloved hand.

The Serpent is gone, but the question—where is The Serpent's family?—still torments him. What if he were the only one left who cared? What if her parents died in some tragic accident when she was 14? What if their Indy blue Mini Cooper with racing stripes drove over some cliff in the Scottish highlands? What if she had been left to some bitter old aunt in Milton-Keynes, a disgruntled youth stuck in a planned community? What if she had become a runaway, gotten in with a bad crowd in an Earl's Court youth hostel? What if her aunt died, her only aunt, and left her nothing, no note of the whereabouts of any relatives? What if she discovered that the friends she had, her bad crowd, couldn't care less? What if these friends didn't come back for their dead, but instead turned a cold eye lest they see their own reflection in the mirror? What if Tres Rawlings were the only one left, the only one who could bury her?

31. RELEASE THE DRAGON.

ALTHOUGH SHE CAN THINK of a thousand reasons not to go back to the St. Francis Psychiatric Hospital, although she wants to have as little to do with the Meticula gene pool as possible, although the brand new Grafton book, *Q is for Quarry*, is burning a hole in her handbag, Sara Bronstein is determined to end this professionally. It is, after all, a psychiatrist's duty, even a young, inexperienced one, to give her clients that all-important closure. Sara has no idea what she is going to do next, but she knows she has to leave here; she knows, that after one last anger management seminar, she is going to get on the phone and use her frequent flyer miles to purchase a one-way ticket back to La Guardia. Rest Stop was just that, a rest stop.

*   *   *

Xerxes is waiting for the hour to change. T minus two minutes. He clicks his refresh button over and over again. When the hour changes, his news screen reads:

Your dragon begins pillaging the lands of Carrot Flowers (47:50)

*   *   *

As has become her custom, in her one hour per week of work, Sara simply sits down and draws like the rest of them. She has learned that the best way to lead the unpredictable residents of the St. Francis Psychiatric Hospital is by calm, collected example. Today she has brought Post-it notes. She opens the packaging and dumps them on the table. They scatter in a rainbow of pastels: light green, light blue, light pink, light yellow. The residents of the sanitarium sit in silence and stare. Leonard, meanwhile, paces behind Sara. Sara has learned not to interrupt Leonard, not to make him sit. It is hard enough for Leonard to pace, hard enough to make him turn from his tendency towards West. Every once in a while Leonard doesn't take his turn, he simply runs head first into the wall. Sara ignores this, keeps doing what she is doing.

Although Sara thinks she is behaving in a calm and collected manner, her silence, and the jerky way she tears open the packaging and dumps the Post-its onto the table, betrays her. The group around the table sits nervously observing. Gabriella, especially, is intent. She stares hard at Sara with her bright, difficult eyes and her furrowed brow.

Sara still hasn't said anything. The crayons are not out this time. Instead, Sara has bought Bic pens. She tears open the packaging and out they fall.

Sara can't look up at the faces. She's finding her cool increasingly hard to maintain. She is surprised that she feels this way, surprised that she cares. Wednesdays without weird Leonard and intense Gabriella; she suddenly finds this hard to imagine.

So Sara simply picks up a pen, red; and a pad of Post-it notes, green; and begins to demonstrate what she had planned to have the group do today. On the top-most Post-it, Sara makes a quick drawing of a stick figure with a sword, and a rather humorous drawing of a dragon, a dragon that really looks more like a big fat duck. She repeats the drawing on the Post-it under-neath, only this time the stick figure with the sword is getting closer to the dragon/duck, and something, which Sara intended to be fire, but which looks more like vomit, begins spewing out of the dragon/duck's mouth. She goes on, drawing quickly to get her point across, until on Post-it note twenty, the stick figure with the sword is nothing but a pile of ashes, and the dragon/duck is lying on its back, with X's for eyes, a sword hilt-deep in its belly.

The group has sat mesmerized, Sara is drawing for them anger in mo-tion. This is new—a unique and unexpected twist in their anger manage-ment seminar. They don't all understand the concept, but they do all understand that what is happening is unusual, and in the world of St. Fran-cis, where the unusual is not often encouraged, the change is welcomed rather silently and gracefully.

When Sara is done, she flips through the Post-its and displays for them her animation. They all start clapping. Sara finally speaks. She says, "OK, now it's your turn."

All of them get to work. Helen draws a house and a woman—a woman pushing a shopping cart. The woman wheels the shopping cart towards the house. The house keeps moving backwards. Eventually the house has fallen off the edge of the Post-its, leaving the woman with the shopping cart all alone, scratching her head, with no house. Joanna draws a needle and a plunger. As she turns the pages of the Post-it pad, the plunger goes in and liquid comes out the needle. Leonard draws a man walking. Although the man is walking, on every Post-it, the man stays in the same place. Objects come at him—saguaros, cows, deer, ranchers, police cars—they all come to-wards the man walking but when they reach him they compress and then disintegrate, as if the man walking had around him some sort of rock-solid force field.

Finally, there is Gabriella. Gabriella only pretends to be drawing. She is more intent on observing. She notices that Sara, who is pretending just to doodle, is actually drawing something as well. Gabriella wants to see what Sara is drawing, but Sara is not letting her. Sara sits with her left arm around her Post-its, avoiding Gabriella's gaze. Their eyes lock for a moment: Sara is aware of the observation; she stays vigilant, keeps her arm in place.

This goes on. There is not much class time left. Ten minutes. Sara is drawing madly, trying to finish, trying to fill the pages. She ignores the goings-on around her. A house going up in flames. A needle doing its dam-age. Leonard walking.

Finally, Gabriella makes her run. She launches herself from her seat. She snatches up Sara's Post-its. She flips the pages. She sees: a man in a bowling shirt that says Dean approaching a woman; a cut to the woman smiling; a large red penis clashing with a dripping red vagina; a cut to the woman smil-ing; the man and the woman in a bed sleeping, the man getting up while the woman is asleep and leaving; a cut to the woman upset; the woman getting up and going to a storefront with the words ST. FRANCIS PSYCHIATRIC HOSPITAL painted on the awning; the woman marching in; the woman with a word bubble over her head that says "I quit"; the woman turning around, grabbing a suitcase, and boarding a plane, a plane with the words TO NYC printed on the side.

Gabriella sees this. She knows what it all means. She knows who the man and the woman are. She howls. It is not a human howl. It is a coyote howl. Sara tries to stop her from this; she tears the Post-it notes out of her hands, says to her, "it . . . it's not what you think." But Gabriella knows that it is exactly what she thinks. Her howl is mournful and sad. The howl elicits a crowd of people in white coats.

*   *   *

He finally has it. He has his revenge. The dragon landed where it was in-tended to land, and now Two-Headed Boy, and the rest of his provinces, their defense has been compromised, and the walls of their citadels can eas-ily be breached.

The Queen Peace & Love but Mostly Love lays her yellow pad next to her. She subtracts all the possible means of protection the *Two-Headed Boy* might have garnered. She takes into account the weakening effects of the dragon. She knows the numbers with all exactitude. She has, up until this very moment, exuded peace. She has simply trained more and more troops, not releasing them on any enemy capable of returning her fire. Her strangely peaceful orcs are now ready to leave their citadel. Their sheer numbers are ungodly. They are all elite troops—orcish spearthrowers, the most powerful offensive weapons in The Realm. The Queen enters in the numbers: 53,302 spearthrowers and clicks "Send." The hourglass on her screen does not spin for long. The central processors maintained by The Lords of The Realm do not need much time. They, like the Queen, know the score. The response is swift; her success monumental:

Your troops have fought a brave battle and won. You have appropriated 1,539 acres of land from The King of Carrot Flowers (47:50). Your army will return from the battlefield in 18 days. Realm T-shirts are now available! Visit The Realm Store at www.therealmstore.com. With your purchase you will receive a 100 acre bonus courtesy of The Lords of The Realm.

The Queen cannot hide her exuberance. She checks the IRC to see who is online. She wants to share the news with sKyLaR, or Raven, or Lord BonZ. None of these names, however, are in bold.

The Queen is surprised at this, surprised at the loneliness she suddenly feels in her hour of triumph. She looks around the room at the clothes on the floor, at the unmade bed, at the flies. Yes, she has won—but what are the spoils? It is no longer the Queen contemplating these things; it is Xerxes. He picks up two drinking glasses from the floor and clinks them together, mocking a toast. The glasses clink with glee. The sound rings hollow.

* * *

The last thing Sara wants to do is call him. Given that she's just told the St. Francis staff that she will no longer be gracing them with her presence, she certainly has no obligation to. And yet, she can't help but feel that Gabriella's new outbreak was her fault, and that, given the circumstances, she owed, not him the call, but her. If there was anyone who could calm Gabriella right now, and better yet, explain the situation to the staff so they wouldn't drug her into oblivion, it was Xerxes. Sara picks up her phone and looks at the digits. She says "damn it," out loud, to herself, and then she dials the number.

★   ★   ★

A voice comes through the intercom in Xerxes's room, "Hey Xerxes, Sara Bronstein is on the phone."

In the wake of waiting for someone to celebrate his success with and finding no one there, Xerxes does not hesitate, although, if he had taken a moment to think, he probably would have. "I've got it, Dad."

Xerxes leaves his room to get the phone. The feel of fresh air—dry, filtered, air-conditioned air—hits him as he opens the door. He feels woozy, punch-drunk. He picks up the phone. "Hello?"

Sara is not expecting this. She'd expected that he'd have his Dad take a message, and that his Dad would convince him to go visit Gabriella. No such luck. She'll get through this. She'll pretend she doesn't care. "I Ii Xerxes, it's Sara. Look, I'm calling about your sister. I was just at St. Francis, at the anger management class, and I was draw . . . telling her that I was leaving and going back to New York City, and she got very upset. I think you should go over there as quickly as you can. She wasn't in very good shape."

"Why—"

"She just started howling, sort of bestially, like a wolf or something. I don't know. I know that they'll medicate her, and that will calm her down, but I think you should go and talk to her. You're very good at bringing her back to herself, you know. She needs you."

Xerxes forces his question through. "Why are you leaving?"

"I need a better place to get my hours. They only give me a session a week here and I'm not progressing fast enough. Anyway . . . that's not why I'm calling—"

"When—"

Sara is choking back her emotions. Hearing his voice, everything was flooding her mind, the way she had felt with him, the hope he had given her for her future. She wants to persuade him that whatever he was doing was dumb, that his passive way of dealing with all circumstances is bound to make him an unhappy man. "Go to your sister, Xerxes."

"Sara? Can I see you again before you go?"

Sara's voice quivers. She's close to breaking. "Good luck, Xerxes. I wish you and your sister the best." And with those final words Sara returns her phone to its cradle.

32. DRAGONS BREATHE FIRE.

CHARLEY'S FIRST-EVER LIMO RIDE had not been the luxury ride that limo rides are hyped up to be. In the ride that had taken place immediately after Kin-Dong and his man had abducted both him and one of his girls, the fourteen-year-old China Jade, he had been unceremoniously tossed into the front seat of the limo. Kin-Dong's man had slipped into the driver's seat next to him, locked the door, placed a finger under Charley's chin, and said, "unlock that door and die." The panel that separated the front seats from the back of the limo was closed, so Uncle Charley could not see China Jade, but when Kin-Dong's man took a pair of silvered, large-lensed sunglasses off the dash, placed them on the bridge of his nose, lit a cigarette with a Zippo, and then, responding to the muffled sounds of struggle coming, despite the soundproofing, from the back seat, began humming the theme to *The Love Boat*—love, exciting and new—Charley knew China Jade's unfortunate fate.

Uncle Charley would have liked to have knocked the sunglasses clean off the driver's face; but he was not the type of man to take dramatic action. He simply sat there and added what was happening to him and China Jade to his list of grudges against an unfair world.

Kin-Dong's man drove the limo up Patpong 1 and out of the Silom District. Traffic was heavy, as always, made worse by the bulk of the limo, and they crawled along, with the man continuing to hum, and the strugglings in the back gaining a certain unmistakable rhythm and meter. Charley, nervous that any twitch could spell his doom, sat up straight in his seat, the cold of the air-conditioned vehicle cooling his sweat and causing him to shiver.

Eventually, they got to a locked gate at the front of a large compound. The man lowered his sunglasses a little and glared at Charley, a glare that very clearly said "stay put," then he got out and opened the back door. Kin-Dong stepped out. "The girl?" the limo driver asked. "She'll come with me," Kin-Dong said. And the man nodded, got back in the limo, and drove Charley north, out of the city.

* * *

"Now isn't a good time to see her," says Rene.

"Why not?" asks Xerxes, looking at his reflection in the one-inch by one-inch window, not particularly impressed with the colicky hair, the bloodshot eyes, or the five-o-clock shadow he sees there.

"She's upset."

Xerxes does not have patience for the assistants of strip mall psychiatrists. "It seems like her being upset would indicate that now is a particularly good time for someone who cares about her to visit her."

Rene has no patience for the snotty twin brothers of schizophrenics. "Wait here, Mr. Meticula, I'll see what I can do."

Rene passes Xerxes and pushes her way through the swinging doors, returning shortly with one of the social workers who monitors Gabby.

"Mr. Meticula," this social worker says, "your sister's situation is delicate today; her routine has been disturbed. She is being irrational. We'd like to sedate her, for her own safety, and the safety of the other patients here, but since you've arrived, perhaps you'd like to see for yourself the state that she's in, so you'll better understand her course of treatment."

Xerxes has no patience for the social worker either, but he behaves. "Can you give me a few minutes alone with her?"

"She's been throwing—"

"It's OK, she's my sister, I can handle her."

The social worker leads Xerxes through the swinging doors and into the hallway. Leonard and another shrink are standing outside the door to the bunk room where Gabriella and all the other "girls" at St. Francis sleep. Xerxes can hear Gabriella behind the door, ranting, "He just throws the card away! Like that. Like it's nothing. What a fool. A fool, fool, fool! A triple, diple fool! You're all fools—foo-uls, foo-uls, foo-uls."

Leonard points at the door, says to Xerxes, "Go in fool."

Everyone—Xerxes, the shrink, and the social worker—look at Leonard. Leonard doesn't speak much, so when he does, he captures people's attention.

"There is so much happening in the *universe!*" comes from behind the door.

Xerxes notices that Leonard has a tooth loose; it had probably come unhinged in his fall. When he said the word "fool," he had tongued it forward, like the swinging door in the foyer.

"You don't all need to stand around," Xerxes says.

The two St. Francis employees back off, giving him room to enter. "If she gets violent . . ."

Xerxes glares at them.

"You know we're not liable . . ."

Xerxes enters the room.

★ ★ ★

Uncle Charley sits in a high-backed chair; his eyes are blindfolded, his ankles are tied to the legs of the chair, and his hands are laying palms down on a table in front of him, secured there by several pieces of duct tape pasted over his forearms and wrists. He can smell the cigarette smoke of the man smoking and pacing behind him. He can hear him grumbling, mingling English curse words with his Thai, "Fuck weather . . . fuck weather." He can also hear the branches of sandalwood and yang trees slapping against the sides of the bungalow to which he has been brought. And he can hear the wind and the rain.

After leaving Kin-Dong and China Jade at Kin-Dong's compound, the limo driver had driven him out of Bangkok to the airport. They had taken a plane south to the border city of Hat Yai, where they had disembarked. The man was met by another man who drove a small blue, rusted sedan. They hurried Charley into the car, drove a short while, pulled off into a muddy alleyway; there they had blindfolded him, tied his arms at the wrist and his legs at the ankle, and placed him in the hot, cramped, and mildewed trunk of the sedan.

Charley had lain this way for hours, his head clunking against the roof of the trunk as the sedan drove over countless potholes. He thought he might die in these confines, but still, he made no sounds. This was his fate, after all, to die in the filth of his own making. Charley slipped out of consciousness.

When he had awoken it was to a pail of rainwater being dumped on his head. Hours may have passed, days; he wasn't sure, but he knew he had been seated in the aforementioned high-backed chair, in the aforementioned bungalow, for quite some time.

The two men get near the butts of their cigarettes, and then, glancing at each other and nodding, turn to Charley. The man who had picked them up at the airport, the sedan driver, presses his cigarette into the back of Charley's hand. Charley tries to move, but he has been secured quite tightly. He screams. The man holds the cigarette in place on Charley's hand. Charley's hand sizzles.

Meanwhile, the other man speaks, "Kin-Dong asked us to take you on this little vacation, so that you could do some thinking, before we returned you to Bangkok. It's very important that you know who you work for. Kin-Dong feels that you may have forgotten your loyalties, after all these years in which he has served you and protected you, so we're here to remind you of your loyalties. Do you understand?"

The cigarette goes out and is removed. Sweat drips down Charley's face. He gulps. "Yes."

"Good," says the man, "Pradeep, gag him."

The sedan driver, Pradeep, gags Charley.

The man continues, "Kin-Dong told us that you are very good with computers, Charley. It is important, I understand, in your line of work, to have quick and nimble fingers. Is this correct?"

Charley just stares at him.

The man slaps Charley in the back of the head. "Answer me!"

Charley tries to speak through the gag. The man slaps him on the side of the head, again, harder this time. "Nod!"

Charley nods.

The man turns, "Pradeep?" Pradeep produces a knife, hands it to him.

"I suppose, that it would be difficult, to do your line of work without any fingers, Charley?"

Charley nods, desperately.

"Kin-Dong, and Pradeep and I, and the rest of the PULO, we are like your fingers Charley, without us you wouldn't be able to do your work." The limo driver places the knife on Charley's forefinger. Beads of sweat make their way down Charley's face. "If we were to remove your fingers, Charley, where would you be? How would you run your business?" The limo driver employs the knife like a hacksaw along Charley's finger; it cuts, first through dermis, then through epidermis; it draws blood.

"Now, Charley, we don't want you to forget who your fingers are, do we? So we're going to have to leave you with a little reminder, so you won't forget." The knife reaches bone. Charley's eyes roll towards the back of his head. "Before we do that, I'm going to tell you what you're going to do. You're going to go back to your Internet café, and you're going to keep running your Web cameras, but now, you're going to turn your money right over to Kin-Dong. And the orphans, when they turn fourteen, and no later, you're going to turn them directly over to Kin-Dong. Do you understand?"

Charley nods again. Again, desperately.

The limo driver lifts the knife from Charley's finger and sets it on the table. He turns to Pradeep. Pradeep hands him an axe.

"Now, Charley, we're going to remove one of your fingers, because we're not sure that you're so good at remembering who you work for, and this way, when you see your hand, it'll be like having a little yellow ribbon attached there. When you go back to Bangkok this time, you're going to find the girl, Persephone, and you're going to hand her over to your friend, the limo driver, and while you're at it, you're going to give him a sack of money, 50,000 bhats; we don't care how you obtain it. Do you understand this?"

Charley nods one more time.

"Now don't move, Charley. We don't want to cut off the whole hand."

Charley tries to do exactly that, to move, but even in his desperation, he is unable to kick the legs out from under his chair, or lift his arms up from the layers of duct tape. Charley watches the axe fall, his eyes big as globes.

★   ★   ★

The shriek is otherworldly, like a lamb's mew before its throat is slit, "YEEEEEEEEEEWWWWWWWWWWWW!!!!!" Gabriella doesn't look at him when she yells it, she just keeps up the pacing and howling she's been doing for the last hour. As she walks, she holds a playing card of some sort on her forehead. On the floor are other playing cards, the majority of them centered in one spot—some facing up, some facing down. Gabriella steps on them as she walks, oblivious to the oddness of their occupation of the room. Gabriella is the only one in the bedroom; it had, for obvious reasons, been cleared of patients, but their detritus, mixed in with the playing cards, lay everywhere: used Q-tips, pink plastic curlers, uncapped sticks of lip gloss.

"Gabby, what—"

"SHUT UP! SHUT UP!"

"Listen—"

"SHUT UP!"

Gabby finally acknowledges his presence, turning and staring him in the eye. She approaches him. The playing cards aren't playing cards at all; they're cards from a tarot deck. She has a card marked The World on her forehead.

"You have it all, right now, and you don't even know it. You have the whole world in your hands."

Xerxes thinks of that Bible school song, *He's got the whole world in His hands. He's got the wind and the rain in His hands. He's the got the tiny, little baby in His hands. He's got the whole world in His hands.*

Gabriella hands Xerxes the World card, kneels down, and starts rifling through the cards in the middle of the floor. She finds two cards that she wants and sticks the first one rudely in his face. "You're fortunate enough to get The Lovers, and what do you do? This!"

Gabriella replaces the first card with the second. It has on it a clown, or court jester of some sort, running down a trail while holding up a dangerously slanting tray. The tray has on it 5 gold goblets. One of the goblets has spilled over, and a red liquid—wine or possibly blood—falls from it onto the trail.

"You waste it. You run away from it. You act like it's nothing. And on top of that . . ."

Gabriella clicks the back of the five of Cups with her forefinger so that it bounces off the bridge of Xerxes's nose. He just stands there, withstanding her verbal assault. Gabriella kneels back down, rifles through the pile of cards again.

"Where . . . where the hell is it?" She looks up at Xerxes from her spot on the floor. "Can't you help me? Are you just going to stand there?"

"Well, if I were to help you, what exactly would I be looking for?"

"You know what I'm looking for."

Xerxes looks down at the mess on the floor. He picks up a card with a beautiful but evil-looking woman on it. The woman is resting on a sword, as if it were a cane. "This one?"

Gabriella looks at him icily. "You're an asshole."

Xerxes decides not to help anymore, there's no telling where picking the wrong card might lead. He hadn't meant anything by showing the Queen of Swords to her—had he?

Gabriella is still shuffling through the cards on the floor, unable to find the one that she's looking for, "That's the thing about the cards, you never get the ones you're looking for. They turn up when you least expect it, Xerxes. When you least expect it."

"Can't you just tell me, Gabby?"

This calms Gabriella. It is his strong point. When you corner him, when you pulled him out of machinations in his head, he is a good listener. "OK, but sit down on the cards."

Xerxes obeys.

"I picked the Empress card to represent your present. The Empress is a sign of fertility. I don't know what this means for you—you have to decide that for yourself—but when I crossed it, it was crossed with The Hanged Man. The Hanged Man is a symbol that whatever the Empress was, probably some creative idea, but it could also be a woman, you've chosen to stifle it with inactivity. You get it don't you—the Hanged Man is just, like, hanging around. That's you, Xerxes, just hanging around. Now, I also did a reading for your past. I picked the 3 of Swords. I thought this was good, because the 3 of Swords is a card that means that you are facing up to painful truths, but when I crossed, I crossed it with The Fool. I don't have to tell you what that means do I?"

"No," Xerxes replies, not at all sure what it means, but not really interested in finding out either.

"Now, none of this. NONE OF THIS!"—Gabriella shouts "none of this" like she has Tourettes—"would matter to me, if it wasn't for the card that was ruling all your houses right now. Because you could just sit around being miserable, and doing nothing, and not facing facts, for a long time for all I, or anybody else, cares; except that what you're doing, right now, is affecting the whole, damn, WORLD!"—Gabriella snatches the World card out of Xerxes's inept hands—"I don't know how, but your actions, whether or not you're aware of this, are affecting a great number of people."

Gabriella gets right in Xerxes face. She sprays him with saliva as she half talks/half shouts at him. "Do you know this? How are you doing it? I never understood you. You're so . . . so blasé. And mellow. And cool. How do you do this? How do you do so little, and yet affect so many people? I don't understand."

Gabriella stops, waiting for Xerxes to reply. He doesn't. At least not right away.

"Gabby—"

"Don't tell me that I'm being irrational."

"Gabby—"

"Or that I need sedatives. *Now, Ms. Meticula, just calm down, Ms. Meticula. Just take one of the blue ones and—*"

"Gabby," Xerxes raises his voice this time. It is enough to get her attention.

"Are you going to listen to me, or is this just another chance for a one-sided Gabriella Meticula rant that nobody wants to listen—"

"NOBODY! WELL, SOMEBODY OUGHT TO LISTEN—"

"Christ, would you—"

"Would I what, KEEP IT DOWN? (Ssssh, Ms. Meticula. Be a little quieter, Ms. Meticula. Let's just turrrrrn down the volume a bit, Ms. Meticula. How bout we—")

This is enough for Xerxes. He has always considered himself a master at handling Gabriella's verbal onslaughts, but her mania is too much for him today. He knows, when he leaves, that the sedatives she was decrying will indeed be administered. He hates doing this to his own sister, knowing that walking out on her would preclude drugging, but, really, how much can he do? Xerxes turns and heads for the door.

"HEY!" Gabriella shouts as he twists the knob.

Xerxes turns to her, resignedly. "What, Gabby?"

Gabriella's voice suddenly goes soft. She speaks in an eerie octave. This is the voice that haunts Xerxes, the voice that she takes when she has become possessed of some weird prescient power. "Does anything get through to you? Anything at all? I don't know who or where you go to, Xerxes, but I know that wherever you go to is an empty, dangerous place."

Xerxes starts to speak, but Gabriella stops him. "Go," she says. "Just go."

★   ★   ★

The finger, separated from Charley's hand just below the second knuckle, lay on the table, marinating in a small puddle of blood. Kin-Dong's man picked it up. Kin-Dong's man said, "Now, Charley, we are your fingers, right? So from now on—Kin-Dong, me, Pradeep, the PULO, you—we're all one, right? So what I'm going to do is I'm going to give you back your finger, so that you remember that we're all one. Isn't that nice of me, Charley?"

Charley, blood exiting his hand at a frightening rate, stared mortified. The man slapped him again on the side of the face, this time with a closed fist. Charley's ears rang.

The man prodded him, "Isn't that nice of me, Charley?"

Charley nodded.

"Take off his gag, Pradeep." Pradeep did as he was told. "Open your mouth, Charley." Charley did as he was told.

The man picked the finger up off the table and brought it to Charley's lips. "Bon appetit."

Charley, realizing what the man was about to do, shut his mouth as tightly as he could. Pradeep, reacting quickly, pried his jaws open, and although Charley bit down as hard as he could, drawing blood, the man was able to slip the finger onto Charley's tongue.

In that last instant, Charley, sweat dripping down his face, tears dripping from his eyes, wanted, desperately, to fight. He shouldn't do what he was about to do. With the finger securely in his mouth, with Pradeep struggling to keep Charley's jaw closed, and with the man shouting, "Swallow it!" Charley did it anyway—Charley, obediently, swallowed his own finger.

When he was done, the man patted him on his head. "Good dog, Charley. Good dog."

★ ★ ★

There is no reason to delay, and yet she is delaying. She should call the movers, arrange the plane tickets, call friends back home, and yet she doesn't. Instead, she's out on the hammock, in the cold, under her flannel blanket, halfway through *Q is for Quarry*.

She reads these books because they keep her focused on the page, and nothing else. Today, however, even a page-turner can't prevent her mind from wandering. She thinks instead of reading the words. The words are a blur on the page.

What she is thinking of, is, of course, Xerxes Meticula. It bothers her that she cannot exorcise him from her mind. Her common sense tells her to drop it; he has, after all, made it clear to her that she is not important to him, and the best thing to do, in such circumstances, is to walk away, as quickly and with as little display of emotion as possible.

And yet, she wonders if this is wrong. She wonders if she needs to diverge from protocol. She wonders if she should go to him, and get to the bottom of his actions. She wonders if she should try to pull him back. This would be difficult to do—it is difficult to go back and feed the dog that has bitten you—and yet, Sara, deep inside, knows that this is the answer, because there is something going on with Xerxes that goes beyond her, something that is deeper, something that needs to be dug out, then burned, and then buried.

* * *

When Xerxes leaves the St. Francis Sanitarium it is no longer day, it is night. The road Xerxes is on skirts a lake. The lake was once a series of small canyons, bare rock exposing layers of geologic history. Now, the canyons have been filled in with water. Now, the rock is nothing but sediment.

What was he going to do? He could not forever sneak in and out of his parent's house in Rest Stop, Arizona. He could not forever hide from the fact that Zahn and Dixie were getting married. He could not forever avoid the inquiries of a very angry group of investors. He could not forever lose people like Sara, people who wanted to engage him and bring him back into the world. He could not forever play this game.

It was true, what Gabriella had said. But even though he knew it to be true, and even though he knew what the solution was—stop, forever stop, playing the game—he couldn't bring himself to do it. The Realm was, in the end, Xerxes's ball and chain. He told himself that this age would be the last, that once these four weeks were up he wouldn't continue, but the truth was he was already devising strategy, already scouring The Realm's discussion boards to find out what the rule changes would be for the next age.

His problem was this: he was caught in an infinite loop. If Xerxes knew the music to put to his problem it would be the music of Dietrich Björnson thousands of miles away—it was Aphex Twin—it was music that demanded your attention because of the lack of change in its notes, music that drove you to fits of insanity or to helpless ennui. His loop was going on-line to play his game, then doing one of two things: mountain biking or seeing his sister. There was a third note that had recently been thrown in, Sara's fluttering flute, but as new as that note was, it seemed to be just blending into the song, a new sound in an old beat.

People had tried to break him of this formulaic electronica—his father, his best friend, his exgirlfriend—but none of these had been strong enough to pull him off the knock, knock, knock of his metronome. He was always back. He was always the Queen tied to a throne.

No one understood the extent of his addiction, the senseless pull that it had. They assumed his distractedness was just the cogs turning inside the head of a brilliant mind. No one knew. No one got that he was always in The Realm, doing the math, processing the politics, trying to find the anomaly that would give his kingdom the jump and the advantage. No one understood how unstoppable was his repetition, how ceaseless its beat had become.

The ending to this would never come. There would be the occasional dangle, the occasional hint of progress, but these were only false illusions to keep him listening to his fruitless song. Back when Xerxes was a kid he would sing a song to his sister. He sang it to irritate her, to watch her slowly lose her cool. It was the song that never ends. He sang it like this: *This is the song that never ends. This is the song that never ends. This is the song that never ends.* He left out the other part, the part that goes: *It just goes on and on my friend, some people started singing it not knowing what it was, now they'll continue singing it forever just because.* He just repeated the one-line lyric over and over, as annoyingly as possible—*this is the song that never ends.* He sang it over and over again while he chased her around the house with his song—her telling him to shut up, her throwing stuffed animals and Legos and Matchbox A-Team vans at him—while he sang with increasing enthusiasm: *This is the song that never ends, this is the song that never ends, this is the song that never ends.*

Xerxes feels hopeless, even more hopeless than he had felt on the day when he was on the bridge counting ten steps down to a leap. This dragon will forever chase him. He will never escape its fiery breath.

But Xerxes, as downhearted as he feels at this moment, as hopelessly addicted, as unsure that he will ever reach the end, doesn't know everything. He can't see, like Gabriella, into the future. His dragon, his prismatic dragon, it isn't the only dragon in the sky. There is a jolly, white dragon from down south. There are two from the Orient. There is a dragon pierced with a sword and smouldering. And there is a metallic dragon, a metallic dragon that will save him.

The moon shines through Xerxes's windshield. The moon is Sacagawea on a dollar coin. The moon is a bald man with scars who is laughing.

BOOK V: THE REVELATIONS

RL TIME: OCTOBER 2000
REALM TIME: YR 17-20

And though they were sad
They rescued everyone
They lifted up the sun
A spoonful weighs a ton

—THE FLAMING LIPS, "A SPOONFUL WEIGHS A TON"

33. YOU CAN LEARN A GREAT DEAL FROM A KINGDOM PAGE.

THE SUN, JUST ABOVE THE HORIZON, is taking a slow spin on a merry-go-round of a sky. Dietrich Björnson is not his usual self. Although the permanent twilight of the Antarctic spring is gorgeous—the sky ablaze 24/7 in violets and reds—Dietrich can't enjoy it; he's worried about a girl.

His first instinct had been to see if she was still playing, because if she was still playing then clearly it had been a hoax. He'd gone to the *Amphibious* kingdom page and checked the stats. The order of the top ten provinces was:

The Kingdom of Amphibious (23:34)

	Race	Acres	Net Worth	Rank
1. Sal A. Mander	Troglodyte	4,148	420,849	King
2. Tree Frogs	Troglodyte	3,982	412,918	Lady
3. Mudpuppy	Troglodyte	2,839	303,983	Knight
4. Spring Peeper	Troglodyte	2,572	289,390	Knight
5. Cottonmouth	Troglodyte	2,528	263,390	Lord
6. Hellbender	Troglodyte	1,748	203,289	Knight
7. The Noc Noc Club	Faery	1,573	163,245	Lord
8. Snapping Turtle	Troglodyte	1,529	169,947	Knight
9. Toad	Troglodyte	1,482	147,940	Knight
10. The Serpent	Troglodyte	990	187,349	Lady

This wasn't good news. The Serpent had dropped from #1 to #10, had been stripped of the monarchy, and was losing a lot of land, a good sign she had gone inactive. Of course, going inactive didn't necessarily mean anything in Real Life; people stopped playing for a variety of reasons, but given the IRC conversation he had shared with her, this information increased his worry.

After checking the kingdom page, Dietrich had resorted to sending her kingdom mates messages, asking what had happened to their Queen. Only a few responded to Dietrich's note, and when they did, they simply told him that she had disappeared—that one day she had been playing, and then all of a sudden she stopped communicating and her growth stopped.

Dietrich hadn't gotten anywhere, and the not getting anywhere was bothering him. In the end, he had gotten desperate and sent a note to The Lords of The Realm, explaining what had happened, and seeing if there was any way that they would share her account information with him—if they could at least provide him with a name—but his story had seemed out-landish to them—how did they know this wasn't just some guy trying to scam a girl's personal information—and they had responded with a terse and mechanical note explaining that privacy laws prevented them from sharing account information with anyone.

Dietrich stares at the sun. Despite the light, Dietrich still lives in dark-ness. He had thought that when the veil lifted over the Antarctic skies, all ills would be cured—that Caitlin would awake from her self-made tomb in Bio-med and that the rest of The Dome's population would stop treating him like a pariah. This, however, didn't happen. There was certainly a new buzz about The Dome, but that buzz was at his exclusion. When he'd been black-balled, new social groups had formed, and those social groups went about their business, oblivious to his isolation.

It didn't help that Caitlin was continuing her self-imposed hibernation, lift-ing her head only to check her e-mail for news about her mother. There was an understanding amongst the Polies that you simply endured. Others had gone through similar crises: a wife had filed for divorce, a child had gone to juvi, grandparents had passed away. These were all reasons to want to hang it up, but not reasons to do so. Those at the Dome felt like astronauts, like they were doing something heroic for their nations back home, like the world was watch-ing their every move. It was important for them to show toughness. It was im-portant for them to continue their work. And since Caitlin wasn't showing this toughness and resolve, she was a dark stain on the whole mission.

Dietrich, for his part, thought the attitude of the Polies was wrong, but there wasn't anything he could do to change their minds. At this place where the nations converged, it seemed to Dietrich that the answer was togetherness; and that the goal should be to pick up those who have fallen. Isolating him and Caitlin because of their lack of toughness and resolve seemed contrary. What they should have done was what he would have done: thrown a party, played some poker, drank some whiskey, talked them out of their depression. Instead they started this nasty cold war, the masses against the weak few. There was no doubt that the masses would win, but in doing so they would lose the one thing that was supposed to make Antarctica different from the rest of the world, that it was a place of global harmony where people were so focused on their mission that they wouldn't let themselves get bogged down in the mire of politics.

In a couple of months, Caitlin and Dietrich will leave. They will go see Caitlin's mother, and hopefully, Caitlin and Dietrich (as well as Caitlin's mother) will recover. But Dietrich wishes he could do something, he wishes he wasn't the pawn of NSF officials. He wishes he could go down to Biomed and tell Caitlin that he'd found a way to get them off the ice and back to a place with normal seasons, sufficient rainfall, abundant fireflies, and annoying—yet tolerable—mosquitoes.

Dietrich doesn't want eventuality to save his wife; he wants it to be his own action. He wants to go to Biomed and hand her a plane ticket. He wants to say, *Look, I love you, let's leave here, let's go home.*

*   *   *

Tres has been watching reruns of The Serpent, sifting through the thousands of movie files that he has carefully cross-indexed, chronologically by date and time, as well as categorically by theme: sex vs. sleeping, alive vs. dead.

Today, Tres chooses serpent280301_sleep.mpg. He cues it up on the monitor that was formerly devoted to her live feed. This is a good one. Mary Lynn passed out on top of her Little Mermaid comforter, stomach down, back up, head sideways, an unusual position for her. She looks innocent and angelic. Over the hours that the mpg plays, a pool of saliva slowly stains her pillow, darkening a starfish a deeper shade of salmon.

Tres can't watch the other movies anymore, the ones of her having sex or the ones of her dying, but he still watches the ones where she's sleeping, where she's at peace. Tres has been doing this, not out of morbidity, but to remind him every day of what was his past, and what he is now determined to make his future.

Over the last couple of weeks Tres's dreams have been of a cold refrigerated room: a cold refrigerated room with wall-to-wall black steel drawers; one of which, the one with the typewritten tab that reads Serpent, The, when opened, reveals the refridgerated body of a woman that he loved, a woman that he loved despite never having seen her in the flesh, despite never having touched her, or caressed her, or even talked to her. Tres never revealed himself to the girl he loved, and this is something that Tres can't let happen again. Tres is determined to no longer accept the blind anonymity of the Web.

Tres is sitting under the posters that his mother hung up in his room. They are pictures of cypress trees, pictures of Big Sur. Big Sur is the place that Jack Kerouac went crazy, the place where he tried too hard to live alone.

Tres sends messages to friends and enemies alike. He tells them who he is. He tells them that he is not just the Two-Headed Boy; that he is not simply the ruler of the kingdom of *Carrot Flowers*; that he is, in fact, an ex-Olympic hopeful who was permanently disabled in a high-speed skiing accident; that he is, now, a very lonely young man who lives in a small room at the top of a very large mansion; that he wants, nothing more and nothing less, to be these people's friends, not just kingdom mates and so-called pen pals, but Real Life friends.

The response is not at all what he had hoped it would be. His own kingdom mates, the people who he has lived with in The Realm age after age, Real Life month after Real Life month, they're not reciprocating. They think this has something to do with a dragon, that Tres is behaving strangely because he's afraid they'll be angry at him for letting their kingdom be outmaneuvered, that he's giving them a sob story so they won't dethrone him. They don't like this change of behavior. They are used to things running smoothly, to the sharing of small intimacies that affect their performance in the game, but nothing more. They know when one member is going to be out for a week at 4H camp with their daughter, or when another will be on an airplane heading out for a conference on the paranormal, but they are left to fill in the gaps, to compose portraits of each other based on fragments. The members of the kingdom of *Carrot Flowers* are utilitarians that have little use for that which is extraneous to The Realm. The Realm is their dirty little secret—the thing that they do late at night while their wives and children are sleeping, or at their computers while their bosses' and co-workers' heads are turned. The Realm is like a mistress that they have every intention of keeping separate from their public lives.

This is disappointing to Tres, but understandable. He is aware that The Realm is a diversion to most people, and diversions cease to be diversions when they turn serious, when the mistress seeks to supplant the wife. Tres is OK with this. He is even OK with them thinking that he is getting weak, that perhaps it is time for another monarch. But he wishes there were somebody, just somebody with whom he could make a personal connection. As he is thinking this a message comes in, it's a message from sKyLaR, the ruler of sKyLaR's PlEaSuRe PaLaCe, one of the players to whom Tres had sent his revelation.

The content of the message is very unexpected. The content changes everything. Tres Rawlings logs onto his IRC.

★ ★ ★

Dietrich does not think the Two-Headed Boy's message is unusual. He has always expressed himself freely in The Realm. But when Dietrich gets the Two-Headed Boy's message, he is not thinking how best to respond, for he is thinking only of a missing girl. Dietrich Björnson conjures up Tron. Dietrich Björnson sends Tres Rawlings a message:

dO yOu KnOw AnYtHiNg AbOuT a PlAyEr CaLlEd ThE sErPeNt? ShE WAs A vErY aCtIvE pLaYeR wHo SuDdEnLy DiSaPpEaReD fRoM hEr KiNgDoM. hEr KiNgDoM mAtEs ArE wOrRiEd ThAt SoMeThInG mIgHt HaVe HaPpEnEd To HeR iN rEaL lIfE. i'M oN IrC @ tHe MaIn PaRlOr.

Signed, Sir sKyLaR of Paradigm Shift

Not long after he got an instant message:

2HB has received an invitation to enter the conference room: tHe MaIn PaRlOr from **sKy-LaR**. Will you accept? Y/N

2HB: Y

sKyLaR: hElLo

2HB: *You said her name was The Serpent?*

sKyLaR: *hEr PrOvInCe NaMe, YeAh. sHe WaS iN tHe KINgDoM aMpHiBiOuS.*

2HB: *Do you know anything else about her?*

sKyLaR: *sHe SeNt Me A jPg. ShE sAiD iT wAs a PhOtO oF hEr BuT I CaN't Be SuRe*

2HB: *Did she have a shaved head?*

sKyLaR: *yEs! ExCePt FoR tHiS dYeD pUrPlE rAt TaIl oN hEr FoRhEaD*

2HB: *Bloody hell.*

sKyLaR: *yOu KnOw HeR?*

2HB: *Maybe. How about tattooes? Did she have tattooes?*

sKyLaR: *yEaH, sHe HaD a TaTtOo Of A dRaGoN oN hEr BaCk*

2HB: *Yikes. I think it is her. Hey, can you send me the pic?*

sKyLaR: *uM, yEaH . . . bUt JuSt To WaRn YoU, sHe'S tOpLeSs*

2HB: *that's OK. I've, um . . . seen her topless.*

sKyLaR: *lOl*

sKyLaR: *P0000012.jpg*

2HB: *bloody hell. It's the same girl.*

sKyLaR: *gOoD, iM gLaD yOu KnOw HeR. i HaD tHiS fReAkY iRc cOnVeRsAtIoN wItH hEr, WhErE sHe SoUnDeD aLl SuIcIdAl. I cOuLdNt TeLl WhEtHeR sHe WaS fUcKiNg WiTh Me Or NoT aNd ThEn ShE dElEtEs HeR aCcOuNt sO i ThOuGhT sOmEtHiNg MiGhT bE wRoNg*

2HB: *skylar, she wasn't fucking with you.*

sKyLaR: hUh?

2HB: she did it

sKyLaR: dId WhAt?

2HB: commited suicide

sKyLaR: sHiT

sKyLaR: hOw?

2HB: She OD'ed. She did it a few days ago.

sKyLaR: fUcK

2HB: Do you know anything else about her? I never found out where she was from.

sKyLaR: sHe ToLd Me ShE LiVeD iN sAn FrAnCiScO

sKyLaR: hOw DiD yOu KnOw HeR?

2HB: I don't really. We were just online friends, too.

sKyLaR: hOw DiD yOu FiNd OuT sHe WaS dEaD?

sKyLaR: dId ShE eVeR mEnTiOn SoMeThInG aBoUt A wEb CaM?

★ ★ ★

How could he tell him this? How could he tell anyone this? He'd been watching this girl for two years. He knew her every tic, her every mood, her every predilection. He'd watched her die, watched her plunge the needle into her arm, watched her body in the beginning stages of decay. And after everything, she had been a player in The Realm. How strange that her life had intersected in this way with his. She had seemed so impenetrable to Tres, so unreachable, and yet, there she had been: maintaining her economy, training her troops, fighting her wars. *Just like him.*

How shameful to tell sKyLaR that this was the closest thing to love he had ever felt. That he loved this girl, this girl who didn't know that he existed, this girl who he'd watched for years against her will. How shameful to say that he was Tres Rawlings, a man to whom touch was denied, a man who only watched. He was the sleazy old man at a peepshow, a hand wrapped in toilet paper for the clean-up.

The Serpent, she was the closest thing to a lover he had ever had; and yet, what right did he have to care?

Tres couldn't answer sKyLaR's question. Telling him how he knew she was dead was too horrible, said too much about what he had become. Tres blinked his left eye, and when he did so, sKyLaR was gone.

34. MOTIVES ARE TRICKY TO DECIPHER.

THE QUESTION—is Two-Headed Boy really an ex-Olympic hopeful paralyzed in such a way that his entire existence is tied to a computer screen?—is not important to Xerxes Meticula. What is important is deciphering what the message is attempting to accomplish. Xerxes can only decipher it as an attempt to win him and his kingdom mates over to his side. Perhaps, by telling them who he is, Two-Headed Boy can convince *Paradigm Shift* to lay off a little bit; and having laid off a little bit, perhaps he can still squeak out a victory. Perhaps, he can still win. This is the only result that can possibly matter to Two-Headed Boy. Winning, undoubtedly, is everything.

For Xerxes, this is a chess match. Now that Two-Headed Boy had made a move, how should he, Xerxes, respond. Two-Headed Boy is a woeful paralyzed boy, now who should Xerxes be?

Xerxes thinks it best to keep up the current illusion, and to push it, to crank it up a notch. He will tell Two-Headed Boy that he is a woman. He will be a girl named Montana—Montana Bronstein. He will make this Montana Bronstein very much like Sara Bronstein, since Sara Bronstein is so desirable.

He will make her American. He will say that she lives in a cabin in the woods. He will say that she has just recently obtained a cable connection in her cabin, and that she is wired up with a cable modem. He will say that she feels lonely (a lonely girl in the woods, that's good). He will say that in Real Life she is a sociologist, and that she is out here in the woods researching fringe groups (that's good—sexy). She became interested in The Realm, he will say, because the people in Real Life who spend so much of their time in The Realm are themselves a part of a fringe group. She thinks she is going to do her master's thesis on this. She's going to call it "A Guide to Survival in The Realm." It's going to be about all these people who would prefer to live in a virtual reality. She herself is a bit of a stranger to this world. She can see how people are drawn in, but she prefers real faces, people she can feel and touch, people she can love.

Xerxes will send a picture of Montana Bronstein to Two-Headed Boy. In fact, he'll send him a picture of Sara, the one he took of her on the gazebo. How could he not be attracted to this woman? How could he not do her bidding?

★   ★   ★

When she wakes up, she is still here, she is still free. Charley has not yet returned. Her only hope, and what a fruitless hope it is, is The Realm. If she keeps playing, perhaps she can sustain the connection, perhaps one day sKy-LaR or the Queen will hop on a plane and come for a visit (something they can do—can you believe it—they can travel halfway around the world with hardly a thought at all!), and when they meet her they will see her talent, they will know what she is capable of, and they will take her into their fold.

This is her plan. She knows it is not much of a plan, but for now it will have to suffice. Gek-Lin continues to do her job—spreading the plague. She does some calculations; she makes another attack on *Carrot Flowers*:

Your troops have fought a brave battle and won. You have appropriated 782 acres of land from The King of Carrot Flowers (47:50). Your army will return from the battlefield in 14 days. Be sure to visit our sponsor sites for additional Realm bonuses.

The King of Carrot Flowers (47:50) has been infected with the plague!

It takes time to accomplish these things. She is constantly aware of this time, how it's passing. She knows she must leave, and yet she can't; this computer, it is her one and only connection, it is her only hope. Gek-Lin goes next to check her messages. She had hoped that there would be more here, something from the Queen or something from sKyLaR, but instead there are only a few messages from lesser provinces, seeking her advice, and one message from a province called *The King of Carrot Flowers*, the province that she had attacked earlier. She is pretty sure what this message will contain, given the damage that she has caused, it will surely be a taunt or a threat, but she opens it anyway. It is not what she expected:

Dear Lord BonZ,

Hello. This is the Two-Headed Boy from the kingdom of Carrot Flowers. I just wanted to introduce myself. My real name is Tres Rawlings. I live in London. I've been playing The Realm for twelve ages, and still don't know any of the other players who I play with. I was paralyzed in a skling accident in 1997 and since then I have been confined to a wheelchair. I've got a device that allows me to communicate via computer with eye movements. Anyway, I hope I can count on your future friendship.

Signed, King Two-Headed Boy of Carrot Flowers

Gek-Lin's heart rate speeds up a notch. She is being offered friendship. Here is someone else with whom she could communicate, someone else who might be able to save her. She does not have time to think of the risk. She does not have time to seek an accurate translation of the entire message. She simply fires it off; Gek-Lin fires off a message of her own.

★　★　★

It didn't take him long to find it. He simply logged onto his account at the public library and browsed through the Death Notices of the *San Francisco Chronicle*:

Mary Lynn Klavich, found September 3, 2000

Person found deceased in her apartment at 1012 Page St. Remains have not been claimed. Identifying marks include a shaved head and a tattoo of a serpent that covers the length of the back. If you have any information about Ms. Klavich, contact the San Francisco Coroner's Office. Burial to take place without ceremony on October 15th at 8 AM in Section N at Woodlawn Memorial Park, located at 1000 El Camino Real, Colma, CA.

Remains have not been claimed. . . . Burial to take place without ceremony. The words strike him like a bullet to the chest. How could this be? How could no one claim her? How could she be buried like that—*without ceremony.*

Tres can't remember ever feeling this low. He'd experienced indifference himself, the quick way he'd been forgotten after his accident, but this, the utter nothingness that had become of The Serpent's life, it was more than he could take. What would happen to him when he died—who would be there to mourn? His mom, his dad, and his put-upon relatives, that would be all. Tres, he was no different than The Serpent.

Tres thought about offing himself then. He thought about activating the device that controlled his wheelchair. He thought about spinning. He thought about spinning his wheelchair until the wires and tubes and shunts and needles that held him together snapped, glucose and saline spraying from the loose plastic tubing, his life pouring out of him in thousands of strands, like the strings of a Portuguese man-of-war.

He thought about it, but there was something new on his monitor. The text read: NEW MSG.

* * *

It surprised him, that she would do this, since their kingdoms had so much bad blood between them. Here his kingdom mates were fighting off a dragon of her making! Here they were attacking each other! And yet here she was exchanging friendly correspondence.

The Queen's real name was Montana Bronstein. She was 25 (Tres's age!). She lived in Arizona, in a small cabin out in the woods. She was a sociologist researching fringe groups. How strange! How cool! She said that she felt like Tres even though she was considered normal. She felt isolated, misunderstood, too smart for her own good. She said that she thought people with handicaps were cool.

She sent Tres a jpg of herself. She wasn't what you would necessarily expect from someone named Montana. There was no red hair or freckles. Instead, she had black hair and short bangs, amber-colored eyes, and an impish smile. She was wearing all black: a black dress that if it wasn't black you'd call a sun dress; and black shoes, black shoes that if she were over fifty you'd call orthopedic shoes, but because they were on a young woman they seemed fashionable. Her hands were on her hips, in a manner once again suggesting impatience with the photographer. She was standing in an old-fashioned gazebo in a town square. There were banners and American flags everywhere.

When he sees the picture he knows what he must do. A vision—it comes to him. The Serpent, she will not die alone. This Montana girl, this beautiful

Montana girl, lonely in the wilderness, she will not die alone. This Gek-Lin girl, this orphan from Thailand, this girl who has also sent him a message, she will not die alone. This sKyLaR guy, this guy full of concern for a woman he has never met, he will not die alone. And Tres Rawlings, because of what he is about to do, he will not die alone.

*sKyLaR has received an invitation to enter the conference room: The castle in the trees from **2HB**. Will you accept? Y/N*

sKyLaR: Y

2HB: *Hey, sorry I cut you off.*

sKyLaR: *tHaT's Ok*

2HB: *I've been thinking . . . that girl's funeral, it's going to be in San Francisco. I found her death notice and it says she's going to be buried without ceremony—she didn't have any Real Life friends or family. I was thinking of maybe going.*

sKyLaR: *pFfFfFfFfFf. I'd Do AnYtHINg To Go 2hB, buT i'M sTuCk At ThE sOuTh PoLe ☺ My WiFe'S mOtHer Is dYiNg AnD wE can't eVeN lEaVe FoR tHaT. iT's ExPeNsIvE aNd DaN-gErOuS to FlY oUt Of Here At ThiS tImE oF tHe YeAr*

2HB: *You really live at the South Pole?*

sKyLaR: *i'M sTaTiOnEd At ThE sCoTt-AmUnDsOn BaSe In AnTaRcTicA*

2HB: *Bloody Christ.*

2HB: *And to answer your question from before. Yes, I knew about the web cam, that's how I knew she was dead—I watched it. I had no idea that she was suicidal or anything, and we'd never shared personal information, I didn't even know where she lived. The whole thing was fucked up.*

sKyLaR: *wHy DiDn'T yOu cOnTaCt HeR kInGdOm MaTeS?*

2HB: *Like I said we didn't share personal information, I didn't even know she was playing.*

sKyLaR: *sO iF yOu DiDn'T sHaRe PeRsOnAl InFoRmAtIoN, aNd YoU dIdN't KnOw ShE hAd An AcCoUnT iN tHe ReAlM, hOw DiD you KnOw HeR?*

* * *

There was a pause here in the communication, and sKyLaR wondered if he was going to disappear again, but after a time more text appeared on sKyLaR's screen.

* * *

2HB: *I didn't really know her I guess. I just watched her. This guy put a web cam up in her room and then left it there, without her knowing it, and I stumbled upon the feed. She didn't seem to have any real friends, she just kept going through people, and I . . . fuck man, I'm paralyzed and home-ridden, she became a friend even though I didn't know her.*

sKyLaR: *dUdE, yOu CaN't gO tO hEr FuNeRaL.*

2HB: *Why not? She doesn't have anybody else. I mean, her death notice said her remains hadn't even been claimed. She needs someone.*

sKyLaR: *iT's CrEePy.*

2HB: *Why is it creepy? It's creepier that they're going to bury a young woman alone. I mean, how much time do you spend in The Realm a week on average: 10 hours, 20 hours, 30? If she was one of your co-workers, and you spent that much time with her, wouldn't you go to her funeral? She was a Realmie, sKyLaR, she spent all her time there. Someone from The Realm should go, and if no one else is going to go, then I am.*

sKyLaR: *wElL, i KiNd Of SeE yOuR pOiNt. If YoU cAn FlY mE aNd My WiFe OuT oF aNtArCtIcA, i'Ll DeFiNiTeLy Go. :p*

2HB: *:P*

* * *

The conversation he has with sKyLaR does not daunt him. It only spurs him on. He's had his parents' credit card numbers for years, abused them in many ways. As long as the credit card says dot-com something-or-other his parents pay the bills without asking questions. A new program, he tells them, a new game, and they let it slide. His parents have paid for thousands of pounds worth of porn. This time will be different, of course, the repercussions will be long-lasting, his parents will never trust him again, but it is worth it to Tres. He has this one chance. He can still make things right. The Serpent, she deserves better than this, better than to end up unceremoniously tossed in the dirt.

Tres makes the arrangements. It is amazing what can be done without what is considered true human interaction. It is amazing that you can take a virtual tour of a chapel: see close-ups of its wall sconces—poor muscled demons doomed to forever carry tapered candles; its stained glass—nine panels representing the nine circles of Dante's Inferno; its organ—a Wurlitzer, polished tin pipes trimmed in gold; its altar—marble, when not covered in a spotless, white altar cloth. It is amazing that you can rent this chapel for "Special Occasions"; that you need only find a time slot on the chapel's on-line calendar, the morning or afternoon session, no questions asked; that you need only use a scroll-down menu to indicate "Wedding," "Funeral," or "Other." It is amazing that you can order flowers to be delivered to this chapel at a particular time on a particular date, that from halfway around the globe you can order lilies. It is amazing that you can find an officiant, that there is a Web site called minister.com where you can look up "Priestess, Pagan" and book her with a mouse click.

These things are amazing and Tres does the amazing. He arranges a funeral in five minutes flat.

There are more difficult things for Tres to do. He must do some convincing. But his family's stature, and global economics, are on his side. The State of California is in a budget crunch, and an old money, anonymous donor from England willing to take a state funeral off their hands is a welcome respite. Once again, no questions are asked. Paperless faxes are sent to Tres, and penless signatures are forged. Tres copies and pastes his Dad's name over a dotted line on his screen. Tres's cornea wields the power of the Internet.

There is still, of course, the matter of the guests. And with the guests, Tres plans to be extravagant. He wants to give them every reason to attend. He books them all First Class, buys them all an extra ticket for a guest. He lodges them in the San Francisco Hilton Downtown, view-level suites. He rents limos. It will be difficult when it comes to the convincing—after all, who in their right mind would attend the funeral of a stranger—but he can market this as a sort of vacation. Tres Rawlings has nothing to lose.

It will be easier if he makes the arrangements first. This can't hurt, it can only bolster attendance, and price is no object to Tres. After all, it's not his money. It's merely the anonymous, unaccounted-for money that can be obtained with multiple titanium MasterCards.

Tres does all this. He is veryexcellenttraveldeals.com's best customer. He purchases tickets for Ling and Manuel, for Ice and Demon, for Asif and Njera, and finally, for her, for Montana Bronstein. The total ticket, hotel, and limo cost is $29,216.69 not including local, federal, or international taxes. He clicks "OK."

There are still some loose ends to tie up. Not all his guests are so easily transportable from plane, to hotel, to chapel, and back again. There is the matter of Dietrich Björnson who lives at the South Pole, where flights enter and exit only a few times a year—not commercial flights but government ones. There is the case of Gek-Lin Troung, a Thai orphan with no identification, who won't be able to fly without a passport.

Tres is prepared for these contingencies. For these contingencies, he has set up the Edward Calvin Rawlings III Foundation. He wrote up The Mission Statement of the Foundation. It can be found on Tres's Web site, ecrfoundation.com:

OUR MISSION

The Edward Calvin Rawlings III Foundation was established in October of 2000 to provide funds for individuals experiencing a personal emergency. The Foundation pools the resources of both commercial and government interests to accomplish its goals. Although the Foundation bears no claim to international authority, it is hoped that all parties will accept the spirit of philanthropy in which these funds are granted, and will do all that lies within their power to see that the needs of the individuals are met.

Tres Rawlings is announcing the generous gifts of the Foundation. The first is a $50,000 grant for Dietrich Björnson.

The grant monies may be used by any federal institution that will provide private air transport for Mr. and Mrs. Björnson from the Scott-Amundsen base in Antarctica to San Francisco International Airport, U.S.A.

The second disbursement of the Foundation is a $5,000 grant for Gek-Lin Troung.

This money may be used by the Government of Thailand to provide private air transport from Bangkok, Thailand, to the San Francisco International Airport for Ms. Troung and a guardian.

These are, of course, still long shots, but today Tres believes that all this is possible, he believes that he has the power to put people in motion and force them to move.

There is only one more thing to be done. He has to send the message. He has written and rewritten the message to get it right. It is right. He pulls up the e-mail addresses of his friends in The Realm on multiple screens. He cuts and pastes his message into each of his four screens. He sends the messages. The messages are like soldiers being sent to war. They march off in formation, one following the other. As they go, they each fire a shot. Tres can feel the recoil.

Dear Friends,

I'm writing this letter to ask for your help. I know that this is very strange, seeing how none of you have ever met me before, but I have spent a great deal of time with all of you online, and consider you real, true friends.

A friend of mine, Mary Lynn Klavich, has passed away. Both of Mary Lynn's parents died years ago, and she has very few friends other than the ones that she made online. She was a fellow gamer, like us. When she passed away, she had no family to bury her, and so I've taken on the responsibility of seeing that she be properly put to rest.

Because she had no family, and very few friends, I've decided to ask some of you to come to the funeral. It is being held in San Francisco, California, on October 20th. I know that this very likely will be impossible, as the notice is short and the distance great, but it would mean a great deal to me if you would come. Besides that, I would love to meet you all in Real Life.

I have taken the liberty of purchasing plane tickets for all of you. You should receive e-tickets in your email boxes on January 1st, YR 17, Realm Time. They will come to you in the mail under the name you have given me. (If I have a false name for you, please let me know right away!) If you have a family and would like to bring them along, let me know and I'll get extra tickets.

I am very sincere in this and I hope to see you in San Francisco. Please write me if you have any questions or concerns.

Tres Rawlings

a.k.a. Two-Headed Boy

35. BEWARE THE PLOT BEHIND THE PLOT.

When the Queen reads the message, she is furious. She had thought that his friendliness was a move of desperation, a whimper before she struck the final blow; but his revelation, it hadn't been that, what it had been was a devious ploy.

Would her kingdom mates fall for Two-Headed Boy's psy-ops? Would all her careful planning, all the time and effort she put into making sure things were perfect, would all these things amount to nothing. All it took was some idiot with a larger-than-life giveaway, some sort of Publishers' Clearing House Sweepstakes, and they would all be off chasing fool's gold.

If any of them went on vacation mode, or worse, canceled their accounts, they would surely drop out of the Top 5, and they'd never catch up with *Carrot Flowers*.

How do you fight something like this? Xerxes doesn't know. His life's failures stand before him like rows of dominoes. Even with all the elaborate schemes, all it takes is one quick push and everything comes tumbling down: maximuminventory.com destroyed by hype and greed; his girlfriend stolen by his flashy friend; his sister taken by mental illness.

All these hidden movements. All this psychological warfare. And now he's going to lose this stupid game. Some chump is promising airline tickets that are, he is sure, fraudulent. All it would take was for one of his kingdom mates to drop out and they would lose the age to *Carrot Flowers*, all the while this Two-Headed Boy chuckling at their folly.

This whole thing is such a dirty trick. The temptation is there to just say fuck it all, to walk away like he had on that fateful day in San Francisco when he had slipped out through the venting. He could log off and go on a long bike ride, take a day trip through Rest Stop National Forest. Hell, he could go even farther with it, pack a backpack, his GPS, and some large bills. He could take a bus to the border, hitchhike to the Copper Canyon, hound the locals for peyote, and then wander around until he lost consciousness and the vultures ate him alive.

Xerxes could escape again, and this escape would be easier than before—
after all, there was nothing preventing him from no longer logging in.

But the Queen is not ready to give in just yet. She is at least going to
warn them, to make sure they know what the Two-Headed Boy's true mo-
tives are. She sends a message to all her provinces:

Dear _____,

The Two-Headed Boy is sending out messages offering us tickets to go to San
Francisco to meet him. This Is a TRICK! It is obvious that he is doing this to slow
down our attacks on him and to try and get some of us to quit before the end of
the age. I know that some of you have expressed interest in getting to the U.S.
Do NOT respond to this message! Do NOT quit!

Signed, Queen Peace & Love but Mostly Love

⋆   ⋆   ⋆

Underneath the note that Tres Rawlings has sent to Dietrich is a postscript:

P.S. sKyLaR—I've made special arrangements for you and your wife. I operate a
foundation which allows me to distribute travel moneys to people in unusual circumstances and I have created a grant in your name to that end. Weather conditions permitting, a flight will leave Christchurch tomorrow, land in McMurdo, and
then fly to the Pole the next day. It sounds like the NSF coordinator at the base is
none too happy about the extraction, but he didn't sound willing to argue with the
Edward Calvin Rawlings III Foundation ;)

It hadn't taken long for the NSF chief to find Dietrich, who was looking
rather stunned in front of his computer, to confirm this news. The Edward
Calvin Rawlings III Foundation had indeed given him an unsolicited grant
for $50,000, for the sole purpose of getting him and his wife off the base a
few weeks early so that Dietrich could attend a funeral, and then take Caitlin
home to care for her mother. The NSF chief did not do what Dietrich
thought he would do. He did not give him the cold shoulder. Instead, he
wrapped his arms around him. Instead, he said, "Dietrich, it was a great winter. Let us know how she's doing." Then he shook Dietrich's hand and told
him he'd let the rest of the base know within the hour.

Dietrich is not sure what to do. He puts on his parka, gloves, and snow boots. He steps out of Biomed and walks to the edge of the Dome. Through the triangles of glass, he looks right into the 9 P.M. sun, sitting just a few degrees above the horizon. Dietrich, with all the pranks and tricks he has performed, with all the mood enhancing and lightening-up he has inflicted on others, had never expected someone to play a trick on him. But here it was. How would he respond?

As he gazes across the great white plain, Dietrich feels arms encircling his waist. He turns. It is Caitlin, the side of her face pressed against his neck. She is there as if summoned, for this very moment. There is, really, only one appropriate response to a trickster—*Go to him, you can't refuse.* And so he tells her, he tells her everything. He tells her about gaming, about the Two-Headed Boy, and how it came about that they got a plane ticket home. When he does this, Caitlin's face lightens up. She smiles at Dietrich like a Snow White awakened by a kiss.

* * *

She is going to America. She doesn't understand the details, isn't sure what a funeral has to do with it all, but she does understand the part about the Two-Headed Boy sending her a plane ticket. Gek-Lin's English is not normally perfect, but today there is not a single grammatical error in the message that she sends to the Two-Headed Boy. Her e-mail to him rings loud and clear:

Hello, Two-Headed Boy. Thank you for doing this for me. You were right to guess that I do not have a passport. Please send it to the British Embassy. My birth date is 04/12/87. Can't wait to see you in the United States of America.

What now? She must leave, as soon as possible, but she needs money for her passport and visa. She could attempt to steal it, but it takes time to steal, and the risks of being caught are high.

Money. She needs it now. Where can she get her hands on some? *Charley's office.* She isn't sure why she hadn't thought of this before, why she hadn't thought of rifling through his effects. Gek-Lin enters the office, begins going through drawers. In the back of one is a cigar box. In the cigar box is money, a lot of money, 50,000 bhats to be exact.

* * *

Uncle Charley is back in Bangkok in another car. Traffic is terrible. He is quiet, sullen. He is missing a finger. The limo driver with the silvered sunglasses rolls down the window, spits.

*　*　*

It's over a thousand American dollars. It's a lot of money. It's all the money Uncle Charley has in the world. Gek-Lin, eyeing it all, considers the quick grab and run that she's performed her entire life in such situations. Any hesitation, when confronted with loose bills, is always a mistake. And yet, as she takes it all into her hands, feels the lovely texture of the paper, as she begins her walk out the door, she realizes that there is no one watching her, that there is no immediate danger.

As much as she resents Charley, and what she knows that he has done, she also knows that he has taught her a lot; that he had introduced her to the game, and therefore the world; that, if it were not for him, this moment, this opportunity for her to go to America, would not exist. A twitch of guilt causes her upper lip to quiver. If she does this, if she takes it all, he will be finished. It already looks bad: he has been kidnapped by some very scary people, and now his orphans—his commodities—have disappeared. If she leaves him like this without any money, without a note, he will surely be finished.

Gek-Lin considers, briefly, his predicament. Charley has made some very dangerous enemies; if he remains here, he will, at best, be Kin-Dong's permanent slave, a fate that, given what he was about to sell Gek-Lin into, is a fate he surely deserves. And yet despite this, and despite the fact that he is running a psuedo-orphanage that clandestinely films children taking showers, Charley has never willingly hurt anyone. What Charley has done is what any orphan would do, he has found an ingenious, if immoral, means of survival.

Before getting out of here, before taking her Hello Kitty backpack, and Psyduck, and a lot of money; Gek-Lin decides to give him a chance. She writes on a notebook: check your computer. Then she unrolls ten 100 bhat notes from the wad in her hand and places them under Charley's keyboard.

*　*　*

The world is acting contrary to the Queen's needs. The warning message, apparently, did not work, or, perhaps did not reach them in time. There are messages on her screen that she cannot bear to read. sKyLaR, fooled into thinking that he will be leaving Antarctica; Lord BonZ (and apparently, since he's running his province, Raven), fooled as well. The Queen is appalled—how could they be so stupid? They've all ceased their attacks on *Carrot Flowers*, and already they're losing ground, have dipped back into the #2 slot.

It is all too much for Xerxes. He feels that there is a conspiracy, that they really are all out there to get him. The feeling of abandonment that he felt that day when he crawled through the air ducts at maximuminventory.com hits him again, at ten times its original strength. *Why not? Why not kill himself over a game?* Of all the reasons he might choose to commit suicide—his company's failing, his sister's schizophrenia, Zahn and Dixie, Sara's leaving for New York City—his loss in The Realm seemed the most logical reason to exit this life. He read once of some primitive contest—it was during the time of the Egyptians, or perhaps it was the Mayans, or the Aztecs, or maybe it was some game the Romans played with the early Christians—Xerxes can't remember, doesn't care to look up the historical text, but during these times the losers, the poor saps who failed to put the ball through the hoop or spear the bull or whatever it was they did, were beheaded (or, possibly, fed to the lions) by the emperor (or king). Losing, in those times, was disgrace, was cause for the forfeit of one's life.

Xerxes is in that mode; he's in that ten-steps-to-a-leap-off-a-bridge space. He goes into autopilot. His destination today is Granite Tower, that place where Gabriella attempted to sacrifice a child. It seems a good jumping-off point. He thinks if he climbs to the very top, and jumps off the back side, that he'll be guaranteed a death. He's not as sure of this as he was sure that a leap off the Golden Gate Bridge, at the right place and under the right conditions, would end in a death, but it matters less, today, what the end result of his leap is. He's more desperate, and desperation leads to a lack of sound judgment. He's aware of this too—and refuses to care. He'll end up a Real Life version of the fictional Tres Rawlings, paralyzed and plugged into a computer, permanently kicking ass in The Realm.

Xerxes knows the way to Granite Tower, sees no need to refer to the maps that litter the kitchen counter. He hops up the stairs leading from the bottom half of the house to the top, taking them two at a time. He ignores the passing glances his parents give him. He enters the garage. He looks over at #8—one last time. He reads the script airbrushed on the tailgate. *Yes*, he thinks, *I have been on this shift too long.*

It's the same thing, all over again. He puts forth tremendous effort, performs Herculean tasks, and ends up with nothing to show for it: a mere score, not even the best score, on his screen. Xerxes is Sisyphus. He stands in the bed of his truck and takes his Cannondale down from the two hooks that secure the wheels to the ceiling of the garage. He turns the bike around, so that its wheels end up on the bed of the truck. He rolls the bike off the truck and onto the floor of the garage. He checks the air in the tires, pumps the back one up a bit. He tests the brakes and then the shocks. He loosens the screws on the suspension to allow for a little more give. He puts on his helmet, his gloves.

He'll try, this one last time, to beat his record. He turns the speedometer/odometer/altimeter on. He begins his ride, flipping the gears shift until he's in 24th. He leaps off the edge of the driveway onto the smooth blacktop of Buena Vista Court. He sails down it, in a tuck, like a downhill skier. His elbows rest on the flat handlebars as if he were on a racing bike and not a mountain bike. His hands are clenched together in front of him. Xerxes looks only at the speedometer/odometer/altimeter; he looks only at the numbers. He's not paying attention at all to the road, that all important, ever-changing, road.

36. UNLESS THE LORDS OF THE REALM DELETE YOU,
YOU ARE VERY DIFFICULT TO KILL OFF.

Q IS FOR QUARRY. FUCK IT. Sara hops into her Jeep Cherokee, the one that she had purchased back when she thought she was going to be a shrink amongst the tribes of the Southwest, and winds her way through the Ponderosas surrounding the road to her house. She drives through downtown, past the courthouse, and towards The Ranch were Xerxes lives. She isn't sure what she will do when she arrives. She hasn't yet determined her approach. She could, justifiably, give him a piece of her mind, tell him off for what he had done. But she has a feeling that she will not be the one doing the talking, that he will be the one explaining, and that she will need to listen before she can judge.

Sara drives the Jeep Cherokee past the smoke shops, casinos, and strip malls. She makes a right turn into The Ranch; she passes the horses, the cascades; she makes her way up the serpentine twists and turns of the road. She makes a left turn onto Buena Vista Court.

★   ★   ★

Uncle Charley finds Gek-Lin's note, and sees the money, the equivalent of about twenty American dollars, that she has left for him. He turns on his computer and reads the Two-Headed Boy's message. It means nothing to him, gives him no encouragement. He agrees, instead, with the Queen Peace & Love but Mostly Love's assessment:

The Two-Headed Boy is sending out messages offering us tickets to go to San Francisco to meet him. This Is a TRICK! It is obvious that he is doing this to slow down our attacks on him and to try and get some of us to quit before the end of the age. I know that some of you have expressed interest in getting to the U.S. Do NOT respond to this message! Do NOT quit!

Charley, too, thinks this is a hoax, a ploy to throw Gek-Lin off so that his kingdom can finish #1. It is cruel what the Two-Headed Boy has done. And yet, understandable. The morality of the Web is different from the morality of the world. Deception is part of the game. Those who are not attune to this are naïve; cyberspace is not a safe place for them. Internet users expect to be flamed and misled. It is all part of the fun.

Of course, the Two-Headed Boy's actions are of no consequence to him. Charley has no intention of finishing out the age. The Realm is an intellectual challenge for him, like chess. It's not an addiction; he isn't consumed by it. He thinks it a good learning tool, and this was why he had introduced all his orphans to it. Through The Realm he could teach them math and English in a way that was interesting to them.

Uncle Charley logs on to The Realm and enters the Preferences screen. He scrolls down to where it says vacation mode. He clicks yes. He will leave the kingdom with the net worth he has gained, he doesn't want to hurt the players who are more involved than he, but he can't keep playing either. He doesn't—actually—know what he is going to do.

Kin-Dong will come sooner or later, expecting the payoff, expecting Gek-Lin, expecting to see Uncle Charley ready to dutifully run Kin-Dong's business. When Kin-Dong discovers that he no longer has either the orphans or the money, he will be very, very angry.

This is it. The end of the road. First, Kin-Dong will torture him, then he will kill him, then he will put his body in the trunk, will attach some stones to his ankles, will find some hidden twist in the Chao Phraya River, will toss his body in. The remains of Charley will then be eaten by piranhas and disappear. All of Charley will be gone. In a way he longs for this, longs for it to end. He deserves this fate—he is a criminal who should die at the hand of criminals. It is a positive Darwinian spin, a good way to keep evil at bay.

Charley returns one last time to the basement where he has spent so much time with his orphans. He goes down to the basement and opens the door to his office. Here are his bookshelves. When he was a teenager, a youth exploited, the books on these shelves were the things that had gotten him through. While he allowed himself to be used by the streets of Bangkok, Charley read the stories of his namesake Charles Dickens. He read *David Copperfield* and *Oliver Twist* and *Nicholas Nickleby*. And he read *Great Expectations*, over and over again.

This was the book that had given him hope. A boy, an orphan, might perhaps make his way out of poverty. He might escape whatever provincial backwater he had come from and make it in a city—a big, English city.

The young Charley hadn't paid much attention to the rest: the part where the young hero falls madly in love with a woman with whom he is never able to consummate his love; the part where the young hero finds out that the man to whom he is indebted for his wealth is a crude, unethical thief; the part where the hero must settle for mediocrity, where he gives up his dreams of greatness and settles for mild comfort; and perhaps, the part most pertinent to Charley, the part where the young hero goes on to ruin those with the same background from which he had come. These parts of *Great Expectations* meant nothing to Charley Hum then, but they mean plenty to him now.

He couldn't take all his books with him, but he hoped to take one. If he was to be murdered, and surely he would be, he wanted to at least take his *Great Expectations* with him to the grave.

Charley takes the book from the shelf and then makes his way out of the basement and into the street. Not knowing what to do, not knowing where to go, only knowing that at noon a band of ruffians was going to be missing his presence dearly, and would, after finding the Blue Moon Internet Café abandoned, quickly begin combing the streets to find him; Charley wonders aimlessly out of the Patpong district, making his way from the city center towards Sukumvit Road, the long road that leads east out of the city, the long road that were he to follow it to its end would take him to the border with Cambodia, the border from where he first entered Thailand. Incidentally, the route that Charley has chosen to wonder aimlessly down, also passes Siam Square, wherein lies the British Consulate.

★ ★ ★

Xerxes raises his eyes from the speedometer/odometer/altimeter for a split-second. A car is there. There is never a car in that spot, when he is bombing down this little stretch of Buena Vista Court—there is only their house, on this road, and his parents are in it, and his sister is at St. Francis, and no one ever comes to visit them, this isn't something that people do, here in Rest Stop, Arizona, visit people's houses. So there is no excuse for the car to be there. And yet it is there. And he is going to hit it. To veer right would send him flying off into a steep slope of stones. To veer left would launch him off a high ledge into a ravine. That leaves riding headlong, into the car, as the only option.

Or bailing, throwing oneself onto the pavement, and letting that pavement do to him as it will.

* * *

It is him. She expected a confrontation, a butting of heads, but not this, him on a speeding bicycle coming right at her Jeep. She was not going too fast, when she came around the bend, and she was heading uphill, so slamming on the brakes has its desired effect. The Jeep stops, quickly, prior to impact. But it is not the Jeep that is going to hit the bicycle; it is the bicycle that is out of control; it is the bicycle that will meet the Jeep.

She sees the split-second decision on Xerxes face. She sees the bail. She sees the bicycle hit her front grill, hears its tire blow out, watches it career to the side. And she sees him for an instant, sliding on the pavement, before he disappears beneath the car, punctuating the moment with a clang.

* * *

Gek-Lin is in an Internet café tapping furiously on her mouse in order to refresh her screen. The e-mail is fifteen minutes late. Her left hand is wrapped around Psyduck's neck. Despite his inanimate nature, Psyduck looks like he's being strangled. His eyes bulge. The stuffing is coming out of his head.

Just as Psyduck bursts, just as his left eyeball pops from its mooring and sadly hangs there by a thread, the ticket comes. With no time to lose, Gek-Lin hits the "Print" button and sprints out the door. E-ticket in hand, she runs, at full-throttle, the half mile to the British Consulate. Patience has given way to panic. Gek-Lin must get her passport. She must get on that plane.

* * *

He is OK. He is lying sideways, in the fetal position, his left shoulder and left hip to the pavement. His head, helmet attached, is crooked and compressed against something metal. He is afraid to move. He moves. He moves his head, just a little. He looks up. At an axle. And the thing—what is it called—that makes the axle spin. He is looking at that, at a drive train. He is OK. Once again, he is OK. Whatever force it is, whatever being is out there, eyeing his progress, has once again played on him his or her or its favorite trick. It has knocked him down, diabolically, and now it is lifting him up, once again.

He is afraid to move. He lets his head fall back to the pavement. He is aware of his injuries. He mentally assesses them. His shoulder, having met the pavement first, is the most delicate, and yet, there are no shooting pains coming from that region. It must be intact. His head, a head that he had helmeted as a matter of course, despite his death wish, having come into contact with the drive train, also, seems, somehow, to be OK. He feels a sharp sting, from where his cheek and lip scraped along the pavement, but there is nothing greater than this. There is pain, also, from his hip and ankle region, but again, there is nothing sharp and telltale wrong with him. How could this be? How could a bicyclist, on the verge of reaching 41.26 m.p.h., come into contact with a moving vehicle and not break something—how could this be?

Xerxes hears a car door open, a black shoe with a silver buckle emerges at eye level. There is shouting. A word enters his head. He says it calmly, querulously, "Montana?"

★   ★   ★

Sara, hands shaking, tries to escape from the clutches of her seat belt, which has suddenly become slippery and octopuslike. She finds the release, eventually, and is free. She opens the car door and gets out. She is shouting before she knows she is shouting. "Holy shit!" "Holy shit!" "Holy shit!" As she is shouting, a word emerges from under the Jeep, in a dove-like voice, almost a coo; she swears the word is Montana.

She is afraid to look at what will surely be carnage beneath her car. She doesn't respond to the word Montana, doesn't consider what it might mean. "Oh my God, oh my God, Xerxes, are you OK? Oh my God."

The voice from beneath the Jeep sounds eerily peaceful, like the ghost of a husband who dies in a tragic airplane wreck and comes back to tell his wife and child that he loves them. "I'm fine."

"You're fine? Don't move, OK? Don't move." Sara decides to look. She has to look. She gets down on all-fours and looks under the Jeep. There he is, in the fetal position, his head against the drive train, his helmet crushed. Her eyes not adjusted, she can't see much in the shadow that the Jeep created over him. She can tell that his shirt, a shirt that reads *We've Come This Far by Faith*, is torn, and she can see some blood, not a great deal, but some, underneath him on the pavement. She is relieved somewhat, the scene is less grizzly than she'd imagined.

"Montana?" Xerxes gazes into her eyes as if she were an angel.

Sara realizes, then, that Montana is a person, probably a lover or girlfriend of some sort that he hadn't bothered to tell her about. This explains things. "No, it's Sara. Do you feel like you can move?"

Xerxes is still staring at her. "I know you're Sara. I like to call you Montana."

There is something wrong with him, probably a concussion. She needs to get him out from under the Jeep and call an ambulance. "Don't try to move, Xerxes. I think there's plenty of clearance if I back the car up. *Don't* lift your head up, OK? I'm going to back up as slowly as I can."

"Good idea."

★   ★   ★

Xerxes Meticula is happy to be alive. It is, most likely, the massive flood of endorphins coursing through his bloodstream that makes him feel this way; but no matter the cause, his accident has knocked a dose of reality into his thick skull. He lays low as the Jeep backs up, Sara putting the Jeep in neutral and inching it back, getting out of the car every foot or so to make sure he hasn't moved. Eventually, he is back in the light, the sun's light, the Jeep having backed up far enough so that he is no longer caught beneath its shadow. He turns over on his back and looks up at the sky. It is aquamarine with fluffy white clouds that look like the soft covering of earmuffs. He turns his head to the right. There he sees the green-gray of Rest Stop National Forest dropping to the yellow of the high desert in the valley, rising back up into the rocky oranges of the Mingus Mountains. Xerxes sees these things, sees that they are beautiful; and he also sees Sara's face, the face of his beloved Montana, there, for whatever reason, to save him.

★   ★   ★

"You moved," Sara says.

"Yeah," Xerxes replies.

"How did it feel to move?" Sara asks.

"Not bad," Xerxes answers.

Sara looks him over. He has some pretty serious road rash on his face, but it looks like the helmet, miraculously, has prevented any major trauma. His chin, cheek, and lower lip are bleeding heavily. The sleeve of his shirt is torn and the shoulder underneath it has a road rash similar to that on his face, running all the way from the top of the shoulder to the elbow. A sock, too, is torn, and a heavy gash is bleeding just above his ankle. "OK, test things out. Can you rotate your neck?"

Xerxes rotates his neck. "Yep."

"Wiggle your fingers."

"Yep."

"Your toes."

"Yep."

"Any pain when you do those things."

"A little."

"OK, follow my fingers with your eyes."

Xerxes does what he is asked, passing her test.

"I can't fucking believe it. You were hauling ass. How did you manage to not seriously injure yourself?"

"I don't know," he says, staring up at Sara intently, looking truly baffled by the question. "It was so strange, when I threw myself off the bike it was like . . . like I just gave up. I didn't try to break my fall or anything. I just relaxed, completely. It was like I said to myself, 'there's nothing you can do, you might as well enjoy the ride.' And that was it. I just sort of tucked my shoulders and slid beneath your car, with a grim, resigned, but somehow peaceful awareness of what was happening. And then seconds later, there was your shoe with the silver buckle on the pavement next to my head."

Xerxes sits up from his reclining position. Pain shoots up his arm; he can tell that some tendons have been stretched past their normal limits, but, miraculously, there is nothing broken, there is no permanent damage. He grimaces a bit, sucks air through clenched teeth.

"You shouldn't move. I'm going to call an ambulance."

"No, no, no," Xerxes says quickly. "I'm fine, seriously. I'm fine."

Sara looks him over, at the blood dripping off his chin and down his arm. "You don't look fine."

"Trust me, I'm fine. Just get me into the Jeep."

"Even if we don't call an ambulance, we need to take you somewhere to bandage you up. You have a pretty good gash on your ankle that's still bleeding and your shoulder looks pretty wrecked. Not to mention that you might have a concussion. And we need to get some Neosporin on your scrapes so you don't end up with a massive infection."

As Sara says this, listing his injuries and discussing how best to bandage them, making sure she gets the details right, Xerxes is thinking about his sister, about what she would say about this incident. The air is fresh today—early October fresh, with a chill in it and the scent of spruce. The sun beats down on the top of his head, the way it does in high altitudes. He can feel the spot where it impacts his head most directly, as if someone is directing it there from a mirror.

Gabriella would consider what had happened to him today a moment, a Biblical moment, a magical moment. She would point to Paul, formerly Saul. She would say that this was his bolt of lightning, the thing knocking him off his horse. She would say that this was something for him to remember—forever—a turning point. Gabriella believed in these things; Xerxes, normally, did not.

And yet here she is, Sara, his potential Savior, the Goddess made flesh, looking down on him, her head surrounded by a Michelangelo sky, offering him suckle. It doesn't have to be so tough. She obviously likes him. She would obviously listen to him. She wants him to speak his embarrassing truths, about his addiction to this game, about how painful is his loss in it—this is her nature, her science, the notion that speaking the truth will heal you.

Just sitting here, not moving, not at all considering his peasants, or his sister, or his fallen business, or Zahn and Dixie, and the guilt he feels for not taking care of these things; just sitting here, not caught up in the math, not lost in his head, not considering all the potential solutions; Xerxes can see past the details to the bigger picture. This fall had taught him something. He is not in control.

One did not get to where one wanted to be by plowing through, by leading invasion after invasion, war after war. Instead, one got to where one wanted to be by having peripheral vision. One had to just hang out, relax, not take things so seriously, and then listen—for outside voices, for some-

thing unusual to poke its way through the routine. And then when it happened, when the intuition was fired up, when the synapses lit up like bumpers
in a pinball machine, when the neurons said, *This, this is it, this is what you are
to do, this is what you are to say*, you had to have the courage to do it, to say it,
to break all the rules and look like an ass.

So Xerxes says it. It is so dumb, such a male fantasy. It is so in his head to
want, and so unlikely to happen. "Give me your shirt."

★ ★ ★

Sara had been watching him watch her. His eyes were somewhat glazed
over. She had thought he might lose consciousness. She hadn't interrupted
him, though. She had hoped he was just catching his breath. Then he said it,
without qualifiers, *Give me your shirt*.

"My shirt?"

Xerxes was still watching her, eerily. He had a big, angelic smile on his
face. "Yeah, I need it, to stop the bleeding."

"Why don't you just use your own shirt?"

"I'm afraid to lift my arms and it's already bloody."

There he was, concussed and bleeding, asking her to remove her shirt.
She knew what he was getting at. This wasn't about stopping the blood flow.
She wanted to tell him off, curse him for leaving her in the middle of the
night. She unbuttoned her shirt, took it off, twisted it to form a tourniquet.
"Lift your leg a bit."

Xerxes obeyed, took a long gander at her cleavage as she bent over him.

She looked at him after tying the knot, saw his stare. She blushed. "Stop
it!" she said, though a smile escaped her, momentarily. "I'm going to help
you up, and then you're going to lean on me, get in the car, and I'm going to
take you to the hospital. Got it?"

"Yes, ma'am," said Xerxes.

They did as Sara had suggested. Sara helped him up, and he sort of
hopped his way to the Jeep. She opened the door for him and he slipped into
the passenger's side. He was tentative, but the endorphins were keeping the
pain from sidelining him. He was still eerily aware, caught in the twisted joy
of being alive, of once again being derailed from the suicide train. "Sara?"

She felt silly, defrocked as she was, goose bumps on her arms, preparing
for the stares and honks as she drove into downtown Prescott wearing only
her bra. This was annoying. Stop the bleeding, my ass. "What?"

"Before we go to the hospital, and things get complicated, and the pain of this hits me, and I'm screaming for Vicadin, I want to explain it all, I want to tell you why I left and didn't call you. It's not going to make any sense, and it's really stupid, but don't interrupt. I want to get it all out in one big monologue. OK?"

"Um, ok." Sara said this sarcastically, her hands clutching the steering wheel, bracing for whatever was coming next.

Xerxes was looking right at Sara, trying to get her to meet his gaze. She wouldn't look back at him. She was intent on staring out the windshield. Xerxes knew by the way she was staring, the way she was clutching the steering wheel, how much he'd hurt her, and therefore, how much she'd emotionally invested, how much she'd cared and wanted this to work. He had done nothing to deserve this from her, and yet it was there. A gift. A winning lottery ticket. It was such a strange thing, the way the world operated. The things you thought were really important, the things you strove for—for Xerxes, success in his business and success in his game—tended to be the things you failed at, the things the world put the most obstacles in your way of achieving; and the things you spent the least time worrying about, the things that you knew were supposed to be important but you never bothered to stop and stare down—they were handed to you, thrown right in your lap.

And yet, you could fuck these things up too, you could choose to not get on the ship when it came to harbor.

"Look, Sara, me leaving that night, it didn't have anything to do with you." Xerxes halted for a moment, trying to decide which "L" word to use. "I . . . I really, really, like you, and I'm very upset that you're moving away. I think, I might, I could, well, it's stupid to say this so soon. I think I could even love you."

Xerxes kept his eyes on Sara. Sara kept her eyes out the window.

"Remember when Gabriella and Leonard ran off, and we were panicking, looking for them, but almost too stunned to actually do anything about it?"

Remember? How could she forget? It was one of the most absurd moments of her life. That day flooded into her memory. Made the pain she felt about leaving this whole bizarre summer behind her that much more sharp. She kept her mouth shut, continued to stare out the windshield.

"I told you that I was a gamer. I know, in a way, this is worse than any other excuse, because it seems so banal, but well, that's what I went to do, that night. I went back to The Realm. That's what the game's called, The Realm."

Xerxes paused for a moment, awaiting a response. He didn't get one.

"Anyway, I'm going to try to explain this. I know you're mad. It's stupid, I know. But this game, it's a game that never ends—it goes on all the time, twenty-four/seven. When I'm not there, bad things can happen, and the longer I'm away the more likely that these bad things will occur. Not only that, but I'm a . . . I'm a monarch, and there's a bunch of people in my kingdom who depend on me: we are one of the top kingdoms in The Realm. So that night that I was with you another kingdom attacked us, and they needed me to lead the counterattack. This is so stupid. I know. But there's this guy, his name is Dietrich, who lives in Antarctica, and a girl, who lives in Thailand, and another guy, who speaks in Edgar Allen Poe poems, we think he's in England, but now there's some speculation . . . well . . . I know . . . this doesn't make any sense. Anyway. We're all on a team. And we wanted to win the game. And it takes a lot of work. So I dedicated a lot of time to this, and that's why I left you that night, to go back to them."

Though she still refused to look at him, though she continued to stare out the windshield, looking at the clouds, and determining animals for them: that one, a rhinoceros; that one, a bunny; she was enraptured by his bizarre tale, by what Xerxes had to say. She was, undoubtedly, sitting next to the world's biggest geek, and yet, she could feel herself being swept up in it, its absurdity, its futurism.

Seeing that she wasn't going to comment, Xerxes went on, "There's this other guy, he calls himself the Two-Headed Boy, he's like the champion Realm player, his kingdom has won the last four ages, an amazing accomplishment considering the number of players this game has, he's like The Realm's Tiger Woods. We finally passed him up. It was stupid to put so much importance into this, but for some reason it meant a lot to me. I needed to be successful in something, even if it was just a game.

"Anyway, today, all fucking hell breaks loose. This Two-Headed Boy, he goes and tells all my kingdom mates that he's some poor kid in a wheelchair who doesn't have any friends, and that there's this girl who he met on-line, who died or something, and he wants us all, since we've all been playing this game together, to come to her funeral. He says he's going to send us all e-tickets to go to San Francisco so we can meet each other.

"It's all a big fucking hoax. It has to be. But Dietrich believes him and logs off, and so does the chick from Thailand. And next thing I know the Two-Headed Boy has the lead again.

"Sara, it's so stupid, but I'm so caught up in it. Today, when I saw all these messages on my screen, I lost it. I wanted it all to be over. All of it. I was going to ride my bike up to Granite Mountain, climb to the top, and jump off. I've never told anyone about this, about how suicidal I am. Back when Gabriella made her first attempt, I had been thinking the same thing, that very day. She called me, from the hospital, just as I was standing on the Golden Gate Bridge, contemplating it.

"So that's what I was doing when I was heading down the hill, just staring at my speedometer, just trying to ride as fast as I could, shutting my brain off and any excuse it might find not to do what I was determined to do. And then, sure enough, wham, you're there driving up the road.

"It's so weird, it's like somebody's trying to tell me something. I don't believe in this shit, you know; but I can't keep hiding from the weird symmetry of things, from the way God or fate or The Great Mover, or whatever you want to call him or her or it makes things work. In that split-second when I was still in the air, pre-pavement, it was like the fog had lifted, like suddenly I could see the whole forest instead of just the trees. I got it, what I was doing wrong, why I kept failing.

"There aren't many winners out there, Sara. There's like 60,000 players in The Realm, more than that in Real Life. The way I've been playing all these games, Sara, the odds are impossible. No matter how good you are, all the cards are stacked against you, and in the end, even if you're really good, the only way to win is to be extraordinarily arrogant and mean—to cheat, to steal, to lie, and then to be one lucky motherfucker.

"When I was in the air, Sara, that's when it hit me. I don't want to be any of those things. I don't want to be a winner. I don't want to do the things you have to do to people to win.

"I had thought, so long, about how unfair this is, how wrong it is that all the people on the top are innately such assholes, and that the rest of us are forced to live by their dictates. I had wanted to beat them at their own game; but I realized, as I was doing it, that I simply became them, that there was no way to win this game and not become one of them.

"Sara, you don't play to win or not to win, you play to play, you play to hang out with all the other players, and when it comes right down to it, if you're sitting there, somewhere in the middle, not willing to make the sort of moral compromises you have to make to get to the top, and if you're not sitting around lamenting that, you're going to have a lot of friends, a helluva lot of friends, and you're going to be happy, and you're going to live a fulfilling life, and you might not end up in the history books as some sort of master of industry, or genius, or whatever, but who really cares, who really cares if history remembers you if you had to be an asshole to get there.

"I know. It's weird. Saying that all of this came clear to me as I'm flying through the air. But that's how it happened. I swear. And while I was flying I saw it, all the things I had that I hadn't appreciated. I saw my sister, Gabby. I saw her, rather than someone to be embarrassed about, as someone to be proud of, someone who was living bravely outside of the common reality. I saw her as someone who was really cool to have around. I saw these people I'd met in The Realm, sKyLaR, and Lord BonZ, and even this devilish Two-Headed Boy guy. I saw them as these amazingly weird people who I was fortunate to have known. I saw Zahn and Dixie. I saw Zahn—rather than the competition, I saw him as the brazen and daring man he is. And then I saw you, Sara, and not only in my mind's eye, I actually saw you, your silly shoe with the big silver buckle. I saw you and what you could be to me, if I let you in, if I stopped playing the game.

"This is why we're here, Sara, in Rest Stop, Arizona. We were supposed to run into each other; you were supposed to almost run me down. We're perfect for each other. This took no work. It just happened. It's something that other people spend their whole lives worried about and looking for, and it just happened to us, without any effort on either of our parts. It's beautiful, Sara."

Xerxes knew he was jumping the gun, presuming things. He didn't care. He went on, rambling, ranting, Zahn-like. He didn't care. He felt powerful, like he had suddenly been granted a third lung and was for the first time exhaling from it.

"Fuck, Zahn should marry her. They should be married. They're perfect for each other. If I'd had the balls, back then, I would have told them that, and backed off. The resentment I feel; it's all petty, base stuff; a stupid, manly thing that's all about evolution and men fighting over women rather than the intellectual reality of the situation, the fact that he's better for Dixie than I am. I think Zahn's totally sincere and I think they're going to work together. They've already set a wedding date. They're getting married, next Saturday. That's nuts, Sara. It's fucking crazy. But yet, I don't know; I just know, I just know they're doing the right thing. And I know that the right thing for me to do, is to bury the hatchet, to show them that I understand, to show them that I know the score. I know I should get the fuck out of here, and that the first thing I should do when I get back is go to that wedding.

"I know that you want to go to New York, but this isn't over yet, there's something else that needs to happen. I need to stop running from things. I mean, it could work, Sara, couldn't it? You, me, we could work."

Sara waited for him to go on, to continue his rant. But it appeared that he'd finished. They sat there in silence, her still looking out the windshield; him still looking at her. Finally, he looked out the windshield, too. She chanced a glance at him. His expression spoke of fear. He must be realizing what he had just said, the risk he had just taken. This could easily end in another rejection.

It wasn't, really, a very good idea to get involved with someone who was as emotionally wrecked as Xerxes obviously was. It surprised her, the extent of it. He had appeared to have it all together, and now, in this moment, she sees the desperation he'd been hiding inside.

Q is for Quarry. But then again, it didn't seem right to simply say no to him, to have come to find him to get this answer, the answer that he had given her, and then to run from that answer.

What did she want? When he had rejected her, the visceral reaction she had was to be hurt, and to get to the bottom of it, but now that he had brought all this to light, now that he had revealed that he liked her, a great deal, but had a number of unrelated things on his mind, how would she respond, *how did she want to respond?*

Sara thought about what she wanted. She could say no. She could go back to New York City, right away. She could escape quickly from these twins and their neuroses. She could have dates set up, very quickly, through cupidsmagicarrow.com, where she would undoubtedly meet some interesting men, most of them in their midthirties and somewhat desperate, looking for women exactly like her, women in their late 20s, attractive in nonblonde kinds of ways, liberated, willing to fuck on a first date, and yet, presumably, willing to settle down too, should, after several such fuckfests, they turn out to be normal enough to do so with.

This would be good for her—a lot of action, a lot of desperate men. She could string a few of them along, appease her carnal desires. She could forget about this, about the introspection that Rest Stop, Arizona forced her into. She could forget about Gabriella, the crazy twin, the one that was eerily prescient and lucid, the one who was the most sane; Xerxes, the normal twin, the one lost in his games, the one who was the most crazy. She could forget Xerxes's story. And she could forget his last ditch effort to save himself by latching on, by latching onto another human being in desperate need. She could forget that he was reaching out, was choosing her from all the fish in the sea, that he was saying, "Sara, I think I could even love you."

Or, she could go to him. That Dylan song began its chorus in her mind, the one that played in Leonard's, the one that played in Dietrich's, the one that plays, so often, the world over. In Rest Stop everything had been stripped from her, all the superficial trappings of her big city social life. Here she had nothing, and because she had nothing, she also had nothing to lose. The song played out its conclusion for her: *go to him you can't refuse.*

"Sure," Sara said, speaking more to herself than to Xerxes, "why not?"

Xerxes was not sure how to take Sara's nonchalance—*sure, why not*—what exactly did this mean in relation to the question he had, well, not really quite asked—*you, me, we could work?*

"So when's the funeral?" asked Sara.

"It's just a hoax."

"Are you sure the funeral isn't real?"

"There's no way. It's scheduled for Saturday. But it's not happening. Trust me."

37. IF YOU ABSOLUTELY NEED A BREAK, CHOOSE VACATION MODE.

WHEN HE WALKS IN, SHE IS THERE, yelling at the glass in front of her. He had walked by the British Consulate, and then, on a whim, if only to smell the electrified air of potential freedom, he had turned around and walked in.

"Why do I need a guardian?" she is screaming, "I already have a ticket." The man behind the glass isn't looking at her, instead he is looking over her head to the back of the room where two men, security guards, are standing. He nods at them and they begin to advance.

Charley is a pragmatic man, and despite the Edgar Allen Poe poems is not one to believe in ghosts. And yet, at this moment, at this unbelievable moment, at this moment when he stands there, frozen in place despite the fact that it is obvious what he should do, he looks up at the high gold-leafed ceiling and sees one. It is her. It is his girl. It is the lovely raven. She is up there, and Uncle Charley knows that it is only he who can release her. He also knows that it is not she that he will be releasing. It is himself. When he does it—if he does it—it is he that will be free.

Uncle Charley hears his own voice. It is not his usual voice. It is not as high-pitched and wheedling. "Wait," his voice commands. He can't believe he is doing this; he is aghast at his own courage. His whole life had been a regret, and now, he has this one chance, this one chance to make good. Uncle Charley, normally passive, is aggressively elbowing his way through the crowd. He feels his arms as he does so, feels his arms as if he's never felt them before. He feels muscle and fiber and tissue. "I'm her guardian," he says, and he can feel the full weight of everything this means to him as he says it, he can feel the lilt his voice just barely avoids. He can feel his almost losing it here, but he doesn't. For whatever reason, he feels somewhat super-human today, as if something he has eaten recently has given him extra strength.

The two security guards have already reached Gek-Lin. They have her arms locked behind her back. She cannot turn to face him and Charley is glad at this. He can't afford to weaken now. Uncle Charley approaches the glass window, he repeats himself, "I'm her guardian," he says, in his best English. "I apologize for my tardiness."

The agent hesitates for a moment. He can nip this in the bud. He can turn them away. There is something, however, in the man's countenance that precludes this. He's missing a finger, and people who are missing fingers, they aren't the kind of people you fuck with. He asks Charley, "ID?"

Charley, wordlessly, hands him his ID.

"And you are associated with the ECR Foundation?" the agent asks.

Charley doesn't know what the ECR Foundation is. He has not read the message from Tres Rawlings. And yet Charley does not hesitate, "Yes."

There is more to this that the man behind the glass should know. For instance, he should know what the ECR Foundation is. But he doesn't, and because he doesn't, he does not want to get flack for it later should he delay these people. The agent makes his decision, it is more likely that he will be reprimanded for delaying this man than it is that he will be punished for letting him through.

"Well, then, sir," he says, "everything appears to be in order. This will be processed within the hour. If you'd please step over there."

★   ★   ★

While his decision about whether to come to San Francisco to The Serpent's funeral had been rather obvious, since it was mostly an excuse to get Caitlin out of Antarctica, Dietrich wondered if any of his kingdom mates were also considering it. He didn't relish the idea of sitting alone with the Two-Headed Boy at the funeral of some girl he hardly knew.

There was another issue too. Dietrich wasn't sure what to do with his province. He couldn't imagine himself playing anymore. Among Dietrich's many charming and magical qualities was his ability to make a peaceful escape. It worked well for him in New York, when he would drop his lovers off at La Guardia, no feelings hurt, the lover happy and content. Dietrich wanted to leave his kingdom mates happy, not angry and resentful.

In order to accomplish this, Dietrich becomes sKyLaR one last time. It is time for him to perform yet another disappearing act.

* * *

He had sworn, while he'd looked up at the drive train of Sara's jeep, when he had seen her black shoe with the silver belt buckle, that he was through, that he would simply cancel his account. One click! That's all it took: Are you sure you want to cancel your account? Y

He had visualized himself doing just that, and he had been absolutely sure that it was exactly what he would do. He'd get home and he'd do it. And then, when he was done, he would get on the phone and call Zahn. He would be very mature and his voice would not waver. He would tell Zahn that he wished to attend the wedding, and Zahn, flabbergasted and thinking how best to play it, would voice his plastic enthusiasm.

This, however, did not happen. When he had gotten home, he had, like he had planned, logged onto The Realm. But rather then go Preferences → Cancel → Y, he had gone Kingdom → News. He had done it without even thinking. Before he knew it he was building on his new land and training his troops. He might have gone on doing this for hours, if, on his IRC, he hadn't gotten a message from sKyLaR:

> You have received an invitation to enter the conference room tHe MaIn PaRlOr from **sKyLaR**. Will you accept? Y/N

> **Peace_Love:** Y

sKyLaR: *sO r U gOiNg To ThE fUnErAl?*

Peace_Love: *errrrrrr. It's a hoax, sKyLaR. the whole thing is a set-up to get us offline. Seems like it's working too . . .*

sKyLaR: *iT's NoT a HoAx, I'm SuRe*

Peace_Love: *And how do you know that?*

sKyLaR: *wElL fOr OnE, hE GaVe ThE nAtIoNaL sCiEnCe FoUnDaTiOn SoMe LuDiCrIoUs AmOuNt Of MoNeY tO gEt Me OuT oF hErE aNd To ThE fuNeRal. tHe EnTiRe CoNtInEnT oF aNtArCtIcA iS iNvOlVeD iN mY eXtRaCtIoN. aNd FoR tWo, He ReAlLy SoUnDeD gEn-UiNe. i JuSt DoN't SeE hOw Or WhY wOuLd mAkE iT aLl Up.*

Peace_Love: *So he could win . . .*

sKyLaR: *nO oFfeNcE tO hEr MaJeStY, bUt I tHiNk YoU'rE bEiNG a LiTtLe PaRaNoId ;D*

Peace_Love: *You really think there's a dead girl? I mean, you read about that guy who was playing The Realm and faked dying in a car accident because he was too embarrassed to tell his kingdom that he was quiting. People do pretty squirrly things here . . .*

sKyLaR: *i DiDn'T rEaD aBoUt ThAt*

Peace_Love: *yeah, the Lords of The Realm put a notice about his death on the website and everything before they found out it was fake. That's why they don't get involved in people's Real Lives any more . . .*

Peace_Love: *Does the NSF actually have the cash in hand already?*

sKyLaR: *dUnNo. ThE fLiGhT hAs BeEn ScHeDuLeD, tHoUgH. iF iT iS a HoAx ThE dUdE iS gOiNg To EnD uP iN jAiL.*

Peace_Love: *This is too weird. I mean, why would you leave Antarctica just to attend the funeral of some girl who you didn't know. I mean, at least the Two-Headed Boy supposedly knew her.*

sKyLaR: i DiD kNoW hEr. ShE wAs ThAt SeRpEnT gIrL fRoM tHe KiNgDoM aMpHiBiOuS tHaT wE wErE aT wAr WiTh. I iRcEd HeR aLl ThE tImE

Peace_Love: you talked to her?

sKyLaR: yEaH, iT's A lOnG sToRy BuT bAsIcAlLy ShE wAs AcTiNg SuIcIdAl OnLiNe. bOtH mE aNd ThE TwO-hEaDed BoY kNeW aBoUt HeR pRoBlEm BuT wE cOuLdN't StOp HeR.

Peace_Love: It was a suicide?

sKyLaR: Y

Peace_Love: Jesus, why didn't you tell me all this stuff as it happened?

sKyLaR: i DuNnO, yOu'Re AlL buSiNeSs AlL tHe TiMe. AnD iT's NoT lIkE wE'rE oN a FiRsT nAmE bAsIs

Peace_Love: Do you have the Two-Headed Boy's IRC address.

sKyLaR: iT's 2hB

sKyLaR: sOoOoOoOoOoOoOoOoOoO

sKyLaR: i'M gOiNg To Be GoInG iNtO vAcAtIoN mOdE fOr ThE rEsT oF tHe AgE aNd ThEn I'm NoT gOiNg To ReNeW mY aCcOuNt In ThE nEw AgE

Peace_Love: Can you wait until I talk to him to go into vacation mode? I still don't trust that this is all happening. Maybe that girl just canceled her account and the Two-Headed Boy made up everything about a suicide. I know, I know, he's getting himself into a lot of trouble. But the whole thing is so outlandish I can't believe it's real.

sKyLaR: iL'l WaIt BuT tHeRe ArE tOo MaNy dEtAiLs 4 tHiS tO bE fAkE.

Peace_Love: hrmmm. I just can't believe it. THX for saying you'll wait, though, I'll let you know what I'm doing as soon as I confirm! ;)

sKyLaR: yOu'Re WeLcOmE! ;)

* * *

What he should do is stop this. The more he knows, the more furious he will be. The last thing he wants now is to be back in that dark space again, back considering a drop off a rocky cliff, and yet he can't, he is compelled. He has to know. He opens up his IRC account and finds him there in bold and green: the Two-Headed Boy, his greatest enemy, his nemesis.

*You have received an invitation to enter the conference room The Strangely Peaceful Citadel of Blue Orcs from **Peace_Love**. Will you accept? Y/N*

2HB: *Y*

2HB: *Who's this?*

Peace_Love: *Queen Peace & Love but Mostly Love from Paradigm Shift*

* * *

Tres Rawlings does not know this, the nerve endings in that region no longer connect to his brain, but when he sees those words, his heart skips a beat. The Queen Peace & Love—he has had so many fantasies about this woman, about who and what she could be. He knows just how impossible these fantasies are, he can't, well, he can't move, and so long walks, and skiing, and sex, are not things that he can do; but despite this, and despite the fact that she is not in the room, and is, instead, 5,233 miles away, he still blushes. He pauses a moment before he types it, but then he does it anyway; he knows she'll take it as flirting, despite the fact that it is partially true:

2HB: *HEY! How's the love of my life?*

* * *

One of the downfalls (or upsides, as the case may be) of playing a woman in an on-line fantasy game, when in fact, in Real Life, you are a man, is that men inevitably flirt with you. This had been, of course, Xerxes's intent in telling Tres that he was a woman in Real Life. He wanted him to be nice to him, in the hope that he could lull him into a false sense of security. Even so, "the love of my life" comment makes Xerxes a little sick to his stomach. He really doesn't want to flirt back to keep up the façade. He decides, instead, that misdirection is the best policy. What he wants from the Two-Headed Boy is proof, proof that this whole dead girl thing isn't a smoke screen; he decides to turn the conversation to The Realm, a much safer place:

Peace_Love: how's that dragon treating you?

2HB: LOL. I dunno I haven't been online lately.

Peace_Love: sure, you haven't . . .

2HB: OK, well maybe a little. So am I going to get to meet you?

Peace_Love: honestly, I don't know yet . . .

2HB: Come on, come on, pretty please

* Peace_Love gags

2HB: Why not? Come on . . . a FREE ticket.

Peace_Love: look, I don't really get this. I mean, OK, you have an online friend and she commits suicide and you want to go to her funeral, even though she lives halfway across the world. Weird, but not entirely inexplicable. But then you buy people plane tickets to go to her funeral, people that didn't know her at all, and people that you don't really know at all. I mean me and sKyLaR hardly know you. why would you do it? it just doesn't make any sense—it's a

Peace_Love: hoax, it has to be. you're just trying to get us to quit playing so your kingdom can win.

2HB: Why would you quit just to go to the funeral?

Peace_Love: we'd have too! or at least we'd have to go into vacation mode for a while. i mean, sKyLaR can't log on after he leaves Antarctica, and then he gets on the plane in New Zealand or whatever, and flies directly to San Francisco, that's got to be almost 2 days of plane travel. And then that girl in Thailand, I don't know what kind of hoops she has to jump through to get on a plane. we'd be doing all this other stuff, and not concentrating on the war with you,

Peace_Love: *and then you guys would kill us. it's the only thing that makes any sense.*

2HB: *. . . that's really what you thought? that doesn't make any sense at all.*

Peace_Love: *no, the thing that doesn't make any sense is spending $50,000 on a plane ticket to get a guy out of Antarctica*

2HB: *ok, back up a bit, what you just said makes no sense. I mean, you have a laptop right, just log on at the airport. And if you're that desperate to maintain your province, and can't do it yourself just have someone log on and do it for you on a public terminal. No offence, but . . . aren't you a little paranoid . . . i know what I'm doing doesn't make a whole lot of sense, but I really am paralyzed, and I really do communicate with the world 100%*

2HB: *through my computer, and so all you guys in The Realm, even though it's mostly just a diversion for you, you're my Real Life friends too. so I don't know. I know it's crazy, but I just did it, I mean, I just bought the tickets. And I'd really like you to come.*

Peace_Love: *has left the conference room.*

2HB: *hello?*

2HB: *still there?*

* Two-Headed Boy sighs

This was it. This was the missing piece. All this time he had sat there, feeling plagued, feeling besieged. The world, all these things that had gone wrong, he assumed that everyone was after him. He lived his life as if it were all a chase scene, with him just running and running. Life had a techno beat, like in *Run Lola Run*.

sKyLaR was right. The Two-Headed Boy was right. His sister was right. There he was, on a trail going down the Mingus Mountains with his hair on fire. How ridiculous he must seem! A hoax? An elaborate scheme? Of course not—he was one of those crazy people, the ones who think there was some sort of cover-up in Roswell, the ones who think aliens are green and have really big eyes and upside-down triangle faces, the ones who think things are more complicated than they really are.

He—it was one of those moments, one of those rare moments when you see yourself as other people see you, rather than the way you see yourself—was a paranoid freak.

All this time he had thought of The Realm as a lonely place, a place where people ran around killing each other off and stealing each other's gold and doing a lot of math, but it wasn't like that for everybody. For some people The Realm wasn't an escape from Real Life but rather a new and unique portal into it. Some people actually met other people there, other intelligent souls, and befriended them. Some people actually thought this world, The Realm, was a *better* place then Real Life, because The Realm was decentralized: you could have your community here, your community of twenty, and in this community you could make your own decisions. Decisions weren't made by some George on a throne. In The Realm, you had power, where so often, in the real world, you did not.

He had missed all of this. All along, he had thought of The Realm as some embarrassing and debilitating obsession. And in the process he had become an automaton. He'd been playing the game and missing the best part of it, that if you were good people respected you, and if they respected you then you could befriend them, and if you befriended them, then you had these weird friends, friends who lived in other parts of the world, friends who you couldn't just meet at your local Baptist church.

All this time Xerxes Meticula has been sitting in Rest Stop, Arizona, he has been thinking that he has nothing, that he has only a college buddy who has betrayed him, parents who don't understand him, and a sister who has gone off the deep end. He holds onto some desperate hope that this shrink he has just met will be his be-all and end-all, but that's about it, these are the only people that can possibly be anything to him. What was so obvious, what was obvious to the Two-Headed Boy and Lord BonZ and to sKyLaR, had never been obvious to him. For him there had always been a line: online friend does not equal real friend. But the rest did not hold this distinction. The Two-Headed Boy, Lord BonZ, sKyLaR, all these considered him (her, really, since he had presented himself to them as a her) a friend.

So Xerxes was not friendless at all, he just didn't acknowledge that his friends were friends. How awkward and one-sided that was! And how easy to change, if he wanted to. Xerxes is sitting in front of his computer. This time he is not her, he is he, he is Xerxes Meticula. And he, Xerxes Meticula, feels transformed. Things, they had not gone his way, but his karma, it had flipped, he was all yin and no yang. Not only did he have Sara, but he also had them, he had sKyLaR and Lord BonZ and the Two-Headed Boy. Xerxes finds himself in an awkward place, but it is easier for him to be honest here than in Real Life. While it is easier to lie on the Internet, it is, conversely, also easier to tell the truth:

Peace_Love: OK, I'll go

* *2HB* nods in approval.

Peace_Love: One thing, though. My real name isn't Montana Bronstein, it's Xerxes Meticula. You'll need to change my name on the ticket.

2HB: that's an odd name

Peace_Love: aye

2HB: and it also means you're a guy

Peace_Love: aye

2HB: oops

Peace_Love: aye

Peace_Love: feel free to cancel the ticket

2HB: no, it's not that. I still think you should come. it's just, you know, kind of weird.

Peace_Love: sorry bout that.

2HB: ;)

★   ★   ★

This is yet another moment when Tres's body cannot do what it would normally do. What Tres's body would do, if it could, would be to exhale, involuntary, the contents of its lungs—namely, air—through a throat that was somewhat narrowed, so that a sound, slightly high pitched, came forth from it. Tres, if he had been able to, would have sighed.

Oh sure, the words springing forth on his computer screen gave no inkling of this. He would not reveal to this Xerxes Meticula, this sudden imposter, his misguided feelings towards someone else, someone named Montana.

Peace_Love: *so when is it?*

2HB: *October 15th at 8 in the morning.*

Peace_Love: *that soon?*

2HB: *aye*

Peace_Love: *Listen, I don't want you to pay for my ticket. I'm sure you're loaded or something, otherwise you wouldn't have done it, but I'm going to bring a friend of mine and it wouldn't be right for you to pay for both tickets.*

2HB: *No, it's cool I already bought it.*

Peace_Love: *seriously, I won't use it, cancel it, OK?*

2HB: *I'm not sure I can*

Peace_Love: *hrmph. Hey, listen, I'll ttyl. there's something I should do right now. All right?*

2HB: *k*

38. AS SOON AS YOU'RE IN VACATION MODE, YOU'LL REGRET IT.

HE DOES IT. He calls Zahn. It happens quickly. Three months of pain healed in thirty minutes. Zahn, he gets choked up, really, genuinely, choked up, not a hint of plastic in his voice, and he asks Xerxes to be his best man, and Xerxes, he isn't sure what to say, since he can't imagine being up there handing him a ring to give to Dixie, and he pauses for a moment, and during that pause he thinks about Sara, what Sara would say about him being a coward, and so he says it, he stands up for himself, he says "no." And it's left that way, at an honest "no," and then Xerxes calls Sara, and he tells her all the things that have transpired, about talking to the Two-Headed Boy and deciding to go to the funeral, and about Zahn and the wedding and about his choosing not to be the best man. And he says all this in a wild outburst, and Sara laughs throughout his mad exposition, and then he asks her, asks her if she'll come, and she says yes, yes she'll come. And then, after he had hung up the phone with Sara, he had gone to the St. Francis Sanitarium, where he needed to tell Gabriella that he was going, and that he would probably not be coming back to Rest Stop for some time. As he had told her Gabriella had only smiled, as if she knew that this would happen all along, and then she had said that she had a request. Leonard, she said, he needs to go, he needs to touch the Pacific Ocean, and then he will be cured, Xerxes didn't know what to say to this. So he said he'd ask her, he'd ask Leonard's shrink what she thought. And then Xerxes had driven home, and when he arrived at home he had sat down, and when he had sat down he hadn't done what he always did, he had done something different. Instead of logging onto The Realm, he had opened only his IRC protocol, and when he looked, sKyLaR was there, a beacon of light in the darkness:

Peace_Love: *hello*

sKyLaR: *hEy! So wHaT hApPeNeD?*

Peace_Love: *well, I talked to the Two-Headed Boy. I guess you guys are telling the truth . . . so anyway, I've decided to come to San Francisco. But there's something you should know, I'm a guy in Real Life . . .*

sKyLaR: *aCk!*

* sKyLaR *slaps* **Peace_Love** *with a wet tuna*

Peace_Love: *LOL*

sKyLaR: *iT's CoOl; It DoEsN't MaKe AnY diFfErEnCe To Me, I'm A MaRrIeD mAn.*

sKyLaR: *hEy sO llsTeN, dOnT gO iNtO vAcAtIoN mOdE jUsT yEt, i HaVe A sChEmE*

Peace_Love: *uh-oh*

sKyLaR: *8P*

★ ★ ★

In her bedroom in the St. Francis Sanitarium, Gabriella Meticula has the World card pinned to the floor with her forefinger. With her other hand she spins it. Around and around. She's been spinning it all day. It has taken much concentration, and she has been much maligned. She will pay soon for her activities with much medication.

But it has been worth it. She can feel the cogs turning. She has done good today. She has set something good in motion. They are all reaching out, going for it. Both she and her brother have done something good.

EPILOGUE: THE END OF THE AGE

It's high time I razed the walls that I've constructed.

—R.E.M., "WORLD LEADER PRETEND"

sKyLaR's plan goes into effect. All the names on *Paradigm Shift's* kingdom screen turn from white to red. Vacation mode. They change colors one at a time, like white driveway lights covered with lenses for Christmas by a suburban Dad. The names on *Carrot Flower's* kingdom screen do the same. One after another, all the top kingdoms follow: a moment of silence in The Realm; a candlelight vigil for the loss of one of their own.

This has never happened before, all the top kingdoms on vacation. The Lords of The Realm take notice. Why would they do this? Why, when the age is almost over, when everything they've struggled for is about to come to fruition, would they suddenly quit? They are worried. What will their sponsors think?

The people behind the names are moving: sKyLaR, Sir sKyLaR, sKyLaR the playboy, sKyLaR is on an Air Force transport plane flying over the hills of New Zealand. Below him is an unbroken carpet of green. This sight gives him hope; there is still room in this shrinking world for new beginnings. sKyLaR's flight is on route to Washington, D.C., courtesy of the Edward Calvin Rawlings Foundation. In Washington, D.C., he will deplane the Air Force transport plane and board a commercial jetliner to San Francisco for the funeral; after the funeral he will go back to Chicago for a layover, and then on to his final destination: Columbus, Ohio. Columbus, Ohio, where he is going with his wife, the lovely Caitlin. Columbus, Ohio, where he will go and care

for Caitlin's dying mother. Columbus, Ohio, where he will go and occasionally drive a beat-up Nissan 4×4, drive it along the Cuyahoga River looking for
car parts. Columbus, Ohio, where he and Caitlin can weld, happily ever after.

Raven, sorrowful Raven, is moving too. Bangkok direct to San Francisco.
San Francisco for two weeks. Then, unbeknownst to anyone, to London,
where he will attempt to start a new life. Next to him, in seat 2B, sits one of
the great loves of his life, the fourteen-year-old Gek-Lin Troung. Oh, how
he'd like to keep her, how he'd love for her to be his own. But he is doing the
right thing. This one, she will be spared.

Lord BonZ, Gek-Lin Troung, sits next to Uncle Charley, who sits in 2A.
Like Uncle Charley, she is flying Bangkok direct to San Francisco, but unlike
Uncle Charley she has no intention of flying back. Her return ticket sits
grease-stained beneath banana leaves in some forlorn Bangkok bazaar.

Uncle Charley is a creep. His stare is on her, as always. But still, he did
this. Made this possible. Killing the bad guy is not always the answer.

Xerxes Meticula is still in Rest Stop, Arizona. He is helping everyone
pack. Gabriella is frantic: *What will she wear, what are the people in San Francisco wearing these days, how cold or warm will it be, what will they think of her,
what if she loses her mind?* Leonard is silent, immobile, twitching. He is
happy that he will finally reach that ocean of his longing, the ocean that
may break his curse. He finds the plane flight, however, daunting. He wants
to shout, *Why can't we walk.* Sara just sits there, too. Smiling at Xerxes.
Watching him work. Her bags are already packed. She isn't helping anyone.
She is here for emotional support. Xerxes must learn to deal with the physical. It's therapy.

Xerxes knows this: they will all miss the plane. The Rest Stop Shuttle to
Phoenix Skyport. A flight from Phoenix to San Francisco. The plane leaves at
5:25 and it's 3:35 already. It will take the shuttle 79 minutes and 30 seconds to
get to the airport. They need to arrive 33 minutes early at the very latest in
order to make their plane. "I need everyone in the car in 7 minutes and 30
seconds," Xerxes shouts.

Tres Rawlings, however, is going nowhere. He is here, instead, in front
of his computer screen, watching the vacation mode lights go on.

Tres knows that this is right. He couldn't, after all, really go. He is too
limited in his movement. How would he have talked Tilda into it; how
would he have convinced Edward? He knows that this is the only way to pay
his respects.

He would have loved to have met them. To have gotten to know them by their real names. But he cannot. He is not physically able. Tres Rawlings cannot abandon one home for another.

Tres Rawlings can only wait. For in twenty-four hours something will happen, a something new and a something hopeful. It will appear, there, on his news screen. It will say, white, on a field of cornflower blue:

The Lords of The Realm have awarded you 200 acres of land and 250,000 gold coins to build your province. You have been assigned to Kingdom 9, Continent 3. The name you have chosen for your province is The King of Carrot Flowers. The persona you have chosen is Two-Headed Boy. Welcome to The Realm.

Today is the first day of the new age.